The Still of Night

KRISTEN HEITZMANN

The Still of Night

BETHANY HOUSE
MINNEAPOLIS, MINNESOTA

The Still of Night
Copyright © 2003
Kristen Heitzmann

Cover design by Lookout Design Group, Inc.

Published by Bethany House Publishers
11400 Hampshire Avenue South
Bloomington, Minnesota 55438
www.bethanyhouse.com

Bethany House Publishers is a Division of
Baker Book House Company, Grand Rapids, Michigan.

Printed in the United States of America

Library of Congress Cataloging-in-Publication Data

Heitzmann, Kristen.
    The still of night / by Kristen Heitzmann.
    p.   cm.
    ISBN 0-7642-2607-X (pbk.)
    1. Illegitimate children—Fiction. 2. Adopted children—Fiction.
3. Birthparents—Fiction. 4. First loves—Fiction. I. Title.
    PS3558.E468S75   2003
    813'.54—dc22   2003014245

To Jim, for believing enough to become one

To Cathy, for the seeds

To Karen, for holding up my arms

To Kelly, for unflagging diligence and insight

Rather, living the truth in love, we should grow in every way into him who is the head, Christ, from whom the whole body, joined and held together by every supporting ligament, with the proper functioning of each part, brings about the body's growth and builds itself up in love.

Ephesians 4:15, 16 NAB

www.kristenheitzmann.com

KRISTEN HEITZMANN is the acclaimed author of eleven novels, including the 2003 Christy Award finalist, *The Tender Vine*, and *A Rush of Wings*. An artist and music minister, Kristen lives in Colorado with her husband and four children.

Prologue

Her legs still shook under the sheet, the smooth skin mottled and stained. The vise had released her, the arcing pain and frantic breaths. All that was past. But her arms would never forget this moment, wrapped around the warmed bundle, its weight transferred from within to her hesitant arms. So fragile, so tiny, yet . . . tenacious. And soon no longer hers. She allowed no internal argument; the ache was punishment enough.

The face beside her now spoke. "It's harder the longer you wait. They need these moments."

She needed these moments. They would have a lifetime.

"You don't want to bond."

She knew it, yet it was beyond her to extend her arms and relinquish . . .

"Let me." Helping hands.

"No." She clutched one last moment before raising the bundle herself. Given, not confiscated . . . or destroyed. She would have that much.

1

Inside the cushion-walled cubicle bathed in morning light, Jill watched Sammi's euphoria dissolve into tantrum tears for the fourth time in less than an hour. The child's medication was obviously out of whack, expressed by excessive displays of inappropriate behavior. They'd be lucky to keep her together until the final bell rang; never mind sending her out to regular classes, where she would overload and self-destruct.

Swiftly Jill snatched Sammi off the floor in a modified takedown motion before the kicking feet made contact with the other students in the special ed reading lab. As Sammi thrashed in her arms, Jill's silent prayers started. *Lord, give Sammi peace. Wrap her in your loving arms. Let her know you're here in her struggle.*

Classified SIED—severe intellectual emotional disability—Sammi, like most of the kids in Jill's caseload, had the ability to learn and achieve, but her emotional upheaval sabotaged her efforts. How did one focus such a mind on phonics and structure when all her synapses were haywire? Might as well expect symphonic music from a nuclear reactor. Jill tried not to question why God made Sammi bipolar or why Joey sat in a world of his own until something irritated him out of it.

"Too loud!" Joey pressed his hands to his ears, ready to erupt.

Jill could hear his teeth grinding in conjunction with Sammi's wails. She pressed Sammi's face to her breast and confined her arms.

Sometimes it seemed the tighter she held her, the more quickly she calmed. She would use a full takedown if it came to it, though she hated to, especially when it would go into the child's report. Had her father forgotten today's medication altogether? The call she had made to him was still unanswered—as usual. *Please, Lord, comfort her.* If Joey lost it, as well, she'd have to call for help. She could not contain them both at once.

She glanced at Pam, who looked over from her group under the window, ready if needed. Quickly assessing the situation as defusing, Jill nodded her assurance to Pam, who returned her focus to her own group. It was a judgment call, but she gave Sammi the benefit of the doubt.

Frequently they flew blind, taking each day, each child in stride— short staffed, underfunded, yet still required to provide free appropriate public education in the least restrictive environment for kids whose functionality would never allow the success Jill wanted so much for them. But she ran the program the best she could.

"Jesus loves you," she murmured too softly for Sammi to hear. Yet it seemed to help. The wails became sobs, which didn't violate Joey's receptors as deeply. He rocked himself, refusing eye contact, and pulled the skin between his thumb and forefinger. It would be raw again before he stopped unless Jill could distract him.

But Sammi first. If she could only control everything that might set them off. In a perfect environment she could even teach them to read. As it was, she'd feel grateful to accomplish Sammi's goal of initiating and maintaining one healthy social contact, and to overcome Joey's lack of receptive language.

Lord, you balance the whole universe. Help me to balance these needs. As Sammi calmed, Jill watched the erupting forces in Joey subside, as well. She glanced at the other two students. Angelica was labeled SLIC: significant limited intellectual capacity. She had brain function that simply couldn't match her desire to learn. Her type A personality would not let her give up, and Jill longed for her success, especially when getting the brighter, more capable kids to even try was a challenge. Some days Angelica was truly her saving grace. She was well named.

And there was Chris. Jill suspected his condition was more likely sleep deprivation than low functionality. The domestic strife in his home was heard all down the block at all hours, and his blank, semicomatose refusal to perform could be partly attributed to that.

Even in the midst of Sammi's tantrum, he looked glazed.

"All right, pay attention. I want to read you a story."

Angelica's round brown eyes found her immediately. She loved stories and curled her legs up under the pink skirt that matched the many pink barrettes clipped onto tiny coarse black braids. Sammi's sobs became gulping breaths.

Jill used a firm, soothing tone. "Do you want to hear the story, Joey?"

He kept rocking but stilled slightly when she said, "It's about a rocket. And a monkey."

Sensing peace, Jill risked loosening her hold on Sammi. The girl was big for eight, a possible growth disorder in addition to her chemical imbalances. Sammi glared at Chris, who had expended the energy to set her off in the first place by making fun of her reading. Climbing down, Sammi deliberately kicked his knee.

"Ow!"

Chris kicked back, and Sammi charged him. As Jill moved to intervene, he pulled a fishing knife from his pocket. Jill lunged for the knife, gripped Chris's arm, and took him down. Chris, who hardly had energy to write his name, fought until she trapped and subdued the scrappy nine-year-old. Jill's heart pounded. This was not some inner-city school where kids knifed each other; this was small-town, middle-America farm country—probably why it was a fishing knife and not a switchblade.

Within moments, Pam had hold of Sammi, and they pulled the children apart, still kicking and hollering.

"Too loud!" Joey pressed his hands to his ears.

Jill couldn't worry about that now. She jerked the knife from Chris's hand. "Where did you get this?"

"It's mine."

"Not anymore." With the knife in one hand and the child in the other, Jill marched for the office. Presenting herself in this sort of situation to Principal Fogarty would not be pretty, but she had no choice. Her kids were rarely armed but invariably volatile. It came with the territory, but somehow Ed Fogarty always saw it as her fault. Still, she had no choice. School policy left no ambiguity in this situation.

As the stress drained, she realized Chris had grown soft in her grip. Why did he carry a knife? Protection? She frowned down at him. "Don't you know better than to bring a knife to school, Chris?"

He had retreated into his stare.

He would be automatically suspended. She could possibly advocate against expulsion, due to his independent educational program. Even so, she would probably not see him until next school year. Disappointment and failure threatened her resolve. But there was no way around things now. She just hoped Pam had kept Joey from harming himself. Pam was a good teacher, but the kids didn't always respond as well to her somewhat abrasive style.

As they approached the office, Chris held back. Jill stopped and turned. "I'm sorry, Chris. You made a really bad choice. Not only did you bring something dangerous to school, you used it as a weapon."

"He'll kick me out."

Jill nodded. "Yes, for a while. You should have known that would happen."

His eyelids drooped. "I'll have to stay home."

Jill heard the anxiety behind his dull words. "Yes, you will. Unless your parents make other arrangements."

He didn't answer, but his eyelids flickered.

"Is there a problem with staying home, Chris? Something I need to know?" She'd checked all year for signs of abuse, given him chances to talk, but he never did. Now he just stood there without so much as a headshake.

She took his shoulder gently. "We have to go in." She opened the door and propelled him into the office. Mr. Fogarty responded to her with all the grace she expected—that of a bull on a tightrope. At least he blew it out with her, and by the time Chris's mother arrived from her job, he was diplomatic and presented a gracious front. The woman looked as dull as Chris, took Fogarty's explanation with hardly a word, then jerked Chris out by the arm. Jill sighed. The best she had managed was to keep things open for Chris next year.

By the day's end she had earned a caramel Frappuccino. It wouldn't spoil her appetite for the evening, just replenish her drained energy. She normally eschewed caffeine, but Dan would come for her in a little more than an hour, with some special plans he'd alluded to. Suggesting she dress up had been especially significant, since they spent more time together in sweats and running shoes. Tonight, she didn't want to look like something dragged through the drain.

She was just to the makeup stage when the phone rang. "Hello?"

"It's Dan, Jill. Do you mind meeting me at Marchelli's?"

Marchelli's? She smiled to herself. And it wasn't even a meaningful occasion. "Running late?" She rubbed a smear of moisturizer into her neck.

"We're on a call. I'm not sure how long it'll take. Could be serious."

She heard radio noise over his phone. "Go ahead, Dan. I'll hold down the table till you get there." She could hardly get upset over his doing his job, keeping Beauview safe and honest.

After an hour and a half of raspberry Italian sodas, the first thing she said to Dan when he arrived was, "I need the ladies' room."

"I'm sorry, Jill." He'd obviously changed in a hurry. His tie was askew and one side of his collar bent up.

"It's all right." But she had spent the hour and a half worrying about Chris. Maybe his inattentiveness was a defensive posture. Maybe . . . She shook her head. It was time to let it go and enjoy the evening with Dan. They'd only dined at Marchelli's once before, on her birthday.

When she came back to the table, Dan had straightened his tie. His bulky neck wanted out of the collar. Not all men looked better in a suit. But she appreciated the significance.

She sat down. "Okay, here's my day in a nutshell. Chris was suspended for possessing and wielding a weapon in the classroom. Sammi's meds were wacko, and Joey had a serious regression in the use of bathroom facilities, probably due to the antagonism between the aforementioned pair. Mr. Fogarty indicated that I do not have control of my caseload and informed me that, contrary to policy, I must reapply for my position as coordinator next year, and I will be considered along with all other contenders, including a new hire I have yet to meet."

Dan frowned appropriately at that. She'd made it all sound comical, but it was starting to eat her up. She gave the best she had to her kids, fought for them, hurt for them. And days like today left her searching for the reason. She closed her eyes and sighed. "I just thought I'd get that out of the way."

Dan laughed softly. "Makes my foot chase of a teenage burglar sound tame."

"Was that the call?"

He nodded. "He was quick, too. Or I wouldn't have been so late."

"Did you work up an appetite?"

Dan raised his brows. "Hungry?"

She pushed aside the menu she had read word for word, including the gratuity policy on parties over eight and the accepted credit cards. "I was too worried about Chris to eat lunch. I haven't had anything but Frappuccino and Italian sodas since dawn."

"I thought I detected caffeine. You either need to become a regular user or avoid it altogether."

"It's more effective on a haphazard basis. Keeps the shock effect at full voltage."

The waiter approached with an air of stiff annoyance at having had his table held up with nothing yet to show for it. "Are you ready to order?"

"Desperate to." She chose manicotti with half clam alfredo and half sun-dried-tomato marinara. Dan ordered the peppered steak marsala. He detailed the chase for her as they nibbled breadsticks and thick, spicy minestrone. It had been one of the more serious calls he'd handled lately. The young man had broken into a home in one of the nice neighborhoods, loaded his car with electronics, and started on the gun collection by the time the private security system brought Brett and Dan to the scene. Brett covered the car to make sure the suspect couldn't double back and escape while Dan chased him down on foot. Dan could run forever, but his speed was not that great. Still, he cornered the kid and took him down, not unlike what Jill had been forced to do with Sammi.

She shook her head. "Do you think it was something in the air?"

Their entrees arrived, and the heavy starch neutralized the caffeine before she was halfway through. She settled down to enjoy the second half. "You haven't told me what we're celebrating."

For answer, Dan pushed aside his plate and looked at her for a long moment, then reached into his shirt pocket and pulled out a photograph. He slid it face up with one finger to the middle of the table between them. Jill looked at the modest house in the photo: some character, but not overly picturesque. She looked back at Dan.

"It's for sale. I was thinking . . . maybe we could do a joint mortgage, fix it up nice, and if things were working out well . . ."

"Things?" Was he actually saying what she thought?

He pulled a slow half smile. "We've had ten great months and . . ."

"And what, Dan?"

"I'm ready for the next step." He pulled his tie loose and opened the top button of his shirt, then gave her his direct cop gaze. "Jill, I know you have reservations. So do I. That's why this is a good—"

"What exactly are you proposing, Dan?"

He winced. "I'm a little leery of that word. I think if we worked into it, made sure we were—"

"Intimately compatible?"

"Exactly."

She stared into his blunt face and wondered if he had any idea that he had just capped her day.

––––––––––

Jill left the restaurant, thankful she had driven herself. She needed some miles behind the wheel. As she drove, she studied the opaque sun, caught like a melon-colored Frisbee in the net of trees along the horizon. Who had tossed it there, and would they come thundering across the sky to snatch it up and send it reeling once again? What careless feet would trip through the branches green with leaf and quickened sap? What eager hand would reach for it?

The Midwestern humidity dimmed it to a lunar impotence, so much tamer than the Phoenix sun. That fiery orb ruled the desert sky like a god, dominating the scaly plants and beasts, breaking their wills, grinding them down to the base elements of survival . . . or so Dan had said when he returned from his sister's wedding this past weekend.

Phoenix had been too hot, even for a man who liked to get out and sweat. He wanted his own exertion to cause it, not the blazing sun. That was Dan, one hundred and ten percent, whether he was running down a punk peddling drugs or pumping iron or racing his bike. The one area he didn't excel in was listening.

How else to explain his proposal? The man she respected, enjoyed, maybe even loved, had completely ignored everything she'd told him since their relationship had become serious. *What exactly are you proposing, Dan?* He'd made it sound so homey, so convenient. So noncommittal. Attending a wedding had no doubt sparked his consideration of the next step. But not influenced it deeply enough.

She switched hands on the steering wheel of her almost new Civic. Almost, meaning less than two years old, but purchased used from her friend Shelly, who won—actually won—a Miata in a raffle. She could still feel the grip of Shelly's hands on her upper arms as they had jumped up and down, laughing in disbelief.

Jill reached over and turned down the air-conditioning that was raising the hairs on her arms. Her plan was to leave Beauview behind and put miles of cornfields and highway between her and home. Dan had probably gone straight home and hit his weight bench. He would work it out through his pores; she'd rather run away.

But not entirely. She had school tomorrow; students depending on her, kids whose lives would be traumatized if she left them to a substitute, even another team member. Consistency was crucial. And in this last week of the school year their stress levels rose, as evidenced by today's stellar performances. Summer vacation was no celebration for many of them. It meant change, and they had spent nine months grasping one set of expectations only to now face a new set.

Some of them she would tutor twice a week through the summer so they wouldn't lose all they'd accomplished during the school year. Three months was interminable for their retention. Without tutoring, she'd be starting from scratch when she rolled up to the next grade level with them.

Even though the highway stretched out before her, she recognized the end of her tether. So at the next exit, she left the highway and started back. Hands had snatched the sun and taken it home. The sky dissolved into dusky hues of peach and lavender, and the farms on either side of the road had that complacent, settled look. Instead of reentering the highway, she followed the country road that would wind back to rejoin it eventually. It would be dark when she got home. No one would notice she went in alone, nor what condition her mascara was in, though tears had yet to come.

With a sniff, Jill fanned her fingers through her hair from the forehead to the crown, then examined the ends hanging midway down her chest, fine and straight and blond. Ash, actually, though she'd never liked that description. It had been silvery blond when she was small; fairy hair, her mother said. It was still thick and soft but lacked the luster it once had. Maybe she should highlight it, frost it, streak it— something with an attitude. But she had no one to impress now, and she was clean out of attitude.

A Mendelssohn concerto, soothing and vibrant, filled the car from her stereo as she merged back onto the highway, but gathering brake lights ahead caught her attention. The lanes were moving, but at a crawl. And the cars veered and wound erratically. What on earth?

Something on the road. No, lots of things. Moving . . . slowly. Turtles! Eight-inch turtles, marching onto the highway from the cornfields, and many not fortunate enough to have made it across. She looked away from the carnage of one she viewed in greater detail than she would have cared to.

Poor creatures. Did they realize they were plodding to their deaths?

Could they see beyond the few feet before them, conceive of something large and fast enough to crush them in less time than it took to take their next step? Their instinct told them to plod forward, relentlessly pursuing whatever. Then splat. Nothing. The great abyss.

At least people were trying to avoid them. She swung her own wheel to the left as one turtle headed for her tires. What was this? Some great turtle exodus? A migration of reptilian pioneers. Whenever a car whizzed past, the turtles would stop, draw in their heads and legs as though the shell could save them from a couple tons of steel. She swerved to the right but heard the crunch anyway. *Oh . . .*

A white Fiat pulled over and two men climbed out, running back along the shoulder waving their arms. Jill watched in her rearview mirror as they worked their way onto the road still waving wildly. Stopping traffic for the turtles? She had to cheer their sentiment. They were young and gangly and idealistic. While one darted out waving people to a stop, the other scooped up a turtle and rushed it to the side.

She smiled. Good for them. The men ignored the honking cars and scooped up one after another. She hoped they got every one of the creatures across to safety. But she was through it now. The cars ahead picked up speed, and she followed suit. How absurd. Who ever heard of a turtle crossing? She pictured the appropriate black-on-yellow highway sign and almost managed a laugh. Why not? They now had crossing guards.

At least she would have a story to tell her kids tomorrow. She wouldn't mention the crushed shells and certainly not the crunch of her own tire. That was too emotional, too risky for her kids. But the parade—that they'd enjoy, and the man scooping them up and carrying them across, protection they couldn't conceive. Even Joey would appreciate this tale.

She only hoped today had not set him back too badly. He'd had more than one regression in the course of the year, and they weren't pretty. That was why Pam and their paraprofessional, Jack, left Joey to her, and in fact she did have better success with him than anyone else had to date. She didn't tell anyone it was prayer that calmed him. That wouldn't go over well in a public school, not with her team. But it was true. Prayer helped. Prayer worked. And she couldn't do what she did without it. These kids, whom everyone would rather forget, push aside, marginalize . . . they broke her heart and gave her purpose. She felt a stab and tried to ignore it, then rose up in defense. Why shouldn't her purpose be other people's kids? Who said happiness could only be found in having her own family?

She parked in the single garage of her townhouse, then went to retrieve the mail from her compartment in the communal box. She had just grasped the envelopes in the box when Mr. Deerborne sidled up.

"Your trash blew over."

Jill glanced to where the rubber can now stood empty beside her garage door, though the gusting wind had stopped by noon.

"Spilled cat litter all over the sidewalk. Safety hazard, that. Someone might have slipped and taken a fall." He waved his cane in the large knuckled hand. "I swept it up for you."

She turned to her neighbor. "Thank you. That was very considerate."

"Saving you a lawsuit is all."

She smiled, though the only one likely to sue her would be Mr. Deerborne himself. "Thanks so much."

When he stalked back across the lot between their buildings, she went inside, dropped the mail on the counter, and looked around. "Kitty, kitty . . ."

The long-haired gray half-Persian-half-who-knew-what jumped onto the counter. Jill scratched his head while he purred his welcome, one of those ratchety purrs that ebbed and flowed. "Hello, Rascal."

He licked her chin, and she tore open a pouch of food to fill his bowl. The phone rang. Shelly. She must have surveillance equipment inside the townhouse. Or maybe Brett had it bugged. More likely she'd seen the light. "Hello?" She slid the mail from under the cat's paws.

"Well?" Shelly's voice always sounded huskier over the phone.

"Well, hi." Jill scooted past the sofa, dropped the stack of envelopes to the ornate corner table she'd purchased at an estate sale, then dropped to the chair upholstered with beige, brown, and black giraffes. An eclectic combination, she admitted.

"Don't keep me in suspense. Was it wonderful? Did he ask you?"

She must also have inside knowledge. "Ask me what, Shelly?"

"Jill Runyan, I'm going to have a coronary, and it'll be your fault." Shelly added a deep exaggerated breath. "I know Dan had something planned, so out with it."

Jill said, "He proposed something, but it wasn't marriage."

"O-kay . . . so we're working into it."

Jill pulled a loose thread from the seam of her chair and rolled it between her fingers. "He wants to live together and see if we're compatible."

"Understandable. His breakup really hurt, you know. His ex was brutal."

All of which Jill had heard before. "Well, I hope I wasn't brutal."

"What do you mean?"

Jill forked her fingers into the hair at the nape of her neck. She hated when Shelly's interrogation happened before she had time to plan her explanation. She was nothing if not methodical.

"Jill, don't tell me you broke up with him."

If only she had a wise or even witty comeback. In truth, Dan was genuinely nice, handsome, responsible . . .

"You are certifiably insane."

Jill sank into the chair's thickness. "You'll never guess what I saw on the highway."

"Don't change the subject, Jill. How could you dump him?"

"Turtles."

"What?"

"A turtle migration or something. There they were crossing the highway, stopping traffic both ways. Ever tried to outmaneuver a turtle with a purpose?"

"Are you falling apart?"

"Of course not." At the moment she hadn't the energy. "And these two guys stopped traffic and started carrying them across, one by one."

"I'm coming over."

"No, Shelly, I'm fine." Jill toed the heel of her left shoe loose and slipped her foot out. "I'm getting into the bath." She took off her other shoe and set them side by side against the chair.

Shelly moaned. "How did he take it?"

"No yelling, no tears, and no personal commitment." Unless one considered a joint mortgage personal.

"It hasn't even been a year. Cops are slow in the personal commitment department. It's a job hazard."

"Your cop isn't."

"Well . . ."

"Shelly." Jill rubbed her eyes. "It doesn't matter. We're coming from two different worlds. What's important to me is . . . incomprehensible to him."

"You mean God?"

"My faith matters to me, Shelly. It's who I am." Not that Dan or

Shelly had a clue what she meant by that.

"You can work out that religious stuff together."

Jill bent a crick from her neck. "We agreed that he had his beliefs, or lack thereof, I had mine, and never the twain shall meet."

"If you're talking poetry, I'm calling the police."

Jill smiled grimly. "Try Dan. He'd love a sympathetic ear."

"Can't you just compromise?"

Compromise. "I don't see how."

"You can't act like the ice queen and expect him to marry you."

Ice queen. Shelly had never been long on tact, but ice queen? Did refusing to sleep with Dan mean she was made of ice? She tried to reconcile that image with the hugs and kisses she poured out on the children, at personal risk. She wanted to love them, to teach and encourage them, to help them succeed. Ice queen. Is that how she seemed to Dan? To Shelly?

"Jill, this is breaking my heart."

"I'm sorry. Just now mine's a little shaky, too. Talk to you tomorrow." Jill hung up the phone. It didn't help that her best friend was married to Dan's partner on the force. Get-togethers were bound to be jolly. At least for a while.

She fought the sudden tears. Why should she cry? So Dan had been personable and caring . . . to a point. The point that ended where her limits began. Ice queen. *Quite a long way from prom queen, Lord. Oh, how the mighty have fallen.*

Jill tipped her head back against the top of the chair and resisted the tears. Falling apart did no good. She should not have dated him in the first place, should have stayed friends and avoided this . . . heartache. But it was hard to withstand Shelly and Brett and Dan's persuasion. Not to mention the loneliness that seeped in sometimes, causing brain lapse in areas where she knew better.

It was nothing against Dan. He just wanted all the elements of a relationship without the legal and moral fetters of a covenant. Or the risk. She knew about risk.

She sniffed and glanced down at the mail. Listlessly she lifted the top card, a reminder of the fifteen-year fund-raiser class reunion. *If the girls could see me now. . . .* She shook her head. How had things changed so much? She'd been on top of the world then, at the top of her class. Until Morgan . . .

Jill dropped her face to her hands. Why did her thoughts go that direction every time she was vulnerable? It was fifteen years ago. For all she knew, Morgan Spencer was married with six kids. And he was hardly to blame for her problems.

But she rolled to her side and curled her knees to her chest in the chair's embrace as tears began to flow. *No, no, no. Don't think about it. Don't add misery to misery.* But the thoughts came anyway. What was she like? Was her hair blond, or dark like Morgan's? It had been dark, but that was newborn hair. Were her eyes still blue, the deep Spencer blue, or gray like her own?

Jill buried her face in the back of the chair and sobbed. She had to get control of this. It had been one awful mistake, and she'd done the best she could with it. She had made the right choice against all the opposition, all the pressure, all the pain. Her daughter was in the best place she could be, with parents who loved her. What more could she do? And Morgan . . .

Jill drew a deep, racking breath. *It had been right. It was the best I could do.* She repeated the mantra until she could stop the tears; then she sat up and took the mail in her lap, forcing her mind elsewhere. She flipped through the envelopes. Junk, junk, utilities, junk. She dropped the stack without finishing and headed for the bathroom.

Some of her best time was spent there, soaking in the oversized Jacuzzi tub, one amenity that had sold her on the townhouse. She started the water. Okay, so things weren't always as she wanted them. That was her own fault. God had planned things better, but she had blown His plan. She couldn't change that.

She hung her sage green blouse and skirt on the hanger at the back of the door and climbed into the tub. Some things she could soak off. Others clung forever. She would spend the night trying to sleep, then go to work in the morning. At least her kids gave her purpose. And the challenges they faced beat anything she could complain about on a bad day.

For a moment her thoughts went to Dan. What was he doing? Probably thinking of all the reasons he was glad to be rid of her. The ice queen.

CHAPTER

2

Morgan maneuvered the white retro Thunderbird up the pass with enough torque and panache to satisfy his mood. The lofty sides of the mountain canyon supported a clear sapphire sky as he scaled the road between them, heading toward the ranch nestled brazenly at the base of one stony crag. Rick's ranch. Rick and Noelle's.

It had been his swift kick that had reunited his brother with the one woman who might have made things different in his own life. Noelle St. Claire . . . no, Spencer. Rick's wife. Thanks to him. Well, partly.

He expelled a sharp breath. He was happy for them. He could say that with honesty, except in those low moments when he'd rather not. Noelle was something special, and he'd imagined . . . Well, better not go there. He'd thought for a time she might be his salvation. But she had proved too fragile. Her own tragedy had almost destroyed her; what did she want with his?

He turned up the CD playing the voice of Mephistopheles deceiving Beethoven in the contemporary rock opera by the Trans-Siberian Orchestra. The imaginary story of Beethoven's last night on earth resonated. The devil coming to claim Beethoven's soul struck a chord in Morgan—especially when Twist and Fate intervened, and Beethoven pleaded his case. Morgan might be damned, but he would have his say and hey—he might even talk his way past old Pete when his time came.

He increased his speed around the bend. His new Thunderbird handled like a dream. Ah, the good life. And it was getting better. In the meantime, his little hiatus ought to hone him to go back in sharp. Mr. Problem-solver. Even at thirty-three he had a knack—Mom called it a gift—for seeing problems and finding solutions. On one of his first consultations he'd accepted stock as payment, and when the small floundering company soared to hi-tech fame and was purchased by IBM, Morgan's name was made. Not to mention capital gains that nicely multiplied on their own.

He slowed as he entered Juniper Falls, the sleepy mountain after-thought Rick called home, though the ranch was another two miles up the gravel road to the right. Morgan considered stopping at the Roaring Boar for a beer before heading up, but he shrugged and made his turn with enough scattered gravel to catch the eye of the man on the porch of the general store.

He gave Rudy a wave, which was returned heartily. One thing about Juniper Falls, the people were friendly . . . and they knew him. Everyone knew everyone. You couldn't lose yourself here like you could in the city. That's why Morgan came. Once in a while, he liked to be real.

He pulled into the yard before the large golden log house, Rick's handiwork, along with the barn, stable, and cabins. Like Dad, Rick had horses in his blood. He looked the part, too: long and lanky in jeans and Stetson, standing between the stable and his Dodge Ram truck. At least it wasn't a Ford. That would have been a little too Texas. This was Colorado Rocky Mountain land.

Morgan killed the music with the turn of his key and climbed out. The spring mountain air was crisp and clean, untinged with the balmy brine of his own home, the view majestic—towering crags over dark, prickly green slopes. It lacked the motion of his ocean view, but its very stasis spoke of perpetuity. It was too much to take in as a whole. It lost meaning in the smallness of the human brain. It needed to be broken down into understandable pieces.

He thought of Noelle's paintings, the watercolors she'd done of small scenes, a gully veiled in pine roots with columbine and rockroses beneath. A single aspen masquerading as a grove, whose webbed roots gave rise to every trunk and leaf. He remembered when she had arrived two summers ago, draped in mystery and too broken to respond to his attentions.

"How are you, Morg?" Rick extended his hand.

They grabbed each other in a brotherly hug. "Never better. Got any beautiful guests we can fight over?"

"If I had any, they'd be all yours." Rick grinned.

"Yeah. Guess you're out of the market. Not that you were ever in it." Sober, celibate Rick.

Rick jutted his chin toward the car. "Traded in your Vette?"

"It's at home. I couldn't pass up this retro dream. Screamin' V8 on a Lincoln chassis; it's a cloud rocket." Morgan looked around the yard and caught sight of a sullen-faced teen on the stoop of the nearest side cabin. "Who's the kid?"

"Todd. He's up with his family."

"He looks happy about that."

Rick sent him a side glance. "He's got problems."

Morgan nodded, then got to the important question. "Where is she?"

Rick cocked his head toward the door. "In the house."

Morgan followed his nod. "You mind?"

"Go on in."

Morgan's mouth quirked as he headed up the broad pine log steps. Rick was cocky to send him in on his own. But then, what did he have to worry about? Morgan pushed open the door and scanned the vaulted main room with the curved staircase at the end.

He'd seen the room remodeled but not redecorated. That must be Noelle's doing—the colored throws, the woven wall hanging above the plain pine cross over the mantel, watercolor landscapes on the walls and the one she'd done of Rick and the ranch. Morgan remembered that one. She'd painted his portrait, as well, and presented it two years ago at Christmas. He'd never had it framed or hung it, though. He closed the door behind him.

"Rick?" Her voice came from the kitchen.

He strolled that way and leaned on the doorjamb. "Nah, he's in the yard. But I'm here."

She spun from the sink with a peeler in one hand and a potato in the other. "Morgan!"

Her hair was honey-colored silk on her shoulders, her eyes the clear gray-green he remembered too often. Her smile was warm and unaffected, and he trailed his eyes down. His glance flashed back to her face.

"Well." He sauntered over and kissed her cheek. "Rick didn't waste any time." He breathed her scent. "When's the little cowboy due?"

"September fourth."

He stepped back half a pace, assessing her. "How are you?"

"Fine." She must know he meant that in more ways than one. So the horror of her childhood kidnapping and later battering was behind her, and Rick and she were on their way to happily ever after. Or did that really exist? At any rate, she was coping, and she looked happy. Leave it to Rick.

"Mind if I stay awhile?"

"Can you stand the quiet?" She turned, rinsed the potato, and set it aside.

"For a while. Be good to rev down some." He leaned on the counter. "Surprised?"

"Actually, no."

"Why not?"

She waved the peeler toward the side counter by the phone. "Your forwarded mail."

He glanced over. "You mean the U.S. Postal Service beat me here?"

She nodded with a raise of her eyebrows.

"Okay, so I had a little detour in Vegas." He didn't tell her how cheap and meaningless it had seemed, though he'd taken in some great shows and had a successful time at the blackjack table. "You know what I think? I think the three . . . no, the four of us"—he waved his hand toward her belly—"should hit the Roaring Boar. Friday night on the town, a little dinner, a little dancing . . ."

She laughed. "Same old Morgan."

"Think we can shake Rick loose?"

"Maybe, but I'm not as light on my feet as I used to be."

He stepped close and took her hands. "I bet you still dance like a dream." He heard Rick clear his throat behind him but didn't let go.

Rick clamped his shoulder. "How'd I know you'd be making a play for my wife?"

Morgan let her go. Had he been? Not seriously, but maybe he'd wanted to see if there was a little flicker there.

Noelle reached for Rick's hand and drew him close. "Morgan wants us to go dancing tonight."

"Uh-huh." He bent and kissed her softly.

That's right, Rick, rub it in. "What do you say? Do we all go, or shall I just take Noelle?"

Rick turned. "Morgan, sometimes I wonder about you."

Morgan laughed, forked his fingers through his hair, and sighed. "Yeah, me too." He turned and scooped up his mail. He had left this as his forwarding address, and he had taken his time getting here, though the days in Vegas had been disappointing. He was burned out on beautiful sirens, late nights, and the false frenzy of the fickle fortunate. He didn't seem to fit anymore. In fact, nothing had been the same since he'd given up Noelle.

He flipped through the mail, stopped at the postcard, and smirked. *Class of '88 Fund-raiser Reunion.* It was a reminder for those who hadn't jumped at the opportunity on the first notice. He flipped the card over and saw the handwritten marker across the picture of high school memorabilia. *Wilson High of '88's most likely to succeed: Morgan, be there and bring your wallet.* "What people won't stoop to." He tossed it onto the table.

Rick picked up the card and looked it over. "Are you going?"

"No."

"Why not?"

Morgan shrugged. "Why should I?"

Rick raised a knowing eye but asked, "It's a fund-raiser?"

"School needs updating—computers and stuff. I'll send a check. That's what they really want." Morgan flipped through the rest of the mail. "Got a room for me?"

"Sure." Rick picked up a couple stray peelings from the floor and tossed them into the sink. "Let's get your bags."

They went down to his car, and Morgan popped the trunk. "Judging by the little guy in the oven, I guess things are working out."

Rick nodded. "Noelle's healing, Morgan. I'd appreciate it if you didn't complicate things."

"That's never been my style."

"Oh, really?" Rick rested his hand on the trunk lid.

"Really."

Rick reached in for a bag. "Are you not going because Jill might be there?"

Morgan reached for the other bags in the trunk. *Jill.* "Just not interested." He hadn't gone to the tenth reunion, wouldn't plan on the twentieth, and didn't care about a mid-decade fleecing.

He set the bags down and closed the trunk. He didn't need this much luggage here, but he'd be moving on to the next project directly. And for that he'd have to dress the part. He had brought his two-thousand-dollar power suits and shirts, his Italian leather shoes, and hand-decorated silk ties, the costume of the consummate professional. The thought left him hollow. He must need this break more than he realized.

Rick paused at the door and turned slightly. "I think you ought to go, Morgan."

Morgan climbed the steps behind him. Rick did not push, especially in personal matters. Why was he making so much of a stupid reunion? Morgan could send them a check for every computer they needed and remodel the ancient computer lab and add classroom connections to boot.

"What's the big deal, Rick?"

"Just a feeling."

Morgan half smiled. A feeling from God, he meant. Rick the prophet, mouthpiece of the Almighty. Go down, Moses. To a high school reunion where he might see Jill? With Rick blocking the door and expecting an answer, Morgan shrugged. "I'll think about it."

Unfortunately, he would. He had been ever since the first packet arrived.

After the final three days of school, Jill had agreed to a Friday night movie fest with Shelly, whose intention was to help her over the heart-ache. Shelly was making more of it than it was. Yes, it hurt to have the void in her life that Dan had filled, and especially to know she'd disappointed him.

As Shelly's best friend, dating Shelly's husband Brett's partner, and forming a comfortable foursome, had been natural. Add to that their similar interests in fitness and outdoor activities, their service-minded jobs—hers to the struggling kids, his to the rest of society . . . on the outside it seemed like a fit. But emotionally, and especially spiritually, they'd missed somehow. Her fault, she knew. Her inability to risk much of herself.

Truth be told, if Dan had an operational faith, she might still resist a next step. Maybe she was the slow one in the personal commitment department. Maybe that's what Shelly interpreted as ice queen, the preserving of self that in essence precluded giving and receiving fully. But love wasn't a game. It wasn't the warm aching inside that had kept her awake the first night Morgan had kissed her. It wasn't anything she could get a handle on.

The pastor at her church talked about love, but it was always in such nebulous terms she wondered if he knew any more than she did. God's love was above hers, self-love a pitfall, and physical love the trapdoor to hell. Maybe a loveless life was best after all.

It was late now as she inserted her key into the townhouse door. A light flicked on across the lot as Mr. Deerborne noted her return from his bedroom window and made sure she realized she had disturbed him. She ignored him and walked into her dark townhouse. Rascal wrapped himself around her legs, arching up to rub his mouth behind her calf as he passed sideways, trailing his tail, then circled back.

Loveless? How could anyone be loveless with a cat? His purr sounded like the Honda's engine on a cold day. She bent and scratched behind his ears, bringing him to his hind legs, front paws curling around her wrist. He licked her fingers. Now if that wasn't devotion, what was?

She dropped the mail on the counter and went to the bedroom to change. Slipping off her sandals, shorts, and sleeveless sweater, she pulled on a nightshirt. She tossed her hair back and caught a glimpse of herself in the mirror. She hadn't changed much in fifteen years. A little thinner in the cheeks, more defined in her features, but not much changed . . . on the outside.

She still looked like the head of the cheerleading squad, the front-page photo of her senior yearbook. She shot the mirror her Miss America smile and almost captured the same expression she'd worn for the camera. Good thing the picture was taken early in the school year and not in the spring, when she was losing her breakfast in the girl's rest room every morning before her first class. She hadn't missed a single day of classes, but she'd been sick enough to hide the pregnancy until the sixth month. She actually weighed less by then than when she'd conceived.

Morgan was the first to know. It hurt to remember the urgency in his face as he promised to stick by her, a promise he had no way to keep once her parents learned of their circumstances. She turned away from the mirror. Maybe it was time for a change. She had an appointment at the salon Sunday with Crystal for a trim, but maybe something more daring was in order.

Jill walked back to the kitchen and flipped through the mail. Nothing important. She remembered the utilities bill from Wednesday's mail and glanced over to the corner table. The stack was still there. She crossed the room, lifted the half-dozen envelopes and the fund-raiser reunion reminder. *Haven't heard from you. Wilson High needs your help. Come share the alum fun.* Good grief.

She slipped the utilities bill free and dropped the rest back to the table. She opened the bill and read the damage, then carried it to her small oak desk and laid it there to be paid tomorrow when she balanced the checkbook. She yawned, scooped up Rascal, and headed for bed.

The phone rang, and Jill rolled over to grab it. 6:32 on the clock. Who would call so early on a Saturday? She lifted the receiver and tried to sound as though she hadn't just been jarred from sleep. "Hello?"

"Can I interest you in breakfast and a bike ride?" Dan's voice sounded chipper, and for a moment she was confused. Had she not . . .

Jill pressed a palm to her forehead. "Dan?"

"I'm sorry. I didn't think you'd confuse me with someone else already."

She cleared her throat. "Hold on just a second." She covered the receiver and yawned, then shook her head and sat up. "Sorry. Shelly had me out late last night."

"I know."

She felt a pang. "Dan . . ."

"We've put almost a year into this, Jill. It's a shame to let it go over . . ."

"Sex?"

He laughed low. "Yeah."

She closed her eyes and rubbed the sleep from them. "I can't expect you to change what you want just because I won't cross that line."

"Sex is really hard on a bicycle."

She laughed, then sobered. "I think the other night showed us both what we needed to know."

"Maybe. But Shelly's concerned that she'll lose one of her close friends here."

Poor Shelly. "I'm not going anywhere."

"Why don't we have a bagel and hash out some sort of friendship agreement?"

Jill dropped her head back to the headboard and smiled at the ceiling. "You are definitely headed for captain, Dan."

He laughed. "I'll be over in thirty."

She hung up the phone. Great. Just what she needed after a late night. Well, Dan had seen her looking worse, and she actually managed to look better than she'd expected in thirty minutes' time. She had dressed in a periwinkle tank with a gray-blue plaid overshirt, sleeves rolled. Her waist-tie cotton khakis were loose enough to ride in if she and Dan decided to after all.

Dan rang the bell at seven o'clock sharp. Punctual to a fault. That was Dan. Reliable and disciplined. She pulled the door open and met his bearish smile. He was burly and compact for a cyclist, but that was from the weight training he did, as well.

"Einstein's?"

"Sure." She locked the door behind her.

"Let's walk." He had locked his bike to her maple tree.

"Okay." The morning was warm and a little humid and smelled of dew.

"So the way I see it, you're set on a platonic relationship, no matter where it might go."

Jill rolled her eyes. "You know, Dan, sometimes prevarication is a good thing."

"Pre...what?"

"Beat around the bush a little, and not with your nightstick." She nudged him with her elbow.

"Sorry."

"That's all right."

Idle conversation seemed to stump him, and they walked quietly for a while. Then he turned his blunt face to her, and the breeze caught the brown hair, thinning a little at the top. "Is it just a religious thing?"

She leaned over and sniffed the flowering hydrangea along the sidewalk, calming the tension his insistent questions brought. She could say yes. Her belief system did not condone premarital sex. She'd been raised in a Christian home with committed parents, taught right from wrong. But the truth was, that hadn't stopped her before. Morgan's love had overpowered her limp beliefs, and the consequences were a far, far more painful deterrent than all the convictions she held now.

She looked at Dan's sincere face. "Mostly." He was trying to understand, and maybe she owed him some explanation.

"I know a thing or two about safe sex, Jill. I teach it, remember?"

Sure he did, a virile, healthy man who believed sex an inevitable part of any serious relationship. He brought the message to the high schools and was wildly applauded. She knew people at her church who felt the same way, in spite of the pastor's sermons to the contrary. But she also knew from personal experience the devastating consequences of having a sexual relationship without that lifetime commitment. She could not make him understand without telling him more than she intended.

He stopped on the walk outside Einstein's Bagels and turned. "How do you know a relationship can work long-term? If you're not willing to give it a trial period, how can you commit to a lifetime?"

"Maybe I can't."

"Why?"

Because I know what it is to lose it. "We've been over this already. I thought we were working out terms of friendship."

With a sigh, he pushed open the door and held it for her. She ordered a potato bagel with cream cheese and green tea. He ordered the seven-grain and coffee. They took their respective bagels to the table and sat down.

Dan rested his forearms on the table edge. "Okay. Let's set the parameters." He picked up the bagel and took a bite, chewed to one side and went on. "No intercourse, obviously. What about kissing?"

"No."

"That'll be hard." He swigged his coffee.

"We'll get used to it."

He took another hearty bite. "What about doing things together? Like this?"

Jill felt tears coming. "I don't know, Dan. Sometimes, maybe."

"Do you want me to leave you alone?"

The tears stung her eyes, but she refused to let them fall.

He reached out and took her hands. "I wish I could just . . . well, we've already ruled that out."

She laughed and reached for her tea, sipping it while he munched his bagel.

Dan studied her as he ate, then swiped his mouth with the napkin and said, "Really, Jill. Can you handle it if we still do things as a foursome? You and Shelly and Brett and me?"

"I don't know. Probably. Can you?"

"Yeah." He tucked the last quarter of his bagel into his cheek. "I'd rather do that than nothing."

She sniffed. "So, we just, um, go back to . . . well, not actually back to the beginning because . . ."

"I kissed you on our first date. Do you think that's what jinxed it?"

Jill covered her face with her hand. "I think I'm just bad luck all around."

"Aw, Jill."

"Want another bagel?" She pushed her plate his way.

"I guess. If you're not hungry."

She sipped her tea, and it settled her stomach. "What's important here is for Shelly to know there are no hard feelings between us. There aren't, are there?"

"Well, I wouldn't say I'm happy about things." He started on her bagel.

"But you do understand. You're not going to start a campaign of parking tickets against me?"

He cocked his fingers like a gun at her. "That would not be professional, my dear."

"I think once we work through the emotions of it . . ."

"Yeah." He chomped down on the bagel and dabbed the cream cheese from the corner of his mouth. The rest of it disappeared in three more bites. He drained his Styrofoam coffee cup and crushed it with his napkin. "So. Buddies?"

"Ohh . . ." She grimaced.

"Come on. We'll ride it off. Nothing like exhaustion to numb the emotions." He stood and took her elbow. "Leg it, lady. The day's a-wasting."

3

Morgan sauntered up to the boy sitting on the cabin porch, scratching the post with a nail. The kid didn't stop scratching or turn, though Morgan guessed he knew he had company. Rick would not be pleased with the word taking shape in the post. Morgan stooped, and at last the boy turned from his graffiti long enough to use the phrase he'd been carving.

Morgan rested his forearms on his knees. "Why should I?"

"Cuz I told you to." The kid fit the word in that sentence, too.

Morgan shrugged. "It's a free country."

Agitated now, the boy gouged a deep line into the post.

Morgan could grab the nail, stop its damaging progress, but instead he asked, "You have a name?"

"Why should you care?" There it was. So far he'd gotten it into every sentence.

"Ever tried a complete sentence without that word?"

"Ever tried to go—"

Morgan raised a hand. "I got the gist."

The kid gripped the nail and dug an ugly curve into the post, then surprised him with "Todd."

"Well, Todd, don't you have anything better to do than vandalize that post?" Morgan wasn't too concerned. Rick could sand it off and stain it up good as new.

"Like ride a horse in a line?" He got it in twice that time. Some kids were afflicted with the word *like*. Couldn't stretch three words together without it. Todd's choice was a little more grating.

But Morgan listened around it. Rick must be taking the family on a ride. Morgan brushed away a brilliant blue-green fly darting in front of his face. "Your folks went riding?"

"Yeah. They thought this dude ranch would be like Disneyland."

"You'd rather be in Disneyland?"

"Take a flying—" Todd started back on the wood, digging in the nail.

"And if they weren't riding in a line?"

Todd turned. "You mean if I could take a horse by myself?" A complete sentence with no profanity.

Morgan shrugged. "Not by yourself. But you could lead the way."

Todd lowered the nail. "Who are you?"

"Morgan."

"I mean who are you on this ranch?"

Morgan quirked his mouth sideways. That was a better question than Todd knew. He waved to the holding corral beside the barn. "A couple of horses right there." It had been years since he'd sat a saddle, but he'd grown up on the same ranch as Rick.

Todd eyed the animals warily, turned back to him with narrowed eyes. "You don't look like a—cowboy." Not a complete cure then, but the word was coming less frequently.

"I'm not. Haven't ridden in years."

Todd formed a sly smile. "Is that your convertible?"

Morgan sent his glance to his Thunderbird parked outside the house. He was lucky Todd hadn't chosen it for his carving. "Rather ride that?"

"Rather drive it."

Morgan moistened his lips, altitude and climate making him dry. "We can take it for a spin."

"I can drive?"

Morgan didn't ask how old he was. Even if Todd were small for his age, he was no sixteen. Morgan dug for his keys. "Why don't you ride."

Todd dropped the nail, and it rolled through the crack in the planks. He stood up. "Let's do it."

They climbed into the car and Morgan started it up. Great engine. He reached his arm between the bucket seats, looked over his shoulder, and backed out in one swift arc. Then he left the ranch, the gravel road trailing behind in a cloud of dust. He spun around at the intersection in Juniper Falls, and they flew back up to the ranch.

Todd's eyes were electrified. He used his favorite word with awe.

"You know, Todd. It wouldn't hurt to develop your vocabulary."

"What should I say? Cool?" But he was grinning.

"In my circle we'd say *excellent*."

"Excellent. Can I drive it?"

Morgan shook his head, "No."

"Why not?" The smile faded and the scowl returned.

"You'd need your dad's permission." Morgan felt fairly certain the kid's dad wouldn't give it. His machine was safe.

Todd swore. "Like that would ever happen." He got out and slammed the door, turned, and kicked it.

Holding his temper, Morgan climbed out and walked around, looked from the shoe smudge to the kid who had stopped in the middle of the apron, breathing hard.

Todd's shoulders rose and fell. "You gonna beat me up?"

Morgan pursed his lips. "Should I?"

Todd glared. "I messed up your car."

Morgan eyed the smudge again. "Nothing a chamois and polish won't take care of."

"Are you rich?" He said it like someone might taunt *Are you fat? Are you stupid? Are you ugly?*

Morgan faced him squarely. "Yeah."

Todd wasn't sure how to take that honesty from an adult. His face showed it. "How rich are you?"

"Nowhere close to Bill Gates."

Todd turned away and stared at the meadow that gradually rose to a stony crag.

Morgan joined him. "Does that bother you?"

"Why should it?"

"It shouldn't." No reason this adolescent time bomb should care one way or another.

Todd picked up a rock and threw it at the creek that ran down the meadow and behind the cabins. "My dad's in jail."

"I thought he was here at the ranch."

"That's my foster family."

Morgan nodded. "What did he do?"

"Killed a guy in a bar fight."

"Where's your mom?"

He shrugged.

No wonder the kid had anger issues. Morgan drew a slow breath. "Life can be ugly."

"What would you know?"

Morgan eyed him sidelong. Why did every kid think he had a corner on the misery market? He said only, "I'd know."

It seemed to sink in. Maybe Todd's mind was receptive to the melancholy that had seeped out with the words. At any rate, the boy didn't argue.

Morgan said, "How old are you?"

"Thirteen."

A shiver went down his back. This kid was almost the same age as . . . Was that why he'd fixated on him, some latent desire to parent someone in place of the one he couldn't? He walked back to the car, opened the trunk, and took out two small bottles of Dasani water. He carried one back to Todd, then opened his and chugged half the bottle. "Do you see your dad?"

Todd drank, too, then shook his head. "Don't want to."

"Because he screwed up?"

"Cuz he's a—jerk." Anger definitely triggered the word.

Morgan nodded. "How 'bout your foster dad?"

Todd scowled but said nothing.

"How long have you been with them?"

"Few months."

"Other kids?" Morgan took a long draw that drained his water bottle, then twisted the cap back on.

"They got three."

"Older or younger?"

Todd drank his water. "Both. One's off in college, one in high school, one almost my age."

"Is that the girl I saw?"

"She's stuck up." Todd crushed the half-full plastic bottle and started to heave it, but Morgan caught his hand and removed the bottle from his grasp.

"They can be at that age." At any age, really, though he enjoyed notching down the ones who really needed it. Especially in the professional world. If they deserved their position, great. He'd work with a woman as easily as a man. It was the ones who'd clawed their way into power through sheer vixen nastiness that brought out his dark side.

"If a stuck-up girl is the worst you have to deal with, you might lighten up a little."

He expected Todd's favorite word, but the kid only glanced up. "If you're so rich, how come you're not out on a yacht or something? How come you're here?"

"I like it here."

Todd kicked the dirt. "That's stupid. There's not even a TV anywhere."

From the trees at the edge of the meadow came the string of horses with Rick in the lead. Mom, Dad, and their dimpled blond daughter came next. Beside Morgan, Todd tensed, then turned around and slunk back to the porch of their cabin. Morgan tossed the water bottles into the barrel beside the barn.

At the end of the yard, Rick stopped the horse parade outside the stable and helped the woman and daughter dismount. They seemed a decent enough family for all the stories you heard about foster care. The dad might be a bit of a milquetoast, but he wrapped his daughter's shoulders with his arm and ambled toward the cabin. Todd was watching through the corner of his eye but averted his face as they approached. The woman spoke to him, but he didn't answer.

Morgan joined Rick. "Hey."

Rick jerked his chin toward Todd disappearing around the back of their cabin. "What was that all about?"

He must have seen their interaction, if you could call it that. "Just getting to know him."

"Good luck."

Morgan grinned. "He is a little prickly. What's the deal?"

Rick heaved the saddle off the mare. "Not sure. He's been in the foster program awhile. Stan's only had him a couple of months. He's flunked out or been kicked out of every school he's attended."

"How'd you get hooked up with them?"

"Stan's a friend of my neighbor. He's trying to keep Todd out of trouble. Needed a place of refuge."

Morgan nodded. "I'm starting to see a pattern."

Rick stripped the blanket and sent the mare up to pasture. "They have the cabin as long as they need it."

"The guy's not working?"

"He's a schoolteacher. Off for the summer." Rick uncinched the last saddle. No doubt he'd given Todd's family the same sort of deal he'd given Noelle when she appeared at his door, wounded and needy.

Rick hoisted the saddle off. "Even though Stan has him at the private Christian school, two rival gangs are courting Todd. Stan thought he'd get him out of Denver, try to make some inroads. We're working out a chore schedule for Todd and his sister—foster sister, or however that works."

Morgan chewed the corner of his lip. "That'll go over well with Todd."

"I hope it'll do him good."

At the sound of the screen door banging, Morgan glanced toward the house. "What about Noelle?"

Rick stared across the yard at his wife. "She's really somethin', Morgan." He said it as though just the sight drew the words from him.

"Tell me about it."

Rick sobered. "We weren't going to take guests this summer, but I think it helps to have other people around. She gets pretty focused."

"On you?" *Rick should complain?*

Rick sent the last horse up to pasture. "It hasn't been that long. God's been good, but sometimes she's shaky."

Morgan watched Noelle spread birdseed on the railing. "You sure a troubled kid is what she needs around?"

"She was glad for the chance. Shifts the spotlight."

Morgan shook his head. His first assessment must not have captured all the nuances of his brother's relationship. Again he had that sense that Noelle had chosen the better man. "Any regrets?"

Rick squinted. "All the things I didn't do right."

Morgan rubbed the back of his neck. "Well, Clark, Lois doesn't seem to notice."

Noelle headed for them, shaking the seed from her fingers and still looking like a piece of Dresden china. "Where'd you go, Morgan? I heard the car tear out."

"Tear out?" He smiled. "Just giving Todd a little ride."

Noelle searched his face. "Really?"

Morgan spread his hands. "What?"

"I just . . . that's nice, Morgan."

"And . . ."

She slid a strand of hair behind her ear. "I know your sisters adore you, but I didn't know you were interested in kids in general. I wouldn't see you spending time with a boy like Todd."

"I'm a sucker for hard cases."

Her gray-green eyes were luminous in the daylight. "I should know that."

His chest tightened. *Sure. Recapture the heartache. Smart, Morgan.* He looked away. "Guess I'll see what's roarin' at the Boar." It was early to hit a bar, even for him. But hey, he was on vacation. He started for the car.

"Morgan."

He turned back to Rick. "Yeah?"

"Did you get a flight to Iowa?"

Morgan frowned. "It's lined up if I decide to go." And he just might want some distance after all.

Rick nodded. "Good."

————————

After biking with Dan out to Finnegan's Pond, twenty-four miles roundtrip from town and back, Jill had spent a quiet afternoon on the patio with Rascal and two professional journals on developing receptive language in autistic children and the use of broad-spectrum antidepressants for various emotional disorders.

Hearing a tap on the glass, Jill pulled open her patio door to admit her friend Shelly, who was waiting with a globe-shaped lollipop. "Tell me what you think of this one." She slipped off the plastic and held it out.

Jill took the lollipop. Not too many people got to be the unofficial assistant to the taste tester for Cartier Confections. Choosing the new test-market flavors was only part of Shelly's job, but she took it seriously and always included Jill for her discerning palate.

Jill eyed the current prospect. "For starters, you've got to blend the colors. This white-and-ecru swirl looks like something someone spit in the parking lot."

"Major concern." Shelly checked it off on her PDA. "No phlegm on a stick."

"What's the flavor?"

"Taste it."

Jill sniffed it. "I'm not much for coconut."

"This is a taste test, not a sniff test."

Jill licked the lollipop, surprised by the sweet, pleasant flavor. "Tastes more like pie."

"Maui coconut cream."

Jill slid the pop into her mouth and spun the stick, coating her tongue for a full dose of flavor. It wasn't bad, less cloyingly sweet than some Shelly had had her try. She'd never make it to the stick, though. In her opinion, they ought to cut the size by half. But they wouldn't market as well. You need size for an eye-catching display, Shelly had told her. "Good flavor. You ought to do one with kiwi. Kiwi-pineapple. You could suck the coconut left-handed and the kiwi-pineapple right."

"Spoken by the girl who has yet to finish one, not two, lollipops at once."

Jill shrugged. "After the tenth suck, the sweet taste buds are saturated."

"Thankfully the majority of our market does not agree." Shelly worked her way into the sitting room.

"So does Maui coconut cream represent a merger, an acquisition, or a new contest winner?"

"None of the above. We're just playing with some summertime variety tastes."

"Definitely try the kiwi-pineapple. Makes people feel like they're on vacation with one lick."

"Hmm." Shelly settled into the giraffe chair and picked up the reunion postcard. "What's this?" She curled up her short freckled legs and switched on the lamp.

"Class reunion."

"Fifteen-year?"

"It's a fund-raiser." Jill set the sucker on the counter and joined Shelly in the front room.

"Are you going?"

"I haven't decided." She glanced at the packet of forms on her desk, the sheet on which to fill in all her vital statistics, and the one to send in with the exorbitant fee. "The school needs work and a quick infusion of cash, so the alumni thought a mid-decade reunion-slash-fund-raiser would help. Get everyone together and appeal to their nostalgia."

Shelly popped her gum. "And *are* you going?"

"I'm not nostalgic. I didn't even go to the tenth."

Shelly reached into the bowl of raw cashews on the corner table. "This is a good cause. You should know the schools need help, and reunions are important. They remind you of your roots, show you how far you've come. Besides, it would take your mind off things."

"Off Dan, you mean."

Shelly raised her hands to fend off the argument. "Dan assures me you worked things out. He's happy; you're happy; I'm happy."

"How's Brett?"

Shelly tossed a cashew at her. "Brett's happy."

"Well, good. Then I don't need the reunion."

"Why not go for the fun of it? I went to my tenth and had a blast. You wouldn't believe the guys who were bald already. And the spreading waistlines . . ."

"Well, I don't care who's bald, and—"

"Where's the paper work?" Shelly dropped the cashews back into the bowl and unfolded her legs.

Jill waved toward her desk, and Shelly sauntered over, then scooped it up along with a pen and returned to her chair. "Let's see. Name, address. Marital status—single; children—none."

Jill flinched. *One.*

Shelly wrote as she talked. "Okay, here's the good part. In fifty words or less, describe your life today and how Wilson High impacted you. Share the good times, the memories, the heartbreaks, and the high points that made you who you are today."

Jill felt her chest closing in. *The heartbreaks and high points that made her who she was . . .*

"I'm waiting." Shelly held the pen above the paper.

Jill scooped Rascal into her arms and nestled him under her chin. "I don't want to do this now, Shelly." She settled onto the couch.

"It's not that difficult, Jill. Favorite teacher?"

"Mrs. Vandersol. American lit."

"Sports?"

"Cheerleading and track."

Shelly shook her head. "That's why you and Dan are so good. You're both physical fitness fiends. Best memory?"

"Homecoming, senior year." *My first dance with Morgan.*

"Elaborate." Shelly held the pen poised.

Morgan in his dove gray tux, her white satin gown, the cluster of lavender roses and baby's breath she'd worn on her wrist, the white rosebud she had pinned on Morgan's lapel, the rosebud he'd crushed when he kissed her good-night.

"A-nd . . ." Shelly looped the pen in her hand.

"And nothing."

"Well, who'd you go with, for heaven's sakes?"

Jill's throat tightened painfully. "Morgan Spencer. We were nominated king and queen, so he asked me to the dance."

"First date?"

"Yes." Though the iridescent hues of her dreams had included Morgan Spencer long before that first date.

"This is good stuff, Jill."

Jill reached over and snatched the paper. "I don't want that written."

"Why not?"

"It's personal."

"That's the idea." Shelly circled her hand in the air.

Jill folded the paper in her lap. "I'll write the rest when I've thought about it."

"Then you're going?"

"Maybe."

Shelly arched her eyebrows and curled her fingers into claws. "I *vant* a promise."

Jill laughed. "All right, I'll go. But I'm not filling up this page with mushy stuff no one cares about. I'll say how Mrs. Vandersol instilled a love for teaching that I've carried with me into my work."

"Oh blah-de-blah-de-blah."

"Sorry."

"You'll get into the spirit when you get there. Let's see . . . it's next week? You're way overdue for sending in to the memory book."

"Rats." Jill clicked her fingers.

"You do not have the right attitude, girl."

Jill smiled. "Well, I'm a little short of attitude these days."

Shelly stood. "I have to run. Brett does expect to eat, even on the weekends, if you can believe it. Here." She scooped up the rest of the envelopes. "Read your mail."

"Yes, ma'am."

Jill walked her out the door, gave her a squeeze. "Thanks for the lollipop." Though she probably would never finish it. As Shelly said, they must have removed her sweet tooth with her wisdom teeth. She turned back inside, flipping through the envelopes that had accumulated while she battled the past week. Her hand froze on the creamy stationery envelope near the bottom. Her breath came in disjointed jerks as she stared at the name on the return label. *Benson.* She closed her eyes and forced her diaphragm to form three deep breaths.

Roger and Cinda Benson. Parents of Kelsey Renée Benson. She had thought it a nice name when they told her. But she had dreamed so many times since that it could have been Kelsey Runyan.

Jill stared at the envelope, the neat rounded script. Her name and address penned by Kelsey's . . . mother. She slit open the flap and took out the letter inside. Her hands shook as she unfolded the single sheet.

Dear Jill,

No, she didn't want to read it. Why would they contact her? Did Kelsey . . . was she old enough to wonder about her birth mom, to want to know, to meet her? The Bensons had been very clear about that in the somewhat unorthodox adoption her aunt had handled. While they knew each other's names, there would be no contact until Kelsey was of legal age, and then only if the child initiated it. Jill had been a child herself when she agreed. She dropped to the kitchen chair and pressed the letter flat on her knee.

Dear Jill,

I'm sure you realize we would not contact you lightly. Please sit down before you read on.

Jill's heart lurched. Something was wrong, so wrong Cinda asked her to sit down, proper procedure when delivering terrible news. She knew that from Dan and Brett. *Kelsey*. Her child . . .

This is not easy to share, but four years ago Kelsey contracted acute lymphocytic leukemia.

Jill watched the words blur. *Leukemia. Four years.* Four years ago, and she never knew. She blinked her eyes clear and forced them to focus. Had Kelsey died and they were only now telling her the fact?

She responded well to treatment and attained remission . . .

No, Kelsey was alive.

. . . until three months ago when the cancer recurred.

Cancer recurred. Those words must be Cinda's worst nightmare. Thinking of the other woman's pain cleared her own head. After all, it was Cinda who had loved and nurtured Kelsey all these years, Cinda who had lived the last four in fear . . . and it was her terror now unfolding.

So why did it hurt so much to read those words? This was the child she'd given away. Jill straightened in the chair. She had given up her right to know her, to be part of her daughter's life. What then? What did they want?

Since her relapse, the leukemia is particularly tenacious. The specialist in charge of her case recommends a bone marrow transplant. If Kelsey has siblings, that would be the best possibility for a match.

Siblings. No, there were no siblings. Kelsey was her only child, her only one.

If not, we are hoping you . . .

Jill felt suddenly weak. *Oh my God. They want me.* Her heart leaped and plummeted in the same moment. She would see her daughter! But her daughter was dying.

Everything paled compared to that. No, not everything. She was being given a chance. There was more she could give her child, more than life alone. Actually, it was like giving her life again. If her bone marrow arrested the disease, cured Kelsey . . .

Jill breathed quickly, too many emotions warring inside. She pored over the rest of the letter. How long had it sat there on her table? Three, no, four days. Had the Bensons been waiting fearfully that whole time? She walked to the living room and dialed the number at the bottom of the page without another thought. After all, what other choice was there? "Yes, hello. This is Jill Runyan." Her pulse thumped in her throat.

"Oh, thank God." Cinda caught her voice in a quick half sob. "I'm sorry."

"No, please. It's all right."

A pause, then, "Thank you for calling. You must have received our letter."

"I just read it. I'm sorry I didn't get it sooner."

"Jill . . . may I call you Jill?"

"Of course."

Cinda drew a thick breath. "I know this is very abrupt and you may not have had time to think through it all, but we're close to a second remission, and the sooner we go forward, the better the chance for success."

"Yes, of course. But I don't know anything about this. What do I do?"

"I'll explain everything involved. If you'd like, we could get together."

And Kelsey, too? "That would be fine."

"Would you be able to come here? To Des Moines? It's hard for me to leave right now."

"Of course. When?" Jill glanced at her calendar, but in truth, nothing on there mattered at the moment.

"Tomorrow afternoon?"

They arranged a time and Jill wrote down directions to the Bensons' house. By the time she hung up, she was shaking like one of the motorized balls she used to stimulate kinesthetic learning. Fifteen years and she was going to see Kelsey.

CHAPTER

4

J ill sat down in the lavender vinyl chair and lifted her wet hair
while Crystal arranged the nylon drape over her. Crystal ran her
fingernails over Jill's scalp and drew the hair out from her head to its
full length. "What do you want?"

"A change."

"Radical?"

"Well, nothing spiked or shaved."

Crystal laughed and scratched the ear that held six rings and a clip.
Her own hair stood in two-inch spikes at the top and hugged her head
like a female crew cut, then reverted to spikes at the back of her neck.
"No, I don't think you're ready for that yet. But I do think you could
consider short."

"How short?" Jill was starting to worry.

"Something playful. Something with attitude."

Jill smiled. "I've been hearing I need that."

"Trust me?"

The nerves shot up her spine, and she hissed a quick breath
between clenched teeth. "Sure." She held that face as Crystal took up
a strand and brought the scissors to within four inches of her head,
then caught her breath and closed her eyes with the snip.

"Now I have to match the rest."

Jill nodded mutely. She'd kept her appointment, hoping a new look might bolster her for the real purpose of her day, and to fill the time until she could go to Des Moines.

"You see the way your bones go here?" Crystal traced her cheekbones with a long-nailed fingertip. "The long, straight hair was ruining that line. And here." Crystal touched the corner of her jaw. "This angle was lost altogether. But you are going to love what I do to you."

Jill straightened bravely. "Then do away." She watched the hair fall in long strands. She could sell it like the woman in O. Henry's "Gift of the Magi." Then she thought of all the combs and barrettes and scrunchies she wouldn't need anymore. *Oh boy.*

Maybe it wasn't a good day for change, not when her whole reality had been inverted by a letter. Suddenly Kelsey wasn't just a memory or a dream. She was real, and she was sick. Jill closed her eyes as Crystal worked. What was she doing worrying about a haircut when Kelsey's thoughts must encompass life and death? It wasn't real yet. That was the problem. Talking to Cinda, making their plans . . . it hadn't penetrated somehow.

It would today, though, and maybe intrinsically she needed something as frivolous as a haircut to ground her. Jill opened her eyes and watched. Crystal was wasted on the little corner shop. She was truly gifted and had an eye to match a face with a style that brought out the best in both. Jill stared at her reflection. "I can't believe it."

"Believe it."

"I look . . ."

"Fabulous. All you needed was a little pizzazz."

Jill shook her head. It felt strange, but she loved it. She looked confident and saucy and elegant at the same time. She faced Crystal. "You are a pro."

"Thank you."

"I mean, really. You have a gift."

Crystal laughed and rubbed her fingernails on her cape. "Got the touch, baby."

Walking out to her car, Jill was struck by the airy breeze in her hair. It felt light and feathery, the thick, soft strands tossing about . . . with an attitude. She drew a long breath, ready to face anything. After all, she was the one who could help. Finally.

Cinda had said they kept Sunday afternoons free. Jill got into the car. She had an hour-and-a-half drive to Des Moines to prepare herself. Emotions surged. She would meet her daughter, though she had sensed Cinda's discomfort. And she didn't blame her. The woman had enough to deal with worrying about Kelsey. Of course she must feel protective. She probably wished there was another way without involving Kelsey's birth mom. Jill's insides roiled. This was her chance.

She contained a surge of tension. How would it be to see her now? How would she look? Surely not the way she imagined her, healthy and rosy and happy. What if she looked . . . Jill shook her head. But it wouldn't matter how Kelsey looked, she was so starved for one glimpse. *Oh, Lord, give me strength. Let me do the right things, say the right things.*

Cinda's directions were clear and easy to follow. Jill found the house and parked at the curb. Pulling into the driveway would be too much like coming home. This was not her home. This was not her child. She had to be careful, to remember what was real. Cinda and Roger were Kelsey's parents. But now the girl would know she had another. She walked to the door, bolstered by the thought.

Cinda pulled it open almost immediately. She was heavier than she'd been the one time they'd met fourteen years and ten months ago, and her brown hair was flecked with silver. Her smile was strained but warm. "Hello, Jill. Thank you for coming."

Jill's throat was too tight for words. This was not going to be easy. She smiled and followed Cinda inside. The small house was a farmhouse style, probably built in the fifties. Wood floors, lots of windows. Cinda pushed open the back screen door and motioned for her to sit on the floral-patterned patio chair. "I thought we'd chat a bit out here, okay?"

"Okay." Jill cleared her throat, glancing about the backyard with a swing in the trees, a small garden along the fence, a cornfield beyond.

Cinda said, "I know this is hard for you. I can only imagine how hard."

"It's hard for both of us. But I'm so thankful you wrote." And she was, even if that letter had thrown her emotions into a whirlwind.

"I would have called, but I couldn't find your number."

"It's unlisted." But she had already given it to Cinda when she responded to the letter. Now she was only a phone call away from any news.

Cinda sat on the edge of the chaise. "I would have preferred to give you that kind of information . . . well, a letter seemed so impersonal. I was afraid you wouldn't respond."

Jill shook her head. "How could I not?"

Cinda looked weary, drained. "You've gone on with your life. I thought maybe you wouldn't—or couldn't . . ."

"Please." Jill leaned forward and touched her hand. "I'll do anything I can."

Tears sprang to Cinda's eyes, and she sniffed. "I swore I wouldn't do this."

"I understand." More than she knew.

Cinda brushed the tears with the back of her hand. "She's just so sick."

"I'm sorry." Jill pressed the fingers she held, sensing Cinda's distress and the small reserves of strength that held it in check. What fear must she wake to every day?

"They weren't sure they could achieve a new remission. It's taken three months to get this close, and they're not sure how long it will last. A bone marrow transplant is her only chance for survival, ten to thirty percent statistically."

Jill couldn't stop the reaction to that bleak figure.

"I know," Cinda said, "but without it, the numbers are zero to five percent. Not that we don't believe she can beat the odds. She's a fighter." Cinda shook her head, then sighed. "It's just that she's already been through so much, things a child should never have to face. But the Lord is good, and He knows best."

Jill nodded. It took a deep abiding faith to believe that in a time like this. Or did she say the words to convince herself?

Cinda straightened, drew a long breath, and gained control. "You need to know Roger and I thought it would be better not to tell her, yet, who you are."

Jill's spirit deflated like a pin-punctured balloon.

"Kelsey knows she's adopted, but the doctor agreed that now might not be the best time for her to deal with any more than she has to. She's very fragile."

Of course that made sense. The sudden anger and hurt were illogical, selfish, wrong. The most important thing was getting Kelsey through this. But how could she meet her daughter and not . . . not what? Take her in her arms and say she was her mommy?

She wasn't her mommy. And Kelsey had grown past that stage. She was an adolescent, though Jill never imagined her that way. At any rate, she saw the protective fear in Cinda's brown eyes. "What do we tell her?"

"We told her you are a donor who shows a promising match. We know you will, because she's inherited at least one complete haplotype from . . . I'm sorry, these medical terms have become a daily part of my vocabulary."

"That's all right. Just explain it."

"Antigens on the lymphocytes are inherited in groups called haplotypes. In the past, transplants have only been possible with a full six-six antigen match or, at worst, one antigen off. So a sibling is the best chance. Even then it's only one in four that another child would inherit the same combination as Kelsey. We didn't expect that possibility, though I had to ask in my letter." Cinda seemed to calm as she spoke, as though focusing on the clinical facts siphoned the emotion.

"But we've found an oncologist who transplants with a single haplotype match using a related donor. There are surface factors they don't completely understand that make a family member a better match."

Jill nodded.

"When you have the first blood drawn, they'll do a test that will confirm a match of one haplotype, three antigens. With your genetic connection, that much is assured. If we're very blessed, there may be more."

Jill's head spun, not from the medical terms, but from thinking of her genetics connecting her to Kelsey, the child she had formed inside her body. She was very aware of Cinda's choice of words. Her genetic connection. *Lord, help me.* How could she not show it? Not betray her motherhood to the child?

"If other tests confirm compatibility, then they would do the extraction and transport the marrow to the center, where Kelsey will have been prepared."

Jill caught those words, as well. She had made assumptions that Cinda might never have meant regarding seeing Kelsey. There were no direct tubes from her body to Kelsey's transferring the marrow. They would not even have to be in the same room, if she understood "transport the marrow." Fighting disappointment, Jill forced the question she had to ask. "May I see her?"

Cinda could say no to even that. But she nodded. "I thought you'd want to. It's complicated, the relationships being what they are."

"If you'd rather I not . . ." *Please, don't say no.* She might never have the chance again.

Cinda smiled gently. "I think it's right."

Jill's throat seized. "Thank you." Like a sleepwalker, she followed Cinda up the narrow wooden stairs that creaked underfoot. Amy Grant's soulful voice drifted from the front bedroom, bright with sunlight. The walls were covered with a small apple-blossom pattern, matched by a ruffled chintz balloon shade at the window. The bed was a white four-poster with an eyelet spread and apple-green-striped pillow shams.

Jill fought the rush of tears as her eyes fixed on the young teen nestled there, pale and bald. She was smaller than Jill expected, more like twelve than fourteen in both size and development. And yes, she looked terribly fragile. The features were her own, but the eyes . . . *Oh, Lord, the eyes are Morgan's.* Jill's heart turned over slowly. Her daughter. Their daughter.

Cinda laid a hand on Kelsey's thin shoulder. "Kelsey, this is Jill."

Kelsey pressed the button on the CD player to stop the music and eyed her directly. "Hi."

Jill forced her voice to come. "Hello, Kelsey. It's wonderful to meet you." *Again.* She flashed on the memory of the tiny newborn she'd held so briefly in her arms but carried a full nine months inside her.

"Mom said you might match my bone marrow?" Her voice was clear and direct. She had a poise and presence beyond her years. Maybe suffering did that. She didn't have time for childish insecurities. Her life was pared down to the basics.

"The chances are good." Jill's voice came out remarkably calm. *This is my daughter I'm talking to!* What would Morgan say? What would he think in her position?

"Do you mind if I ask why?" Kelsey was no fool. How had they explained a stranger offering bone marrow to her? How did the unrelated donor program work? She should have read about it before coming.

Jill fumbled. "I work with kids who have problems. I believe in organ transplants and any kind of medical procedure that helps people survive." Where had that come from?

"So it's like a ministry or something?"

"A ministry?" She looked at Kelsey's eyes, so, so blue. "Yes. In a way." A ministry to her daughter, a chance from God to—

"Have you given marrow before, for someone else?"

Throat tightening, Jill shook her head. "No. This will be the first time."

Kelsey's lips tightened. "It's painful." Her eyes were red rimmed and far too large for her shrunken face. "Even though they sedate you, it hurts for days." Her gaze didn't waver.

Was she testing her commitment? "It'll be all right." She touched

Kelsey's hand. The skin was soft and warm, and an almost electrical thrill passed through her with the touch. Her daughter. *Oh, God, she has to live!*

Kelsey smiled, and it wrenched Jill's heart. "I didn't know someone would care enough. I mean . . ." She glanced at Cinda. "My parents would do it, if they could, but I'm adopted."

"Oh." Jill's voice was hardly a whisper. "I'm sure they've done a lot more than this for you."

Kelsey smiled at Cinda, and Jill ached at the relationship she saw between them. *Oh, God, oh please, God . . .*

Cinda patted Kelsey's shoulder. A simple, familiar gesture. Jill wished she could touch her daughter that way. Did Kelsey notice their likeness? Jill wanted her to, hoped she would guess. But that was self-ish. Kelsey didn't need to deal with anything more. Cinda and the doctor were right.

Kelsey turned back to Jill. "Why did you choose me?"

Jill's heart jumped. Was there more in the question than Kelsey let on?

Cinda touched Kelsey's cheek with the back of her fingers. "You know that's not how the program works, Kelsey. It's all matching anti-gens."

Kelsey's gaze remained direct. Was she one step ahead of them? Did she guess, did she know? "If I were healthy, I'd donate, too." Kelsey settled into the pillows. "It helps people live."

"You do enough by giving people hope." Cinda looked up. "Kelsey has a Web page—she calls it her Hope Page. She answers the questions and fears of other kids with leukemia, and sometimes their parents. Mostly she shares Christ's love." Cinda rested her fingers on Kelsey's head. Jill absorbed every one of those touches, imagining them for her-self.

"Mom?" Kelsey's eyes suddenly took on Morgan's intensity.

"Yes?" Cinda met her daughter's gaze.

"God could do this, couldn't He?"

Jill felt a jolt, sensing Kelsey's fear.

Cinda fought her tears. "Of course He can."

"Like a miracle."

Cinda smiled. "Yes."

Jill's throat went dry and cleaved together. *Please God.* If anyone deserved a miracle, it was the child before her.

Her daughter's eyes pierced her. "Thank you for coming to see me. And for the rest of it especially."

Jill nodded, her voice trapped in her throat. And that was all she would have, fresh images to play through her mind of her daughter. Not as she had ever imagined her, but real true images. Somehow she walked out.

Downstairs, Cinda handed her a sheet of information and a business card. "This explains what you need to do to begin the process. If the testing indicates we can go forward, Kelsey will enter the Yale New Haven Cancer Treatment Center."

"Okay." But nothing was really sinking in.

The drive home gave her time to think and to pray desperate prayers that left her empty and afraid. *Why like this? Why couldn't I find her whole and healthy?* All her fairy-tale imaginings of Kelsey in the perfect life, with every happiness, shattered and spilled about her. "It's not fair! I've already paid!"

Angry tears dammed up inside. Why now? She'd gone on, just as Cinda said, though it was a battle sometimes. She had the kids at school, and her work meant so much to her. To help the ones who struggled for too many reasons.

Now Kelsey. It hit her again like a blow. She had already lost her child once. How could she do it again? Even with the brave smile and intense eyes, it was obvious that Kelsey was terribly sick. Jill was caught in a vortex, spiraling down. She had to focus on what she could do. Otherwise she felt too helpless for words.

––––––––––

After Jill had left, Kelsey sat at the desk near her window. It seemed like a small miracle to have that much energy. This last round of chemotherapy had been worse than the others, since her second remission had proved harder to achieve, and it was taking larger doses to maintain. But she'd napped a couple hours and felt better.

She opened the laptop computer her parents had given her last Christmas and brought it to life. Yes, she was a whiz. Not that she could take much credit for that. Because of all the hours she'd spent in a hospital bed, and since she didn't watch TV, the computer was a godsend, one her parents could scarcely afford these days with the mounting medical bills, but the computer had provided a chance to reach out.

It had been her roommate's idea, actually, to start a Web page. Sort of the Ann Landers for leukemia kids. A man from the church had helped her create it, but she had taken over from there. With an animated DIF and a MIDI, she'd added graphics and music, just to make it fun. But really, as Mom had said, it gave her the chance to share Christ's love.

She opened up the mail section. Four letters today. She clicked to open the first from a girl newly diagnosed. That was the hardest time, before your sickness became the reality of your life. She raised her fingers to the keyboard.

> Dear Amy,
> I know it's scary. I was scared, too, and confused. How could this be happening to me? Maybe they're wrong. It's all a bad dream. Then when chemo started, I knew it wasn't a dream. It was real, though I still didn't understand why. The only thing I knew was that Jesus was in control. He is the best, best friend.
> When other kids were afraid to come see me, or even grownups didn't know what to say, I felt like a freak. But Jesus was always there. I trust Him with my life. You can, too. Write me back if you want to know more.
> Jesus loves you and so do I. Kelsey
> www.kelseys_hope_page.com

She moved on to the next. Some days she was so tired it was hard to think what to say. Then she trusted the Holy Spirit to give her the words. Days like today, her words came easily, maybe because seeing Jill gave her fresh hope herself.

> Dear Samantha,
> Yes, there are days I feel sorry for myself. I say, why me? But the answer is, why not? Would I wish it on someone else instead? What if they didn't have faith or courage? Jesus gives me what I need even when I forget to ask. And sometimes I do. Sometimes I even get angry and think it's not fair. But God's Word says, "In all things God works for the good of those who love him, who have been called according to his purpose." So I know He uses even leukemia for some good thing I can't see. Trust Him and He'll give you peace.
> Jesus loves you and so do I. Kelsey
> www.kelseys_hope_page.com

When she finished the mail, she surfed the Web awhile, then stopped and stared out the window. Kelsey bit her lip. The thought of an allogeneic bone marrow transplant scared her. There were so many more complications. But autologous transplants, taking her own marrow, treating it to kill the cancer and putting it back in, didn't work well for leukemia. No, they'd have to wipe her marrow out and hope Jill's worked.

She felt like a geek knowing all that medical stuff, more than Mom or Dad guessed that she grasped. But as she'd told Amy, leukemia was her reality, her life. It would maybe be her death. She'd gone three years in remission and dared to feel cured, even though five was the magic number. When the markers showed a recurrence, she almost didn't believe it. But then, she'd been feeling punky again—and ignoring it as though it would go away. She knew better. Leukemia didn't go away, no matter how much you wanted it to.

It was a battle between good and evil. Though the drugs made her sick and ugly, she pictured them as bright angels with fierce faces and long swords hacking down the demon cells that tried to kill her. She'd gotten the idea from the psychotherapist who counseled kids on the ward. Dr. Blair called it imaging and suggested they picture what was going on in their bodies in a positive way.

What was going on in her body seemed no less than the war in the heavens. So angels it was. In between fevers and nausea, the angels didn't look quite so fierce. Sometimes they raised their swords to her and smiled. Then she felt seriously certain they would win.

But when her mind wandered with spiking fevers and her body swelled and her hair fell out, it was hard not to see the slimy black horde beating back her army. It only helped to know that whatever happened inside her, ultimately she had the victory.

———

A lingering scent of scorched macaroni and cheese clung to the main room as Morgan showed Todd his assignment on the game card: act out the cameo for his team to guess. And the word was *nun*. This ought to be good.

Morgan had purchased the game Cranium at Starbucks to liven up the evenings and dispel the interpersonal stiffness infused into the ranch by Todd's family. Stan was uptight and insecure, the mother, Melanie, an exercise in frustration, and the daughter, Sarah, a teacher's pet sort of girl, whom Todd had pegged pretty accurately. Todd fit with them like a scorpion in a bunny cage.

But it was just the sort of challenge Morgan thrived on in the corporate world, bringing people with disparate strengths and expectations into a common vision and equipping them to move forward. This was simply a small-case scenario. So far he'd explained the rules and they were having a practice round in each category before playing guys against girls for blood.

"No way," Todd said, looking from the card to him.

"Come on. You know what it is."

Todd shoved the card at him. "I'm not gonna be that."

Morgan pulled him close and whispered, "You want to wax those girls or don't you?"

"I can't act like a—"

Morgan pressed a hand to his mouth, turned so both their faces were away from the group. "Now what do nuns do?"

Todd shrugged. "Nothing fun."

Morgan grinned, responding too easily to Todd's recalcitrance. "So make your face sour. Now what?"

"Pray," Todd whispered.

"That's right. Put your hands together."

"This is stupid."

Morgan pressed Todd's hands into a flattened peak. "Now get on your knees and if they don't get it, show them you're wearing a veil."

"I'm what?"

Morgan pushed him out to the center of the circle. Todd dropped grumpily to his knees, then closed his eyes and looked heavenward with a better imitation than Morgan had expected.

"He's praying," twelve-year-old Sarah guessed.

"It's a person," Morgan reminded her.

Todd stroked the sides of his head to his shoulders, then prayed again.

"A nun!" Melanie called out, and Todd pushed up from his knees and sagged into his chair. But there was a prideful flicker behind his glare.

"Good job, Todd. Last category is 'creative cat.'" Morgan took the tub of clay from the box. He passed the clay to Stan, who looked utterly defeated when he realized he had to model DNA. Noelle could do it. She'd ice them all in the artistic category, even the sensosketch category, where the artist's eyes had to stay closed. The time in the hourglass passed before Stan had done more than wad the clay back and forth in his hands with a pained look that rivaled the roll of Todd's eyes.

"That's okay, Stan." Morgan stuffed the clay back into the tub.

"We'll count on you for the datahead category." He caught Noelle's smile across the room and returned it. Rick might think chores would settle Todd with a sense of responsibility, but unless this family got to know one another, those gangs would look better than ever by the end of the summer.

As the evening progressed he felt like a camp director. Boys and girls, can't we all get along? Was he the only one who understood communication? It was a small victory that by the end of the game, he'd at least gotten them to laugh. Noelle especially, but then, she already appreciated his sense of humor. By the time Todd's family headed back to their cabin, she turned shining eyes on him and murmured, "That was nothing short of amazing."

"What?"

"The way you drew them out, got them working together."

"Once I ascertained Stan did have a pulse, and Sarah and her mother could smile, and Todd wouldn't murder anyone . . ." He spread his hands. "It was clear sailing."

Rick adjusted his seat on the couch, stretched his legs. "Not everyone has your stamina, Morgan."

"Stamina? We are talking basic interfacing."

"Well, not everyone has your gift of gab."

"But Morgan's right." Noelle laid her hand on Rick's arm. "When Stan had us all rolling with his mermaid impersonation, I think everyone felt a surprising camaraderie. That family needs to laugh."

Morgan sent her a half smile. "I definitely think your asylum charade topped the event."

"So I do insane well." She polished her nails on her chest with a smile. Was it only months ago she'd hidden herself away, too broken to face life and love and laughter? "But *you* are the consummate ham."

"Well." He stood up. "It's good for people to push past their inhibitions." He jutted his jaw at Rick. "You might even find a latent thespian in that man you married, Noelle."

Rick shook his head. "It's not inhibition. Just not my style."

Morgan smiled. "Give me a while."

"Morgan, you've had thirty years of working on me, pushing me into things I wanted no part of. I think I am what I am."

Noelle reached up and kissed his cheek. "Just the way I like you."

Morgan ran a hand through his hair. "Well, it's getting thick in here. Guess I'll check my mail."

"I thought you didn't work on these hiatuses." Rick wrapped his arm around Noelle's shoulders.

"I have a few things hanging. Denise'll have my hide if I go completely incommunicado." Though he regularly drove his zealous professional assistant crazy that way. "Good night, lovebirds." He headed up the stairs.

5

Jill wondered for the umpteenth time why she had come. The week had passed too quickly with all the end-of-the-year reports and evaluations, the meetings with the parents whose children she would continue to tutor. And then there'd been the blood test and the stress of waiting for those results and the thoughts and memories churned by the whole situation.

She should have skipped this event even after paying the fee. She'd done her duty for the fund, more than she could afford, and it was ludicrous seeing these people, hearing who was driving a Porsche, who practiced law, who was in jail. None of that mattered to her. She shouldn't have come. It would drain her reserves.

She saw him walk in, as though some inner radar had been tuned for that moment all evening. She hadn't been watching for him, but his entrance had drawn her gaze immediately. How could it not?

He looked better at thirty-three than he had at eighteen. What man didn't? But Morgan more so. He'd grown into himself, filled in the spare places, yet stayed fit and handsome . . . heart-seizing handsome. He carried himself with confidence and ease as he joked with the attendants at the reception table.

That was Morgan, quick with the jokes and smooth with the lines. He pinned his name tag on, probably the only person there whose yearbook picture wasn't adolescently stupid. He always had been photogenic, easy before the camera, something he had done better than she.

Jill felt her chest tighten as he surveyed the room. Would he see her? The new haircut Crystal had given her was so different, he might look past without knowing. Yet what was she thinking? What would she do if he saw and came over? She turned away, concentrating again on the conversation of the groupies who had reattached to her.

Her friends. The girls who had gone to every dance, who'd won every popularity contest, who had turned down dates from boys who were too dweeb or pimpled. And she'd been at the front of the line, except that she'd also excelled in academics. Now she looked at them, a couple overweight, the others attractive and sure of it, most of them married, two divorced.

She wished she hadn't come. She glanced back over her shoulder. It felt strange not to have the weight of her hair slide with the motion. The short soft edges brushed the back of her neck instead. Where was he?

There, talking with Randy Beech and Glen Stevens, his old buddies, though they looked as if they could choke with envy. He must be wowing them, as only Morgan could. He turned and caught her eye, quite by accident, she saw in his expression. He held it only a second, then turned back to respond to Glen's question. A burst of laughter from the three of them.

"But tell me, Jill, where have you been?" Lyssa's voice had deepened from the cigarettes she'd experimented with and found she liked too well. "I heard you were back in town. The committee wanted to enlist you, but you're not in the phone book."

Jill turned back to Lyssa and saw that half the group had drifted away. "It's less complicated that way." A simple precaution any single woman might consider, even one living across the yard from patrol officer Brett Barlowe, husband of her best friend, Shelly.

Lyssa rolled her eyes. "Isn't it pathetic what we have to do to avoid the pervs?"

Jill startled. Had Lyssa read that into her comment? No, probably just shared the concern. She was divorced, lived alone, as well. Jill noted the line of lipstick across the tips of Lyssa's front teeth. She still had her overbite, though her figure had become voluptuous. Implants? Not exactly the way to avoid notice, if Lyssa was concerned about unsavory advances.

Jill shrugged. "It probably doesn't matter, but I unlist it anyway."

Dan had insisted on that precaution when he came onto the scene.

Lyssa rolled her eyes. "I mean half the entries in the book are initials, like the kooks don't know that's a female?"

Jill sipped her 7-Up. Lyssa obviously had issues and probably experience. "Unlisted is safer."

Janice touched her arm. "So what are you doing these days?"

Jill turned. "I teach. Special ed." *I'm waiting to learn if I can give bone marrow to my daughter, who's dying, but whom none of you know exists.*

"Really?" Janice scanned the room, already dismissing her work as unimportant.

"Is there a man in your life?" The voice was husky.

Jill turned to Babs. The woman had been waiting to pry, just as she had fifteen years ago, wanting every detail, the first to sniff out a new crush or, at the other end, who was tired of whom. "No, not currently."

"Well, don't look now, but Morgan Spencer came in alone."

"I know. I saw him." She *must* be made of ice. She managed to say it with such lack of emotion even Babs deflated some. But not enough.

"I can't believe the two of you aren't together. I thought nothing in the world could break you up."

Actually it took very little. Only living with it all these years had been hard. Jill shrugged. "High school romance."

"Be real, Jill." This from Janice. "Have you taken a good look at him?"

No. I'm trying to avoid any glimpse, can't you tell? Of course they couldn't. She was too good at hiding it, a skill she'd developed along with the scar tissue on her heart.

"Well, he's noticed you."

Jill hazarded a glance. Morgan was seated at a small side table. Melinda Blake and her husband stood over and chatted with him, but he looked her way again, this time intentionally.

"Why don't you talk to him?" Babs was on the scent, trying to make things happen. Did nothing ever change?

Jill forced a smile. "So what are you doing, Lyssa?"

"Legal secretary. Fitch and Norton."

"Married. Two kids." Babs was clearly bored. "Really, Jill . . ."

"Give it a rest, Babs." Lyssa touched her arm.

Babs rolled her eyes. "Whatever."

Janice bumped Lyssa's elbow. "Hey, there's Mary, Mary McBride. Isn't she some senator?"

Lyssa turned. "State rep, I think."

"Let's go." Janice tugged and Lyssa followed.

Jill made a move, but Babs cut her off. "Here's your chance. He's all alone."

She felt desperate to go the other way, any direction but to where Morgan sat. However, that would give Babs all the ammunition she needed to spread the word through the whole assembly. Jill tipped her head. "Well, why not?"

She handed Babs her empty soda glass and turned with more non-chalance than she thought possible. Morgan was sitting alone, though not for long, she was sure. She wished she'd brought Dan as a buffer, then realized how unfair that would have been. Still, they couldn't go the whole evening avoiding each other. Already more eyes than Babs's were on them.

It was human nature. How would two old flames react to each other after fifteen years? Especially when the flame had been snuffed so mysteriously. Did any of them suspect? Not even her closest friends had been told, but did they guess? What was it her parents had said? A summer mission trip? Come on.

She drew a long breath and started toward him. It felt as if every eye in the room was on her, but that was her own nerves working overtime. With more determination than she felt, she approached Morgan's table. He watched her with the slow, suave appraisal she remembered, only now much more suave and . . . cynical. He looked fantastic in spite of that.

She stopped less than two feet short of the table and managed a weak smile. "Hello, Morgan."

He raised his glass in salute. "Still the best body in the room."

She felt the fire in her cheeks, too aware suddenly of the flattering cut of her black sheath, and almost turned away without another word. But, then, he had a right to despise her. Hadn't he tried to do the honorable thing, at least as he saw it? *Oh, Morgan.*

"How are you?" It sounded stiff and stupid in her own ears.

He nudged the extra chair out with his foot, then stood and seated her. She remembered the feel of his hand across her shoulders as he eased the chair in. He slipped off his suit coat and hung it behind his chair before sitting down with the easy grace that came naturally to him.

His shirt fit as if it was made for him, and she realized his coat had, as well. He was obviously doing well, or had he succumbed to the reunion madness of pretending to be what you weren't? No, Morgan cared too little what people thought to do that. Why didn't he say something?

She shifted in the chair and tried again. "It's been a long time." Why did she keep saying these inane things? *Morgan, I've seen our daughter. She's so beautiful. She has your eyes.*

"You've graduated."

"What?"

"From Vanilla Fields." He drew a long breath in through his nose. "Obsession."

She flushed. Of course he would be up on women's fragrances. He was always so sensual. "Yes. But I still wear Vanilla Fields sometimes."

He smirked, then glanced at her hands folded awkwardly over her maroon leather clutch on the table. "No wedding ring?" Again he sliced her with his tone.

"No."

"Divorced?"

She swallowed. "No."

"What are you drinking?"

"I'm not. I have an early commitment in the morning."

He fingered his own drink. From the look of him, he'd had a few before coming in tonight. He lifted the tumbler and drank. When he put it down, his eyes were like shards of antique glass, deep blue and dangerous. "Well, you've satisfied appearances. Don't let me keep you."

The words reached out and slapped her. She stood up woodenly, and again he rose in the gallant gesture, but she saw the hatred in his eyes. His position kept it hidden from the rest in the room, but it was clear to her. She walked away trembling, her legs taking her straight to the hall and down to the ladies' room. She went inside, locked herself into a stall, and collapsed. She pressed her quivering knees together and dropped her head to her hands.

What was she doing? Why had she come? She jerked a swath of toilet paper from the roll and pressed it to her eyes, refusing even the semblance of tears. Did these people mean anything to her? Her friends, the popular clique, the beautiful people—they were all the same, still obsessed with appearances, still self-absorbed. Had no one changed but she?

Morgan. He had changed. The fun-loving rogue had become cruel and cynical. He'd always had a teasing streak but underneath held such a tender heart, kinder than any boy she'd known before or since. She released a slow breath. He was cruel now in a way he'd never been before. But maybe the real cruelty was hers. She had left town without a word, left him believing she'd aborted their child, left him as her parents had insisted. And they'd been right.

It took her a long time to see it. At first she'd wept continuously, clinging to a single hope. Her parents consented to her carrying the child on two conditions: one, that she give it up for adoption, and two, that she not see Morgan again. But she had hoped against hope that he would find her.

It was a foolish juvenile hope. Morgan was eighteen, hardly more mature than she, and certainly no more qualified to raise a child. Maybe he would have tried. Maybe he would have married her, but how could it have lasted? Somewhere along the way she'd stopped waiting, stopped crying. Even though her actions had been dishonest, bordering on illegal, she had done the right thing . . . for her child. And God willing, she'd have the chance to do it again.

From the entrance of the ballroom, Morgan watched Jill leave the building. Maybe he'd hurt her more than he thought. Maybe she wasn't as heartless as he believed, at least when it came to herself. Never mind that she'd done away with their child. All legal and neat, of course.

He looked down at the ice in his glass, naked without the booze. He could take care of that easily enough, but he didn't. Maybe it was nostalgic sentimentality that permeated his system, but he decided to feel it instead of killing it in drink.

Fifteen years ago he'd been one raging hormone. But beyond that, there had been something special about Jill, something he hadn't found anywhere before or since. Not even Noelle, if he were honest with himself. He'd loved Jill, pure and simple.

He set the glass down on the rectangular pillar that held the gilded pot of artificial florals. He looked out into the night where she had disappeared. Maybe he should have held his tongue. She had felt awfully good under his hand. They could have danced, for old times' sake. He could have held her. Now *there* was a painful jolt.

Maybe he'd have that drink after all. But he looked into the room, massed with people he'd left behind, and shook his head. He'd given his check, made an appearance. And the only reason for coming had left. He did, too.

He took a red-eye to Denver, redeemed his car from long-term parking, and headed for the mountains. Soon he'd go off again to conquer giants and prove his prowess. He had set the guys on their ears talking about his recent years' successes. But after all, he *had* been voted most likely to succeed.

And succeed he had. He drove from the airport, his Thunderbird handling like the sweet road machine it was. His blood alcohol was probably more than marginal after several drinks on the flight, but he was in control. Juniper Falls came into sight sooner than he'd made it before. He'd rocked those curves tonight.

The ranch was dark, naturally, with Rick and Noelle snuggled up together in the master suite Rick had remodeled so capably. Rick's baby was probably sleeping between them inside his mother as content as a little cub could be. Why not?

He pulled to an abrupt halt before the porch, climbed out, and staggered slightly. Whoa. Not so clear as he'd thought. He gathered his senses. Just stiff and tired. He climbed the stairs and let himself in with the key Rick loaned him.

He stood in the darkness of the vast main room and looked up the winding stairs to where his brother and sister-in-law slept in marital bliss. On second thought, maybe he wasn't quite ready for sleep. He went to the kitchen and opened the cabinet he'd stocked on arrival.

Ah yes. Crown Royal. Just the ticket. He sat down at the kitchen table and unscrewed the lid of the bottle. No glass? And he was drinking alone. Dangerous, Morgan. He lifted the bottle in lonely salute. *Here's to living dangerously.*

He heard the soft step before he got the bottle to his lips. Noelle, in a green floor-length velour robe. Her hair hung loose and her eyes were sleepy as she came in and sat down across the table. He gripped the bottle protectively.

Gently, she covered his hand with hers. "Don't, Morgan."

He formed a wry smile. "Those words are inseparably joined in your mind, Noelle." But he let go the bottle and took her hand instead, remembering all the times she'd pulled away, all his efforts she'd rebuffed. Of course, he hadn't known then how she'd been hurt. He'd only seen someone who might have filled the void.

She said, "You saw Jill?"

He raised a single eyebrow. "I guess Rick's been blabbing."

"He told me a long time ago. Not her name, though. That I learned tonight."

He looked down at the diamond on her finger, remembering the first time he'd seen it, the day Rick had put it on there. Morgan had kissed her anyway and rendered his brother an avenging angel.

She slipped her hand away, stood, and reached for the coffee beans and grinder. Ah yes, coffee to sober up the drunk.

"What's she like?"

He shrugged. "I knew her at seventeen." He tipped the bottle to his mouth, pouring the booze down his throat. May as well perfect his condition before she waged war against it. "I was not the judge of character then that I am today."

"What was she like at seventeen?"

He clunked the bottle to the table. "You don't want to hear this."

She sat back down and took his hand before he could wrap it around the bottleneck again. "Tell me, Morgan."

"She was every guy's dream. Cheerleader with brains, accelerated a full year, even. Great sense of humor and class. She danced—as well as you, only looser, not so trained. Her smile . . ." He sighed. "Her smile sank in like syrup." He shook his head, then squeezed his temples with his free hand. "She killed my kid. Did you know that part?"

"Yes."

He made a fist inside her palms. He was babbling, too drunk to stay unemotional. He would never bare himself like this otherwise.

"She was very young, Morgan. You don't realize the kind of pressure . . ."

"I was young, too, Noelle." Too young to know anything about anything. Though he'd thought he had all the answers.

"But you weren't the one with the immediate problem. You could have walked away."

He jerked his hand out of hers. "I didn't walk away. I would have taken care of her."

"She was a minor. It wasn't up to you or to Jill."

He closed his eyes and hung his head back. "They acted like I was the arch fiend."

"It was their daughter."

"They wouldn't let me see her. Wouldn't let me talk to her even once. It all came down the week we graduated, and then she was gone. She never even tried." She could have found him. His parents would have told her he was at Wharton. One phone call. But she'd never made it. Sure they were kids, and they'd screwed up. Rick would say they had violated God's law. Morgan knew that, and maybe that was why he actively courted hell.

He sat in morose silence, then said, "She had her hair all cut short. It used to be long like yours, and I liked it that way. But she looked even better with it short. All kind of puffed and feathery around her face like Meg Ryan on a good day."

"Is it blond?"

He nodded slowly. "Kind of silvery, not golden like yours. Gray eyes. She's kept her figure, too, not like some of them. But then, they've had kids." The words tasted bitter.

She didn't let him stay there. "Did you speak with her?"

"Not very nicely." He said it with regret. What if he could have been civil? Would he be sitting now with Jill instead of his brother's wife?

"Don't blame yourself, Morgan."

He slumped. "Who else is there?"

Rick was awake when Noelle crept back into bed in the dark. He'd heard their voices but stayed where he was. He raised the covers, drew Noelle close, and said, "Morgan?"

She nodded against his neck. "He saw Jill."

Rick released a slow breath. Maybe he shouldn't have pushed it, but he'd really thought the Lord would provide some closure so Morgan could quit punishing himself. "How bad is he?"

"He passed out the minute he hit the bed."

No surprise there.

"He once accused me of hiding inside a shell. Alcohol is his."

"How long were you downstairs?"

She tucked her head into the hollow of his neck. "Long enough for him to vent instead of drowning it. I wish I knew how to help."

"He's too successful to hit bottom and get real help."

"Why can't God—"

"It doesn't work that way. We pray for him. Mom's worn her knees out, and Dad, too. But God doesn't force the cure. Morgan has to want it."

"Then what's the point in praying?"

Rick shifted her in his arms. Noelle's faith was new and as fragile as her emotions. He felt the responsibility of nurturing and protecting her. "Lots of points we don't see." He stroked the hair back from her temples. "Like keeping him alive long enough to find his way. How many curves did he take tonight?"

She closed her eyes, probably picturing the mountain highway.

"And keeping others safe when he drives with no one to stop him. All the things we can't see that might bring Morgan to his knees. Maybe even what happened tonight."

"He was cruel to her."

Rick tightened his arms around her. "Well, it's complicated."

"Do you blame her, too?" Noelle's voice had the thinnest edge.

He must tread carefully. Abortion was murder. He knew that in his deepest soul. Nothing would change his mind, no mitigating circumstances no matter how difficult. But Noelle wouldn't necessarily understand, having been victimized. Maybe Jill had been victimized by Morgan's advances. Certainly Morgan should have known better. But to kill the baby . . . what that had done to Morgan and the pain it had caused his own family . . .

He released a hard breath. "I can't judge her."

"But you blame her." Her voice had a tremor. Some part of her own woundedness had been triggered. "You have no idea what fragility forced her decision."

Fragility? Noelle was fragile in body and spirit, broken as a child by a perverse fiend. Jill was not fragile. His memories of her were vibrant, peppered with touch football and pompons and long legs running hard. Morgan had fallen for her in pure Morganesque abandon and hadn't stopped falling yet.

"I'm not sure he wasn't the more fragile of the two."

Noelle considered that for a silent moment. "He pretends nothing fazes him, but he's not very good at it. It must have really hurt."

Rick stroked a strand of hair from her cheek. "Partly because of how it came down. Jill was ripped out of his life with no real closure."

"Still, it was so long ago."

"You'd understand if you'd seen them together. And he didn't just lose Jill." Rick spread his hand over her belly. "How do you think I'd feel if you took this life from me now? Destroyed our child and there was nothing I could do?"

She pressed her hand over his. "Don't even say that."

"I just want you to see why Morgan can't let it go."

She stroked his forearm. "That's why you wanted him at the reunion."

"I don't think it was me. I think the Lord wanted him there. I have . . . a great unease in my spirit."

"For Morgan?"

Rick nodded. "We don't agree on much, but he's been there for me in more ways than I can name. Even before you made things interesting."

She pushed his chest softly.

He kissed her temple. "Go to sleep. Soon enough we won't have these long, quiet nights."

She nestled in and they both dropped into silence. Too soon he woke with a jolt to find her trembling and thrashing. He caught her tightly in his arms. "Noelle. Stop. It's just a dream."

She opened teary eyes and gasped, "The baby."

Rick placed his hand there, instinctively protecting the life inside. "The baby's fine."

She pressed her face into his chest. "I dreamed he took her."

"Michael?" The ex-fiancé who had battered Noelle and triggered memories of her early abuse.

She shook her head. "No. It was the other face."

The kidnapper she had thought of as God. "He can't hurt you." But Rick wondered again if she would ever be free of it. If sharing Morgan's trouble triggered her pain . . .

"He's out there somewhere. They never caught him."

Because she'd been released as soon as her father gave up prosecuting the case. No one knew then what damage had already been done. Rick rubbed his hand over her belly. "Our baby's safe. That's why you have me."

She looked into his face, green eyes awash. "Hold me, Rick."

He did. He kissed her mouth. "I love you." It swelled up and filled him until it almost brought tears of his own.

"I love you, too," she whispered.

And he settled her in tight to his chest. She was the Lord's gift, no matter how painfully it had come.

6

J ill looked at the little faces, diligent in their task. The Sunday school class was balm to her soul, second-grade children of dedicated families with no problem worse than an occasional runny nose. It was especially healing after last night's fiasco. The smell of Crayola crayons and newsprint mingled with the cheese crackers on napkins and the tart apple juice she poured into bathroom-size Dixie cups.

After today's lesson she'd given them time to draw their favorite Bible stories. With the snack laid out and ready, she walked around to see their progress. Emily drew stick figures well below grade level, but Jill was not there to assess potential learning difficulties. She wanted these children to know their faith, to learn the Bible and all the wonderful truths it held. To know Jesus.

She felt closest to that herself when she was with them, more so than when she sat upstairs for the service or even when she prayed alone. In this class with these eager little lives she could almost remember how it had been for her before everything went wrong.

Stop it. Don't think about it. Don't wonder how Kelsey had looked before the cancer, how she might have huddled over a page with crayons in her hand.

Jill stopped over David's picture. She stooped down and engaged him at face level. "David, did you understand these were supposed to be pictures of your favorite Bible verse?"

He nodded. "It is."

She looked down at the picture of bubble-eyed monsters.

"It's what Pastor talked about today."

Jill racked her brain to put sense to the picture in light of the youth pastor's talk on loving everyone even when they were different.

He rubbed his fist into his cheek. "The aliens. The verse said to love the aliens among you."

Jill glanced quickly into his eyes, caught the sincerity, and contained the humor and joy that exploded within her. She barely controlled a laugh but smiled unashamedly. "It's wonderful, David." She stood up and continued around, full of the gift of that child's innocence. *Thank you, Lord.* And she laughed silently. *That's just what I needed.* She worked with too many problems every day, and now her own had caught up with her. But there was David's picture, and she buried it in her heart.

She carried the joy home with her after the service, but it faded when she walked inside to change clothes. Her black sheath lay across the chair where she'd tossed it after running home like a scared Cinderella. But Morgan had been no prince. She pulled on Lycra shorts and a baggy T-shirt, socks and running shoes, and walked over to Shelly's. Together they headed for the running paths through the woods behind the complex.

"I don't know why I agreed to walk with you." Shelly panted, holding her side. "You have track legs that hurdle everything in your path and make my poor stumps into jelly."

"I'm sorry." Jill slowed her pace. Frustrated not to be running, she'd unconsciously strode out.

"Synonyms for walk are words like *amble, stroll, saunter.*"

Shelly was not Dan. "Sorry, Shell."

Shelly sucked air into her lungs in two long draws. "I'll forgive you if you tell me about last night."

Jill did not want to talk about it. She was ashamed of leaving in tears just because Morgan Spencer snubbed her. If Morgan chose to hate her, that was his business. It was the other emotional pressure: fear for Kelsey and having her daughter suddenly in her life at all. And maybe a little bit of Dan. Those were a lot of stress factors. Any test would say so.

"Hello? I'm the short, chubby friend you're walking with?"

"You're not chubby." She wasn't, just solid.

"About last night . . ."

Jill sighed. "It was all right. I didn't stay long." She'd agreed to walk after church with Shelly instead of running or biking with Dan. Now she wondered if Dan wouldn't have been an easier choice. But she did not want to miss church. She needed grounding right now. Shelly slept in late on Sundays and was just about rallied by the time Jill's service ended.

"Are you going to the picnic today?"

Jill shook her head, unconsciously picking up her pace, then realized Shelly was dragging. She slowed down again.

"Why not?"

"It's just not important to me, Shelly." Why give Morgan a fresh target and Babs more ammunition? What had once been precious was broken past repair.

"You need a social life."

"I have friends." Though none as close as Shelly. The members of her team at school were not kindred spirits, and they clashed so much professionally that Jill spent most of her time trying to keep peace between one faction or another.

"You need a love life. If you won't accept Dan . . ."

Jill turned, caught Shelly's hand. "Let's make a pact. You don't nag about my love life, I won't nag about your weight."

"I'm working on my weight."

Jill didn't have a ready reply. "Well, good." She started walking again.

"Was he there?"

Jill's breath shortened. "Who?"

"Morgan Spencer."

"Yes." She picked up her pace. It would do Shelly good to work a little.

"Bald?"

"He looked terrific. Want to jog the downhill?"

"Want to do CPR?"

Jill laughed.

"Did you talk to him?"

"Briefly." So briefly her head still reeled. *"You've satisfied appearances. Don't let me keep you."* In other words, get lost; I can't stand the sight of you. It shouldn't matter, but it did. She didn't hate him. She had as much cause, didn't she? Why would he bear her such malice all these years?

"Come on, Jill. What did he say?"

"We didn't really talk. We were interrupted." By too much pain.

"Then go to the picnic and get reacquainted."

"There's no point, Shelly. He doesn't live here anymore." The memory book listed a P.O. box in Santa Barbara.

"You never know."

Oh, but she did.

———

Morgan cracked his eyelids open, and pain from the sunlight sliced into his brain. A shadow moved across the window and settled in front of his face. He risked a quick peek again. Rick's chest and a steaming mug that smelled like coffee. Morgan groaned. "That better be spiked."

"Try it this way." Rick held out the mug.

Morgan rolled and raised himself up on one elbow. He took the mug and slurped. Not bad, even if it would do nothing for the pounding in his head.

"Starbucks fresh ground." Rick studied his face.

Morgan could guess what he saw. He sucked in another swallow and tried to sit up. What was Rick doing in his bedroom? He usually left him to sleep it off and went about his morning chores like the responsible citizen he was. As far as Morgan knew, he had induced the only hangover Rick had ever experienced.

Rick sat down. "Is it bad?"

"Yeah." Morgan set the mug on the corner of the nightstand where Rick sat.

"Noelle's worried."

"Sorry." He sort of remembered seeing her last night. Probably made a fool of himself.

"She said you saw Jill."

Morgan leaned back and groaned. "It's too early for this."

"It's past noon. We've been to church and back hours ago. You've missed breakfast and lunch."

Morgan's stomach recoiled. "Good." Especially at the thought of Noelle's fare. He reached for the mug and gulped, then sent a sideways glare at Rick. "Two subjects are off limits, little brother. Food and Jill."

"How was she?"

Morgan shook his head.

"Married?"

"No." Though why on earth not, he had no idea. Any man alive would find her attractive, adorable, addicting.

"You were supposed to go, Morgan. I know it."

"Fine. I went." The coffee coursed down his throat. It needed a shot of Johnny, but at least it was strong.

"I wish you could have worked it out."

"I did." Morgan replaced the mug on the night table and straightened enough to know his head was in truly sorry condition. "If I never see Jill Runyan again—"

"Morgan." Something in Rick's tone stopped the thought in Morgan's mind. "Look at you. You're a wreck."

"Thank you very much."

"You have more natural ability, more God-given talent, and Lord knows the lion's share of the Spencer looks."

Morgan stared at his brother. Where was this going?

"And you've spent the last fifteen years trying to destroy yourself."

Morgan cleared his throat. "I've found a little success along the way."

Rick huffed, shaking his head. "More success than you needed professionally and financially. I know what you've accomplished, in spite of yourself."

"Does this have a point?"

"How long are you going to let this thing with Jill drive your life?"

Morgan stretched his fingers over his forehead. "This thing with Jill ended a long time ago."

"No it didn't. Face it, Morgan."

Morgan rubbed the back of his neck and ignored him.

"You thought Noelle could make you forget."

"All right!" The force of the words through clenched teeth sent pain rippling through his head. "Do you know what it's like to see the woman who killed your child? To feel the visceral poison of the attraction you once had, still have? The wanting, the hating." He swallowed hard and cursed Rick.

Rick gripped his shoulder. "If you don't forgive her, it will destroy you."

Morgan slapped his hand off. "Get out." He threw off the sheet and tried to stand, then collapsed back on the bed.

"I know how much you love her, Morgan. I know how it hurts. You pulled me out of the pit when Noelle left."

"That's my job." Morgan felt drained. "I'm the big brother."

"Well, maybe it's time you listened for a change. You're lucky you didn't die last night, driving up here in your condition. Is that it, Morgan, a death wish?"

Morgan didn't answer. Let Rick say his piece.

"You owe God more than that, and somewhere inside you know it."

"The Lord made a bad investment in me." Morgan shrugged. "He can sell it off anytime."

"But He won't."

Morgan closed his eyes. Definitely easier on the head that way.

"Accept it, Morgan."

He didn't want to know what.

"Peace and forgiveness. That's what you need."

Peace. That sounded good right about now. If he didn't open his eyes, would Rick go away? Pain thrummed. And not just in his head. Seeing Jill had awakened the ugliest parts of him. Maybe he should get out, go somewhere else. Paris—the Champs-Elysées. Australia. Norway. Antarctica. Would any place be far enough?

He opened his eyes at the tap on his door. Rick had left it open and Noelle peeked in. "Are you decent?"

His mouth quirked. "If I'm not, it's your fault." He vaguely recalled her pulling back the sheet so he could collapse into bed last night.

She came in with a small glass, brown and fizzing. "Here."

Morgan took it. "Bitters and soda?"

"I found the bitters in your cabinet. All I had was Sprite to mix in." Her eyes were shadowed. The last thing she needed in her condition was sleep deprivation.

Morgan raised the glass in toast. "To my savior."

Rick frowned, but Noelle just looked sad.

Morgan couldn't stand that. He gulped the bitters, which would help the state of his stomach, if little else. "Now get out and let me clean up." He seriously needed the bathroom, and he'd had all he could take of their concern.

Rick wrapped Noelle's shoulders with his arm and led her out. Morgan chugged the rest of the bitters, then dragged himself up and staggered to the bathroom. He closed the door with a groan, then emerged later, toweling his head dry. It had been a long time since he'd messed himself up this bad. He rubbed his face and dropped the towel.

Gingerly he pulled on some navy Ralph Lauren cargo shorts and a coordinating yellow-collared shirt. His shoes had to be somewhere. He pulled one loafer from under the bed, holding his head as he stood up, and slipped it onto his bare foot. The other was nearby. Now to pack a few things. Within half an hour, he was ready. He picked up his bag and went down the hall.

Noelle was in her studio, painting a watercolor still life. He'd noticed she tended toward even smaller themes these days. This one was a glass vase with cut flowers and a blue-and-white cloth bunched beside it. She was washing the upper edge of the paper, and with her arm raised, the bulge in her belly was more pronounced. She turned, took in his bag. "No, Morgan."

"Gotta learn one of those words without the other, my dear."

She laid down her brush as he approached. "Why are you leaving?"

He set down his bag and cupped her shoulders. "You're in no condition to play nursemaid to a prodigal."

Again that sadness in her eyes. It twisted his gut. "Besides, I have places to go." He slid his fingers into the hair that hung over her neck. "I'll think of you while I'm strolling the Champs-Elysées. We never had the chance."

"Please don't go like this, Morgan." Her tone was sincere. Just his luck that by the time she begged him to stay, she was already married to Rick and carrying his child. He knew very well where her heart was, and what did that leave for him? Pity? He swallowed the bitterness in his throat. He needed to get control, and he couldn't do it with Rick preaching and Noelle worrying.

She rested her hand on his arm. "That's not all your things. Are you coming back?"

He shrugged. "I might."

"Morgan . . ."

He bent and kissed her cheek, then remembered another just as smooth, accented with feathery blond hair. What if he'd kissed Jill last night, taken her into his arms as he'd wanted to when he saw her approach—just stood up and pulled her into his arms and kissed her? His pulse raced as he slid his hands from Noelle's shoulders. "Be good."

Her eyes held his. "Can I say the same to you?"

He smiled. "Gotta have fun doing it." He chucked her chin lightly. "Tell Rick good-bye."

She didn't try to stop him, just watched as he went out the door with one last wave, then headed down the stairs and outside. The sun tortured his eyes as he reached the gravel. The ache in his head defied the aspirin he'd swallowed. He squeezed his shoulder blades back with a low grunt, then opened the trunk and put in his soft leather travel bag. He turned when Todd sauntered up.

"Where are you going?"

Morgan eyed the kid. "Not sure."

Todd's pointy face glared. He leaned close, staring, and sniffed, then backed off. "You're messed up."

"No."

"Yes you are. I smell it."

"I brushed my teeth." Who was this punk kid to jump on his case?

"It's in your skin."

Morgan scowled. "I showered."

"It comes out anyway. I remember."

Expelling a hard breath, Morgan rested his hands on the open trunk frame. "Your dad?"

Todd kicked his toe into the dirt. "Why'd you get drunk?"

Morgan squinted. Why in heaven's name had he come to Rick's ranch? "I don't answer to you."

"Yeah." Todd's face was all snarl. He walked away with a bigger chip than he'd come with.

"Todd." With a sigh, Morgan caught up to him, grabbed his arm, and turned him. "You're right. I got messed up last night, drank more than I should, and right now I feel like something you don't want to step in."

"Why?"

Morgan looked at the angry, defensive kid. He did not have an answer. He had no answers at all.

Todd's eyes darted to the side. "I wanted you to talk to Stan."

Morgan's head throbbed. "What about?"

"You and me doing stuff."

Doing stuff? Morgan swallowed. This kid was not his responsibility. Some undersized, overcharged kid . . . Then he realized Todd had not sworn even once. His chest squeezed. "What sort of stuff?"

Todd shrugged. "I've got all these chores now. Like they think it's gonna help me get responsible." He shot him a glance. "But after . . . we could talk or somethin'."

What had he started? "Don't you talk to Stan?"

Todd shrugged.

"Why not?"

Todd kicked his toe into the dirt in a steady rhythm, raising a little cloud. "He gets all mad if I swear or say something he doesn't want to hear."

Morgan sagged. He did not need this. He looked at the car waiting to carry him away, somewhere, anywhere.

"Go ahead." Todd must have followed his gaze. He turned away.

"Where is Stan?"

Todd glanced over his shoulder. "What do you care?"

Nothing. Morgan almost turned and headed for his car. Instead, "I've got time if you want me to talk to him."

"What difference does it make if you're leaving anyway?"

Morgan sighed. "Todd, would you get Stan?" Why was he standing there begging the kid?

"He's in the cabin. Hold on a minute."

Morgan waited. Todd came out of the cabin with Stan, and Morgan took another good look at the man. Taller than average height, though he stooped, sandy hair thinning, perpetual bags under the eyes but a strong chin.

Stan shook his hand formally as though they hadn't just spent the week in some proximity. Though counting all the "sightseeing" drives the family had taken, they hadn't connected as much as they might have. "Todd says you'd like permission to do things with him?"

Morgan glanced at the scrawny spin artist, then back to Stan. "Thought we could try out some hiking trails, take in a movie or two."

Stan rested his hands on his hips and nodded. "Since you're Rick's brother, I don't see why not."

Yes, any brother of Rick's must be good as gold. Stan's sense of smell must not have Todd's acuity.

Stan nodded toward the bag in the trunk. "Were you going somewhere?"

Todd's eyes darted and Morgan's met them. "No." He could tell himself the word came without thinking, but it hadn't. Somewhere between tossing the bag into the trunk and shaking Stan's hand, he'd decided not to leave.

Stan's eyes ran over the rest of the car. "What do you do, Morgan?"

"I'm a corporate consultant, troubleshooter. I solve people's problems."

Stan nodded. "Must do all right with it."

Morgan formed a quick smile. "Yeah."

"He's not as rich as Bill Gates," Todd said.

"Todd." Stan frowned.

Morgan laughed. "That's okay. I told him that."

"Well. Todd has some work to finish up." Stan raised a hand. "Just let me know when you want to put something together—with Todd, I mean."

Morgan nodded. "Sure." Stan seemed a decent enough guy, though he'd jumped to a conclusion comparing him to Rick. Still, Todd could do a lot worse. As they walked off, Morgan pulled his bag from the trunk and started back into the house.

Noelle had begun the vase and stems when he went back upstairs. She turned and smiled, guessing in advance his change of heart.

"I guess I'll stay awhile, unless you've fumigated my room."

She shook her head. "What changed your mind?"

He glanced behind him. "Todd."

Noelle's smile spread, reading more into it than there was. But then, maybe not.

"Just a few days probably. That's all the quiet I can stand."

"You're welcome as long as you like. You know that."

He did. Though he and Rick were as opposite as two brothers could be, there was a bond between them. Maybe more so since Noelle had entered the picture, strange as that seemed. Someone less than Rick might be jealous and suspicious, especially when Morgan pressed the limits. Instead he freely offered his home, his family. Morgan nodded. Sometimes he needed that.

7

Jill stared at the letter, an impersonal sheet of paper typed by uncaring hands, the scrawl of a signature at the end. She felt light, as though gravity had suddenly released her, then realized with a crash it had not. Her head struck the edge of the table. Pain.

"Jill!" Shelly rushed in, slamming the measuring cup onto the table and crouching beside her. "Did you faint? Are you sick?"

Jill cleared the shock from her head. Sick? No. But her heart did not believe it.

"You have not been eating, girl."

That was true. Yet she'd gotten up at dawn every morning and run, hoping the exercise-induced dopamine would suffice. She had poured herself into tutoring the students who qualified for the extended school-year program while she had waited to hear the results. And now . . .

"What's this?" Shelly snatched the letter.

Feebly Jill tried to take it back.

Shelly stood up. "What is this?" Her face paled, her mouth hung slack. "Pre-transplant bone marrow test results? Jill! Are you dying?"

Jill dropped her face to her hands. "No," she said flatly. "My daughter is."

Shelly dropped her hip against the cabinet, mouth open, staring as though Jill had suddenly turned green and sprouted antennae.

"A bone marrow transplant is her only chance for cure." Tears stung

and her throat burned. "I don't match, Shelly." And she broke down, shaking with the terrible sobs that came. "I don't match." She was vaguely aware of Shelly rejoining her on the floor, arms coming around her. She buried her face in Shelly's neck. "Oh my God, my God." Would He ever stop punishing her?

"Shell? Burgers are on the grill; we need—" Brett stopped just inside the patio door.

Shuddering, Jill looked up and saw Dan come in behind him.

He pushed past Brett and dropped to the floor. "What's wrong? Are you injured? Did you fall?" He touched the lump on her head.

"Shelly, what's going on?" Brett demanded.

Jill snatched the letter and pressed it to her breast, sending Shelly a beseeching look.

But Shelly shook her head. "No way. I'm not letting you face this alone. We're your friends, Jill. At least I thought so."

Jill dropped her chin, fresh tears flowing. What did it matter? What if the whole world knew? Her daughter was dying, and she could do nothing to stop it.

Dan came around behind her and lifted her to a chair at the table. "Could someone tell me what's going on? Face what?" He looked at Shelly.

Shelly shrugged and eyed Jill expectantly.

Jill looked from one to another. Her three closest friends. Shelly must have come to borrow something across the narrow yard that separated their patio doors. She could smell the smoke from their grill and remembered she'd been invited to join them but had turned down the invitation. She dropped her forehead to her palm, then pressed the letter flat on the table. "I can't donate bone marrow to my daughter." She looked up and saw just the expression on Dan's face that she expected.

His jaw hung slack and his brown eyes searched her face as though he'd never seen her. "Your daughter?"

She smiled dryly. "Safe sex, just the way you teach it."

He frowned. "Jill . . ."

Shelly pulled out a chair and sat. "Brett, sit down. Dan, stop hovering."

When the table was full, Jill looked at her friends again, Shelly's face sympathetic but hurt. Brett, uncomfortable. Dan . . . poor Dan. Jill wanted to laugh. It was so . . . but tears came instead. She fought them away. "I was seventeen. I gave her up for adoption." Her throat tightened, looking into Dan's face. She saw understanding dawn.

"A few weeks ago, I got a letter saying she had leukemia." Her voice broke. Grimly she contained the horror that word still gave her. She'd read everything she found on the Internet about the disease and spent hours sifting the library catalogue for the best available books on the subject.

"The parents knew where to find you?" This from Shelly.

"I always update my address with them just in case." In case Kelsey wanted to find her, not in case she needed to die.

They all sat in silence. Of course, they didn't know what to say. Her friends were all revamping their image of her, trying to catch up with the truth but needing to discard so many appearances, starting with chaste. Jill flicked a glance at Dan.

He reached over and took her hand. "Why didn't you just tell me?"

"Why didn't you tell me?" Shelly's tone was betrayed. "It's not like we'd pin a scarlet A to your dress."

Jill shook her head. "It was fifteen years ago, long before I knew any of you. I—it was behind me." Except for all the times she'd imagined her child, longed for her, and cried.

Dan's hand was warm, his eyes gentle, almost relieved. Maybe now he considered her "normal." "What's her name?"

"Kelsey. Kelsey Renée Benson. She's fourteen. She's . . ." Tears stung again.

Dan's hand tightened. "These are the kinds of things you don't try to handle alone, Jill."

She sniffed back the tears. What could they possibly do? Kelsey was going to die and there was nothing they could do.

Shelly picked up the letter. "So they asked you to donate marrow to stop the leukemia?"

Jill nodded. "Without a transplant there's no chance of cure. The initial test result was good, but the cytotoxic antibody screen gave a positive reading for anti-HLA class one antibody." Stabbing pain shot through her chest as she babbled. Like Cinda, she spouted the right medical terms, but they did not siphon the pain. "If they did the transplant, Kelsey would reject my cells. I can't help her."

Shelly looked up from the letter. "What about her father?"

Jill's spine went cold. *Morgan.* She hadn't even thought it. *Oh, God, I can't. You can't ask it.* But it seemed God could ask anything. Go to Morgan? Tell him her daughter, their daughter needed him? Wouldn't he have the other haplotype match and possibly no antibody cross match? In spite of the June heat in the kitchen, she started to shake.

Dan shot a glance to Brett and chafed her hand. "Take it easy, Jill."

But Shelly had fixed her with a piercing gaze. "It's Morgan Spencer, isn't it?"

Dan looked confused. Jill could almost read his thoughts. Should he know something here?

"Um." She raised a shaking hand to flick back the soft strands falling into her face. "He doesn't know anything." She had lied to the judge at the termination hearing, listed the father as unknown, and served notice to all putative fathers in a newspaper in her aunt's county where she knew Morgan would never see it. "My parents told him I had an abortion."

Shelly drew a long breath and sat back in the chair. "Well, maybe it's time to enlighten him. Where do men get off thinking if the woman has an abortion it magically all goes away? I bet he was just so relieved."

Jill bit her lower lip. She hadn't been there when her parents told him, but she'd seen his face when she first mentioned it, and she'd heard her father yelling at Morgan's over the phone. No, she didn't really think the Spencers, or Morgan, had felt relieved. But what could she do?

"So," Shelly said, forcing the issue again. "Do you know where to find him?"

"Only a post office box in California."

Shelly's face reflected Jill's own uncertainty. As much as she would like to, it shouldn't come to him in a letter. And she had just seen him! Could have told him, but instead they'd exchanged stupid words that meant nothing.

"His family lives near here." At least they had. She pictured the classy Spencer farm where she'd spent some wonderful times. "I guess they'd know where he is." She sniffed back tears and noticed a distinct smell.

"Oh no!" Brett shot up. "The burgers." He hurried out, the rest of them staring after him.

Dan said, "Those burgers will be charcoal. Shelly, why don't you and Brett go out for dinner? I'll stay here with Jill."

Shelly looked from him to her. Jill sensed her indecision but knew she would obey. Anything Dan wanted. Even if it meant she wasn't the first to get the whole story. Weariness settled like a blanket.

Shelly stood up. "I'll talk to you later, okay?" Shelly's expression left no doubt that she would.

Jill sent her a bleak smile. What if she said no? Did Shelly ever take no for an answer? At the door Shelly glanced back, then went after her husband. Jill sat without speaking, her hand cupped between Dan's.

"So that's the real reason, isn't it?" Dan spoke softly, but there was an edge in his voice.

She looked into his blunt, suntanned face. He was the guy they'd call for a good-cop/bad-cop routine. His was the face you would trust. But she hadn't. She lowered her eyes. "I meant everything I told you. I believe in marriage. Intimacy belongs within the covenant. All of that is true."

"Now."

She drew her hands away. "I was seventeen years old, Dan. I had people like you telling me I could and should be sexual."

"And of course Morgan Spencer." Again the clipped tone. Was he jealous?

She sat back in her chair. "I don't need this now. Yes, I learned the hard way. Does that make the lesson less valid? If I had done things right, do you think I'd be sitting here begging God not to make me tell Morgan the truth, and praying he doesn't hate me so much he'll let our daughter die?"

"Real boy scout, is he?"

Jill pictured the cold, cynical man Morgan had become and started shaking again. "I don't know. We were kids. He was eighteen years old; what do you expect, Dan? My parents gave us no choice. They blamed it all on Morgan and sent me away before I could even see him again."

He released a long breath. "Okay. I'm sorry. But we've been together almost a year and I had no idea. I thought I knew you. This is the kind of thing that scares the you-know-what out of me. If we can be in a relationship this long and you keep something like this to yourself . . ." He shook his head. "It's Liz all over again."

Jill knew it was his hurt speaking, but that was uncalled for. "I never lied to you, Dan. And I certainly didn't cheat on you." And now anger covered her hurt. "And the fact that I have a daughter is really none of your business at all." She tried to stand, but he caught her wrist.

"Jill. I'm sorry. That was unfair."

She settled back, wishing the anger wouldn't subside. But it did, leaving only the terrible fear and disappointment.

"What are you going to do?"

Her chest tightened like a vise. "Find Morgan." She didn't want to say it, but she had to. Kelsey needed any chance there was.

Dan rubbed her hand. "You don't look too good."

"I don't feel too good."

"How's your head?"

She reached her fingers to the bump. "It's all right."

"Why don't I start you a hot bath? While you soak I'll make us something. . . ."

"Dan." Jill covered his hand with her other. "No." Then she drew both her hands away. "I need to be alone." To think. To pray. But she didn't say it aloud. She was already a hypocrite.

He was hurt. He wanted to make something happen between them that she knew now was not going to happen. Just the thought of facing Morgan was enough to keep her from ever risking that kind of intimacy again. She took the letter, folded it, and slipped it back into the envelope.

Dan stood up. For a long moment he looked down on her, wanting to change her mind. She kept her eyes on the envelope, so innocuous from the outside, so devastating within. Then he went out.

Jill closed her eyes. She sat there in numb silence. This couldn't be real. Why had Shelly even mentioned Morgan? Of course the father could be the donor, but *her* mind hadn't made the leap. She had not allowed it to because the very thought meant she would have failed. *Oh, God. Please don't ask this of me.* She would call the number on the letter, the number for questions. And she would ask, could it be a mistake? Could they retest?

They'd had difficulty with her vein, and she had bruised and hurt afterward. But it would be less painful by far than going to Morgan with the truth. She couldn't. God couldn't expect it.

"Why?" She threaded her fingers together and pressed the knuckles of her fists to her lips. "Lord, I was so naïve." And she'd been so in love. Nothing could have prepared her for Morgan—Morgan as she'd known him then. She had worshiped him. And God was a jealous God.

She could walk away. Cinda would learn the results, know the marrow didn't match. Jill tried not to think how devastated all the Bensons would be right now. She had tried, but she couldn't save her daughter's life. *Could Morgan?* She didn't know. He bore the other half of Kelsey's antigens, but there was the lymphocyte cross-match test. Morgan might be no better match than herself. She might go to him, tell him everything, for nothing.

Forking her fingers into her hair, she pressed her forehead to her palm. Did she have the right to not take that chance? *Oh, God, why?* She suddenly sat up straight. She could let Cinda tell him. She could give Cinda his name and let her write, call, or go to him. Jill pictured Morgan hearing the news, the shock and disbelief. She sagged.

She refused to be that much of a coward. He deserved to hear it from her. *Okay, Lord. If you want me to tell him, show me.* She got up and went to the shelf where she kept her Bible. She knew it well enough from a Sunday school perspective—had all her Old and New Testament stories down pat. But she wasn't very adept at applying Scripture to her own life. She depended on the pastor's sermons for that.

One of the women at church had told her that she got answers by opening the book at random and reading the first verse that caught her eye. Jill had thought it crazy, but she was desperate enough to try anything. She let the Bible fall open in her hands. It was roughly in the middle, the book of Jonah, and her eyes landed on chapter three. *Then the word of the Lord came to Jonah a second time: "Go to the great city of Nineveh and proclaim to it the message I give you."*

Trembling, Jill closed the book. It was crazy to think that had been a divine message. It was nothing short of gambling. Of course the book would fall open in the middle, and she could probably read anything into what she found there. She opened the Bible again. This time it was Isaiah, an oracle to Edom, wherever that was. *Someone calls to me from Seir, "Watchman, what is left of the night?" Watchman, what is left of the night?" The watchman replies, "Morning is coming, but also the night. If you would ask, then ask; and come back yet again."*

Meaningless words. But that just proved it. She could open a hundred places and get a hundred different passages. *If you would ask, then ask; and come back yet again.* She had come back and the passage was no clearer than the first reading. She closed the Bible and sat down on the giraffe chair. Then, picturing Kelsey's sweet, sweet face, she dropped to her knees. "I'm asking, Lord. What do you want me to do? How can I help her?"

Announce the message. But that was to Jonah. Nineveh didn't even exist anymore. She dropped her face to her hands. Why was this so hard? She had no trouble praying for Joey when he was violent, for Sammi's tantrums, for the others when they were hurt and rejected and misunderstood. She could pray for the children. Maybe it was Kelsey she must focus on now.

She pictured her daughter's face again. *"Is it a ministry?"* What fourteen-year-old girl thought of help and kindness as a ministry? Had Jill even understood the word at that age? She moistened her lips. *Lord, what do you want from me?* But she knew. In her heart she knew. If it were anyone but Morgan. And she saw again the utter disdain in his eyes, the hatred he felt for her.

Did that matter? It was for Kelsey's sake. Sighing, she opened the Bible a third time, not looking for some supernatural answer now, but just comfort. She flipped to the Psalms, number forty: *I waited patiently for the Lord; he turned to me and heard my cry. He lifted me out of the slimy pit, out of the mud and mire; he set my feet on a rock and gave me a firm place to stand. He put a new song in my mouth, a hymn of praise to our God. Many will see and fear and put their trust in the Lord.*

Peace settled inside her. She loved the psalms. This one seemed especially encouraging. Maybe God had a purpose, even if she couldn't see it. Right now she was sure of nothing. It was too late to call about retesting. But in the morning, she would ask her questions. And if there was no other way, she would find Morgan.

Morgan secured the pack onto Todd's back, tightened the left strap, and patted the boy's shoulder. "Let's go."

"Why do I have to carry it?" Todd stepped away from the car toward the trailhead. He'd hit Morgan up that morning to do something, though he didn't seem overwhelmed with the prospect of hiking the national park trail.

"Because I'm the guide."

"So?"

Morgan gripped the walking stick he'd picked up at one of the tourist shops in Juniper Falls. Normally he didn't darken their doors, but he couldn't resist the stand of natural sticks, gnarly but sanded smooth, and got one for himself and Todd.

"Just imagine I'm Gandalf and you're Frodo."

"I'd rather be Strider."

The night before, Todd's face had been more animated than Morgan would have guessed when they'd gone to see the *Lord of the*

Rings movie that had finally made it to Juniper Falls's single-screen theater. Surprisingly, Todd had never seen any of them, and the impact it had on the kid was remarkable. Todd had responded powerfully, and Morgan sensed a longing for something truly heroic.

"Well, if you're Strider, you'd better step it up." Morgan set the pace along the narrow trail where he'd taken Noelle on their first hike together. It had a fabulous view at the top.

"Why do we have to hike?" Todd trudged, a sour look on his face.

"Expands the lungs, opens the mind."

Todd used a profane phrase that translated "Who cares?"

Morgan shrugged. "You should. You want to be scrawny all your life?"

"You're not exactly Arnold Schwarzenegger."

"Don't want to be. Buff shoulders don't fit well in a suit. But I'm fit and strong, and that's what matters."

Todd swore again.

It would be a long hike if Todd meant to argue with every word. Just fifteen short hours ago, the movie night had been magical, and not only on the screen. Todd had lit up like the wizard's wand, let down his guard, and conversed. This outing was not proving as promising.

"So what is it you like about Strider?"

Todd made his voice powerful. "Let's go hunt some orc."

Morgan smiled. "Aha."

"And when he hacked that one orc's head off. That was really cool."

At least the kid was talking instead of swearing. "What about when he healed Frodo with the herbs?"

Todd scrunched up his face. "Oh yeah. When the elf girl came?" Obviously not as memorable a scene. But Todd seemed to have snapped out of his funk. "And when he fought off the black riders! Their screams were awesome."

Morgan quirked an eyebrow as he walked. "Like to have them on your trail?"

"No way." Todd glanced back down the slope. "But if they were . . ." He gripped his walking stick like a cudgel and swung. "Back! Back before I knock your heads off!"

Morgan laughed. At the moment he hardly believed this was the kid he'd caught carving profanity into Rick's post. "But they don't have heads."

"Well, they sort of do. Strider lit them on fire."

"That's true. Must have a sort of body, though they're neither alive nor dead." There had been some days Morgan felt that way himself, and it was a toss-up which outcome he'd prefer. But not since Todd had called him on it two days ago.

"They should have made you Strider."

"Me?"

"You have black hair and blue eyes. And you look more Strider-ish."

Morgan cocked his head. "And so you think I look foul and feel fair? 'All that is gold does not glitter, not all who wander are lost'?"

Todd screwed up his face. "What?"

"Oh, that's from the book. They left it out of the movie." He started climbing again. "When they first saw him, the hobbits were skeptical of the ranger. But Frodo's heart could tell Strider was trust-worthy, even though he looked like a rogue."

"A what?"

"Bad dude."

Todd grinned, the first yet. "Rogue. What else did they leave out?"

"A lot." Morgan rounded a bend in the trail. "No way to catch it all in a movie. Even three hours long. You ought to read the books."

Todd hacked a bush with his walking stick. "Don't have 'em."

Morgan planted his stick and turned. "We'll have to see about that."

"I don't like to read anyway."

"Don't like to read! Then you've never found the right books."

"I can't do it good, okay? I'm stupid—so what?"

Morgan eyed him. If that was true, no wonder the kid couldn't succeed in school. "You're not stupid, Todd." Anything but. The kid was more cunning than most grown-ups. "Does Stan know?"

"Just get off it."

Morgan started on. They had reached a steep section and puffed upward without speaking, then stopped for a water break. The sun overhead gave everything a sharp-edged brilliance. Morgan pulled two water bottles from the pack on Todd's back. He chugged his and urged Todd to do the same, though he resisted. "Gotta stay hydrated. Need a snack, or should we move on?"

Todd kicked the dirt. "I don't care."

"We'll snack at the top, then." Morgan put their half-empty bottles into the pack, still secured on Todd's back, and slid the ties shut. "Come on."

Todd rolled his eyes but followed. They climbed until they reached the summit, then stood and gazed out at the rippling range and golden hills. Not so long ago Morgan had stood there with Noelle, tried to make her trust him, tried to break the shell that trapped her in. He'd failed.

Todd pulled himself up tall. "Which way is Mordor?"

Wiping his face with his forearm, Morgan looked out across the scene and imagined the ruined, tortured land of fiery darkness. A slow breath escaped his lungs with a sudden sense of futility. "Mordor is wherever you make it, Todd."

8

Dear Kelsey: My three-year-old, Annie, thinks she sees angels when she has her treatments. Is it possible?
Kelsey's fingers went to the keyboard.

> Dear Susan,
>   Yes, I believe your daughter sees angels. Jesus said, "See that you do not despise one of these little ones, for I say to you that their angels in heaven always look upon the face of my heavenly Father." Annie's too little to understand what's happening to her. But Jesus knows exactly what she needs. He loves her so much. Why couldn't He show her the angels watching over her? I was taught how to visualize my comfort, but I don't find it hard at all to believe that Annie can truly see hers. Especially if it helps her not to be afraid.
>   Jesus loves you and so do I. Kelsey
>   www.kelseys_hope_page.com

Kelsey rested her fingers on the keyboard and read over what she'd said. And though she hadn't written it, sometimes her army had become so real she might truly see them, as well. Annie was only three, and her cancer was acute myelocytic leukemia, the one with the lowest cure rate. Kelsey's eyes teared. Maybe Jesus was showing her heaven so she wouldn't be afraid to go.

Swiping her eyes clear, she read the next question and started her answer.

Dear Micah,

Choosing to be part of a study could help others in the future. I like to think we've been chosen for a purpose. Though it seems like just our bad luck, what if our whole reason for being sick is to help all the other kids later on? If no one takes part in the studies, how can the doctors find a way to win? But your parents are afraid, too. They're hurting as much as you are. Pray for help to make the right choice. And trust Jesus.

He loves you and so do I. Kelsey
www.kelseys_hope_page.com

In spite of the bad news about Jill's bone marrow not matching, she'd had a good day. Her friends had come over after school to play Taboo. Mom made her favorite oatmeal no-bakes and Rice Krispies treats. The good thing about being sick was she could eat anything she wanted. At least during the times between chemotherapy when her stomach wasn't upset and everything didn't taste like dirt. But she guessed even if she weren't sick, she had the kind of body that would not get fat easily.

Like Jill's.

She got up and peeked down the hall stairs. Mom and Dad's voices murmured below, but it would be a while before they came up to bed. She crept to the study and closed the door softly behind her. The walls on three sides were lined with bookcases, and the closet held boxes of photos and old schoolwork and all kinds of stuff. The big desk in the middle was piled so high the ancient typewriter was buried. Stacks of papers climbed from the floor up the sides of the desk almost to its top. Where would she start?

———

Jill looked in the phone book, almost hoping the name would not be there. But as her finger scanned the Spencer listings to Hank, her mouth went dry. Who would answer the phone? And could she bring such news to them on the telephone? It was better face to face. She noted the address, still off Wilmington Road.

Jill closed her eyes, accessing her determination as she once had before a race. She had called Cinda last night with the possibility of finding Morgan. She had to know if that was an avenue they would consider before she risked the heartache it would involve. She had tried not to sound too positive because she had no idea how it would turn out. But both Cinda and Roger had grasped the possibility. Cinda had almost let her off the hook, too, offering to contact Morgan herself. But Jill had said no.

Cinda could have no idea how painful it would be to go to Morgan with the truth. She knew nothing of the lies, the deception, only that it might be difficult to contact him. Jill sighed. The responsibility was hers. She would face Morgan. But she must find him first, and shooting a note off to his P.O. box was not the way to do it. What sort of man had a P.O. box for an address? Maybe he traveled. By his snazzy suit, he appeared to have the money for it. Whatever the case, she had her starting point.

Closing the book, she grabbed up her keys. Protocol said to call the Spencers first and set up a time. But that meant talking to them without explaining the situation, or explaining it all over the phone, and she already knew she would bumble that. No, she would take her chances.

She drove across town and out into the country, past regiments of cornstalks on either side. The Spencer farm was one of the nicest properties out there, and Jill had loved seeing the horses Hank raised, though she had a healthy fear of riding them. Morgan never pushed. He wasn't a horseman like his father and Rick. Thinking of Rick made her consider the rest of the family: Morgan's mother, Celia, and four little girls.

Not little now, she realized. Therese must be grown, maybe gone. Stephanie, too? She couldn't remember their exact ages. There was a sizable gap between Rick, two years younger than Morgan, and Therese, the oldest sister. What had she been, five or six? Jill pulled into the long lane that led up to the low gray ranch-style house. It was well kept and hardly looked any different, except that the trees and shrubs had grown some. The white trim was neatly painted and the door was now a slate blue, updating it but still not changing the sedate country appearance.

She pulled up in the gravel circle, heart pumping. Would they know her? Probably all too well. *Lord, give me strength.* She climbed out, walked to the door, and debated between the brass knocker and the bell.

Before she could do either, the door opened and a fresh-faced girl with the Spencer blues looked smartly at her. "Hello."

Jill studied the face, trying to imagine one of Morgan's cherubic sisters in this lanky adolescent frame. She dug for the baby's name. "Tiffany?"

"Nope. She's out blading."

Hadn't Tiffany been the baby? "Then you're . . ."

"Tara. Can I help you?"

Yes, Tara was the baby. Tiffany had been a toddler. "I was wondering if your parents were home."

"Yep. Come on in."

Jill walked into the house where she'd eaten family dinners while Morgan was alternately amused and annoyed by the little girls and Rick quietly appraising, and Celia . . . It would be easier to face Hank. He'd always been so warm and accepting.

"Mom, there's someone here." Tara's voice had a buoyant ring, and Jill realized with a pang she was close to Kelsey's age, though healthy and much taller. "She's in the study. Just a minute."

Jill almost considered telling her not to bother, that she'd talk to her father. But then, what would she tell Hank? You remember that baby my father told you I'd aborted? The things he hollered about your son and your own moral values? Well, guess what . . .

Celia came down the hall, dressed in a blue-print housedress and sandals. Her hair was more gray than brown, but her eyes were the deep chocolaty tone Jill recalled. Tara was on her heels, eager and nosey as any adolescent girl.

"Yes?" Celia's tone was reserved and polite; then she stopped and stared. "Jill?"

"I'm sorry to barge in on you like this." She should have called.

Celia stood a long moment not speaking.

Tara looked from one to the other of them curiously, then with a Morganesque wave of her hand, said, "Why don't we all sit down."

Celia turned to her daughter with a faint smile. "You go out, Tara. I'll talk with Jill alone."

Tara looked both surprised and disappointed, but she turned with a dramatic sigh and walked away.

"Come in, please." Celia led Jill into the living room, bathed in the diffused sunlight of hazy clouds and foliage. "Do you want some tea?"

Jill shook her head, remembering Celia's scrupulous hospitality. She would offer tea to her worst enemy, and Jill just might fit that description. "No thank you. I won't be long."

Celia motioned her to a side chair and sat across in its partner. "Well, you've taken me by surprise."

"I'm so sorry I didn't call. I thought it would be better to explain things in person. I should have called."

Celia waved her hand. "Don't worry about it."

God, give me strength. "I'm here because I need to find Morgan." She realized her mistake by the sudden closed expression on Celia's face. This was going worse than she'd imagined. "Mrs. Spencer . . ."

"Call me Celia."

Jill collected herself. But how could she put into words her family's deception, the grandchild Celia didn't know she had, that child's condition?

"What is it, Jill?"

"My daughter has leukemia." Of course that told Celia nothing, though her face softened with concern. What a stupid thing to blurt out. Her daughter? Cinda's daughter, Morgan's daughter. It was all so confusing.

Jill faced Morgan's mother. "Celia, I never had the abortion." There, it was out, and a ghost of understanding passed over Celia's face as Jill rushed on. "My parents allowed me to carry the child if I gave her up for adoption and . . ." Tears stung her eyes. *Lord, don't let me fall apart!*

Celia's stare held confusion and dismay. She said, "I'll get some tea."

An excuse to leave the room, but Jill was grateful, as well, for the chance to gather herself. She dropped her face into her hands when Celia left. That was probably the worst she could have done with this. Why did everything jumble up when she tried to deal with this head-on?

Please help me. I'm trying to do the right thing. Jill heard murmurs in the kitchen, probably Tara and her mother. *Are you okay, Mom? No, you can't join us. Is something wrong? Yes, everything.* Well, maybe Celia wouldn't actually say that to her daughter. Jill composed herself, trying to order her thoughts. Sitting there by herself in this house that held so many family members, she realized how truly alone she was.

That was one thing she had deeply envied of Morgan: his large, happy family. Though he and Rick teasingly bemoaned the arrival of their sisters, Jill had felt the love and connectedness in the Spencer house. She was one of only two children, and her brother was four years older. She had hardly spoken to him in two years—not through animosity, just lack of interest.

Celia returned with two glasses of iced tea and a sugar bowl on a tray. She set it on the table. "Sugar?"

Jill shook her head. "Just plain, thanks."

Celia doctored her own, then sat down again. "I think I'm over the shock now."

"I'm sorry. I'm doing this badly."

Celia smiled a little, no mirth reaching her eyes. "So you had Morgan's child after all."

Jill nodded. "I gave her to a wonderful couple. I would never have troubled you with this except . . ." She swallowed the tightness in her throat. "As I said, Kelsey has leukemia and needs a bone marrow transplant."

"Kelsey," Celia murmured.

Jill would break down if she asked for details, description. She forced herself to focus on her purpose. "I've been tested but disqualified as a donor."

"And so you think Morgan might do?" Celia had jumped ahead, guessed her purpose.

"There's a chance." Jill sipped her tea, allowing its icy bite to moisten her dry mouth and throat.

"And otherwise you would have kept all this to yourself." There was an edge to Celia's voice.

Jill lowered her glass, cupped it between her palms in her lap, and stared into its tawny depths. She didn't know what to say. Yes, she would have kept it to herself. Even now she dreaded telling Morgan.

"Do you have any idea what it did to Morgan to think you aborted his child?"

Jill heard the cool fury of a mother. She knew what she would find in Celia's face if she looked.

"From the time the kids were small they understood the value, the utter preciousness of life—my boys no less than my daughters. In this family we treasure children. If you had told him anything else . . ."

Now Jill did look up and caught the bitter pain in Celia's eyes before it smoothed into her normal frank gaze. What could she say? She murmured, "I'm sorry. I'm so sorry." Yes, it had been her parents' doing . . . at first. But she hadn't considered that the lie might wound Morgan still, after all this time. Was that why he hated her so much?

"You'll find him changed."

I know! But she couldn't think of that. "Will he help her?" She couldn't stop the question. She felt terrible for Morgan, but it was Kelsey who needed help.

Celia's mouth hardened. "Do you imagine he won't?"

Jill took another drink, more to hide from Celia's ire than any-thing. What did she imagine? His hard blue eyes had haunted her sleep, his sardonic smile, the cutting words. None of that mattered. "I only found a post office box in California. I didn't want to tell him in a letter."

"He's staying at Rick's ranch in Colorado right now."

"Rick's ranch?"

Celia stood. "I'll write you directions from the Denver airport."

"You will?" She had hoped, yet expected Celia to refuse. Or maybe she'd hoped Celia would refuse.

Celia fixed her gaze flatly. "Would you tell him this over the phone?"

She had considered that a mode of least resistance, but Jill shook her head. "No, I intended to do it in person, though I wasn't sure you'd agree that was best."

Celia lifted the tray. She paused. "I know you're trying to make things right. But the truth is, great harm was done. I don't know any better than you how to set it right. But there's a young girl who needs help, quickly, I surmise. The best way to get through to Morgan would be to go there."

Jill nodded. "Then I will."

Celia went again into the kitchen. Jill heard the tray bang and the glasses clank as though she'd set it down too hard. She waited, hands gripped together.

Celia returned, handed her a slip of paper. "Here are the directions to the ranch. It's in the mountains. You'll want to rent a car that can take a grade."

Jill nodded silently, then, "I'm very sorry."

Celia looked into her face. "You did the right thing. You gave your child life. I just wish you could have told us the truth." Her eyes teared.

Jill didn't want to see it. Not in Celia of all people. She looked down at the paper in her hands. "Thank you. For this." She held it up. It would cost a fortune to fly on such short notice, but there really was no other way. "Should I call him first?"

Again Celia's mouth tightened, and her eyes grew immeasurably sad. "No." Was there some reason behind her certainty? Jill's chest seized. What was she going into? But there was nothing more to say except, "May I give you my phone number . . . in case you need to reach me?"

"Yes, thank you." Celia's voice was tight.

Jill reached into her purse and took out her business card, which included her home phone. Only certain people received those. But she wanted Celia to have it now. She didn't know why. She left the house completely drained. If it took so much to tell Morgan's mother, how would it be to tell Morgan?

Her stress intensified when she got home to a message from her own mother. Ordinarily, she would call right back and they would share a pleasant, if superficial, conversation. Now she felt like a traitor. It was tacitly understood that Kelsey was not a subject for discussion. That unhappy incident was behind them. It had never occurred to Mom how much Jill had needed her when Kelsey was born, how it might have eased the pain for the months afterward if she could have told her what the baby looked like, how long and hard she'd pushed, how tearful and ecstatic the Bensons had been.

But Mom's first words to her when she came back were, "It's over and forgotten, Jill." She had meant it kindly, perhaps, but besides burying the pain, it had left a superficial façade between them they both worked hard to maintain. But now, how could she leave Morgan's mother grieving the situation and say no word to her own about the circumstances that were turning her life upside down?

She went to find Shelly. A friend was definitely in order. Shelly opened immediately at her knock.

"Can I use your computer?" Shelly's DSL line would be faster than her Internet service, and she wanted things put into motion before she lost her nerve.

Shelly grabbed her arm and dragged her in. "Yes, on one condition, and you know what it is."

"I'll tell you everything, but first I need to buy a plane ticket for this weekend."

Shelly gripped both arms. "To find Morgan?"

Jill nodded, more bleak inside than Shelly could know. "He's at his brother's ranch in Colorado, and it's going to drain my account getting there." Not to mention her courage and fortitude. But this was what she had to do. She would gather her energy for the hurdle and leap. How she landed was up to God.

Taking his keys from the hook in the kitchen, Rick crooked an eyebrow. "Sure you won't come?"

Morgan shook his head. Rick's little mountain church service was not calling to him. He glanced at Todd, standing with Stan's hand on his shoulder, obviously feeling the same way. His face was drawn down in his typical scowl, but he was not Morgan's responsibility. If Stan was surprised he didn't rush off with the rest of them to worship, it was a good lesson in making assumptions.

Todd's sister, Sarah, waved as they all left the kitchen. She wasn't as stuck-up as she'd seemed, probably just shocked by the arrival of a foul-mouthed, sullen kid in her life. There still wasn't much interaction between the two, but that took time. Stan's wife, Melanie, was the last through the door, and Morgan released a slow breath of relief.

Noelle was home but upstairs fighting a virus. Rick had assured him she'd be all right sleeping off the bug, and he could use some time alone. With the roar of Rick's truck fading from the yard, the house grew quiet. Just now that felt fine. Ascon had contacted him again, but the current CEO, the daughter of Ascon's creator, was still playing games. She expected his consultation to give her suggestions she might want to consider. He didn't work that way. Following his initial viability analysis, she'd have to commit to the measures he had outlined in order to give her company any shot at the New York Stock Exchange.

It was his reputation as much as her corporate success.

She knew what he could do, and the board was running scared enough to pressure her, but she still resisted his involvement as a "rent a CEO," as she had quaintly, though not originally, put it. If she waited too long, Morgan would look elsewhere. He didn't waste time on lost causes. There were plenty of challenges with potential, and he could choose where to spend his energy.

Taking the mug of coffee, he went to the front room, where he'd stashed his kangaroo leather briefcase and spread his proposal over the table. He'd faxed it to Ascon already, but he studied it now for any flaw, any improvement.

He had addressed Ascon's particular situation without disclosing the exact measures he would take to correct the problems. Once they contracted his services, he'd give Ascon their money's worth. Morgan read through the pages, satisfied. Marlina Aster would have to take him on reputation or not take him at all.

He moved on to his laptop to study his next options. He'd researched several corporations who'd queried his program, and he studied the different files now, sorting them according to likeliness. Those he found most promising, he'd send a follow-up proposal. And there were any number of fresh possibilities with the unstable economy. He sent an e-mail to his professional assistant with the names of the companies he'd chosen to look at next. She'd make the initial contact, then he would go in person to assess the need and either take charge himself or send out a team.

Car tires grinding on gravel in the yard signaled a visitor, but he remained focused until he heard the knock. He could hardly expect Noelle to answer in her condition, so he went to the door and pulled it open. The greeting died on his lips with the high-tension jolt to his system.

It had been bad enough the other night at the reunion when he'd half expected to see her. The incongruity of finding Jill on Rick's porch now left him without remark, though for so many years he had imagined her showing up one day and explaining it had all been a terrible mistake.

"Morgan, I . . . I guess you're wondering why I'm here."

Wondering hardly seemed sufficient for the high-speed RAM spinning in his head. Obviously some errant thread had reconnected them the other night and now formed a noose around his throat that stifled any words. He had imagined this meeting on his terms, in a place he controlled, not Rick's ranch, where he went to hide, to let down his guard and be real. Jill's presence violated his intention.

He looked from her face down her blue knit tank and waist-tie pants that fluttered in the wind, then back to her face framed with that short, sassy hair. Whatever her reason for being there, it wouldn't be good. But what else was new?

She drew herself up with determination. "I need to talk to you."

The muscles pulled tight in the back of his neck. "I thought we covered it all the other night." His tone iced even him, but he would not give her the advantage.

She looked to the side, a stark extremity in her expression that tugged at his gut. "No, there's more that needs to be said."

The wind fanned her hair as she returned her gaze to his face, imploring . . . what? What could she possibly want from him? Absolution? "If you're confessing, I forgot my collar."

And there was the telltale fire in her eyes. She hadn't come to grovel; there was purpose behind her supplication. "Will you please listen to me?"

It was rude and went against his grain to let her stand there. Even facing off with business adversaries, he maintained a calculated courtesy. Now his first instinct was to shut the door and walk away. And regret it for the next fifteen years?

Jill's fingers shook as she caught a strand of hair from her eye, tearing up from the gusting wind—not as composed as she wanted him to think. "I would have called, but Celia recommended I not."

He gripped the door's edge. "You spoke to my mother?"

"I needed to find you."

A surge of anger. She had no right. What could be so important she had braved his mother, and Mom had directed her to him? Cold dread washed over.

"I had to, Morgan. Just let me explain."

Irritated, he stepped back and motioned her in.

She paused inside the entry, glancing around the main room. "This is Rick's place?" An attempt at normalcy, like the small talk she'd made the other night to polish the splintered gash between them.

"His humble abode." He closed the door, hoping she felt as trapped as he did.

"It's nice." Her gaze paused on the grand piano. "Who plays?"

Morgan nodded up the stairs. "Rick's wife. She's sleeping off a flu—

especially rough, since she's pregnant. Happily, if you can believe that." He passed by her. "Drink?"

"No thank you."

As she followed him around the couch to the gathering space before the huge stone fireplace, his nerves rose up in static electric response, each nerve isolating from the next, drawn irresistibly toward her. He resisted by putting as much space between them as the setting allowed.

Her hands gripped the handles of her purse. Where was her confidence in the charm and acceptance that had always drawn people to her? Why did she suddenly draw from him a traitorous compassion?

"Morgan . . ."

He pressed a forearm to the massive half-log mantel and fixed her with a lionlike stare. "Yes?"

"Could we sit?" She lowered herself to the dun-colored couch.

He ignored the suggestion. She was not as beautiful as some of the women he'd dated. But there was an attractiveness that went beyond her features, her long, toned figure. A personality and intelligence that hollered "get to know me." She'd had the same spark fifteen years ago, and it angered him to acknowledge it still.

His gaze sent a satisfying flush up her throat, but then she seemed to be fighting tears. He hadn't expected that. She must be more keyed up than he'd realized. He resisted moving toward her as he might have. Why should he comfort her? Yet it tugged anyway. "You had something to say?"

"Yes, I . . ." Her voice broke and she pressed her hands to her face. "I don't know how to tell you."

That from the girl who had already given him the best and the worst news in his life? She'd shown up without invitation, begged her way in, and now thought she could stammer and cry? Losing patience, he crossed over, sat down, and took her hands from her face. Her gray eyes were awash with some hurt, deep and terrible. Was it catharsis, forgiveness she wanted? Dread and calm mingled. "Just tell me."

She drew a deep breath. "Morgan, I never aborted our baby. I gave her up for adoption."

He dropped her hands, denial searing his mind. Their baby wasn't dead? Comprehension grew. The images that had formed his guilt were false. The disgust, which had grown like cancer inside him every time he remembered the girl he had loved . . . He shoved up from the couch unable to stand her closeness. Fifteen years, believing he had fathered a child she'd chosen to destroy. And now . . .

"It was the best thing for all of us. She's had a good home, a Christian family."

His throat cleaved. It had all been a lie. Why? He searched her face as though the answer could be found there. Grief, anxiety, and fear—but nothing he could grasp. And then the realization washed through him. She had lied to be rid of him and their child.

Hands clenched, he strode to the window. It was her so-called right—her body, her choice. So what brought her here now? Why this tearful episode, this encroachment on his life? Even if the other night had shown her he was doing well financially, she could hardly sue for child support. Not when she'd given the baby away—without his consent.

"What do you want?" He spoke to the glass but, shaded as it was by the porch, even that held her reflection.

She pressed clasped hands to her knees. "Morgan, she has leukemia. Acute lymphocytic leukemia."

He took that in with no sensation, his responses uncharacteristically inactive.

"They treated her four years ago and controlled it. But she came out of remission and chemotherapy isn't working. She needs a bone marrow transplant from someone genetically connected."

He expelled his breath and dropped his head as the pieces clicked together. "You don't match." His voice was dust.

"No."

"Why else would you need me?" He turned from the window.

"Morgan, I . . ."

He walked to the mantel and leaned, but it offered scant support. A child. A daughter out there somewhere, the fruit of his love for Jill. Not dead. But dying. Her words sank in. Leukemia. He knew the gravity of that disease. His daughter had leukemia. He clenched his hands and the muscles of his arms pulled like ropes.

"Morgan . . ."

"Just tell me what I need to do." He turned enough to see her blink back her tears. What did she expect?

"There are initial blood tests." She reached into the purse at her feet and drew out a card. "This is the oncologist at the Yale Cancer Treatment Center. You can contact him for instructions. If there's a match, he'll tell you what happens next and they'll . . . let Kelsey's family know."

"Kelsey." His voice rasped, and his own hand shook as he rubbed it over his hair. His *daughter*. "I want to see her." The words were out before he thought of all that would mean. Then he turned fully. "I want to see her."

Jill struggled again for words. "It's not that easy, Morgan."

Easy? Did she think this was easy?

"She's very sick, and Cinda . . . her parents don't want to add stress."

Her parents. A mother and, of course, a father. He dropped his chin to his chest. He was nothing but the sperm donor. The girl out there knew nothing about him or anything he'd accomplished or ever would. He couldn't see her; he could only make another biological donation.

Jill scribbled a number on the back of the card. "In case you need to reach me. I'm sorry, Morgan."

He didn't answer. Anything he said now would draw blood.

Jill started to stand, but a motion overhead caught her eye. A woman walked out across the balcony, amber hair hanging just below her shoulders. One hand rested on her swelling abdomen through the sage green robe that hung to midcalf. It must be Rick's wife, and she was beautiful.

She came down to the bottom of the stairs and gave Morgan a smile just touching her lips but deep in her gray-green eyes. She cared for him, cared a lot. Then she turned. "Hello. I thought I heard voices." She stifled a cough and cleared her throat.

"You shouldn't be up." Morgan's concern was real, and Jill felt a spear of envy.

"I needed some tea." Her voice rasped. He moved toward her, but she held up her hands, palms forward. "I don't want to share my germs." She looked again to Jill.

Resigned, Morgan said, "This is Rick's wife, Noelle."

Jill stood up, her throat tightening when he didn't present her. "I'm Jill Runyan."

As Noelle sent a quick, knowing glance to Morgan, cold needles pricked Jill's flesh. Noelle knew who she was. Had they talked? Had Morgan told her all about their difficult past? She had to go. She'd done what she had come for.

Morgan said, "I'll get your tea," and strode to the kitchen.

"Thank you."

Jill had a hard time picturing her as a mountain rancher's wife. Her bearing suggested graciousness and culture. In fact, Jill more easily imagined her with Morgan than Rick. Another spear. That was absurd, but seeing his solicitude toward this woman after the raw anger he'd shown moments ago . . .

Jill reached for her purse, but Noelle took a seat on the piano bench, far enough away to avoid contagion. "I'm sorry if I interrupted." Her voice was hoarse and weak. Why had she come down? Had she sensed Morgan's distress?

Jill sighed. "I was just leaving."

"Can't you stay awhile? I'm sure it was a long drive up."

Not long enough. She had been as unprepared for Morgan as she'd been for Kelsey. And at the moment, she wasn't sure which meeting had hurt more. How could she gracefully decline?

The last thing Morgan wanted would be her staying another minute after the news she'd brought and the wounds she'd opened. But that wasn't Noelle's problem. It was no one but hers, and now Morgan's. If only she hadn't needed to drag him into it. The look in his face would stay with her too long, and his words. *"Why else would you need me?"*

She met Noelle's soft gaze. Healthy, she must be stunning. But just now her expression probed. "Is Morgan all right?" Again the concern in her tone.

"I gave him some difficult news." Jill looked down at the floor, hearing the hum of the microwave in the kitchen. In minutes Morgan would be back.

"It's not his family?" Noelle's love there was obvious, too.

Jill imagined her with all Morgan's family, his sisters and Rick and Celia and Hank, people she had once imagined—she stopped that thought. "No. It's personal." Tears threatened again. She blinked them away.

Noelle tried to speak but coughed, then, "I'm sorry. I didn't mean to pry."

Morgan came in with a steaming teacup and handed it to Noelle. He gently raised her chin. "You should go back to bed."

That was not a simple brother-in-law relationship. But then, was any relationship with Morgan simple? Jill ached in ways she had not begun to explore but knew she would whether she wanted to or not. She gripped her purse. "I need to go."

Noelle stood up. "It was nice to meet you, Jill." She coughed hard.

An engine sounded outside, the crunch of gravel. Morgan left Noelle's side and took Jill's elbow, more to hasten her out, she suspected, than any courtesy. Had they covered it all? Would he do what was needed?

Jill wanted to escape, but the door opened before they reached it. The space filled with Rick, taller than Jill remembered him, and he'd filled out from the lanky youth he'd been to a muscular man. He stopped short, resting one hand on the knob, his eyebrows darting up at the sight of her.

"Jill."

Wonderful. A family reunion. How many more Spencers must she face before this was over? "Hi, Rick." She forced herself to meet his eyes. He must hate her as much as the rest of them, though his expression was enigmatic.

She'd done what she had to; now she wanted out. Morgan had taken his pound of flesh, and he was the only one with cause. The questions were there in Rick's face, but she owed him nothing. Morgan could tell him whatever he wanted.

Morgan pressed his hand to her lower back. "She was just leaving." He eased her past Rick and onto the porch, kept his hand on her all the way to the car, then turned her abruptly. "What does my mother know?"

The gusting wind robbed her breath. He moved to block her face from the wind, but his expression battered her more.

"I had to tell her why I needed you." That was poorly phrased, and he didn't miss it. "To find you, why I needed to find you."

A momentary amusement washed his face, at her awkwardness, she was sure. "You certainly know how to go for the gut, Jill." It was the first time he'd spoken her name, and it didn't sound endearing. "Dare I hope this is our last encounter?"

"You can handle everything through the center." The wind slapped her face, and she raised a hand in defense. "But it has to be soon."

His face hardened. "I'll do whatever it takes."

A swelling of relief. "I know."

"Do you?" There was such poverty in that question, it hurt. What sort of father would he have been? Interactive and warm like Hank? Upright like her own—with whom she had not really spoken in too long, not since her pregnancy had put a wall between them. She'd disappointed them so badly. Her family, Morgan's. And herself.

She reached for the car door, but he opened it first, a shade of his old chivalry. She got in and he closed the door without another word. Before she had the key in the ignition, he turned and went into the house.

10

Morgan went straight through to the kitchen, took the bottle of bourbon from the cabinet, and started for the back door.

"Morgan."

He ignored Rick, but the second swing of the screen told him his brother had followed him out. He turned. "I'll talk to you later."

"After you've killed it with the bottle?"

"Yeah."

Rick gripped his shoulder. "What is it? What did she want?" His extra inches made Morgan squint up in the brightness to meet his gaze.

Wind gusted, then passed. Morgan raised the bottle in a toast. "Congratulate me. I'm a father."

"What?" Rick dropped his hand from Morgan's shoulder.

"It seems Jill didn't abort my daughter; she just gave her away."

Rick stared at him, taking it in as slowly as Morgan had. "She came to tell you that?"

"No. That information was not important enough."

Rick shook his head. "What, then?"

Morgan's chest constricted. "My daughter has leukemia. She needs a bone marrow transplant. Jill thought I might fill the bill." He watched Rick grasp the situation as his face matched the turmoil threatening his own control. He closed his eyes, trying to imagine his daughter. Kelsey. "Rick, I need to be alone."

"Then leave me the bottle."

Morgan gripped its neck. "I'll just buy another."

"Not on Sunday."

The screen swung and Noelle came out, squinting in the sunlight, its brightness illuminating her illness. She didn't need this. Why was Rick making it an issue?

She shaded her eyes. "Come back in, Morgan." She coughed and kept coughing. Rick wrapped an arm around her shoulders and sent him a look. Don't make it worse. Don't make her worry. He should never have come. If he hadn't gone to Rick's, he wouldn't have attended the reunion, wouldn't have seen Jill . . . What was he thinking?

He had a daughter who needed him. She must be fourteen, just a little older than Todd. Whatever he was doing for Todd was nothing to what he could do for his own daughter. But just now he needed a drink, needed it badly, though at eleven in the morning that didn't look good. He expelled his breath. All he wanted was to be alone. His stomach burned, and his mouth watered for the oblivion he'd find two-thirds into the bottle.

"Come on, Morgan. Let's talk it out."

"Noelle needs to go to bed." And this was getting blown out of proportion. He knew what he had to do, and he'd do it. If God had any kind of mercy, he'd match better than Jill and be what his daughter needed. There was no reason for Rick and Noelle to get involved.

Noelle leaned on Rick, obviously achy and weak. Whatever germ had her was no cakewalk, and it had to be worse pregnant.

Morgan softened. "Go to bed, Noelle."

"I will if you come in with Rick. I won't rest otherwise. I'll worry."

Morgan shot her a smile. "Heart of steel, remember? I can handle it." But he followed when Rick motioned him back inside. So he'd put off the stupor awhile. He surrendered the bottle, and Rick put it away.

"I'll be right back," Rick shot over his shoulder as he led Noelle through the kitchen.

Morgan heard them on the stairs. He sat down and rested his head in his palm. Where had the sense of control gone? His laptop sat in the other room, but none of that meant anything. Marlina Aster and her daddy's company could drop off the face of the globe for all he cared. Every one of the corporations could belly-up and he would not lose one night's sleep. Jill had wiped out the last fifteen years, and he shook like a scared kid again.

Rick tucked Noelle into their bed, saw the questions in her eyes. He pulled the sheet over her. "That was Jill Runyan, Morgan's—"

"Former girlfriend, I know. Why did she come?"

Rick smoothed the sheet about her neck. "I guess she never aborted the baby. She gave her up for adoption."

Noelle searched his face. "And she came to tell Morgan?"

"That, and their daughter has leukemia. She wants him to donate marrow."

"Oh no." It came out a pained sigh. "Did he agree?"

Rick sat down on the side of the bed. "I haven't gotten the whole story, but do you think he wouldn't?"

She shook her head. "I should go down. He'll need to talk."

Rick stroked her hair. "Noelle, I know you care for Morgan . . ."

She caught his hand and pressed it to her cheek. "You know where my heart is."

Rick smiled. "That's not what I meant." He bent and kissed her forehead. "He's confused and hurt and God knows what else. He turned to you before, to get past Jill."

"He knows I love you. He made me see it."

"That doesn't mean he's stopped loving you." Rick knew only too well how impossible that was. Jill had torn Morgan's heart out, and Noelle was the only one who came close to repairing it. She might think her solicitation was helpful, but would it keep Morgan from what he really needed?

"Maybe this is the fall, Noelle. The thing that will turn him back to God."

She wheezed and coughed, then dropped her hand. "Okay." She looked weary enough to give in to anything. Was the pneumonia coming back? "If you're not feeling better tomorrow, we'll see Dr. Bennington."

She smiled. "My hero."

"Him or me?"

She laughed and it made her cough. It reminded him of the day he'd found her too ill to know her heat and power had been turned off. He'd taken her home and discovered his heart was hers. Things had not been easy even so. And they wouldn't be easy for Morgan, but Rick sensed God's hand. This all had to be part of the burden he'd been taking to prayer these last weeks. He stroked Noelle's cheek. "Pray, will you?"

She nodded, her eyes closing already. "He loves her, Rick."

"I know. He's tried to replace her in all the wrong ways. But she's the only woman he's loved. And maybe you."

"Poor Morgan."

Morgan looked up from the kitchen table when Rick returned. "She's all tucked in?"

"Yeah." Rick frowned. "I'm worried. After that last pneumonia . . ."

"Don't take any chances." But loving anyone was a chance. Morgan studied the grain on the table. Were love and pain always linked? He'd hoped at least for Rick that wasn't so.

Rick went to the refrigerator and took out two small oranges. He set one before Morgan and sat down across the table. "Ready for my brotherly advice?"

Morgan quirked his mouth sideways. "No offense, Rick. But there's nothing you can say that I don't already know."

"So what's the deal? What do you have to do?"

"Get a blood test."

Rick dug his thumb into the end of his orange and tore up an edge of peel. "Probably not a bad idea anyway."

"I'm healthy, Rick. They're not going to find anything that keeps me from helping my daughter." Now his life had a purpose—to save the baby he'd thought he lost.

Rick's expression revealed his doubt, but Morgan doubted booze was an issue in bone marrow donation. Then again, what did he know? He swallowed the dryness in his throat, stood, and filled a glass with water. He chugged it at the sink, set the glass there, and sat back down. "If I have to stay sober, I can do it."

"Why don't you, then?"

"It's not an issue for me. I enjoy a drink or two."

Rick held his gaze. "A drink or two doesn't leave you in a stupor."

Morgan didn't answer that. Instead he said, "She told Mom." He still quaked at that thought, wanted to wring Jill's neck, but if he touched her, he would kiss the breath from her instead. Where had this rage come from? And how could it still be connected to so much want?

Rick chewed a section of orange and sat back. "You ought to call her."

That was not going to happen. Did his sisters know? His dad? Were they worried for him all over again? Why was he thinking about that? Somewhere out there his daughter was fighting for her life, the life she almost lost before she came into the world. Had Jill intended to kill her and changed her mind? Or had she intended all along to lie? Did it matter?

He rubbed his hand over his mouth. "It's better to leave it alone." He tore the peel of his orange in a spiral around the top.

"Did she tell you the girl's name?"

"*The girl* is Kelsey." Morgan continued the spiral around the sides and down. He shook his head, pausing his peeling. "She's been out there all these years." He looked at his brother, trying not to show the bleakness of that thought.

"At least it wasn't what we thought. At least Jill gave her life."

Morgan focused back on his peel, tore around the bottom, and pulled it free. "She didn't give her us."

"She was a kid, Morgan. So were you."

Morgan tore the sections apart, separated one, and held it. "Rick, you can't begin to understand."

"I know."

Morgan bit the section in half, chewed slowly, then added the other half. He was actually glad Rick had stopped him from running off with the bourbon. It hadn't destroyed him yet, but too many more years of it would. And he wanted alcohol-free blood for the test.

He pulled out the card Jill had given him. It was someone from the Yale Cancer Center, but Jill's number was written on the back. He had noticed she gave no phone number in the reunion information. Must keep it unlisted. Probably tired of being hit on.

"What's that?" Rick swallowed his last section of orange.

Morgan softly huffed. "My link to the woman I owe it all to."

Rick took the card, read both sides, and handed it back. "A lot of men would have let this go, Morgan. Most would have been relieved and grateful their girlfriend took care of the problem. It says a lot that it didn't leave you unchanged."

Morgan looked at him. "Is that supposed to be comforting?"

"There's good inside you that couldn't stand what you thought Jill did. And there was good in her that couldn't do it. God had His hand over both of you."

God's hand? Morgan tensed as a surge of pain shot through him. Was it good for her to let him believe their child had died? Good to disappear and never try to contact him, to explain? To leave him aching for what they had and would never find again? Sure, it had changed him. And not for the better. "Forgive me if I don't see it that way. It's kind of pathetic to think my little girl's out there praying for a miracle, and I'm all she's got." He stood abruptly.

Rick looked up. "Where are you going?"

"Boulder."

"Why?"

"To have blood drawn."

Rick stood also. "Do you want me to come?"

Morgan grinned. "I think I can handle it. But thanks for the offer."

"Are you coming back?"

Morgan sighed. "You're worse than Mom."

"You won't be any good to your daughter if you smash yourself up on the road."

"I know what I'm doing." Morgan picked up the rest of the orange. "I do manage to live without you most of the year."

Rick gave a slow nod, unconvinced. But what did it matter?

"Kiss Noelle for me."

Rick said nothing. Well, he had been pushing a button there.

"All right, kiss her for yourself." He picked up the card and folded the instruction sheet into his pocket, in case the hospital in Boulder would need to contact them. He went out, pushed the keyless remote and disarmed the alarm, then reached for the car door.

"Morgan!"

He expelled a hard breath. Todd he did not need.

"Where you goin'?"

"Boulder." Morgan pulled open the door.

"Can I come?"

"No."

His tone must have communicated more than he meant to because Todd kicked dirt at him and walked away.

Morgan didn't stop him. He owed the kid nothing. His daughter needed his focus and attention. But he closed his eyes and turned. "Todd."

Todd kept walking.

Morgan got into the car and brought the engine to life, then put the window down. In his rearview he saw Todd look. He put the car in reverse and zoomed back across the apron to where he stood. "I can't take you this time."

Todd just glared.

"Next time." Morgan pulled away. If that wasn't good enough, fine. He spun gravel, left the ranch and reached the highway, cranking up the strains of Fate's voice in the *Beethoven's Last Night* CD. If he could just get a grip on the situation. Why wouldn't it make sense? It should. Jill had been a good girl. She would have wanted to do the right thing. It had never fit that she would abort the child. Morgan knew that now. So why the lies?

To be rid of him. But now she needed him. No, be very careful there. Jill did not need him. Kelsey did. That was his focus.

In spite of the traffic, he reached the Boulder Community Hospital soon enough and explained that he needed to give blood for bone marrow typing.

"Do you have a doctor's order for this?"

He showed the man the business card from Kelsey's oncologist and the instruction sheet and chafed while the man read over it all. "Let me call over to the lab."

From the end of the conversation he heard, Morgan guessed there was a problem. Why did they always have to make it difficult? To maintain an aura of importance, mystery even? *Just take the blood!*

But the man hung up and said, "We don't do this draw. You'll have to arrange it with the University Hospital in Denver. Call them in the morning."

Morgan took back the business card and instruction sheet. Had Jill gone through all this? She must have hoped she'd match. Must have wanted to be the one to help their girl. Must have wanted to avoid his involvement. He felt a flicker of empathy as he imagined her realizing she had to go to him with it. He'd never been nasty to her until the reunion—hadn't had the opportunity—but that night had set the tone. No wonder she'd been shaking.

He walked outside. The afternoon was fresh, no wind. Either it had passed or only haunted the upper elevations. Plenty of bikers and walkers along Boulder's streets. He drove to Pearl Street and parked at the western end of the outdoor mall, set his alarm, and walked along the brick-paved street mall.

A rangy man with a ponytail held a long pipe that reached almost to his knees and played an endless combination of three notes. He had a stiff upturned turban before him on the ground, but Morgan didn't think the music worth much. He passed a man on a crate. "Attention, everyone. I am going to perform an illegal act." That drew the crowd. "I am"—he shook out a cigarette—"going to light this cigarette in public. That's right. In a public place, in sight of everyone, I will light and smoke this cigarette." He flicked his Bic, held it to the cigarette, and inhaled.

Morgan passed on. He noticed the gaze of two women sitting on a planter in the second block of the mall. They smiled encouragingly. He kept walking. A little dog came and yapped around his legs and the woman at the end of the leash tried to hush it. "She has a thing for hotties. What can I say?" She pushed the plum-colored hair back behind her ear.

Obvious. Too obvious. Morgan left her to her dog. He was hungry. He'd had nothing but coffee that morning and the small orange he'd eaten on the drive down. He took a table in a street-side café. A waiter brought his menu and asked, "Can I get you something to drink?"

Morgan's throat tightened. "Coke." He looked down at the menu. "And a burger."

"Which one?" The waiter indicated the column of burgers, everything from whiskey sauce to Cajun blackened. "Just a burger. Fries." Morgan hadn't had anything so mundane in years. As his man waltzed away, he looked back out to the mall. The two women strolled past and caught his eye again. Two of them, looking with open invitation, and he wasn't the least bit interested. He frowned into the Coke, which arrived by another hand, then sipped the too sweet fizz.

Why hadn't she told him the truth? Why had she carried the baby, given it away, and never told him the truth? A jazz sax started somewhere and kindled his melancholy. By the time his burger arrived he was sufficiently gloomy to order a Manhattan. When it came he gazed at it in its cone-shaped glass with two cherries on a plastic sword.

He lifted the sword and looked at the shockingly red cherries. A drip of bourbon dribbled down his fingers. He laid aside the sword and sucked the drip, then took up his burger. After the first bite he realized he wasn't hungry after all. He left a twenty on the table and walked out into the mall.

On a sudden thought, he took out his cell and touched a speed-dial number—not Bern Gershwin's office, but his home. Their relationship had surpassed professional and had moved to racquetball every second Tuesday and the occasional barbeque with Bern's family. But this call would take things to a new depth.

"Bern, here. What's up, Morgan?"

"Got a minute? I have a situation to discuss."

Bern muffled the receiver. "Take that outside, boys. Your mother will skin you alive." Then back on the line. "Of a professional nature?"

"Yes and no."

"Well, I'm in my study now. We'll consider what follows confidential. Go ahead."

Morgan stared ahead as he walked, trying to think how best to express the bomb dropped in his lap. "When we set up my estate plan we stated no kids. That's changed." He explained what Jill had told him, not surprised by the pause on the other side.

Then, "Hold on, Morgan. I'm going to start from scratch on this." Thorough lawyer that he was.

"Shoot."

"What makes you think the girl is yours?"

That sent a jolt through his system. Morgan frowned, stepping off the sidewalk and circling his car. He hadn't considered anything else. "Bern, Jill wants me to donate bone marrow."

"A little more creative than some. Convince me."

Morgan disarmed the car and got in. "Fifteen years ago, she was pregnant with my child. I was told she had an abortion, but . . ."

"So she lied."

A flash of fury. Yes, she had lied, or others had for her. In fifteen years she'd never tried to correct it.

"When was the last time you saw her?"

Morgan settled back against the seat. "A week ago. Class reunion."

"Interesting timing."

Bern had a point. "Wouldn't she ask for money, not blood?"

"You'd be surprised. Talk to our estate guys about the heirs that come out of the woodwork." Bern huffed his disgust. "This bone marrow plea could be the ploy that opens your vein and starts the money flowing."

Morgan tried to picture Jill scamming him for money. That thought had occurred, but only in conjunction with Kelsey being his daughter and child support issues. Once she'd described the leukemia and produced the medical center information . . . that had to be true. "I don't think she's making it up. I just want to know how this affects things."

"That's up to you. Operating on the possibility it's legit, I can talk to a colleague in the firm and get back to you. You need to know how you want to proceed. Proof of paternity, etcetera."

Morgan closed his eyes. How much more complicated would it get? "I've agreed to the testing for a bone marrow match. Wouldn't that tell us all we need to know?"

"For medical purposes, perhaps. Not legally without a suit unless you're on the birth certificate."

He seriously doubted that. "Look into it for me, Bern." Then he risked making it more personal still. "I want to see her."

A pause. "You mean that?"

Morgan cleared his throat. "What are my chances?"

"I have no idea."

But he'd find out.

11

Jill would not allow herself to think what might happen if Morgan's stem cells didn't match. As she sat on the flight, buffeted and jostled by the wind, she imagined Kelsey getting stronger, Morgan's marrow fighting the disease inside her. It would all be worth it. God would not have sent her otherwise. He was not fickle. His love was everlasting. She knew that, even if she couldn't capture the surety just then in her heart. She didn't have to feel it to believe. She had maintained that position for years.

If it was feelings she sought, they were there in plenty. Too many. In his casual designer shorts and seersucker shirt, Morgan had looked as good as he did the other night. And he'd certainly not been dressed to impress anyone this time. The white retro Thunderbird outside the house had to be his. And she had noted the Dell laptop on the table. What was she doing crashing into his life when he'd obviously done so well with it?

She stared out through the oval Plexiglas at the sun setting beneath her. It was for Kelsey—regardless of the feelings that had threatened to make it personal. What attraction there was between them was fatal. No one could bridge so much pain and betrayal. At least Morgan had made it clear he never wanted to see her again. A spark of defensive anger rose inside her. They were agreed on that.

After landing, she collected her overnight bag and drove home.

The message light flashed on her phone. Lethargically she pressed the button. Her mother's voice: *Jill, I didn't hear back from you. Everything all right? Call me, dear.* Then Cinda: *Jill, this is Cinda. Could you give me a call at your convenience? Thanks.* She rattled off the number, and Jill noted the nervousness in her tone. She must have agonized over whether it had worked out with Morgan.

Rascal plastered himself against her leg as Jill picked up the phone. Cinda first. "Hello, this is Jill."

"Oh, Jill. Thanks for calling. How did it go?"

Jill leaned on the counter. "I found Morgan and he'll have the blood test."

"Praise God! Jill, I can't thank you enough. How was it?"

"He wants to see Kelsey."

A long pause. "What did you tell him?"

Jill repeated what she had explained, at Cinda's request, that it would be too stressful for Kelsey. If the stress still surging inside Jill was any indication, Cinda was right.

Cinda spoke flatly. "It isn't the same as with you. We had . . . some connection. You delivered Kelsey. You gave us our daughter. He . . . Jill, I appreciate what he's doing, but . . . Kelsey's confused enough. If she has to try to conjure feelings for a stranger and . . ."

Cinda had already expressed all that when Jill raised the possibility of Morgan as a donor. She assumed the message was intended for her, as well. "I understand." She'd seen Kelsey's spunk but also her vulnerability. As Morgan was now, he could say and do things that . . . hurt. Kelsey had to be protected.

"Are you all right?"

"Fine." Nothing in her voice betrayed how very un-fine she was. "I'm relieved he agreed. I guess we wait to hear." She threaded her fingers into her hair.

"Yes. Too much waiting. Like Jesus on the Mount of Olives." Cinda sighed.

Jill scratched under Rascal's chin as he stretched himself up to her lower thigh, demanding recognition. "Did you tell Kelsey about Morgan?"

"Only that there's another potential match."

"I guess that's best." Jill heard Morgan again, saying he wanted to see his daughter. He meant it, but he didn't understand. Did she? She tried to see it from Morgan's side. She was asking so much and giving nothing. How could she begin to make up for the hurt? Morgan would understand—once he was over the shock and thinking clearly. At least his fury was only for her and not his daughter.

"On the other hand, and I know this sounds inconsistent," Cinda paused, "but Kelsey would like to see you again."

Jill's throat tightened. Why would Kelsey ask that? They could explain her first trip easily enough, donor-recipient connection. But she was no longer the donor. Another visit, when there was no longer a medical connection, when she didn't match? What would she say? How could she carry out the charade? And didn't it violate what Cinda had just said? Keeping it simple for Kelsey surely didn't include another visit.

"I explained that she couldn't expect you to come again. But she insisted I ask."

Jill pressed her hand to her eyes. "What do you want me to do?"

The silence lingered, then, "To be honest, it's not what I wanted. But I don't have the heart to deny something she wants so much. I certainly understand if you can't come, especially now that there isn't a match."

"You have to know that if Kelsey's asking, I can't say no."

"I didn't think so." There was a smile in her voice. She understood Kelsey's magnetism.

They worked out a time on Wednesday between Kelsey's maintenance chemotherapy and after Jill had finished tutoring her students. Then she hung up and stared at the floor. Had she been disloyal to Morgan? Should she have urged Cinda to reconsider? How selfish was it to see Kelsey herself, then side against him for the very same?

It wasn't her decision. Quickly she punched in the speed-dial code for her mother. A rush of relief when she got the answering machine. "Mom, everything's fine. Hope all's well with you and Dad. Talk to you later."

God was merciful. She scooped up Rascal, and he curled his paws around her neck. She snuggled her face into the fur beneath his head, letting his purr vibrate her cheekbone. Then when he had established his ownership, he wiggled out of her arms and jumped to the floor.

Just as well. She had little to give in the wake of emotional overload. The phone rang. She picked it up. "Hi, Shelly."

"I saw your light."

"Um-hmm."

"Can I bring you some brownies?"

Jill smiled. "Brownies are definitely what I need." Even if it meant she'd relive the day for Shelly. Maybe talking about it would give her some perspective. Shelly was always good for perspective.

The knock came while Jill was halfway into her nightshirt. Shelly called from the kitchen. "Dr. Brownie's here."

Jill tugged down the nightshirt and met Shelly in the kitchen. "I had to change. I might fall asleep at any moment."

"Not until I've heard it all."

Jill reached for a papery-topped gooey brownie. No one made them like Shelly.

"Milk?"

Jill nodded. "Sure."

Shelly poured them each a glass. Jill took the plate into the living room and sat in the giraffe chair. Shelly curled her legs up on the couch, setting the two glasses of milk on the corner table between them. "So tell me."

Jill bit into her brownie and chewed the bittersweet confection. "Not until I'm fortified." She followed the brownie with a long chug of milk. Was there anything so good? In spurts and rushes she told Shelly about Morgan, how he'd been that day, and how he'd been at the reunion, and how he'd been before. She shook her head. "I feel like I've ruined his life."

Shelly was actually quiet. She pressed a brownie crumb up from her knee and said, "Does Dan know you're in love with Morgan?"

Jill stared at her. "Shelly, that's not what I said."

Shelly met her gaze. "Yes, it is."

Jill shook her head. "I admit he's entangled in my psyche, especially at the bad points, but . . . he's not the person I knew. I've grown past him." When he didn't come for her, when she put their baby into a stranger's arms.

"That's the real reason you and Dan didn't get anywhere. Not a difference of beliefs or—"

"That's not true." Jill clenched her fist. "Morgan hates me. And it's just as well."

Shelly sank back on the couch. "You are so blind."

Jill said nothing. This was not the perspective she wanted. Shelly was wrong. "I went to Morgan because Kelsey needs him." Cinda's phone call niggled. Why did Kelsey want to see her? "Don't read more into it than there is."

Shelly rolled her eyes. "You're the religious one here. Why do you think all this is happening?"

"To save Kelsey."

Shelly hunched forward. "Then God could have used you."

"Maybe . . . maybe He wanted Morgan to know; maybe it's for Morgan, too."

"But not for you. God doesn't care about you."

Jill huffed out her breath. "Of course God cares. Jesus died for me. I wish you understood that. It's more than I deserve, more than I can ever repay. But I don't have to. It's His free gift of salvation."

"So after this life you can be happy."

It sounded so wrong, yet how could she refute it? Shelly knew she wasn't happy. "It's just all the stress. When Kelsey's better, when it's all over . . ."

"What? You and Rascal will grow old together?"

"You're married, Shelly. You don't understand that some people can be alone and be happy, complete, satisfied. Especially if they know and love Jesus as I do." It was true. If she could ever love Christ as completely as He loved her, she would need nothing more. And marriage to someone like Dan, who didn't share her beliefs, was worse than being alone.

But marriage to Morgan, who also didn't share her beliefs? That was a treacherous thought, one that had once filled her waking and dreaming moments. She had forsaken what she knew was right because his kisses were more potent than her faith. If she loved him still, it was God's punishment for her making Morgan an idol.

"Shelly, it breaks my heart that you and Brett don't know the Lord."

Shelly spread her hands. "Frankly, I don't see the benefit."

Jill dropped her chin. That was her fault. She was a dreadful witness. But Shelly knew her too well. She could hardly pretend to be rapturous. "I couldn't face this without Him."

Shelly sighed. "What if it's not about facing it? What if you're supposed to do something?"

Jill collapsed in the chair. "What else can I do? It's out of my hands."

"And in God's?"

"Yes, Shelly." Jill willed her to believe it.

"Well, sorry if I think that's a cop-out. Brett's arrested too many kooks who think God ordained their crimes. If He's such a good God, so all-powerful, why is there so much misery?"

"Because the world is messed up."

"So save the planet?"

Jill tossed a chunk of brownie at her. "You know that's not what I mean."

"Well, from my point of view, those of you who believe are not in any better position than those of us who don't. If Dan had seen it differently, he'd have been born again and married you."

It stabbed. Had her lack of joy poisoned Dan, as well? She thought of the good times they'd had together, then the discussions. She'd maintained the party line, but had the truth of it ever come through? Had she ever demonstrated a radiant faith?

"Sorry, Jill. I shouldn't have said that."

"No, it's true." Jill closed her eyes against the sting of tears. She could talk, but had she ever lived her faith? Maybe with the children she taught. Maybe there.

"Dan will not be happy I told you what he said."

"It doesn't matter."

Shelly reached over and grabbed her hand. "I'm sorry."

Jill smiled. "You may not believe it, but you make a terrifying prophet."

Shelly scrunched up her brow. "Will I be struck by lightning?"

"No, but I might if I don't take what you said to heart." Jill squeezed Shelly's hand. "I want you to see the joy of serving God, the hope, the peace."

"Well, if you can accomplish that with all this going on, then I'll believe there's something to it."

Jill drew a deep breath. No matter what lay ahead, her trust had to be real. Her friends knew her too well to buy a false gaiety. "I have to sleep now. I'm worn out."

"I'll leave you the brownies."

After Shelly left, Jill took out her Bible and the concordance that went with it. Using the two, she would read every "joy" entry in the Bible. If she focused on that, would it fill the hollow of her heart?

Morgan heard the strains of Rick's guitar when he walked in, saw his brother perched on the hearth. Noelle was curled up on the couch, listening with a look so enraptured it hurt. Her expression changed to one of concern when she saw him. He hated that. Why couldn't he burn all by himself?

Rick set the guitar in its case. "How're you doing?"

"Sober."

Rick nodded. "I could tell."

Morgan sat down in the corner chair. He settled back, the immensity of his situation pressing him down, the unfathomed revelation still unreal to his mind even when he spoke it aloud. "I've got a fourteen-year-old daughter." *Maybe*, Bern's doubts whispered, but the truth shouted louder.

Rick set the guitar aside. "I guess we misjudged Jill. It must have taken a lot for her to stand her ground."

Morgan didn't want to think about Jill and how it must have been for her. He didn't want to remember how she was, as great in a tag football game as she was on the dance floor at the prom. Talented and intelligent, she hadn't been obnoxious or overbearing, just eager to give her best all the time. She had challenged him as few people did, but it was her genuine joy of life he'd loved. He closed his eyes.

Maybe he'd been immature. Certainly he'd messed up. But they'd had something special, something worth fighting for. Why didn't she fight for him the way she'd fought to have her baby? He silently groaned. No hangover had hurt like this. It took everything he had to hide it.

They sat with the night deepening around them. Noelle's eyes grew heavy, then closed, her breath deepening to a rasping wheeze. "Is she all right?" he asked softly.

Rick studied her. "She's worried. She cares about you."

Now that she was married to Rick. It didn't matter anyway. Noelle was irrelevant. So much of his life was irrelevant. He was irrelevant. Unless his marrow matched. He didn't know how any of that worked. He rubbed his face, overwhelmed by his ignorance. How could he have a kid in the world and not know it? A daughter dying, and he spent his time on business plans to revive flailing corporations. "God, Rick."

"Just God."

Morgan peeled his hand from his face and shook his head. "It wasn't a prayer."

"It could be. Don't you miss it, Morgan?"

"What?"

"Someone bigger to lean on."

Morgan cocked his jaw, fighting the pain like a failing dike. "That's not reality."

"It used to be. I remember you training me to serve on the altar, the reverence you had for all things holy."

Morgan quirked a smile. "The times we found the tiniest hand towel for old Father Quinn?"

"God enjoys a joke."

Morgan's voice rasped, "I'm not laughing."

Rick didn't push it. The lamp glow wrapped around them in silence.

Morgan swallowed. "I want to see her."

"Jill?"

Heat surged through his body. "I meant Kelsey."

"Is that possible?"

"I think I'll have a little clout. If there's a match." He ignored Jill's warning against it. The concerns of Kelsey's so-called parents were not his. She didn't have to know who he was, didn't even have to see him. He just wanted to look at her, to see what he and Jill had created. To wipe out the images of what he thought had happened.

Tears stung the backs of his eyes. It was insane. He'd spent fifteen years proving himself. He had everything he wanted: a four-million-dollar home with an ocean view, the fastest cars, the best wines. He could choose his projects, travel, entertain . . . anything he wished. No, he wasn't financially independent yet, but he'd carved a niche and virtually assured himself continued success.

As Rick said, another man would have put this behind him without a thought. Sometimes he did. He sure hadn't spent the last fifteen years feeling like this. He'd felt great, triumphant, satisfied. As long as he didn't probe too deeply. He knew what his looks could get him, what his brains could do. He was packaged for success. And whatever Rick might say, he'd found it. So what that it sometimes felt hollow?

If he wanted to marry, he could. If he wanted kids . . . *I have a daughter.*

Rick said, "We should get some sleep."

Morgan wasn't tired. His mind was on overdrive. "I think I'll have a drink." What could it hurt?

"Go to bed, Morgan." Rick stood up, lifted Noelle into his arms. It was a sight so gallant Morgan wanted to holler as his brother carried her up the stairs. It could have been him. At any stage in his life he could have found that happiness. If he had just let go and forgotten the love that had formed and transformed him, and the severing that could not be cauterized. Why hadn't Jill told him? Could the truth have hurt her so much?

It was only steps to the kitchen. What did it matter, since the blood test was delayed? He took down a bottle and a glass, carried them back to the front room, and sat. The bottle was familiar and comfortable in his hand as he tipped it into the glass. He took the bourbon into his mouth, swilled it gently over his tongue, and swallowed. He wouldn't sit long. Just finish his drink, then try to find sleep.

He was in the place where Jill had sat earlier. He should not have upset her. It had been reflex after what she'd done. Only she hadn't done it. That thought re-impressed on his mind. She'd saved their child, if not their relationship. Maybe that was best. If they had stayed together, their love might have failed. He took another swallow. It was the amputation that kept the ghost pains alive.

12

Kelsey startled, staring into the darkness around her. It wasn't pain or nausea that woke her, nor fear, but the sense that someone was close. "Mom?" she whispered, but nothing stirred in response. Sometimes Mom knelt beside her bed, praying silently over her while she slept; sometimes that penetrated her sleep. But that wasn't it. Still, she had the strangest feeling she wasn't alone.

"Dad?" Again nothing. Kelsey sank into the pillows. The feeling intensified, as though not only was someone watching her but was so near it raised the hairs on her skin. Yet there was no fear, and she closed her eyes, absorbing the presence in peace. Then, behind her eyelids, she saw a girl with a tiny baby in her arms. The baby was wrapped in blankets, and she couldn't make out any more than the shape and the fine down of its hair, dark hair, but she knew it had fallen out and come in pale.

That was the first time I lost my hair, she thought. But why had she jumped to that conclusion?

The girl was sitting in bed with a sheet over her legs, and she bent and kissed the baby's head. Waves of sadness washed over Kelsey with that kiss, sadness so wrenching she almost opened her eyes. But she wanted to know more. A strand of pale blond hair slid from the girl's shoulder, and Kelsey almost felt it brush her own cheek.

Tears started and washed the vision away. Kelsey opened her eyes.

She had found nothing in the cluttered study any of the three times she'd looked, none of the documents she'd hoped would be there, but she knew. She knew.

———

Jill ran alone. It was something she'd promised Dan not to do. Young female joggers were an easy mark, especially in a treed place like the park near the townhouses. But she needed it.

The last few days had left her tied in knots, and today she was going to see Kelsey. She stretched her hurdler's stride and let the drumming of her paces drive everything else away. The air was moist beneath the trees, the scent of humus rich and satisfying. Though she'd never been a farm girl, she appreciated the scent of good earth. It conjured a sense of well-being she needed at some visceral level.

Then Morgan's face intruded, shattered the peace her mind had almost attained. "It's out of my hands." She said it aloud. "I've done my part." The roll and jar of her paces quickened. Sweat drenched her back between the shoulder blades, her chest and neck. Her arms moved easily at her sides, her body synchronized in a movement as natural as breathing. She was made to run. That's what her track coach had told her.

She'd worked hard at it. Morgan, too. He was a sprinter, not suited for the long haul but possessing Mercurial heels in the hundred-yard dash and quarter-mile. She had run the mile, gaining strength and confidence as she ran. But the hurdles made her shine.

She remembered the times Morgan had tried and ended up kicking the hurdles, not from inability but annoyance. He didn't like things in his path. He'd rather clear away the hurdles than leap them.

She thought of Kelsey, so small and underdeveloped. How would she have been if disease had not struck her? Athletic? Strong? By fourteen, Jill was head cheerleader of the sophomore squad, already a track contender, and a mean tag football player. Kelsey looked ready to blow away.

A sob broke in her chest, and she lost her stride. *Oh, God, why?* Why did He allow Kelsey such misery? She thought of Shelly's question. It haunted every Christian at some point in their lives. Why suffering, God? Why evil? Why pain and loss and death?

Sin. But had Kelsey sinned? What could she possibly have done to draw such vengeance upon herself? Unless it was Jill's sin, and Morgan's. Was Kelsey paying the price? Jill struck out faster. God wouldn't do that. God was love. Jesus loved her unto death.

Then why, why, why? No amount of dopamine would drive that question away. She just had to face it and somehow find joy in the midst. Besides, it was time to shower and go tutor her students. She completed the loop and ran hard for her patio, slowing at the sight of Dan's cruiser parked at the curb and his uniformed self leaning on her post.

She came to a panting stop, wiping her sweat and hair back with her forearm.

Dan pursed his lips. "I told you not to do that."

Hands on her hips, back arched, she drew several long breaths. "I know."

He pushed off from the post, turned off the staticky radio hooked to his belt. "I want to talk to you."

"I don't really have time."

"It won't take long. I just want to ask you something." He cleared his throat, then looked off to the side.

Jill pressed her shoulders back to relieve the stress. "What, Dan?"

He turned back abruptly. "Why don't we get married?"

"What?" She searched his face. Had he actually said the "m" word? He was ready to make that commitment now, when everything was so messed up?

He took her hands. "I know I've been burned, and that made me cautious. . . ."

Jill shook her head. "Stop it, Dan. You're on a rescue mission."

He pulled her closer, tucked her hands against his chest. "I'm worried about you."

"So we should get married?"

"At least you wouldn't be running alone."

She flattened her palms on his chest. "Don't worry about me."

"Jill, I've been thinking a lot about things."

"So that's what's been burning." She grinned, but it didn't alleviate the seriousness in his eyes.

He hooked his arms over her shoulders, hands clasped behind her neck. "I wanted to know we were sexually compatible. I thought . . ."

"I know what you thought." His insecurities over losing his wife to another man were understandable. She pulled out of the loop of his arms. "You don't have to explain. But I do have to shower and go teach."

"Have dinner with me tonight."

"I can't. I have plans." She started for her door. He would not be happy she'd left it unlocked to get back in that way, but she slid it open.

He frowned. "Do you listen to anything I say?"

She turned back with an apologetic glance. "I hate running with a key." At his expression, Jill raised her hands. "I know. I won't do it again. I promise."

"What plans?"

She stopped and sighed. "I just can't, Dan. I'm too confused."

He nodded. "Fine. I'll run with you tomorrow."

"Dan . . ."

"I won't say a word."

She forked her fingers into her hair. "I don't need a bodyguard."

He rested his hands at his hips, all cop, but she couldn't give him the wrong idea.

"I have to go in. I'm going to be late."

He stepped back. "So go." But his gaze followed her as she stepped inside and slid the glass closed between them. Dan's vigilance and misplaced concern she did not need. It was enough that she'd laid Morgan's life to waste. She didn't want any more casualties.

———

Morgan took the call and listened with no surprise to the person informing him that his blood was a single haplotype match with his daughter's. They'd already sent him information explaining the genetics, so if that hadn't been the case, Bern's doubts of paternity would have stood. Now Morgan agreed that the next steps in the process should be done at the UCLA medical center nearest his home in Santa Barbara, the place that might actually perform the procedure. For sure he would have the second test, the one that had disqualified Jill, and if there was no cross-match problem, they would proceed with physical exam, mandatory counseling, and whatever else they wanted to do with him.

He had to go home. Rick's ranch had served its purpose and more than he'd intended. He walked outside and found Todd in the stable. Until he noticed him watching, Todd seemed to enjoy running the currycomb over the horse's sides. Once he realized Morgan was there, he put on his sulky face and shortened the strokes.

Morgan leaned on the stall. "Hey."

"It stinks in here."

Morgan shrugged. "You get used to it. Good quarter horse manure."

Todd swore for the first time in the three days since Morgan's trip to Boulder without him. They'd patched it up with another movie and two trips for ice cream.

"Almost finished?" Morgan stroked the mare's muzzle as Todd curried her hindquarters.

"Two more stinkin' horses."

Morgan pushed back from the stall. "Come find me when you're done. We'll shoot some hoops." He went back outside to the clear mountain sunshine. It was almost brutal on the eyes, firing a too sharp image to the brain. He missed the hazy blue of the coastal sky, the beating of the surf, the palms waving, and the profuse floral palette. He missed his bedroom with windows on three sides overlooking the sea from the cliff above, the little trail that led to the narrow beach. He missed the sunset on the water, the lights of the crystal ships offshore, the cry of the gulls gliding overhead, the seals barking just close enough to hear, and the dolphins making graceful arcs in the early morning tide.

He passed under the basketball hoop Stan had hung on the side of the barn. As far as he'd seen, it hadn't done much toward building communication between the man and his foster son. Stan was uncoordinated, made one shot in ten, often chased the ball, and dribbled it off his shoe. He tried, though. Which was more than could be said for Todd. The kid must never have touched a basketball. How did you get to be thirteen and not know that rolling motion that looped the ball up and in?

Morgan shook his head. He'd hate to see the kid on a surfboard. On second thought, maybe he'd enjoy it. Maybe he'd like paddling Todd out over the bouncing breakers to the rolling swells to catch one big enough to get a ride. Morgan picked up the ball leaning against the barn wall. A three-step layup sank it with nothing but net. He dribbled on the hard-packed gravel. Not wood or pavement, but it worked.

He spun and shot. Swish. By the time Todd joined him, he was into his game. But he sent Todd the ball and said, "Just dribble. Cover the court one bounce to each step."

"What court?"

"Don't get smart."

Todd dribbled, no rhythm or regularity, some bounces high, some
he had to stoop for.

"Get it even."

"I'm trying."

"I know." Morgan took the ball and demonstrated. "Don't watch
the ball, just feel it, let it come back to your hand, but look ahead
where you want to go."

Todd tried again.

"Better. Much better. Keep going."

"Aren't we going to shoot?"

"Maybe." Morgan shrugged. "If you want to."

"You're the one who wanted to play." Todd caught the ball and
held it.

"Okay, shoot."

Todd tossed the ball. *Like a girl,* Morgan thought.

"Here. Come stand in front of me." He took hold of Todd and the
ball and mimicked the motion. "Two hands to here, then this hand
takes it up and over. Feel the arc."

Todd missed, then chased the ball down and tried again. They
played until Stan's Subaru Forester pulled into the yard. Todd's bones
and muscles seemed to morph into putty. His shoulders and face
sagged; his pants slid lower down his rear. He handed the ball to
Morgan as though he'd just realized it might contaminate him.

Stan climbed out of the car and waved. "Hey, I'll join you."

"We're done." Todd trudged toward him.

Stan's body followed Todd's example. "Did you finish your chores?"

"I'm sure you'll find something I didn't do."

Todd slunk past him and went behind the cabin. Melanie and
Sarah had gone back to Denver for some activities of their seventeen-
year-old son, who was holding down the home front—or maybe just
for some semblance of normalcy. Noelle had been hospitalized for
pneumonia, its treatment complicated by the pregnancy, and Rick was
keeping vigil. For the last few days, it had been just Stan, Todd, and
Morgan fending for themselves on the ranch. His exit could prove
interesting.

Stan joined him on the court. Morgan handed him the ball.

Stan looked at it. "I'm really bad at this."

Morgan guessed he wasn't referring to his athleticism.

Stan rolled the ball between his hands, glanced briefly toward where the boy had disappeared, and pursed his lips. "We're worse off than when we came, I think."

"His anger's less."

"With you, maybe. You should have heard how he talked to Melanie the morning before she left."

Morgan could imagine.

Stan stooped and rolled the ball to the barn wall and asked, "How are you getting through? Why does he trust you?"

Morgan rested his hands on his hips. "I don't know. Maybe I'm not trying so hard. I don't have as much to lose."

Stan nodded. "I'm trying. Every minute I think, what can I say, what can I do to make a difference."

"Why don't you just take the minutes that come? Let change happen on its own."

Stan shook his head. "It's affecting everyone. It's like we brought in a virus, and little by little we're all getting sick."

"If you think of Todd that way, no wonder you're struggling."

Stan rubbed his face. "I know. It's not right. But we were happy. We thought it'd be such a blessing to reach out to a kid in need. In the schools I see so many who just need . . . something."

Morgan didn't have a quick answer to that.

"I think he tries to shock us."

"Then don't be shocked."

Stan frowned. "That's fine for me. But Melanie and Sarah are not used to that language, that level of hostility. Sarah's been in private Christian school all her life. Melanie married me right out of Christian college. I thought *we'd* influence *him*."

"Just listen to him, Stan. Don't try to change him."

Stan opened his mouth and expelled a sharp breath. "Is that spoken from experience?"

Morgan cast him a glance.

Stan raised both hands at his sides. "I shouldn't say anything, but I'm observant. You and Rick . . . you're not very much alike."

Morgan half grinned. "What was your first clue?"

Stan smiled. "There've been a few. Morgan, the truth is I don't have any idea how to reach Todd. When Melanie first talked about doing the foster program, I thought sure. We've got a lot to be thankful for, three great kids, not abundant resources but enough. Let's share the blessing, you know?"

Morgan cocked his head noncommittally.

"I've always been, well, good. I don't have a testimony like some, how God turned my life around from drugs or promiscuity. I just do the right things and serve the Lord and love my family the best I can."

"Like Rick." Morgan looked across the yard. They made it sound easy. But somehow it hadn't been that way for him. Choices. It all came down to choices.

"Sometimes, when I see that wall in Todd's eyes, I wish I had somewhere else to come from, some other perspective."

"Be careful what you wish for."

"I know, but I think maybe that's why you can reach him where I can't." Stan stood a long moment. "I'm grateful for the time you take with Todd. I know he is, too."

Morgan nodded.

"Were you . . ." Stan gave a short laugh. "Don't take this wrong, but were you like him?"

Morgan considered that. "Maybe. Not at that age, but later." After he'd messed up so bad he couldn't find his way back. "I sure thought I had all the answers."

Stan sobered. "Tell me what to do."

Morgan shook his head.

"That's what you do, isn't it? Tell people how to fix their problems?"

Morgan sighed. It was businesses he saved, behemoth entities in a capitalistic system. But he engaged Stan's eyes and held them. "Stop considering Todd a problem."

Morgan headed for the house. If he reached Denver in a couple hours, he could find a first-class seat and be home by nightfall. He could sleep to the sound of the surf, and Todd and Stan would have the ranch to themselves. Trial by fire. Wasn't that what Stan was asking for?

With less than her usual confidence, Jill mounted the stairs toward her daughter's room alone. Cinda had simply said that Kelsey requested a private chat. But why would Kelsey want to see her alone? Why did she ask to see her at all? To thank her for trying? Jill sighed.

There was still hope. Morgan's first test was the same match as hers, Kelsey's other haplotype. If they could just get a negative cross match . . . Jill stopped outside the door. *Lord, help me.* Last time she'd taken her cues from Cinda. Now, seeing Kelsey alone . . .

"Come in," Kelsey said before Jill knocked.

Jill pushed the door open with a smile. "How did you know I was there?"

Kelsey blinked slowly. "I heard you on the stairs. I know every creak and snap." She sat atop the bedcovers, propped up on pillows. "Come in and sit down." She drew up her knees to make room on the bed.

Jill sat down.

"Thanks for coming."

"Sure. I was hoping to see you again." But now that she did, she couldn't help noticing her frailty. If this was how Kelsey looked in remission. . . Her head was uncovered again, pale skin on a rounded skull that made Jill think of her as a newborn, even without the fine dark halo she'd been born with.

Kelsey caught her glance. "My hair used to be your color."

"I guess it will be when it comes in again." Jill took the chair beside the bed.

Kelsey shrugged. "I'm getting used to being bald."

"I thought it was radiation that made the hair fall out."

"Strong chemo drugs do, too. They had to use some big guns to get me in remission this time." She sighed. "I would have lost it once we found a match anyway."

"Why?"

"Conditioning radiation."

"Oh." Jill wasn't sure where to take that. She'd read about the conditioning regime that virtually wiped out the patient's immune system to be replaced by the donor's, though nowadays they were trying less extreme methods.

Kelsey shifted up slightly in the pile of pillows. "It's all really toxic. Messes up all kinds of things. That's why I haven't developed . . . you know, breasts."

"Breasts aren't everything." Jill glanced down at her own. "Confessions of a flat-chested woman."

Kelsey smiled.

"It's a decided plus for a runner. Nothing bobbing around, flapping in your face."

Kelsey laughed, then grew serious. "The worst part is I probably can't have children. But I don't expect I'll be around that long anyway."

Jill jolted. "Of course you will!"

Kelsey looked her full in the face. "Will you promise me something?"

Jill nodded.

"Will you be honest with me?"

"I really believe you'll live, Kelsey. They'll find another donor. . . ."

"They already have. Did you know that?"

Jill swallowed. Kelsey had just asked her to be honest.

"Yes, I knew that."

Kelsey settled back. "I had a dream the other night. I won't call it a vision, but Jesus does send me visions."

Again Jill wasn't sure how to answer. "What kind of visions?"

"Just things He wants me to know."

"You must feel very close to Him." And Christ to her. What a wonderful thing. Kelsey's was the vibrant faith. What a witness she would be to Shelly, to anyone.

"I love my mom more than anyone besides Jesus."

Jill followed the change of subject. "It's obvious how much she loves you."

"But she wasn't in my dream. You were."

Jill fumbled a response, unprepared for Kelsey's frank declaration. "Well, that's . . ."

Kelsey looked away. "When I say visions, it's not like floods or the end of the world or anything. It's just little things He buries in my heart."

Jill stayed silent. She knew what was coming and had no answer ready. Surely Cinda wouldn't want her to lie.

"I look a lot like you, don't you think?"

Jill's throat stuck.

"But I must have gotten my eyes from my dad. My bio dad, I mean."

Tears stung. Jill dropped her gaze to the hands in her lap and realized they were gripping each other for dear life. "Yes, you have Morgan's eyes."

"He's the new donor, isn't he?"

The tears pooled and Jill blinked them away. "Have you talked to your parents?"

"You promised to be honest."

Jill met her daughter's gaze. "Yes. He is."

"Because they wouldn't do a single haplotype match with an unrelated donor. Just like they wouldn't let me meet you before the transplant if you were just a match in the donor pool. It violates the one-year rule."

"One year?"

"No contact between unrelated donor and recipient until one year after the procedure. I've read all about it on the Web sites, donor pages, medical pages."

Jill stared. So Kelsey had known.

Kelsey formed an impish smile. "When I asked to meet you, I knew the only way was if we were actually related. Mom couldn't do it otherwise. She had to have a source of contact outside the donor program. Like adoption records."

The little imp. "So you knew from the start."

Kelsey nodded. "You didn't hide it very well."

Jill dropped her face and smiled.

"Mom worries so much how I'll handle things. She tries to protect me, but I know a lot more than she thinks."

Jill nodded.

"What's he like?"

Jill drew a jagged breath. She didn't have to ask who. "Well, he's handsome. Dark hair and your color eyes. And he's done very well. I don't know much else anymore. I hadn't seen him in years."

"Why didn't you marry him?"

Jill faced her unabashed daughter. "I was seventeen. My parents were furious. They wouldn't let me see him. They did what they thought was right, just as yours did by not telling you—"

"I know that. But sometimes they think I'm still a little girl. I know I look like it."

"But you're a brave young woman. And bright." Jill gave her a wry smile. Not only had the child figured it all out, she'd maneuvered her into confessing and providing the rest of the information, a tactic Jill might have used herself at that age.

Kelsey pierced her suddenly with Morgan's eyes. "Why did you give me away?"

Her heart staggered. "I obeyed my parents." Jill would not tell her daughter she'd fought just to save her life. "But I've thought of you so often over the years."

Now Kelsey was silent. They looked into each other's faces without guile. Jill didn't know this child, but then, she did. They'd shared the same blood, the same nourishment, the hope and heartbreak. "I'm sorry, Kelsey."

"Don't be. God knew where I needed to be. I just wanted to know."

Jill's heart split. *God knew where she needed to be?* Had God taken her baby because she could not have handled Kelsey's illness? How would she and Morgan have dealt with it all? Would it have torn apart an immature relationship, left them reeling and fighting? Her heart staggered in her chest. Was she so shallow, so inept? Anger burned up inside. She would have done her best. The same way she'd protected Kelsey from the secret solution of her problem, she would have protected her from . . . leukemia?

"You can tell Mom we talked." Kelsey smiled. "I'm sure she's guessed, since I wanted to see you alone."

Jill nodded.

Kelsey moistened her lips. "You said his name is Morgan, right?"

"Yes."

Kelsey looked away. "Did he say . . . anything when you told him?"

"He wants to see you."

Kelsey was quiet a long time. "I'll have to wait. And pray."

Oh, Lord, the child's astute.

"But thank you for asking him to be tested. I'm sure you did."

Jill met the pert smile with her own, but it was forced. "He wanted to help."

Kelsey nodded. "I'm tired now."

Jill stood, letting her eyes linger on this child she'd birthed. "Good-bye, Kelsey."

Kelsey raised her fingers with another smile. "Thanks."

Jill closed the door behind her, drew a breath, and fought back the tears. She descended the stairs, wishing she could just go home, but Cinda waited in the living room, and Roger had come home from work and joined her. Jill spread her hands. "Kelsey guessed. I couldn't lie to her."

Cinda nodded. "We wouldn't want you to."

"She also asked about Morgan." Jill looked toward the window, wanting to get out, to be alone.

"It's all right, Jill." Cinda stood and put a hand on her shoulder. "Thank you for coming."

Jill nodded, rolling her lips in against the tears. That would probably be the last time she saw Kelsey, or any of them. It was now their life, as it had been for fourteen years. She turned for the door.

Cinda murmured, "Would you like me to keep you informed?"

Jill paused. Did she want to know if Kelsey died? But she wouldn't die. Morgan's marrow would cure her. It had to. "Yes, if you don't mind."

Roger joined them at the door. "We're very grateful." He was a quiet man with a soft voice that seemed incongruous with his heavily callused hands and cracked knuckles.

Jill smiled in response, then went out and drove home to Beauview. She went into her townhouse in stunned silence, came to a stop in the center of the living room and moaned, clutching her head between her palms. She dropped to her knees, but no prayer would come. How could she talk to God when He had deemed her unfit?

Had they all known? Her parents, her aunt who kept her through the pregnancy and daily reminded her not to grow attached? *"God knew where I needed to be."* Such innocent words, yet they tore open her spirit and left it writhing in pitiful shreds. Worthless, they cried. Worthless.

13

Morgan loved the rugged shore of the Santa Barbara coast. The public beach, a couple miles south of his home, was not that great, and his narrow strip at the base of the cliff could hardly be called beach at all. But the view and the power of the sea—that was worth every cent he'd spent on his coastal property. He sat a long while on his balcony, long after the citrine and ruby hues had faded over the water, and now there was only the restless sound of it. He nursed a snifter of Courvoisier in the starlight and thought of Jill.

It had taken a lot for her to come to him, to find and tell him the truth and ask his help. All for a child she'd sloughed off at birth. But Rick's words were true. It could not have been easy for Jill to stand up against her parents and have the child. It meant embarrassment for the family, especially one so "Christian."

Morgan well remembered their condemnation. He might have been the anti-Christ, not a foolish kid in love with their daughter. His youth bore no consideration, nor the fact that Jill had willingly participated. No, he was the accursed, and she . . .

He raised his glass. "Here's to you, Jill, my sweet fall from grace." He drank her toast, thinking of her eyes awash with tears, and how he'd wanted to kiss them away. "Blissful iniquity." Strange how porous the self became in the still of night. His chest constricted and he took the brandy into his throat as he took the night into his soul.

Jill opened her swollen eyes to the tapping on her window. What? She rolled out of bed, crossed the room, and pushed aside the curtain. Dan. He motioned to her, and she trudged to the front door and admitted him. "I'm not running today."

He chucked her chin. "You look awful."

"Thank you."

"Are you sick?"

Yes. Unto death. "No."

"What is it, Jill?"

She headed for the kitchen, poured two glasses of orange juice, and sat on the iron stool at her counter. Dan took the other stool and swigged down a gulp of juice. Jill let the tangy sweetness refresh her mouth, though it was a surface reaction at best.

"Tell me what's up."

"I don't feel like talking."

Dan rolled the juice glass in his large palms. "It's Morgan Spencer." He spoke the name as he might some punk he'd run down and cornered.

She raised her eyes. "It's not Morgan. It's . . ." She drew and released a breath, stood, and walked to the glass door. The morning was damp, the sky dull. The wind would blow it clear, but then the sun would reveal everything in sharp chiaroscuro. She didn't want to see clearly. She didn't like what she had seen already.

Why was Dan here? Why wouldn't he leave her alone? She closed her eyes. "I doubt my faith, Dan. I don't know what to believe anymore." She glanced over her shoulder at him.

His face was kind and frank. "Maybe you've just grown up. Isn't that from the Bible? When I was a child I spoke like a child, but now I'm a man?"

Jill's soul constricted. Was that it? Was she finally seeing through a myth? Was Shelly right, that there was no difference between those who believed and those who didn't? They were all in the same mire, mucking through the best they could? She tried to think of one definitive prayer God had answered.

Maybe Joey calmed because she held him, not from any divine favors dropped from heaven. All those countless prayers she'd uttered were probably waving out into space in unending futility. It was nothing. A great empty nothingness.

She looked back out into the milky sky. Was there no heaven beyond? No hell beneath? Or was it something more profound than her limited faith could frame? *Prove yourself to me. Make me know.*

Dan stood and crossed to her. "Things happen that open our eyes. I gave religion a try, but it never made any difference. I find my own answers now." He took her waist in his hands, his badge cutting into her shoulder blade. He pressed his cheek to the side of her head. "Why don't we run?"

"In your uniform?"

"I brought a change."

She leaned into him and shook her head. He kissed her hair, her ear. She pulled away. "Stop it, Dan."

He let her go. "What's the matter?"

Couldn't he see she was a wreck?

"I thought we'd solved it, Jill. The things that stood between us."

She turned and looked into his face. What conclusion had he drawn?

He spread his hands. "If you're done with your concerns and I'm done with mine . . ."

"What are you saying, Dan?"

He caught her shoulders. "Your faith is no longer an issue, and I don't have to prove myself competent to please a woman." His face was earnest. "We've taken away the obstacles. That's how life works."

She pressed her fingertips to her temple, then shot her gaze through his eyes. "Obstacles? Do you understand I'm questioning everything I am?"

He rolled his eyes. "Jill . . ."

"Get out, Dan."

He let go and stepped back, then picked up his hat and left. She drained her glass of orange juice and got into the shower. Motions. She had to go through the motions. The hot water removed the night's film from her skin, but inside, her spirit was limp. She shampooed and bared her teeth to the water, filled her mouth and swished.

Apple-scented steam rolled over the mirror and walls when she opened the curtain and stepped out. Rascal meowed outside the door, and she opened it just as the phone began to ring. Jill scooped Rascal up and dropped him on the bed as she picked up the receiver. "Yes, I told him to leave, no I won't reconsider, and no I don't need brownies or milk or a shoulder to cry on."

"Okay," the woman's voice said.

"Hello?" Jill caught the towel to her mouth.

"This is Anita Rawlings. I wanted to let you know Angelica's sick and won't make her tutoring today."

"Oh, Anita."

"It's okay, Jill. It sounds like you could use a day off."

Jill drew a shaky breath. In truth, she might lose her mind. "Thanks for calling, Anita."

"Are you all right?"

"Yes."

"I'll pray for you today."

Jill said nothing. They'd spoken in the past about faith in general terms, the usual platitudes. Did she want Anita's prayers? What difference did it make? "Thanks." She hung up and pulled on her running shorts, sport bra, and tank. She tied on her Nikes and headed out the sliding glass door. It was backward to shower and then run, but since she was not teaching after all, she had to do something.

She slid the door shut and hurried past Shelly's patio. She thought Shelly had been watching Dan leave. Most of her life was a drama for Shelly, but if she'd been thinking, she'd know her friend would not be awake yet. Brett was probably just getting up and starting his morning routine before Dan joined him to go to the station. Dan had allowed time for a run.

Jill reached the path and stopped to stretch. Already the air was muggy. The cornfields might love it, but it oppressed her as she started to run. Or was it more than the air? Her own spirit was muggy, weighing her down. She forced her legs to move in a steady, constant battle over lassitude. Each stride was one more than the last. She could do that much. Too many things were out of her control, but she could make her legs run.

Just over an hour later, she left the park and headed back to her patio door. She blew the bedraggled bangs from her face as she passed Shelly's, noting the cruiser outside. She'd almost made it by when Shelly opened the door and called to her, holding a yellow-green lollipop as a bribe.

The last thing she wanted was to go inside with Brett and Dan there. Why weren't they at the station already? Shouldn't they be gone? But maybe it was earlier than she thought. She went through Shelly's door and met the lollipop straight on. "What's this one?"

"Your suggestion. Kiwi-pineapple."

Jill took the sucker and glanced at Dan standing in Shelly's kitchen, one hip to the counter, eating an éclair. The sweet did not help his expression as the lollipop would not help her. *Get out* were strong words to him.

Shelly put on a mock New York accent. "Taste it already."

Jill licked the sweet obediently, identifying pineapple at once but less kiwi. How did kiwi taste anyway? She'd only named that flavor symbolically. Dan gobbled the éclair and dabbed cream from his fingers onto a napkin. Should she say something? Apologize? No, it was better that they face it. They couldn't remain in limbo, neither together nor apart. At least this way it was settled.

Brett came out of the study with whatever he'd needed to retrieve. He nodded and the two of them headed out the front door. Jill followed Dan with her eyes, but neither had said a word.

After he left, Shelly hung her head to the side. "I see I've missed something."

Jill stared at the lollipop. "What have you missed, Shelly?"

"Gee, I'm not real sure. Whatever it is that has Dan acting like Robocop around the woman he loves."

"We're friends."

"No. Huh-uh. That was not friends. That was devastation in a uniform."

Jill looked up. Honesty was always best with Shelly, and the sooner the better, or she'd wheedle it out anyway. "He asked me to marry him; I said no."

Shelly's face formed just the expression Jill expected. "He asked you—I thought you said you weren't in love with Morgan."

Jill sighed. "Could you please give me more credit than that? My whole life is falling apart. It's hardly the time to get married."

"But, Jill." Shelly dropped to a chair. "Do you know what it took for him to ask you? That was the greatest statement of trust he could make."

Jill's heart wrenched. "I'm sorry."

"Is there anything you can say that I'll understand?"

Waves of bleak despair washed over her. "I don't think so."

Shelly dropped her head to her hands. "You're on a kamikaze mission."

Shelly could be right. Since leaving Kelsey's bedside, a spiraling depression had seized hold unlike anything she'd known since being torn away from Morgan and having her baby alone. *Worthless*, the voices murmured. When had she ceased to matter? When her marrow didn't match? When she gave away her baby? When she gave up her virtue to Morgan? She was so empty, she couldn't cry even if she'd let herself.

Shelly must have caught her expression. "You are not spending the day alone. I'll call in."

"You don't have to do that, Shelly."

"You're more important than Cartier Confections. The boss can answer her own phone for one day."

Jill hadn't the strength to argue. She held out the lollipop.

Shelly eyed the sucked sweet. "Do you think I want that?"

Jill realized what she was doing. "No, I guess not."

"You didn't give me your opinion. Here I had them create your very own flavor, your 'I'm on vacation' flavor to double with our Maui coconut cream—"

"It's good, Shelly."

"And utterly irrelevant in the scope of life."

That actually brought a ghost of a smile. "Something like that."

"Go shower while I inform the president her assistant needs a personal day to deal with something infinitely more important than sucker flavors."

Jill obeyed. Spending the day with Shelly might just be what she needed.

They went to a movie, but she could not have named it afterward. Then they went to the mall.

"That does it."

Jill forced herself to focus. "What?"

"This is like *Night of the Zombies*." Shelly's earnest face confronted her. "Since when is puce with polka dots 'nice'?"

Jill looked at what Shelly had just shown her. The short set was appalling, actually. "No, I don't like that. Do you?"

Shelly's mouth dropped open. She waved her hand slowly in front of Jill's face. "Hello. Anybody home? I mean the real Jill, not some changeling of vacant mind."

Jill dropped her gaze. "I'm sorry, Shelly. I don't know what's wrong."

Shelly moistened her lips. "You need to talk."

Jill shook her head, but as always, Shelly ignored her. Seated at the café court, a mocha latté between her hands and Shelly's face before her, Jill realized there was no escape. "I don't even know where to start."

Shelly's eyes softened. "Well, something happened since the last time we talked."

Yes, something had happened. She had lost her surety of a good and loving God. She had lost the point of her salvation, the relevance. She shook her head. Maybe it was stress overload that numbed her, not the realization that she was worthless in God's eyes. Maybe even that was delusion. What if there was no God? She'd rather believe that. It hurt less.

"Talk to me, Jill."

Jill tried to form her desolation into words. She'd made her confession and been baptized at nine. Her parents were so proud, and their approval meant more than any spiritual awakening involved. She had measured up to their expectations and made the false assumption that she also measured up to God's.

She looked into Shelly's face. "I think maybe it's all been a hoax. That, as you said, there *is* no difference between those who believe and those who don't. We're no better off believing than not."

Shelly threaded her fingers. "What have you always told me? Circumstances don't matter. It's what you know by faith that counts. That Jesus Christ gave His life to bring salvation once for all." It was almost comical hearing the words from Shelly's mouth.

"My daughter is dying. She's fourteen. She'll never have a child. And even if Morgan's bone marrow halts the disease, there's no certainty of a cure." Even as she said it, she knew that wasn't the heart of her desolation. Her soul rent inside her. "Shelly." Her voice caught. "Kelsey told me not to regret giving her away, that God knew where she needed to be. With a different mother." Jill stared into her friend's eyes. "God rejected me."

And suddenly her resistance ruptured and pain burst from her in scalding tears. Shelly snatched a wad of napkins from the nearest food booth. Jill pressed them to her eyes until the sobs ebbed.

Shelly spoke softly. "Maybe God did you a favor. Maybe he knew a young girl, alone and immature, could not support the upcoming difficulties in that baby's life."

The words were sensible from Shelly's point of view. Jill acknowledged that much. But shame mingled with sorrow to clog her throat. God saw it, too, what they'd all seen. *Unworthy.*

Others talked in such glowing terms of their relationship with

Jesus. She did everything they did, but she was like the wannabes who hung with the cheerleaders, hoping some of the magic would rub off on them. Jill knew from the inside, there was no magic. It was all illusion.

14

Noelle was back at the ranch when Morgan returned by taxi a week later. He found her on the couch looking almost well, but he read weariness in her posture. He bent and kissed her cheek. "The prodigal returns."

"Me or you?"

He smiled. "Now there's an interesting thought. Done anything worth repenting?" He sat and slid an arm around her shoulders.

She nudged him with an elbow. "I'm too tired even to think of anything."

"Yeah, yeah, yeah." He removed his arm to a respectful position.

"The good news is, in spite of my pneumonia, the baby grew two centimeters."

"Two centimeters. Imagine that."

She rested her hand on her abdomen. "It's significant."

"Then good. I'm glad to hear it." And he was. Noelle's baby was a beacon of hope, of what it could and should be like. His first awareness of her pregnancy had been difficult, hammering home what he'd given up, what he could have fought to have for himself but had given Rick instead. Now he was just grateful the baby thrived.

"How about you, Morgan? Tell me what's happening with you and Kelsey."

Hearing his daughter's name from Noelle gave him a jolt. Hearing it connected to him brought the ache. *With him and Kelsey?* Nothing. How could there be? She'd been ripped from his reality before he ever laid eyes on her. Maybe it was some flaw in his nature that made it matter so much. Why couldn't he just let it go? So he had a kid. So what?

But as the oldest of six, he'd been a natural caretaker. Rick teased that their bane had been the arrival of the little sisters, but he had adored every one of those babies. Mom knew. She'd seen his soft heart and appreciated his automatic nurturing. He would come home from school and let the little girls swarm him. He tickled, hugged, even changed their diapers. He would have made a good dad.

"Morgan?" Noelle touched his arm.

"Yeah." He gathered in his thoughts. "I don't know what's happening with Kelsey. I've done my part. It's scheduled."

"The transplant?"

"It's actually called a harvest on my end. Rescue on Kelsey's. Imagine that, Morgan Spencer to the rescue."

Her gaze rested on his. "I don't have to imagine. I know that masked man."

He looked up at the vaulted ceiling, noted a few cobwebs at the junctions of crossbeams. He cocked his head. "You ought to let me get Marta up here."

"You'd never get her away from her grandchildren."

"Wanna bet?"

Noelle smiled. "No. Your silver tongue is notorious. But I'm all right."

"I think you could use the help. And frankly, this place isn't the same without her."

"You mean my cooking."

He winked. "What say I cajole her for a month or two?"

Noelle laughed. "Morgan . . ." Then she sobered. "It is tempting."

He stood up. "She still with her son's family in Littleton?"

Noelle nodded. "Last we heard. Aren't you going to call first?"

"No. The personal touch is more effective." Though it hadn't been with Noelle. She'd resisted his touch like no woman before or after, until he'd used his magic to reunite her with Rick. Something was wrong with that picture. Why could he make things work for everyone else but himself? If he consulted on his own life, would he find the answer?

"I'm so glad you're back, Morgan."

That warmed him more than it should have. "I'm not staying long." With a quick wave, he strode out and saw Rick riding Destiny, his sorrel stallion, down from the high pasture. He ought to run the plan by him, as it was his brother's ranch. He waited in the yard while Rick dismounted the impeccably behaved horse. Hard to believe it was the same fiery-tempered animal upon which Rick had charged into the yard the first day Noelle arrived. Morgan half suspected Noelle had married Rick for Destiny.

"Hey, Morgan. You're back."

"Sort of."

Rick crooked an eyebrow.

Morgan pulled his keys from his slacks pocket. "I'm going to fetch Marta for a couple months to help Noelle out."

"Oh, you are, are you?"

Morgan smiled. "With your agreement, of course."

Rick propped his hands on his hips. "First off, Marta won't come. She's crazy about living with her grandkids. And secondly, I can't afford to pay her what she's worth. Since we're not taking guests this summer, aside from Stan's family, I have only the sale of the foals and the occasional riding party. With Noelle's illness . . ."

"Let me do it."

Rick shook his head. "I know you can afford to, but—"

"All the times I come up here, eat your food, take up a room, gaze at your lovely wife. I owe you."

"Sorry, Morgan."

"Ever heard of the deadly sin of pride?"

Rick studied him a long moment. "It's not pride, it's . . . well, okay, it is." He dropped his chin. "It's not easy having the daughter of old money for a wife."

Try not having her. "Let me spring for Marta."

Rick frowned. "Man, you're annoying."

"Come on."

"Don't make her think I put you up to it. And don't make her feel guilty if she refuses."

Morgan started for his car. "She won't refuse."

———

And the really annoying thing was that she wouldn't. Rick was sure of it. He watched Morgan take off in his Thunderbird and knew his brother would do whatever it took to get Marta up to the ranch to cook and clean and order them around. Not that it was a bad thing, especially with Todd and Stan still baching it, and Noelle hardly past the pneumonia.

That had been a bad scare, and she was still weak and tired. Soon she'd be cumbersome. Marta was exactly what she needed. It just rankled that Morgan thought of it. And yes, it was pride. Morgan might have his faults, but he sure had his gifts, as well, like seeing a problem and providing a solution. Rick looked over the ranch. A good part of his relative security was thanks to Morgan.

He'd gotten him into the ground floor of a few prospects that had made a tidy profit. Nothing like the first company that launched Morgan into big-time money, but enough subsequent suggestions to buy into one or another of the corporations he was turning around. It was a risk, of course. If Morgan's plan didn't work, there would be no profit and maybe losses as well. But that had yet to happen.

Still, Rick guarded those investments carefully for his family's future. The ranch income was normally sufficient for their everyday needs. At least he owned it outright, had no mortgage to concern him, only the property taxes, insurance, and expenses. He wanted to be a good steward over all that he had. And Noelle seemed content. But Morgan saw things with an outside eye and didn't hesitate to intervene.

Rick stabled Destiny and went inside the house. Noelle was asleep on the couch. He stood a long moment watching her, love swelling inside him like the baby that enlarged her belly. The hours beside her hospital bed had brought back too clearly the ones spent there after her fall on Aldebaran, the mare she'd ridden over the flaky shale slope.

That had taught him too well not to lose his temper with her. She was so fragile in so many ways, yet she was strong, too. And the Lord would make her stronger still as she grew in faith. Looking at her now, he could understand Morgan's wanting to help her. Some women just brought that out in a man.

Even Jill, the day she'd come. He had spent a lot of years blaming her, but when he'd stepped in the door and seen her there, his first instinct had been to reach out, say something more than her name. But Morgan had moved her out too quickly.

Noelle stirred, opened her eyes, and smiled. "What are you doing?"

"Watching you sleep."

She patted the couch next to her, and he sat down, curled her into his arms, and kissed her. She caught his vest lapels and drew a breath beside his cheek. "You smell like horses."

"Yep. Aldebaran's foal tangled with something last night. Had to bandage up his leg."

"Is he all right?"

Rick kissed her eyebrows. "He's fine. Sort of put me in the doctoring mood, though."

"Oh yeah?"

"Know anyone who might need some TLC?"

"Mmm." She snuggled into his neck.

"This is not the place." He scooped her into his arms, then carried her up the winding stairs. While they had the house to themselves he ought to take advantage of it.

Morgan returned four hours later with Marta and six bags of groceries. Rick had to hand it to him. Morgan made you want to do his request. Marta would not have stood a chance. She looked smaller somehow but just as spry, her gray hair wrapped around her head in braids. It took her all of two minutes to shoo them out of the kitchen so she could get started on supper. In the front room, he gripped Morgan's shoulder. "What did it cost you?"

Morgan smiled. "A gentleman never tells."

Rick wrestled him by the neck, but Morgan refused to talk. Whatever it was, it would sure be nice having Marta again. If just for a while. He went down to Stan's cabin and knocked. They'd been taking most of their meals at the big house already, but he and Noelle hadn't put together anything spectacular, and while she was in the hospital, he'd just given them the run of the kitchen.

Stan opened the door. "Hi, Rick."

Rick glanced in and saw Todd with his back to them, hunched over a Game Boy. "I wanted to let you know we've got our cook back. Her name's Marta. Used to be here every summer, and believe me, she's amazing."

"Hey, that's great."

Was that relief in his face? Noelle might not be the best cook. . . . Rick caught that thought and pressed on. "Morgan talked Marta into a couple of months. You'll get some terrific meals."

Todd looked up. "Morgan's back?"

Rick nodded. "I'm not sure how long."

Stan stepped out and closed the door behind him. He glanced back, then spoke low. "Rick, I'm debating the effectiveness of this venture. The few days with just the two of us, I almost threw it in." He spread his hands. "That just now was the first interest he's shown in anything."

Rick studied the man's face. Discouragement definitely. "That's your call, Stan. You have the cabin as long as you like."

"If I could think of anything else . . ." Stan raised his hand and dropped it limply. "I was hoping for a breakthrough before I took him back into real life."

Rick nodded.

"It was too much for Melanie and for Sarah. They needed some normalcy."

"Are you sure of your call?"

"To foster care?" Stan pursed his lips and stared at the floor of the stoop. "I don't feel released."

Rick gripped Stan's shoulder. "Then run the race."

Stan nodded. "Maybe now that Morgan's back . . ."

"Stan." Rick dropped his hand. "Morgan outshines most of the male population. You can ride his shadow, but is that going to accomplish what you need?"

Stan sighed. "Probably not."

"Fight for the kid, Stan. Morgan's magnetism won't outlast your faithfulness."

Stan drew himself straight. "You think?"

Rick nodded.

"That's what I heard in my prayer time. Persistent widow and all that."

Rick smiled. "Keep knocking." He started off the stoop.

"Rick, is everything all right with Morgan?"

Rick released a long breath. How did one answer that? In the world's view Morgan was king. In God's eyes . . . "You could keep him in your prayers."

Stan nodded. "I will."

They all sat down that evening to blackberry-glazed pork chops, scalloped potatoes au gratin, fresh string beans, and oatmeal muffins. She complained, but Morgan insisted Marta sit at the long table with them.

"None of that hiding in the kitchen, Marta. You'll eat with the rest of us or the deal's off." He gave Rick a taunting wink.

Rick frowned. What was the deal? He'd get it out of him one way or another.

Noelle clasped her hands at her throat and gazed at the fare on the table like Cinderella at the ball. "Now I know I've starved my husband."

Rick gave her a smile. "I did not marry you for your cooking."

"Good thing."

Rick bowed his head and blessed their meal with special thanks for Marta, who prepared it. For the second time that day, his heart swelled inside him. God was good. He glanced at Todd, pleased to see a semblance of appreciation on the boy's face. And close to hero worship when the kid looked at Morgan.

Stan had a fight ahead, but something inside told him Morgan was playing a part there, too. Just as he had with Noelle.

Still riding the wave of the coup he'd accomplished, Morgan winked at Todd, although the kid had been sullen and silent throughout the meal and seemed less appreciative than he ought to be. Once he had more of Marta's great cooking to fill him out, he'd be more than grateful. The rest of them already were, especially judging by Stan's portions.

Morgan smiled to himself. When he'd shown up at Marta's door, she had literally shaken him by the shoulders. "Where have you been? Why haven't you called or written? I hear from Rick and from Noelle. Do I hear from you?"

"I'm here now."

"And full of mischief, I'm sure."

Morgan gave her his best smile. "No mischief, Marta. Just a little of the devil."

"You don't fool me." She'd tugged him inside. "Come see my angels."

So he'd met the family, all suitably impressed by the things Marta told about him. And he'd shown equal appreciation for the boasts she made on the children. Then he'd thrown the offhand, "By the way, I've come to kidnap Marta." They had argued of course, though he could tell she was not only flattered, she was tempted. But what had really gotten her were the small educational trusts he'd promised to set up for the two grandkids. Yep, he knew her soft underbelly.

Once she'd decided, they all seemed open to the break and Marta had packed up her things and said good-bye. She'd actually teared up with joy when he drove her into the ranch. She'd dabbed her eyes furiously. "Don't you tell."

He'd kissed her cheek. "Your secret's safe with me."

After the meal, while the others chatted in the dining room, Todd cornered him on his way up the stairs. "Why'd you leave?"

Morgan leaned his hip to the banister. "I needed to go home."

"Where's that?"

"California."

Todd stuck his fingers into the loosely woven throw across the back of the couch. "You just flew there and back?" The use of his prime swear word in that sentence betrayed some fresh animosity.

"That's right."

"You have your own plane or something?" There it was again. Were they starting from scratch?

Morgan dislodged a shred of pork chop from between two molars with his tongue. "I flew Delta. Is that all right with you?"

Todd scowled. "You just took off. I didn't even know you'd gone."

Morgan shrugged. That's how he operated. He came and went as he pleased.

"Why'd you go?"

"I felt like it. Missed the waves on the rocks." The control of his own place. And of course he'd had all the medical reasons, which he was not about to elaborate to Todd.

Todd kicked the bottom edge of the couch, a nervous rhythm. "Rick said you had something happen. He thought maybe you wanted to be alone."

"Maybe I did."

"What happened?"

Morgan considered the kid, saw more behind his questions than nosiness. But he was not ready to discuss his daughter. He'd spent every day at home trying to figure it all out. The second matching test had determined a lot more than Kelsey's immediate future; it had altered his.

"How did you and Stan like having the ranch to yourselves?"

Todd swore again.

Morgan rubbed the back of his neck. "Why don't you come up and see what I brought you?"

"You brought me something?"

Morgan started up the stairs, Todd following. Part of what he'd brought should make Todd ecstatic. The other part would be a tougher sell. With Todd's present mood, it would be tougher yet. Morgan hadn't realized how much he'd shaken the kid by leaving. That was not a good sign. Todd needed to attach to Stan, develop that trust.

They went into his room, and Todd immediately honed in on the laptop on the dresser.

"Don't touch it."

"Why not?"

"It's booby-trapped."

"Liar."

"Calling me a liar, kid?" On impulse, Morgan grabbed him around the shoulders, wrestled him over, and tossed him down onto the bed.

Todd's face reddened and he flailed wildly. He was scrappy but too small to defend himself. He hollered, "Cut it out."

"Why should I?" Morgan pushed him down, grinning.

Todd pressed him back with his fists, but he had little natural strength. He'd be an easy mark for any bully. As soon as he sat up, Morgan pushed him down again like an inflatable toy with a sand bottom. "You think you're so tough."

Todd resisted the next push. "You think *you're* so tough!"

Morgan leaned his hip against the pine log that formed the foot post. "Uh-oh. You've got my number."

Todd grinned in spite of himself, gave Morgan's arm one last shove. "So where's my present?"

Morgan cocked his head. "Actually I have two. One you'll like more now, and the other you'll appreciate the rest of your life."

Todd glared. "Great. It must be *good for me*."

"And the deal is, you can't have one without the other."

Todd swore.

"You have to agree."

"No way." Todd shook his head. "I don't even know I want the first one."

Morgan walked over to the closet and eased out a box. He set it on the bed beside Todd and watched the kid's eyes widen. Todd tore open the carton and pulled out the portable TV. "You've gotta be kiddin' me!"

He'd gauged that one well. Rick, and even Stan, might spend their days just fine with no television, but Todd had griped constantly. He let the kid ogle the set until he'd satisfied himself, then looked up.

"What's the other thing?"

Morgan went to the closet again and pulled out the phonics and reading program he'd ordered from the radio after hearing the ad. *Any one of any age can learn to read with our back-to-basics program.* He set it on the bed beside Todd. "The deal is you work on this with Stan and learn to read." Stan was a teacher, after all. "The TV's your reward."

Todd stared at the plastic carton that held the reading program and chewed his lower lip. "I know how to read."

"That's not what you told me before."

"I can read some stuff. I just don't know how to figure all of it out."

"So here's your chance." Morgan hoped the lure of the TV would be enough to win him to the idea.

Todd stared at the TV a long moment, then shrugged. "I guess."

Morgan smiled. "Let's run it by Stan." He slid the TV back into its carton and handed it off to Todd, then took the reading program and led the way downstairs.

Rick and Stan were still in the dining room, though Marta and Noelle had gone into the kitchen. Both men looked up as Morgan motioned Todd in around him, gripping the carton protectively. Morgan waited in the doorway as Todd approached his foster dad.

"Morgan gave me this." He looked at Morgan, then back. "I can have it if you teach me to read."

Not exactly the words Morgan would have chosen, nor the tone, confrontational and defensive at once.

Stan drew his brows together. "What do you mean?"

"You probably thought I was stupid. But I didn't get to school much when they taught the kids how to read. Morgan thinks that'll help." Todd jerked his chin toward the reading program. Morgan handed it over.

"You never told me you couldn't read." Stan looked from one to the other of them as he took the program.

"Yeah, well, I don't really care. But I don't get the TV unless you teach me, so are you going to?"

Morgan winced. Maybe he should have spoken for Todd.

Stan looked down at the package, turned it over and read the back, then looked up. His expression was similar to Jimmy Stewart's in *It's a Wonderful Life*, sort of pleading and betrayed. Didn't he see it was his chance to bond and help Todd succeed? What kind of teacher was he?

Stan swallowed, then spoke softly. "I'll be glad to help you read, Todd. But we'll have to talk about the TV."

"The deal is I learn to read, I get the TV." Todd turned to Morgan. "I can have it while I'm learning, right?"

This was not going the way he'd expected. What was Stan's problem? "Why don't you leave it on the table for now." Morgan jerked his head toward the doorway. "Let us talk."

Todd did not want to let loose of the set, but Morgan sent him a confidential look that penetrated his resistance. Todd put the TV down and stalked out the door, swearing under his breath.

Morgan turned to Stan. "He told me a while ago he couldn't read very well. I thought this was an opportunity to correct that."

Stan's gaze was more direct than he expected, and there was a flicker of anger. "I don't believe in bribing kids."

"It's not a bribe. It's a reward. Something to strive for." Hadn't Stan ever heard of incentives? What thriving company didn't offer a bonus program for achievement? What teacher didn't stick stars on a chart?

"And what if he needs to raise a math grade? Do I get him an Xbox? Or a go-cart if he gets to class all week?"

Morgan glanced at Rick, typically silent but listening and observing it all. "The kid's going crazy with no TV. What does it hurt to let him watch an hour or two?"

"It's the precedent." Stan bore down on him doggedly. "I can't keep up with you, and I don't want to."

Morgan dropped his chin. So the TV was a big deal. He'd wanted a big deal to get through to Todd. He hadn't expected Stan to get worked up. It wasn't about keeping up or impressing Todd. It was to motivate, encourage him. But Stan did have a point about future expectations.

Morgan rested against the doorframe. "It's your call."

Stan stood up, still holding the reading program. "I appreciate your concern and your letting me know there's a problem. I just wish you'd've come to me first." He didn't add that Todd was his responsibility, but that was implicit.

Morgan nodded. "I'm sorry. It's my style to find a solution and act on it."

"Sometimes there isn't a quick fix. Putting a Band-Aid on a rotten limb won't keep gangrene from spreading. I could buy Todd's trust. But I'd rather earn it."

An admirable sentiment, which Stan was not accomplishing. But Morgan had overstepped. "What do you want to do?"

Stan shrugged. "I'll think about it, and pray about it."

And in the meantime Todd might combust. Morgan stepped out of his way. Stan left with the reading program under his arm. If he tried to make Todd learn and refused the TV, Morgan did not want to witness the result. He turned to Rick. "Hope he makes the right choice."

"You put him on the spot." Rick's voice was low as always, softly controlled yet annoyingly firm.

Morgan pulled out a chair and sat down. "It's called incentive. Everyone works better when there's something in it for them."

"Morgan . . ."

"I know. I made Stan look bad. But he didn't have to. He could have seen it—"

"Your way?"

Morgan leaned the chair back on two legs. "What's he so uptight about?"

"Come on, Morgan. You drive in here with a hot new convertible, take Todd off for all kinds of fun—"

"Nothing Stan couldn't do himself. He thinks a thirteen-year-old kid wants to sight-see and scoop horse manure."

"It's his kid. At least his responsibility. What are you trying to prove?"

Morgan's throat tightened. "I'm not proving anything. I just want Todd to have what he needs."

"Why?"

Morgan looked hard at Rick. What king of inane question was that? "You think a kid should go through life dropping out or misbehaving because he's lacking a skill that could turn it around?"

"That's not what I asked."

"What, then?"

"Why does it matter to you? You drop in here on a lark three, four times a year, but you think this kid's trouble is yours to solve?"

Morgan rocked on the back chair legs, Rick's words penetrating.

"Stan has the kid every day of the year. He's volunteered to raise him, to deal with his language, his attitude, his physical, spiritual, and emotional needs. And you come in like Santa Claus buying the kid gifts and making promises and undermining everything Stan's trying to do."

What really stung was how the truth sunk in. He had done that for years professionally. He could go in and blaze, then move on to the next project with little thought for the dimmed leaders in his wake. But Todd was not a project, a consultation; he was a person with a whole life ahead of him, a life that Morgan would not be a part of.

When had simply befriending Todd become a mission to right

every wrong in his life? When he learned about Kelsey and felt the overwhelming helplessness? He'd been on a crash course to save the world since he entered Wharton, graduated with honors, and accepted the kind of positions men would kill for. A few years of that and he knew he wanted to be out on his own. His mind was tailor-made for turn-around management, but that didn't always apply to personal life.

He set the chair legs down and rested his elbows on the table, head dropped, hands clasped behind his neck. "You're right. I was way out of line."

"Your heart was in the right place."

"Doesn't make it easier for Stan." Morgan blew a slow breath through puckered lips. "Good thing I'm leaving."

"You just got here."

"A stopover on the way to Beauview."

Rick raised his eyebrows. "Going home?"

Funny how he and Rick both still called it home when it hadn't been home for either of them for years. But Morgan shook his head. "No. I want to see Kelsey before the transplant. I want her to know . . ."

"What?"

"That I had nothing to do with sloughing her off."

Rick dropped his gaze. "Morgan." Disagreement, obvious in his tone, but he didn't argue. They both knew his mind was made up.

Rick finally looked up. "Are you leaving in the morning?"

"Right now."

"Driving through the night?"

Morgan shrugged. "It'll be easier than sleeping. I will, however, make my apology to Stan. He deserves that much. And say good-bye to Todd."

Rick nodded, then stretched. "Thanks for fetching Marta. That'll help a lot. I know it cost you."

Morgan smiled. "And you're dying to know how much."

"I'll get it out of Marta. Or Noelle will."

Morgan shook his head. "We made a pact. If you break her, it'll be an international incident."

Rick laughed softly. "Have it your way. I'm just glad she's here."

15

Jill sat with Shelly and Brett around the table in her kitchen nook, determined not to give the suffocating depression a fresh foothold. She thought again about her tutoring session with Joey that morning. It helped to focus on the kids. Her primary purpose through the extended school year was to keep them interacting and maintain their base-level skills. She didn't introduce anything new, just played with what they'd learned through the regular school year. She did, however, encourage development in personal areas like correct conversational responses and self-control.

Joey's mother desperately wanted him to get potty trained and insisted that at nine, he could learn it if he wanted to. Jill had explained again that his brain didn't receive that signal as something he could process and act on, that it was common with autism. He might never connect a sensation to that behavior. But she understood the frustration, and at some level, so did he. He'd been particularly disruptive and agitated that morning.

She sighed and started picking up the cards Brett had dealt her. He was out of his uniform, wearing a Beauview PD T-shirt and sweats. He tossed a handful of M&Ms into his mouth. Hearts was Shelly's favorite game, so they sat now and arranged their final read-'em-and-weep hand. Jill held enough stinkers to consider shooting the moon.

They'd invited Dan, but he had plans, so they played three-handed, which meant more cards and a kitty to the taker of the first dirty trick. Jill wondered what Dan's plans were, or if he meant to avoid their foursomes altogether after the last encounter. At this point so would she.

The phone rang, and the machine took it immediately, since she'd been disinclined to answer most of her calls.

"Hello, Jill. This is Cinda."

Jill rushed up and grabbed it, leaving her cards and her friends waiting. "Hi, Cinda." She leaned on the counter and forced herself to calm. Cinda had promised to keep her informed, but if it was more bad news . . .

"Jill, Morgan's cross match was negative, no reaction between donor and recipient. They're compatible."

Jill dropped her head back, eyes closed. *Oh, thank you, Lord.*

"I'm calling from New Haven. They've admitted Kelsey for the pretransplant conditioning."

A rush of painful joy seized her. It was happening! Morgan matched. *Forgive my unbelief!* "Cinda, that's wonderful."

"I'm so grateful to you."

"Don't even say that. What happens now?"

"Her protocol requires myeloablative therapy, total immune destruction, because her remission was so difficult to achieve and the cancer is tenacious. There's a tremendous risk of infection and so many factors. But we're hopeful." Cinda sounded weary, as well.

"How's Kelsey?"

"Excited. Very weak."

Jill shook off the sudden dread. "I know this will work. Is Morgan—does Morgan know what to do?"

"The center is in communication with him. He gave the final consent and passed the physical exam that accompanied his counseling. Once Kelsey is ready, they'll do the transplant."

Oh, Morgan. She tried not to envy him.

"Keep praying."

"Of course." Only she hadn't. She'd let a few innocent words drive her faith away. What right had she to question God's wisdom? If He judged her unworthy, who was she to argue? Twice the Lord had found her unacceptable. Yet now He received Morgan? *Stop it! He was God. He could choose as He liked. This wasn't about her.*

"Yes, I'll pray, Cinda."

"Add one or two for finances. I don't know how we'll pay for everything. We've already mortgaged the house and ... well, just include that in your prayers. I couldn't bear to refuse Kelsey a treatment simply because we couldn't pay."

Jill's heart thumped. "No, of course not. That's an important prayer."

Cinda sighed. "It doesn't sound right to worry about money. I know the Lord will provide."

"It's still important to ask." Jill took a chance. "Give Kelsey my love."

"She sends you hers."

Jill gripped the receiver. Was that just a platitude, or had Kelsey actually said it? She pressed her free hand against the sob rising in her chest. The sweet balm of the possibility chased away the shadows. "Let me know if there's anything else I can do." She rolled her lips in tightly as tears threatened. "And how things go."

"I will."

"Thank you." She hung up and drew a deep breath, then turned to Shelly and Brett. "The transplant's on. Morgan matched."

They both congratulated her and asked more questions than she could answer. Morgan would have the answers. Doubtless he'd been given all the details he'd need in order to go forward, to help their daughter, to save her life. Jill played the last hand without thinking and ended up with all but two of the points, but she didn't care.

Kelsey was going to be all right. After Shelly and Brett went home, she took out her Bible and read the Psalms. *Praise be to the Lord, for he has heard my cry for mercy. The Lord is my strength and my shield; my heart trusts in him, and I am helped. My heart leaps for joy and I will give thanks to him in song.* Peace filled her. She felt closer to His love than she ever had. Sweet consolation. Had she ever known it so completely before?

She went to bed, knowing she would sleep better than she had been. She dropped off right away, but there was pain, tight wrenching pain that seized her belly from the sides and across her lower back, then funneled up the front in mounting intensity. Push. She had to push. Sweat ran into her eyes and her mouth was arid. Push! She cried out and someone told her not to. Direct the pain, make it work for you.

Her belly seized, a swollen mound, glistening with sweat. Push! Without her will, her belly pushed. The baby emerged, streaked and creamy, into hands that glowed with golden light. Too bright. The hands were too bright.

Those hands took the baby from her womb into their grasp, stilling the cries and jerking limbs. Jill reached, but both baby and hands were gone. She woke, gasping, and stared around her in the darkness as though she might find them there. She closed her eyes and pressed a hand to her racing heart. She'd dreamed of Kelsey's birth before, but never like that.

She rubbed a hand over her eyes and settled back down, the image of those glowing hands still in her mind.

———————

Kelsey lay in the bed at the Yale New Haven Treatment Center, her second night in that medical center. Dad had gone to grab them some cafeteria food and Mom to call Jill. Mom didn't seem to mind talking to Jill. She was part of it all. She'd made it happen. No one else would have known to find Morgan. *Morgan.*

Kelsey touched the Hickman catheter in her chest, used to administer the chemotherapy that had achieved her remission and would receive the new doses to wipe out her immune system. After radiation and the killing drugs, it would be the channel to receive the bone marrow from her father, her biological father. Why did she keep thinking about him? What was he like; how did he look? Wasn't it normal to wonder?

She had to be careful, though. Mom and Dad were touchy about it. Didn't they know her wondering didn't change her love for them? She just wanted to understand. Had he cared about Jill? About her? Did he do this transplant out of guilt, or did he really want to help? Jill had said he wanted to see her.

Why would he want to see her? She was ugly, bald, pale, and bruised. Who would want to see her? Who would ever look at her and think she was anything but a cancer patient? Certainly no boy. No man would want to marry her someday. But her bio-dad? Would he look away, embarrassed by her?

Jill hadn't, but that was different. Jill was . . . a mom. No, that presupposed that dads were less accepting, and she knew that wasn't true. Kelsey shook her head. She wasn't sure why she doubted Morgan. Maybe because he hadn't married Jill, hadn't taken care of her when she needed it. Jill said it was her parents' fault, but Kelsey wasn't sure she believed that. Anyway, she couldn't risk it. Jill worked with kids who had problems. She was used to it. Morgan wouldn't be. No, the one-year rule of no contact was a good idea. At this point he might take one look and decide to keep his marrow to himself.

If she was still alive in a year, maybe then. When she had hair. Waves of nausea rose inside from the first treatment she'd had that day. And it would only get worse. Was it even worth it? She closed her eyes and pictured her army of dispirited angels looking to her for their strength.

"I don't have any," she said to the darkness, then realized others were fighting for her, as well. The nurse who'd been so funny earlier, the oncologist and all the staff. Even her bio-dad, who was scheduled for the marrow harvest. She couldn't give up now. Everyone expected her to fight, to stay positive, to be hopeful, the giver of hope on her Web page, the sharer of Jesus' love. But it was so hard.

She thought for a minute, then turned on the tiny reading lamp beside her bed and opened her laptop. Instead of going to the Web page, she opened e-mail. She had some new messages from her friends, but she clicked "Write" instead. Maybe she shouldn't do this, but there was one person who had promised to be honest. Maybe she could be honest back, too.

Hi, Jill. I hope you don't mind that I got your e-mail address off the card you gave Mom. It's late here; I guess it is there, too. Maybe you won't get this until tomorrow, but I wanted to talk, to tell you . . . Kelsey paused. No, this was her chance to say what she couldn't say out loud, couldn't tell Mom and Dad, who loved her too much. *I wanted to tell you I'm scared. I know you'll understand, cuz you must have been, too. When you had me. Did it hurt very much? Who was with you? Did you get to see me?* She hadn't intended to ask about that, but it took her mind off the rest. *What was it like when I was inside you? Did you hate me very much? Were you sad I was there?*

She almost erased that part, but no. This was her place to be honest, to write whatever she wanted. If Jill didn't answer, she'd understand. It still helped to write it, just to get the thoughts out. *I'm really sick right now. All I think about is throwing up. Were you sick with me? Then you know how I feel. Not like I have the flu and will get better in the morning. It goes on and on. I try not to show it because Mom and Dad get so sad. It hurts them when I hurt. They feel it, too. I was hoping I could just tell you about it sometimes.*

I have this army inside me, fighting to make me well. But when I feel like this, it's hard to believe that will ever happen. My roommate is scared because her cancer went into her brain. I don't think I could stand that. I feel selfish for dreading the cells in my spinal cord. But soon they'll be wiped out, and then Morgan's marrow will start making me well. I wish you could tell me more about him. I keep wondering. Especially now since I might never turn eighteen. That's when Mom said I could make a decision on finding him or not. I think I might die without seeing him.

Again Kelsey paused. *I shouldn't say that, I guess. It discourages the angels inside. I should explain that. I imagine the chemo and radiation and my own good cells are an angel army fighting the bad demon leukemia cells. When I get discouraged, my army falls back, the others start to win. Prayer helps. When I ask Jesus, He sends new troops. I should ask Jesus now because I really, really feel sick. Thanks for listening. Bye now. Kelsey*

She closed her eyes and prayed, *Jesus, help me,* then gathered her will and told the angel host to go kick butt, a phrase Mom would not approve of but which seemed somehow completely appropriate. And she went on to imagine them doing just that—bright, glowing feet booting the black demon host right out of her body.

———

Morgan walked up to the cabin door and knocked. The sky spread out above him in blazing color, a gaudy display that would fade soon, and then show off again in starlit splendor, but he'd made his decision and meant to act on it. His stomach was full of Marta's great meal, and he really could drive through the night better than he'd be able to sleep, now that his mind was made up.

Stan opened the door but didn't speak.

"I need to apologize, Stan. I put you in a bad spot."

The corners of Stan's mouth rose slightly. "I'm sure that wasn't your intention."

"Doesn't clear it up for you, though."

He shrugged. "I'll pray for wisdom."

Meanwhile Todd might blow the place up. "May I talk to Todd a moment? Is he up?"

Stan turned. "Todd, Morgan wants you."

Todd came from the back bedroom with a T-shirt in his hand and wearing sweats hung low enough to show half his boxers. "Yeah?" He looked sullen and angry.

"Can we talk a minute?"

Todd glared at Stan, but the other man didn't leave. Probably wise.

Morgan rested a shoulder on the doorjamb. He didn't really care if

Stan was included. "Two things. I didn't use good judgment in making you that offer. Learning to read better would be a good choice, but that's between you and Stan. I'll leave the TV at the big house. He can determine if you should watch it sometimes."

Todd's eyes blazed. "You can't just take it away."

Morgan smiled. "Then make your case with Stan. But do it right."

The slow boil that followed was probably worse than the kid's usual kicking and swearing.

"The second thing is, I wanted to say good-bye."

"You're leaving? Now?" Todd glanced out at the moonlit yard.

Morgan nodded.

"You just got here."

"There's something I have to do."

"What?" Todd shot the word like a missile. What could Morgan possibly have to do that was more important than hanging out with him?

"My daughter's sick. I want to see her before she has a serious procedure."

Todd gaped with no subtlety whatever. "You've got a kid?"

Stan looked surprised, as well. So Rick had kept that confidence. Now was not the time to go into it.

"Good-bye, Todd."

Todd turned without a word, stalked back into the bedroom, and closed the door.

Stan ran a hand over his hair. "That's the looks of it, these days." At least he didn't ask about Kelsey, no doubt reading the subject-closed body language.

Morgan held out his hand. "Good luck, Stan."

Stan shook it. "Are you coming back?"

"I don't think so."

"Well, it's been nice getting to know you. And thanks for everything. He might not show it, but it mattered to Todd, the time you spent and all." Stan scratched the back of his neck. "I'll pray for your daughter."

Morgan turned from the door. "Thanks." He went out and crossed the yard to his Thunderbird. He'd already told Rick, Noelle, and Marta good-bye, and there was nothing now to do but to climb into the Thunderbird and go. He opened the door and caught a motion from the corner of his eye.

Todd tore across the yard and rammed both hands against the car door, slamming it hard. Then he kicked it again and again until Morgan snatched him up and pulled him away. Todd turned his fists on him, shouting every vulgarity. Morgan caught his arms and pinned them at his sides, then pulled the boy tightly into his arms.

"I hate you! I hate you!"

Morgan held him. Another string of profanity. Morgan kept his arms around him. Todd pressed his fists into Morgan's abdomen and started to cry. He let the boy cry. So much anger and hurt had to come out some way. After a while, Todd swiped his arm under his nose, bunched his shirt, and rubbed it against his face.

Morgan held his shoulder. "You all right?"

Todd pulled away. "Yeah."

Morgan reached into his pocket, handed Todd his card. He had intended to give it to him at the cabin, if Todd hadn't walked away before he could. "This has my cell phone and e-mail."

Todd looked at the card.

"If you want to talk, you've got your choices."

Todd looked up at him.

Morgan smiled. "You're a good kid, Todd. Give Stan a chance."

Todd stood there as Morgan climbed into the Thunderbird and started the engine. He raised a hand, and Todd did also, holding on to the card. Morgan smiled. "Be good."

"You too."

Morgan laughed. "Okay." He backed out and drove down the gravel drive, settling in for the long haul. He cranked his tunes and tipped his head back. Another beautiful night in the Rocky Mountains, but he'd be leaving all that behind.

Jill climbed out of the shower and toweled dry. She had run earlier than usual, troubled by Cinda's phone call. Yes, the promise was overwhelming to have Morgan match, to be going forward with the only lifesaving option for Kelsey. But Cinda's other comment hung heavily this morning. *"I couldn't bear to refuse Kelsey a treatment simply because we couldn't pay."*

Through all this Jill had never thought of the expense. How could money be attached to life and death? Last night she'd felt peace, believing in the Lord's goodness. Yes, as Cinda said, He would provide, just as He had allowed Morgan to match, at least closely enough to go forward.

But the Lord helped those who helped themselves, and her thoughts now were on funds. What could she do to help? It must be bad if Cinda mentioned it to her. Jill went into the bedroom and dressed in blue shorts and a yellow shirt. She shook her hair, spritzed it with a light mousse, and now could let it air dry.

The sun had just risen and cast the room in pearly tones. She sat down at her desk and booted up her old computer. One of these days she'd update, but for now it worked for searching the Web and keeping her prayer journal. She started to open that document but saw she had mail and went there first.

A message from Kelsey. Jill opened it at once and read with surprise, heartache, and joy. Kelsey trusted her with her fears. She had turned to her with the thoughts she could share nowhere else. Though it broke her heart to read it, Jill exulted. There still was something she could do for her little girl. *Hi, Kelsey. I'm so glad you wrote.* She went on to answer her daughter's questions. Yes, she had been sick and afraid but never hated the baby inside her. *There were times I wished it hadn't happened. I'm sure you know how that is. But when I held you the first time—the only time—I was so glad you were in the world, even though I wouldn't get to know you. You were special even then.*

She told her about Morgan's playing football and running track, how he beat her in a sprint, but she could outrun him in a long race. She told her how smart he'd been without trying, but how it annoyed him that she'd been accelerated a full year and could still keep up academically. She had teased him with that. Then she thanked Kelsey for being honest about her fears and illness. *You can tell me anything, Kelsey, and don't worry how it sounds. I'll understand. I'm praying right now for lots and lots of angels to fight your battle. Hang in there. Jill*

She went into her prayer journal and thanked God for the opportunity she'd just had. She asked Him to keep that channel open as long as Kelsey needed it. She prayed for strength and courage for her daughter, and for the family's finances. She read her devotional section for the day and journaled about it. Then she closed down the computer and was just standing up when the doorbell rang.

She glanced at the clock. 7:05? It had to be Dan, though they hadn't spoken since her invitation for him to leave.

Rascal rushed past her, whisking his tail against her legs like a feather duster. He always pretended to race her to the door, but when he came to it, he shrank back as though the great outdoors might reach in and swallow him up. She nudged him aside and peered into the peephole, then caught herself against the door. Now she knew how it felt. Her lungs squeezed and her hand trembled as she opened the door.

"Morgan . . ."

He shot her a smug smile. "Surprise."

She'd had a reason to spring herself on him. Why would he possibly be reversing the shock? "What are you . . ."

"The cross-match was negative."

"I know."

"We're doing the transplant."

She nodded. "Cinda told me. I'm so glad, Morgan." But didn't he have to be somewhere else to do it?

He raked her with his gaze, his eyes cobalt shards, hard and dangerous. A flush burned up her neck. She glanced at his white Thunderbird glinting in the parking space across from her door. If that didn't draw her nosy neighbor's attention she couldn't guess what would. "Morgan, what do you—"

"Want?" He caught her waist and drew her onto the stoop. "What do you think?"

She had to tip her head to look at him. What was he doing? Why was he there?

He caught her shoulders and pressed her against the doorjamb, staring at her lips until she started to shake. Then he met her eyes and said, "I want to see my daughter."

Her breath escaped in a rush. "You can't. They've transferred her to Yale, preparing for the transplant."

He frowned. "When?"

Jill shook her head. "I just heard last night. They've started conditioning. Only her family can be there."

"Her family. Does being her father count?" His tone was cold and clipped.

She turned her head to the side, but he caught her chin and turned it back. "Is that family enough, Jill?"

"Morgan. I can't see her, either."

He stared at her hard and clearly skeptical. "Really."

"Why would I lie?" Even as she said it, she knew what he was thinking.

"Why indeed."

She dropped her gaze, not wanting him to have the upper hand, leverage against her. He was too unpredictable, too different from the laughing boy she'd known.

"I know you're angry and frustrated, but I can't change anything. I'm doing the best I can with all of this, as I've tried to from the start."

His eyes were acetylene torches. "Honesty from the start might have helped, instead of letting me believe the worst."

Indignation rose up. "You believed it easily enough. Didn't you remember how hard I cried when we first discussed abortion?"

His hand tightened on her arm. "You suggested it, not me."

"I asked if that was what you wanted. I had to know."

"I told you no."

She closed her eyes, held them a moment, then faced him again. "I didn't know my dad was going to tell you that. They wanted a clean break, nothing you could use to . . ."

"What?"

"Stay involved."

His grip loosened, but he didn't release her. "And it never—" He stopped at the sound of an engine and flashing lights behind him. She looked past him to the police cruiser pulling to a stop behind Morgan's car. Brett and Dan climbed out, eyeing them.

Morgan turned, obviously surprised to see the cops. "Is there something I should know?"

Watching Brett and Dan, she felt more awkward than she could ever remember. Why were they staring so menacingly?

"Step back—slowly," Brett said, and Dan rested his hand on his gun.

What on earth?

Morgan let go of her. "This is better than the last time."

Jill stepped off the porch. "Brett—"

"Over here, Jill." Dan motioned her.

This was not how she'd imagined their next conversation. Was this some macho jealousy thing? Had he lost his mind and brought Brett along? She went down the three stairs and the length of the walk. "What are you doing?"

Dan kept his eyes on Morgan but answered, "Your neighbor called in an assault."

She looked from his face to the townhouse across the parking lot. She didn't have to ask which neighbor. She let out a sharp breath. "That's a mistake. You know Mr. Deerborne." She glanced back at Morgan, standing by the door with a wry look. Could their interaction have looked like assault? She pressed her palm to her face, embarrass-ment washing over in waves.

Dan let go of his gun and jutted his chin toward Morgan with the force of his ire. "You know him?"

She nodded, seeing the suspicion of Morgan's identity dawn in the narrowing of his eyes, the clench of his jaw. He wanted to say more, ask more, but kept his mouth shut. After a moment, he circled back around the cruiser and climbed into the driver's seat. They must still have been at Brett's to get over there so quickly. They probably had yet to go in to the station. And Deerborne would have called Brett directly, as usual.

Brett looked from her to Morgan and back. "So you're all right?"

She nodded. It wasn't police protection she needed. She glanced at the opposite townhouse, where the old man was probably pressed to the window, though the daylight reflection kept him hidden. Anyone who thought women had the market on nosiness and gossip had never met Mr. Deerborne. He made a habit of calling Brett at home over the smallest things, but he'd never called the police on *her* before.

As the cruiser pulled away, she joined Morgan back on the porch.

"Very interesting." Morgan settled his back against the wall and crossed his bare ankles. His legs beneath the navy shorts were tan and muscled.

Jill shoved her fingers into her hair. "Come inside. I'll explain." The sooner they were out of Mr. Deerborne's view, the better.

She led Morgan to the kitchen and poured two glasses of cranberry juice.

He picked his up and studied it. "This the strongest thing you have?"

"What . . . else . . ."

"Coffee? I've been driving all night."

He'd driven all night and still looked that good? "I might have some instant."

He winced. "That's all right." He drained the juice glass.

Jill took a gulp of hers, absorbing the tang. The way her head spun already, any caffeine would put her over the edge. She needed to stay calm, get calm.

"So are you going to tell me why Beauview's best are guarding your door?" He raised his eyebrows.

"Brett's my neighbor." She waved toward the townhouse outside the patio door. Then she pointed toward the front window. "And my other neighbor, Mr. Deerborne, is the self-established watchdog." She drained her juice glass. "Do you want something to eat? I baked scones yesterday, lemon pecan." She was babbling.

"Okay. But I've got to have some coffee, real coffee. I passed a Starbucks back in the strip mall." He pulled his keys from his pocket. "There won't be a SWAT team waiting when I get back. . . ."

She smiled, almost able to find it funny, and shook her head. "I'll let the National Guard know you're cleared."

"Yuh." He went out, and for a moment she wondered if she'd dreamed the whole thing. She leaned on the counter, staring at the door he'd left slightly ajar. His car pulled out from the lot, and she drew a cleansing breath. She had to pull herself together.

She poured another swallow and drank it, just tart enough to tighten the tissues of her mouth, leaving it refreshed and invigorated. In her mind, juice beat coffee any day. She carried both glasses to the sink and washed them up. Then with a damp cloth, she wiped her clean counters and swept a few cat hairs from the floor.

Scones. Why had she offered him scones? If he'd driven all night, he probably wanted something hearty like steak and eggs. What was she thinking? She couldn't cook for Morgan as though he were . . . someone in her life. Even if she'd had eggs or steak.

Pull yourself together. He'd come to see Kelsey, and once he realized that was impossible, he'd go away. A scone was sufficient to show hospitality. She jumped at the tap on the glass and turned to see Shelly standing on the patio. Jill hurried over and let her in. "What are you doing up so early?"

"Deerborne's call woke me." Shelly shoved her glasses up her nose. She only wore them upon waking and at night after removing her contacts. She looked around. "Doesn't look like an emergency. You're alive anyway. Did Brett come over?"

"Brett and Dan both." She pictured Dan's face fixed on Morgan.

"What happened?"

"Our favorite paranoid overreacting."

"To what?"

Jill moistened her lips. "Shelly, Morgan's here."

Shelly's eyes darted.

"He's not here this minute. He went for coffee. But he drove all night and just showed up."

"Morgan Spencer. *The?*"

"Yes, Shelly. *The.*"

Shelly plopped her hands on her hips. "Did Dan see him?"

"Oh yes." Jill pictured the scene exactly as Dan must have seen it, pulling into the parking lot and up to her door.

"So tell me everything."

Jill sighed. "He wants to see Kelsey. I guess he thought I could arrange it."

"Can you?"

Jill shook her head. "She's at the treatment center in Connecticut. Even if she were in Des Moines, the family would have to want it. And they don't."

The Thunderbird's engine sounded outside and Jill braced herself. A minute later, Morgan tapped a knuckle to the door and pushed it open. Shelly gasped. Morgan had that effect.

16

M organ took in Jill and the other woman with a casual glance. So she'd called in reinforcements. He closed the door and joined them at the counter, setting down his double espresso. Normally he liked the morning blend, but this morning a direct infusion to the bloodstream seemed in order.

"Morgan, this is Shelly, my neighbor and best friend, and the wife of one of the officers who came earlier. Shelly, Morgan Spencer." She obviously had no terms to describe him. Understandable. He hadn't even introduced her to Noelle when she came to the ranch.

He squeezed Shelly's hand with a smile. "Hi." He could sense Jill's nerves like a leftover odor filling the kitchen. Had she run for her friend before he'd cleared the lot? He reached for his coffee and slurped it softly. Man, he needed that. The half he'd downed driving back was only now clearing the fog.

"Well, I guess I'll . . ." Shelly headed toward the patio door.

Morgan raised his cup. "You don't have to go on my account." Especially if Jill needed the buffer.

Shelly caught the door handle. "You two probably want to talk."

He glanced at Jill. Did she? What would they have to say? But Shelly closed the door behind her with a wave, then started across the yard. Morgan watched her go into the opposite patio door, then turned back. Jill's hair was drying into that careless mop that was surprisingly alluring, saucy, and vulnerable at once.

She smelled faintly of apples, and he guessed her shampoo. No other fragrance covered it. It seemed an appropriate Iowa girl scent. Jill took out a Ziploc bag of scones from the refrigerator. "I'll just warm them." She took down two salmon-colored plates and put the scones into the microwave. Soon their aroma covered hers. He was not much on breakfast, especially this early, but without sleep something in his stomach would be good.

He leaned his elbows on the counter. "Seems I'll have to guess."

She turned to him. "Guess?"

"The one giving orders was Shelly's husband. The other one . . ." He watched her color rise. He'd guessed correctly. "You should have told me your boyfriend might shoot."

"He's not. Anymore."

Morgan took a swig of espresso. "Ah, another pawn sacrificed."

She opened the door and checked the scones, then set them to heat again. "My neighbor has an overactive thyroid, and way too much time on his hands. He calls Brett over any disturbance and imagines threats in every shadow."

Threat, disturbance. Telling words. Morgan eyed her. He wanted access to his daughter, and Jill was the key to that. He'd have to play nice.

She pulled open the microwave and handed him a scone on a plate. "Butter?"

"This is fine." He doubted he would even taste it.

She took her plate to one end of the counter and sat down. He took a bite. The scone sent a burst of sweet lemon into his mouth, a pleasant surprise.

"They seemed to take this call seriously." He caught a crumb from the corner of his mouth, picturing her muscle-bound cop, another jilted suitor. She'd made it an art. But it didn't matter. Morgan swallowed the bite. She'd sent him a "Dear John" no imbecile could ignore, and he wasn't there about her. Kelsey was the part of his life he wanted reattached. Not permanently, certainly nothing detrimental to the girl, just the certainty that she actually existed, hadn't lost her life as he'd imagined too clearly.

The match in their haplotypes was proof enough, but it wasn't tangible. He needed to lay the ghost to rest before he could move on. And only seeing his flesh-and-blood daughter would accomplish that. But it was complicated if they had already moved her to Yale for conditioning. He knew what that entailed and doubted they would admit him—assuming it was true that she was there at all.

He only had Jill's word for it. He knew better than to believe her without checking it out for himself. So the best thing was to continue with his plan. "What are you doing today?"

"I'm tutoring."

"Find someone to cover you."

"What?" She set down her untouched scone.

"We're going to Des Moines. To see Kelsey."

Jill pressed fingers to her temple. "Morgan, she isn't there."

"We'll see." He did not want to be ugly, but the tightness of his stomach betrayed how much he needed her to agree.

She stared down at her scone, one edge of the glaze melted to a sheen. She had to know he couldn't trust her, had not driven all that way simply to give up on her word alone. He would see his daughter, one way or another.

Jill spread her hands. "Okay. I'll call the Bensons and see—"

Morgan shook his head. "I'd rather talk to them in person."

"They won't be there."

He sipped the espresso. "Ready?"

Jill let out a breath. "Don't you need to sleep first? It's over an hour's drive."

He ought to, but that might give her the chance to back out. He tapped the paper cup. "This'll do the trick."

"It'll take me a minute to arrange things."

"Fine." He nibbled at his scone while she made her phone call and gave instructions. She sounded professional and concerned, but not overly tense. That probably meant she was telling the truth, but he was not ready to concede.

"I've had a situation come up that I have to see to," was all she told the substitute. Cool. Very cool. She'd learned to hide well.

Jill hung up and cleared their scones, then accepted the inevitable. She slipped on a pair of white leather sandals, the sort that went between the first two toes with slender straps to the sides, and caught Morgan's look. He'd always said she had great feet, the toes aligned in a sloping arch, neither blunt nor overlong. She'd been amazed he would even notice her feet when the other guys were absorbed only with other anatomy.

She slipped her purse over her shoulder and locked the door

behind them. What was she doing? Proving her honesty? They would drive to Des Moines and see that she had told him the truth. It was a waste of time, gas, and energy, and she was letting her kids down to do it. Why? Because Morgan cocked his finger? That rankled.

She stopped at the door. "Do you want me to drive?" Since he was tired . . .

A quick smile. "No." He led her to the Thunderbird retro convertible that looked no more than a few hours old. It was a great car, though hardly the macho machine most thirty-something men would choose. But then, Morgan wasn't most men. He'd always had an eclectic bent, much broader in his tastes than other guys. Even in high school he had appreciated museums and art galleries and theaters.

"Do you like it?" He held the door for her to climb in.

She got in and ran her hand over the red leather seat. "It's really nice."

He got in and made sure she was buckled, then gripped the red enamel stick shift and put it into reverse. The moment he set the car in motion, she knew why he'd chosen it. Its ride was amazing, and Morgan liked comfort. That was another thing she remembered, and she laughed at the thought.

He turned. "What?"

She hadn't meant to share it, but she told him anyway. "I was just remembering the first time I went to your parents' ranch. Hank was teaching Rick to break that colt."

Morgan drew his brows together, searching for the memory and probably wondering what it had to do with anything.

"I asked if you were going to take a turn, and you said you were the only man in the family with nerve endings."

Morgan glanced sidelong. "It's true. Rick still spends half his life getting tossed to the dirt. And he hasn't the sense to stay there." He returned his gaze to the road. "Me, I'll take a hot tub and a flute of champagne."

She smiled. Yet he'd played a terrific wide receiver and taken the tackles without complaint. His speed had protected him, but he never had the size to take it past high school, or so she assumed. His physique now did not display laxity, yet neither was there brawny bulk. He might work at fitness, but she guessed not with the fervor Dan employed. And mostly it was genetics anyway. Both his parents had been slender, as were hers, which gave Kelsey her willowy frame.

Jill fixed her mind on the image of her daughter and realized

Morgan had no image of his own. Her throat tightened. That didn't seem right. Why would the Bensons let *her* in but not Morgan? Maybe it was just the timing. Or the fact that they'd never met him in the first place. Their only contact had been with her, however brief. Morgan was never in the picture at all.

But he was now. And he wanted to see Kelsey. Why? He could anonymously donate his marrow and go on with his life. Why was he making this a crusade? Her tension notched up higher. What would happen after he saw that Kelsey was not in Des Moines? Did he expect to find her in New Haven?

A turtle on the side of the road recalled to her the scene she'd witnessed, was it only weeks ago? She told Morgan about it.

"Had it rained a lot?"

She nodded. "It was really wet for a couple weeks."

"They were probably seeking higher ground. The road would be a haven from the flooded field."

She hadn't even thought of that, but it was so obvious. Her ideas of exodus and crossings seemed silly next to his pragmatic explanation. It also meant the creatures probably turned around and climbed back up after their rescuers left the scene. She sighed. What an image of fallen creation.

Nothing else to say came easily to mind, so she watched out the window in silence. Morgan drained the last of his coffee and replaced the empty cup in the holder, then draped his wrist over the steering wheel. She wanted to ask what he'd done all these years, how he'd done so well. Would he find it awkward to answer? To talk about his life?

"What is it you tutor?" Morgan's question caught her thoughts up short.

So it was her life they'd discuss. "It's actually an extended school-year program, for kids who need a continuum. I teach special ed."

"You always wanted to."

"Well, first I wanted to be an arctic explorer. The polar bears looked so cuddly."

Morgan slanted her a look.

"But you're right, by high school I was pretty settled on working with learning-challenged kids." She bit her lip. "I hope they'll be okay with Pam."

"I'm sure you can take a day off now and then."

She shook her head. "Even though it's basically playgroup in the summer, maintaining skills and interaction, any disruption in routine throws the kids off."

"Does Kelsey know about me? That I'm her donor?" He slid it in so smoothly it had to have been planned. Get her loosened up and talking, then hit her with the real questions.

Jill licked her lips, the air rushing past, stealing the moisture from her tongue. At least she could give him that answer. "They didn't tell her, but she guessed. She knows her stuff, all about the protocols for this type of transplant. She knew they wouldn't use a single haplotype unrelated donor. She had already guessed my relationship, so that meant the new donor must be you."

"So it won't be any surprise for her to see me at her door."

Oh, it would be a surprise, and not one Cinda or Roger would appreciate. That they weren't home was the only reason Jill had agreed. "She isn't there, Morgan." How many times would she have to say it?

"How's Kenny?" Did he mean to keep her jumping from subject to subject? Now it was her brother. What next?

"He's in Pensacola, pastoring a church. No one calls him Kenny anymore. Actually, I haven't spoken to him in a couple years."

"Why not?"

Because he's ashamed of me. She had embarrassed him at the time he was developing his theology. "We don't have much in common. I send birthday cards to his kids." She pulled a windblown strand of hair from her eye and groped for a change of subject. "I guess you see a lot of Rick."

"I make it out there a few times a year."

"From California?"

He nodded.

"How did you end up out there?"

"Silicon Valley."

"You're in computers?" She could not see him as a geek.

He shook his head. "I graduated Wharton, put in some years as a corporate finance officer for a few tony companies, then decided that was limiting and went into turnaround management. The first companies I worked with were in Silicon Valley. One had super potential and poor vision. They were about to crash before ever getting off the ground with a great idea. I saw what was needed, accepted stock as payment, then propelled it to greatness, reaping my share of fortune and fame."

He'd said it tongue in cheek, but it had to be fairly accurate by the other clues she'd already seen of his success. That potential had been recognized early by the National Honor Society and plenty of scholarship programs. She was glad he'd actualized it. Then it hit her that he couldn't have if she'd been there like a ball and chain with a newborn daughter in tow. Her disappearance was the best thing to happen to him. She looked out the side at the farms they passed.

As they entered Des Moines, she directed him to Kelsey's house, and he parked in the driveway, no doubt leery of leaving his car on the street with the more well-used vehicles. He got out and came around for her. How long had it been since she waited for someone to let her out of a car? Yet she'd instinctively remembered Morgan's training.

He had explained to her on their first date that it had nothing to do with her inability to open the door for herself, but that anyone with class wouldn't expect her to. She got out now and led the way to the door while he alarmed the car. He needn't have bothered. In two minutes they'd be climbing back inside.

Jill knocked at Kelsey's door, expecting a lull, then a second knock, proof to Morgan that the Bensons were not in Des Moines. She startled when the door was opened by a young woman, maybe nineteen or twenty years old, with thin brown hair and a triangular mouth that lengthened its base when she smiled. "Hi. Stuff for the fund-raiser?"

Momentarily confused, Jill shook her head. "No."

Morgan came up close behind her.

The girl flashed a smile. "Oh, I'm sorry. I've had people coming all day to bring stuff for the yard sale. It was in the newspaper."

Jill glanced behind the young woman into the house. Were the Bensons there after all? "Is the sale for Kelsey?"

She nodded. "To help with medical costs." There it was again, the financial reality that the fight was not in Kelsey's body alone. Jill wished she had brought something for the sale.

"It's this weekend, if you want to come."

"I live in Beauview. I, we"—she motioned to Morgan—"came to see Kelsey."

"She's not here. They transferred her to Yale New Haven."

Jill glanced at Morgan. Now would he believe her?

The young woman turned to him. "I'm Rebecca. I'm house-sitting while they're gone and collecting the stuff for the youth group fund-raiser."

"Can you tell us about it?" His voice was low and tight.

"Sure. Would you like to come in? I made sun tea this morning."

There was no point if Kelsey wasn't there. But Morgan returned Rebecca's smile and said, "Tea sounds good."

Did he think he could search the house if he just got inside? Jill followed Rebecca inside with Morgan behind her. Maybe he hoped to grill this girl about his daughter. But he stopped at the photo wall in the living room and looked at the portraits. Kelsey's was not updated. She had hair, light blond hair. The other two showed her even younger with Cinda and Roger. Jill watched his face. What was he thinking?

Rebecca came back with two glasses of tea. "I'm sorry you drove all the way out here for nothing. Would you like to sit?" She offered two chairs in the living room.

Jill glanced at Morgan. It wasn't for nothing. Now he knew she had told him the truth. They took the chairs and she held out her hand. "I'm Jill, by the way. Jill Runyan."

Rebecca smiled. "I guessed that, when you said you'd come up from Beauview."

She had?

"Cinda is my mentor. We're pretty close. She mentioned you, and you look a lot like Kelsey."

Jill drank the icy tea and glanced at Morgan. Would Rebecca notice his eyes were Kelsey's? He could introduce himself if he wanted to, though she hoped word wouldn't get back to the Bensons that he'd been there.

He said, "Is the yard sale the only thing going for medical costs?"

"Right now." Rebecca pulled out a card and handed it over. "This is Kelsey's emergency fund account. We've had donations, but not nearly enough. We're trying everything we can think of to reach the goal: garage sales, bake sales, even boxes with Kelsey's photo in the grocery stores."

Cinda's financial concerns were real. For the first time in her life, Jill wished she were rich. What could she do? Take a summer job in addition to tutoring? But that would take too long, even if she found extra employment. Sell her townhouse? With the financing she'd found, she spent less on it than she would renting, and she had to live somewhere.

Rebecca sighed. "It's just incredible how much her treatment costs, especially the transplant. It's cutting-edge medicine, the only chance she has. But there's less than a week until it's scheduled and . . . well, we're praying for a miracle."

Morgan's eyes narrowed. "What do you mean?"

"The treatment has to be paid for by the time of service. Roger has tried to find loans, but they already have a second on their house and debts from the previous treatments. So far they haven't found a lender." She spread her hands.

Jill opened her mouth to confirm the awful understanding that was forming in her mind: Kelsey wouldn't get the transplant? The thought was so staggering she couldn't make a sound. She *would* sell her town-house, her car, anything.

"What does he do?" Morgan asked softly.

"Contracting. Drywall. He works hard. It's just when you're self-employed, you don't get, like, the greatest insurance."

Jill sensed Morgan's tension. *Please don't make a scene.* The Bensons were obviously doing the best they could.

He pocketed the card Rebecca had handed him. "Thanks."

Jill moistened her lips. "How is Kelsey?"

Rebecca shook her head. "I haven't heard for the last couple days, but she has so much spirit. Nothing has mobilized our youth group like her sickness. Everyone wants to help Kelsey. It's just hard to do enough."

Jill stood up. "Well, thank you for filling us in. I'll do what I can." Her heart rushed. What a stupid platitude. What else did she have? There was nothing superfluous in her life. Oh, maybe her bike and a few pieces of clothing. What good was that?

Rebecca picked up the tea glasses. "Help pray for the miracle. That's the best thing."

Jill smiled. "I will." A miracle. Did she believe God could work in a big way? Did Morgan? She had no idea where he stood with God. Would he pray for—her breath caught suddenly. Morgan. Could he do more than pray?

They went out to the car, and by the stiff hand on her back, she gauged his still heightened tension. But Morgan didn't speak as he pulled out of the driveway and started back the way they'd come. He could at least acknowledge that she *had* told the truth. That would give her the courage to broach the other subject. What was she think-ing? She'd already braved the lion for Kelsey. She'd jump into his jaws if . . .

She drew herself up. "Morgan—"

"I'll do what I can." He didn't look at her, just gripped the wheel and muttered, "Drywall."

It wasn't a question, so she didn't answer. He had already told her he would do whatever it took. He must be in a better position than the rest of them financially. He'd said as much on their drive over. She'd seen his toys. Her heart thumped with expectation. Maybe that was the real reason they'd made this drive, for Morgan to see his child's picture, to hear for himself how great her need was. Maybe the Lord had put him at her door that morning to begin the miracle Kelsey's friends prayed for.

Her spirit swelled with expectation. *Oh, Jesus.* All the pieces could come together according to the Lord's perfect plan. She had to trust. She bit her lip as Morgan reached the highway and headed back toward Beauview. She wanted to pepper him with questions, wanted certainty that he could do what he'd tersely indicated. If he did, maybe after the transplant, when Kelsey was well, Morgan could meet his daughter.

Yes. The thought warmed inside her. She would help him see Kelsey. The day was bright; the air smelled of earth and tar and new leather, and for the first time since learning about Kelsey, the dark clouds inside her lifted. It was hard to believe she was riding beside Morgan. But it had to be part of the plan, the intricate details the Lord was weaving together.

He needed sleep. He'd spent thirteen hours on the road to Beauview, four hours round trip to fetch Marta. Add to that the time on the plane to Denver and the taxi drive to the ranch. He'd had no sleep and more caffeine than even he could handle. He was getting shaky, probably a blood sugar crash. Marta's dinner last night was his last meal except for the few bites of Jill's scone. He had to get back to her place, about half an hour, he guessed, from where they were now. He could make it that far. He shook off the hypnotic effect of the road.

"Are you all right?" Jill must have noticed the wide stretching of his eyes, that last shake of the head. He'd thought she was absorbed in the landscape.

"Yeah." He switched hands on the wheel and chewed a flake of dry skin from the side of his lip, pulverizing it between his front teeth. He'd left Santa Barbara with one purpose in mind: to see Kelsey. He had tried to go through the doctors, but they told him the program required a year from the transplant date for unrelated donors, which he was considered to be, since he had no legal connection to his daughter. And they had confirmed what Jill had said—the Bensons believed it would stress Kelsey to meet him.

How would it stress her to know he cared? That elfish face in the portraits looked wiser than any of them. She might look like Jill, but he saw plenty of himself in her expression. She would handle it. It was their own position that her parents worried about. And well they should. Jill might have pawned her off, but he'd had no say in the matter. If it was legal connection they required . . .

Morgan rubbed the back of his neck. He wasn't being vindictive. It just wasn't right. None of this was right. That little girl deserved more than people dropping change into boxes with her picture. And the card in his pocket was one huge opportunity to make his point.

He pulled up in front of Jill's townhouse, new enough, nicely landscaped, each unit with a garage. That was important for a woman living alone. He got out and walked around to her door, gratified that living single hadn't made her too feminist to accept the courtesy his family had ingrained.

Jill climbed out, and he walked her to her front door, which she unlocked and pushed open.

When she hesitated, he said, "Mind if I come in awhile?"

She held the door wider. "You must be exhausted."

"I could use a rest." He yawned and followed her in, waiting while she slipped out of her sandals just inside the door and left them next to her Nikes. "Still running, eh?" And he eyed her legs, remembering them flying over the hurdles with speed and power.

She nodded.

"You excelled in that." Especially the last run right out of his life. That won her the gold medal. He settled onto the couch, every muscle crying for rest. He had one purpose in being there—Kelsey. Then he looked at Jill and stopped lying to himself. It wasn't thoughts of Kelsey that had driven him all these years. Love and pain vied like twins inside him.

"I'm sorry you didn't get to see her." She sounded sorry, and it was in her face.

"I will."

She nodded. "Maybe after the transplant, if . . . if she has it."

"She'll have it."

Relief and gratitude bloomed in her face. Didn't she realize he would have done anything for them?

"Thank you, Morgan. I wish there was something I could do."

He sat down on the couch. "Come home with me for the procedure. You can be my nurse while I'm laid up." She didn't believe him, he could tell. He wasn't sure where it had come from himself. "Wouldn't you like to be part of it?"

She searched his face.

"I'll be doped up and crippled. At least for a few days." He stretched. "And Consuela is not the kind of woman I want rubbing my back."

"Consuela?"

"My housekeeper."

She crinkled her brow and looked away. "I can't, Morgan."

"Why not?"

"I can't just pick up and leave. I have responsibilities. . . ." She spiked her fingers into her hair. "I can't."

"Consuela lives there with her brother. There's also my professional assistant, Denise. You wouldn't be alone with me."

She stood up and walked to the window, more distressed than he'd expected. "Why are you doing this?"

If she needed an answer to that . . .

She shook her head when he didn't give her one.

Fine. He was certainly not going to beg. He leaned back and closed his eyes. Bone tired. Deeper than the muscles, it went to his marrow, which he would soon be depleting for a little girl he wasn't even allowed to see. "Mind if I rest awhile?" He slipped off his loafers and stretched out on the couch. Getting prone felt great.

CHAPTER

17

Jill watched him sleep, his exhaustion apparent in the brief moment it took him to succumb. It must have been the exhaustion that prompted his invitation. Didn't he realize how painful it would be to spend time together? Yet he was doing so much, everything she had wanted to do for Kelsey. Did she owe it to him?

She pressed her hands to her face. *Lord, show me. I know you have a plan here, and I don't want to get in your way.* She'd spoiled his plans before. *Show me clearly, Lord.*

She left Morgan sleeping and went to get groceries. If he was awake at lunchtime, she'd make a crab salad. She was sure he'd be gone by supper but bought a flank steak to marinate just in case. New potatoes and scallions, canned corn for the recipe she made with cream cheese and green peppers, and fresh tomatoes from the vegetable stand ought to do it. One good meal to send him on his way. And she bought a can of coffee, even though she'd have to borrow Shelly's coffeemaker.

"Jill, how are you?"

She turned. "Oh, hi, Anita. I'm fine." She did not want to go into details with a mother of one of her students.

Anita caught her arm. "Are you? Pam indicated you had an emergency that made you step out for the summer."

For the summer? How had taking one day off turned into the whole summer? Jill hoped the principal wasn't behind that one, though she wouldn't be surprised. She'd knocked heads more than once with Ed Fogarty, and he'd take any chance to rid himself of his number one headache. "It was just today. I had something come up." Some*one* who now slept on her couch. And a sick child no one knew she had. Didn't that warrant one day?

"I was worried after we talked."

Jill's mind jumped to the last time they'd talked, when she'd confused Anita with Shelly on the phone and snapped about Dan. "That was a difficult day." She smiled. "You know what they're like."

She nodded. "Well, I'm praying for you."

"Thanks." Jill pushed her cart forward, and it hit her squarely that she needed to pray, too. Was something going on? *Lord, give me wisdom. Guide and sustain me.*

What did Anita mean, the whole summer? A misunderstanding. It had to be. But it would be just like Fogarty, who had resented her ever since their argument early in the year over the appropriateness of terminating defective life at birth. He not only disagreed with her contention that all life had value, he resented her believing it. She and Fogarty were fingernails on chalkboard.

Jill sighed. She paid for her groceries and went out to her car, steeling herself to go home. Morgan was still asleep when she went in, and Rascal had curled up at his feet. She hoped he wasn't allergic to cats, since he wore no socks and Rascal had flopped against his bare ankles in happy abandon.

She stood for a moment, overwhelmed by the fact that Morgan Spencer was stretched out on her couch with her kitty at his feet. Not that Rascal was standoffish, but just the incredible unlikelihood of Morgan's being there at all . . . She crept to the kitchen as he slept and put away the groceries as quietly as possible.

She had already straightened the kitchen, so she crept down the hall and cleaned the bathroom. The bedroom needed only a touch-up, though he would not set foot in it. At last she went back to the kitchen and put together a salad with chunks of imitation crab, butter lettuce, ranch-flavored sliced almonds, and wedges of tomato.

Should she wake him or eat by herself? She was hungry and needed fortification. She went over and touched his shoulder. "Would you like lunch, Morgan?"

Without opening his eyes, he muttered, "I'll just sleep."

She went to the counter and drizzled her portion with Greek dressing, putting aside his for later if he got hungry. She had no idea what his eating habits were. In high school they'd both been more conscientious than some, since their athletics demanded it. She recalled his eating frequently, but what teen boy didn't?

She carried her plate to the nook and sat at the small wrought-iron-and-glass table. The salad was tasty and fresh, but maybe it wouldn't have satisfied a man's appetite. Dan would wolf it down and scour the place for something he could sink his teeth into. She should have gotten meat or carbohydrates. But she'd shopped as she always did, whatever looked good at the moment.

And she'd been distracted by Anita's comment. Maybe she should call in, see how the morning session had gone. No, that was paranoid. She had a right to take a personal day if she needed to. Of course, she had taken several others when she'd been so down before. But her attendance during the school year was exemplary. It was absurd to even be concerned.

And she wouldn't be if there hadn't also been the disciplinary action for "forcing religion" on the children, as though her kids could even understand. But she'd shared with Anita how prayer calmed Joey, and Anita had felt led to pass it on to Joey's mother, Charline, who did not appreciate it.

That session with Fogarty had been especially unpleasant. His suggestion that she might do better in a Christian school, with parents who went for that, was rife with threat. Well, she hadn't opened her mouth about prayer or faith or anything since. But he knew and collected every complaint from her team and those parents who were more willing to blame their child's lack of success on her than any inborn limitations. Even some of the other teachers who didn't appreciate her insistence that they integrate the kids as well as they could. In short, it was a hostile environment, and that accounted for the tension she felt now. That and Morgan Spencer's presence.

While he slept she'd just run by the school and see how things were going. That should alleviate at least that factor. She gathered her purse quietly, slipped back into her sandals, and went out. The school wasn't far, and she pulled into the lot, noting the cars parked there, Fogarty's especially.

She went inside and started for the special ed room, but he called to her from his office. This was not good. Had her apprehension been founded? She joined him at his desk.

"I thought you were sick."

"No. I had a personal situation I needed to handle."

He nodded. "Have a seat." His neck had that red turkey skin one expected on a farmer, not a school administrator. His eyes were limpid green under albinolike brows. He cut to the chase. "I've made my decision for next year. I've offered Pam the coordinator position."

Jill stared at him. Though she was permanent to the district, the team leader and coordinator positions could be shifted by the board or administration each year—if warranted. Usually that depended on competence, but she'd done everything she could with her program, and a cold steam erupted inside. "What was the basis for your decision?"

"I feel you're too confrontational with your team and the other teachers."

Confrontational? "I fight for what the kids need." And even then she was careful not to offend.

"In your opinion."

Jill fought against the overwhelming impulse to shove his desk into the circular mound of belly that looked like a seven-month gestation. "I think I've handled the position with exemplary care and thoughtfulness toward all aspects of the situation."

"I disagree." He folded his white fingers. "I've had more complaints than I've addressed."

"What more?"

He leaned forward. "Jill, I suggest you accept Pam's leadership. She has a more global view of education."

Jill swallowed hard. An understanding that matched Ed Fogarty's. This could not be happening. What had she done but pour herself out for children who needed a champion? Pam did fine. Jill would give her that. But she would not make waves, not fight for their budget, not insist the kids be integrated wherever possible.

Was it sour grapes? Fogarty had made his decision, but if there were other complaints she'd know. She did not believe for one minute he hadn't jumped on her for every one. No, he had given the position to Pam because she was an agnostic humanist with the politically correct opinion on everything.

"There's another small matter. I've heard from several sources that your personal situation seems to be distracting you. We've hired a new teacher with a degree in severe and profound handicaps, and I'd like to integrate him before the school year begins. I think it would be a good thing for you to take some time this summer to deal with your situation, and give over your extended year caseload to Don."

Jill stood up, stunned. Her legs had moved automatically. With her permanent status, Fogarty could not get rid of her directly, not without cause. But he could make her presence so pointless that she'd leave on her own. And that was exactly what he was doing. Yes, they needed another special ed teacher, but not one whose training rendered her irrelevant. He was counting on her quitting.

If it were one of the kids being wronged, she would fight, argue, plead. But she was too stunned just now for any of that. She turned and walked out, her mind scrambling. What was going on? This couldn't be happening. Those kids were her life.

Stepping into the sunlight, she pressed her hands to her face. Was it possible she had let them down, not given her all? Yes, she'd been stressed, confused, depressed. But had that affected her performance? It must have if Pam had noticed. She'd said not one word to Pam about Kelsey or any of it. Jill drew a long, slow breath. This new man, Don, might be just what they needed. With an SLIC degree he must be compassionate, dedicated. But where did that leave her? In a daze, she drove home, parked in the garage, and went inside.

Morgan still slept on the couch. His head was cradled in his arm and his mouth hung slack. He was a man, asleep in her home, as out of place as a Picasso on her walls. But was it any stranger than everything else happening to her since learning of Kelsey's illness? Her life was unraveling. Again.

Lord, please. She wasn't sure she had it in her to fight. Then she thought of Kelsey and the fight her daughter faced. This was nothing compared to that. It was hard to press on, but she had to. For Kelsey's sake. A thought shot into her mind. Was this all happening for a reason? Had God just freed her for her real purpose? That thought brought grim comfort. She hadn't meant to lose her job when she asked the Lord to show her clearly.

But was that exactly what this was? Maybe she could go with Morgan, be a part of the process. Maybe this was God's hand, not Ed Fogarty's. Though he liked to play God, Fogarty was nothing but a pawn in the bigger picture, whether he knew it or not. Jill's heart thumped erratically. She should be devastated, terrified to be losing the underpinning of her existence—not to mention the impact on her finances.

Yet relief trickled in and watered her soul. She looked at Morgan. She could stand it. They could be civil; their drive today had proved that. Maybe this was the nudge from the Lord she needed. A sharp pang stung when she thought of her kids. How would they respond to a new teacher? They would ask for her. What would they be told?

But if this was God's will, shouldn't she trust even that to Him? She pressed her hands to her face. *Lord?*

It wasn't peace exactly, but a sense of submission. If she'd been urged to fight, she would have. But that was not her leaning. She moistened her dry lips and hoped she wasn't making another mistake with her life. It was possible, given the simple fact that Morgan was involved.

Something moved against his legs, soft, yet prickly points on his skin. Morgan stirred, opened his eyes to the cat at his feet. It stretched with a raspy meow, and he noticed it was the claws of the cat's back foot in his skin. He rose up on his elbow and studied the cat, puzzled.

Jill spoke from the nook. "He's a cuddler."

Morgan stretched and stifled a yawn, maneuvering his legs from under the cat and swinging them to the floor. He held his face and his stomach growled. "Did you say something about lunch?"

"A few hours ago. It's closer to dinner now. But you could have the salad still." She got up and took a salad from the refrigerator. "Greek, or blue cheese?"

"Either." He was still foggy, but he needed food.

She set his meal on the table. He didn't get up right away but sat still, holding his head.

"Are you all right?"

He turned. "Yeah."

"I hope you like crab. I just grabbed what looked good at the store."

He pressed himself up and stretched again. "Can I wash up?"

She motioned to the kitchen sink. He went to the sink, scrubbed his hands and face, and toweled dry with her dishcloth. Jill looked dazed. She couldn't still be that disturbed by his invitation. After all, she'd started the process. He joined her at the table, studied the salad, and picked up his fork.

"If you'd rather have something else, I can—"

"This is fine."

"I know it's not awfully filling."

He glanced up, then took a bite.

"Not everyone likes butter lettuce or imitation crab. I should have thought—"

He swallowed his bite. "It's good."

She continued, "I'm marinating a steak for dinner. Do you like cheesy corn?"

What on earth had turned her into this babbling brook? He leaned back in his chair with a smirk. "Sure." So she was assuming he'd stay that long. He took another bite, unsure himself where to take it all.

"Would you like something to drink?"

"Do you have anything I'd want?"

"Just milk or juice. Or water."

"Water. Thanks."

She stood up and poured him a glass from the filtered pitcher. She set it before him and sat back down, fidgeting.

Rascal came and rubbed his legs, then went to her. She lifted the cat to her lap.

Morgan took a drink. "Does he have a name?"

"Rascal."

"Doesn't appear to have the energy to warrant that."

She snuggled Rascal under her chin. "Not since he got neutered. But as a kitten it certainly fit."

Morgan watched her, more unsure of his motives than before. What was he doing there talking about dinner with a woman he wanted to throttle? Or did he? Eating crab salad, watching Jill with her pet, in her home, in the town that deep inside was his home, too, it was hard to hold on to the anger. But it was harder still to understand.

He wiped his mouth with the paper napkin. "Thanks for the salad."

"If you're still hungry—"

"I'm fine." But he wasn't.

"Morgan . . ."

Here it came, he could tell by her expression. Something she didn't want to say but felt compelled to. What other bombs did she have in her arsenal?

"I was thinking about what you said, about being with you for the bone marrow harvest. Did you really mean it?"

He backpedaled to get there with her. "Yes."

"Why?"

"I told you, Consuela's great with a meal and a mop, but—"

"I mean really, Morgan."

He studied her stroking the cat under the neck, an expression in her eyes of both concern and hope. "Jill, I didn't think it through that deeply. If you want to come, come." Definitely not the answer she wanted. He leaned back in his chair. "Can you arrange it at school?"

Something flickered in her eyes. "Yes. I have as much time as I need."

He shrugged. "Then come."

She stood up and walked to the front window. The stiff line of her back showed her ire. What did she expect? For him to jump for joy? He was still trying to weather the tide.

But he got up and joined her. "Since this involves both of us, we ought to see it through together."·

She turned. "I'm grateful for you doing this, Morgan. I thought I could show it by supporting you. If you don't need that . . ."

He slid the ends of his fingers inside the waist of his shorts and resisted the unrealistic tug of her words. "I'm long past need, Jill."

She gathered herself. "Good. Then I'll come as a friend and . . ."

He quirked his mouth sideways. "Rub my back?"

"If you need—if you want—if that's what . . ."

His grin made her squirm. "Got a football?"

"What?"

"A pointed spherical pigskin?" He made the passing motion.

She glanced at her front closet. "Yes, but I doubt it's inflated." She opened the door and dug it out from a box on the shelf, squeezing it a little too much.

"Air pump?"

"On my bike."

He followed her into the garage, warm with the day's captured heat and smelling of cat box and rubber. He took the small hand pump and the needle she scrounged and made the football firm. "Throw it around?"

"Okay."

They had to go back inside and out her patio door to get to the long strip of property between her row of units and the next, where her friend Shelly and the cop lived. Morgan pulled back his arm and sent Jill a soft spiral. She caught it easily, and her return throw was strong and straight. She'd been a natural for the game, equally capable of throwing and catching, and a speed hound in sight of the goal line. She didn't mind mixing it up but took it personally if she got tackled.

He sent the ball back sharper this time. She stepped to her right and caught it, sent it back. His muscles appreciated the motion after the long drive and his nap on the couch. "Go out for one."

She started running, and he led her just enough with his throw. She drew it in to her chest, turned, and burned it back. He had to dive but caught it, then landed and rolled.

"Sorry."

He lay on his back in the grass until she stood over him.

"Are you all right?"

He gripped her ankle. "What do you think?"

She swooped down to capture the ball and tried to tug free of his grip, ending up sitting hard on her backside. He rolled, knocked the ball free, scooped it up, and ran. She charged to her feet too late to catch him before he raised his hands and the ball high in victory.

She jutted her chin. "That was holding. Ten yards."

"This is holding." He clamped her waist with one arm and held the ball up higher than her reach.

"Cheater."

Three middle school neighbor boys came into the yard. "Can we play?"

Morgan let her go. "Don't know, can you? Let's see your stuff." He sent the nearest boy a spiral. It glanced off his fingers, and the next kid over caught it. "Now that's teamwork. You two can be on Jill's team. She needs the extra help. I'll take you." He pointed to the third and smallest of them.

The boy ran to his side.

"What's your name?"

"Eric."

"Eric, we are going to take 'em out early, and I'll tell you how." He drew the boy's head close and whispered the first play. "Got it?"

Eric grinned. By the end of their possession, a tomboy girl named Alli and a balding electrician had joined in. It was no surprise when Brett stepped out his patio door dressed in a Beauview PD T-shirt. They rearranged the teams to accommodate him and his wife, who had just gotten home from work. When Shelly missed the third easy pass, he put her on the line to block her husband, who knew his stuff. Marital devotion might confuse the man.

Morgan had his team running like a machine, but they were still having trouble with Jill's speed. Mark, the electrician, had a long throw and when they connected, she easily outdistanced Morgan's defense. He ordered Alli over farther to the left and winked at Eric to rush the passer, but Mark still got off his throw and Jill sprinted for the goal line. It was up to him. He cut the angle but had to lunge to get both hands to her hips. His momentum brought them down, rolling just before they hit, so he got the ground and she landed atop.

She held on to the ball but scowled. "Two-hand touch."

"I did."

She pulled onto her knees. "No, you tackled."

Lying on his back, he could hardly argue. "It was momentum."

"Intentional."

He punched the ball up through her hands and caught it. "Crybaby."

She shoved his chest. "Thug."

He sat up and stared her down. "What are you gonna do about it?"

She ripped a handful of grass and shoved it down his shirt, then scrambled to her feet and stood hands on hips.

Morgan stood up, shaking the grass from his shirt. He did not reciprocate, just sent her a smug glance and called his team together. "Fourth down. Let's stop them." He read the next play as it unfolded, their electrician quarterback lacking ingenuity. Morgan intercepted the ball almost out of Jill's hands, a rush of old memories flooding in as he did—all their competitions, the many times she came out on top, but the times he bested her as well. Football, track, academics—she'd been an essential element in his formation.

As her hands tagged his hips, he couldn't help but miss all the challenges they could have given each other over the last fifteen years. She had sharpened him like no one else before or since, the final pass over her pumice leaving his edge too keen to touch. He set his jaw. He was treading dangerous waters. But when had that ever stopped him before?

———

Shelly was more proficient with the flank steak, skewered shrimp, and new potatoes on her patio grill than she'd been with the football. Jill finished grating the cheese and set it aside for the corn, then set Shelly's table for four, a different foursome than their past norm. Morgan and Brett were in companionable conversation, though Jill suspected in Brett some defensiveness on Dan's behalf.

She lifted the plate of tomatoes she'd sliced and peppered. "Do you want these in the fridge until we're ready?"

"No, keep them room temp. Don't you know that, midwestern girl that you are?"

Jill smiled. "I know that's what they say. I just prefer them chilled."

Shelly crossed to the sink beside Jill and rinsed her hands. She whispered, "You didn't tell me he was Apollo."

"He's not." Morgan was far too human.

"Could have fooled me." Shelly hooked the first can of corn under the opener and whirred the lid off.

Jill took the cans from Shelly and poured the corn into the pot. She turned on the burner and put the pot's lid on. "Shelly, I'm going with Morgan to be there when they extract the marrow." If she was crazy, Shelly would say so in an instant.

Shelly wiped her hands on a towel. "Where?"

"The UCLA Medical Center. It's the one nearest his home."

"He doesn't have to go where Kelsey is?"

Jill shook her head. "He'd like to. He wants to see her. But that's not how it works."

"My stomach's growling, Shell," Brett called from the living room. "Don't forget the grill while you're standing there with your heads together."

"Last I looked you weren't paralyzed," Shelly called back.

Brett grinned. "Fine. I like my steak rare." He got up and headed out the patio door.

Jill caught Morgan's gaze. During the game he'd been playful and exuberant; Morgan did always shine in a crowd. Not that he played to an audience necessarily. He just liked people, and they liked him. Now his expression was inscrutable, though he didn't look away when their eyes met. If ever there was a crazy mixed-up situation, this was it, and he was probably as confused as she.

Brett came in with the plate of grilled meats and browned new potatoes. Jill would have baked them with scallions, but Brett liked them from the grill a little crisp and smoky. She stirred the last of the cheese into the corn with the already melted cream cheese, peppers, and onion. They gathered and she said a silent prayer for all of them. Morgan winked at her when he took a bite of corn. That was the Morgan she remembered.

The steak was done to a perfect medium rare, thinly sliced and running juices over the plate. The shrimp was charred and lemony, and the tomatoes, bursting with crisp, fresh flavor, contrasted nicely with the creamy corn. A lingering scent of smoke drifted through the screen from the grill.

Morgan ate, but with none of Dan's voraciousness. He did appear to appreciate the fare and said so twice, once actually making Shelly flush. This was not good. Getting Morgan out of town was gaining significance. Shelly was way too much the romantic to ever let it go. She would not understand the utter impossibility of anything developing between them again.

———

After dinner, Morgan walked Jill back to her townhouse and stopped outside her front door. Probably better not to go in again. He took his car keys from his pocket and bounced them in his palm. "You can be ready in the morning?"

She looked into his face. "If you're sure you want me to come."

"I don't make idle offers." He might not have thought it through completely before he threw it out to her, but once he'd said it, he wasn't taking it back. He didn't operate that way, even if the next few days might be close encounters of the worst kind. He'd acted on instinct, and that usually paid off.

"Then I'll be ready. Are you going to stay with your family, or did you want to . . ."

He quirked his mouth. "I already sampled your couch. I'll get a room."

"In a motel?"

He took the house key from her hand and unlocked her door. "I spend most of my life in hotels."

"Not the kind you'll find here."

Why was she pushing it?

"Good night, Jill."

He waited until the door closed and locked behind her, then went to his car. No doubt it was absurd to stay in a roadside motel when his family was twenty minutes away. They would have a bed for him, and they would want to see him. But he had put them through enough the first time. The less they knew, especially now that Jill was going with him, the better it was for all of them. Mom would not let it go until she had probed out every nuance, and Morgan had no answers except that he intended to find his daughter and improve her situation by any means he could.

The motel bed was at least better than Jill's couch, and he was tired enough it would do. The lack of a minibar was disappointing, but not enough for him to go find a liquor store. That would only be an invitation to traipse down memory lane, and that was one trip he'd rather skip. The football game had been enough to quicken memory and more. He needed to keep his purpose foremost. He never wanted to feel that helpless again.

18

Kelsey sat in the hospital chapel, breathing hard just from walking. Like it was some major thing to move her legs! How discouraging was that? But she tried to hide it. Mom was worried enough, and Kelsey hated to make it worse. She had begged to come to the chapel, even though Mom was concerned about infection, and rightly so. But there was so much fear and sorrow in the oncology ward it had overwhelmed her spirit.

Her roommate had been taken to intensive care with fever spikes of a hundred and six. She had mumbled loudly in the middle of the night until Kelsey realized she was delirious. She'd buzzed the nurse and they had taken Rachel away.

Kelsey lay waiting for her own fever to spike, but the antibiotics they'd started at the first sign of fever yesterday seemed to be controlling it. So far. She'd asked the nurse for pizza and eaten it at 2:20 A.M. It tasted bad, but the milk shake with it helped, and for once she'd been hungry.

Mom settled into the chair beside her in the chapel. Dad was making phone calls. There were so many people praying for her. Peace permeated the quiet chapel in the middle of the busy hospital. How many scared cries had gone up inside these walls? She closed her eyes and asked Jesus to give Rachel strength. She'd had her surgery yesterday, and from the faces of the oncologists, they were optimistic.

Jesus, don't let this infection stop her healing.

Rachel was twelve, and her fifteen-year-old brother had been a constant visitor before the surgery. His broad face had more coppery freckles than anyone Kelsey had ever seen. Even his fingers were freckled. He'd smiled at her when he came in to see his sister. "Hi, there. Mind if I barge in on you and Rachie for a while?"

Kelsey shook her head. "Barge away."

They'd ended up playing Scrabble on Rachel's bed, laughing at the ridiculous letter combinations Josh tried to pass off as words. Since they didn't have a dictionary to prove him wrong, Kelsey accessed one on her laptop and gleefully pointed out his errors. Now Rachel was in intensive care, and Kelsey once again faced her own condition.

It was dumb to think she couldn't die. Even if she had made it to five years on her first remission and been declared cured, she wasn't sure she'd have believed it. God had numbered her days regardless of all the Cytoxin and radiation the oncologists had to offer. Lately she felt stretched and flimsy, like a musical story she'd heard as a child where the character had become "see-through-ish." That's how she felt.

She smiled when Mom took her hand. "It's a nice chapel, isn't it?"

Mom nodded. "It's good to have a place set aside for the Lord."

"Besides our hearts?"

Mom smiled. "I don't know how people are coping here without God's grace to strengthen them."

Kelsey nodded. "Please pray for Rachel. She doesn't think Jesus loves her anymore. She told me something I can't tell you, something she's ashamed of, and now she thinks Jesus can't love her."

"It's easy to believe the devil's lies."

Kelsey drew in a slow breath. "It was. But everything seems clearer now. Like I'm not expecting so much anymore."

Her mother's face tightened. Had she hurt her? She hadn't meant to.

"It's not like I've lost hope. I just feel different. I can't explain it."

Mom squeezed her hand. "I love you."

Kelsey squeezed back. "I love you, too." She closed her eyes and let the quiet of the chapel settle inside her. That's how it felt, like the peace moved from the room into her body. Maybe she breathed it in, or it went in through her skin. Maybe into her blood that didn't know what it was doing anymore.

Would Morgan's bone marrow teach hers how to behave? Morgan

Spencer. Her dad. No. Her friend? That felt more like it. She should have told Jill she would meet him. It wasn't her decision, but if she asked enough she could make it happen. When she got back home. Maybe. Right now she'd pray for him, and for Jill. This couldn't be easy for them. At least Jill loved Jesus. Did Morgan?

He must be a nice guy to go through it all for her. He could have said no. Maybe Jill would tell her more about him. It was nice to e-mail her and know they had a truth pact. When she got back to the room, she would write her again. But right now she was in the chapel to pray for Rachel and all the kids she'd written to and all the others in the ward. Even though it was hard to focus. *Jesus, I'm too tired to think of all their names. But you know us. We're your little army, fighting with the big angel soldiers. It's just that I'm tired. So tired.* And she fell asleep in the chair.

———

Jill checked her mail, trying not to hope for a note from Kelsey, but when it came up, a little thrill passed through her.

Hi, Jill. My roommate, Rachel, had brain surgery and is in intensive care. I'm so glad my cancer is not in my brain. Her brother Josh is really nice. He doesn't care that I have no hair. He's used to bald girls. Says he prefers it. He has so many freckles it makes me laugh and he's a terrible cheat at Scrabble. I know I'm too young, but he's the kind of person I would like to date someday, if Dad ever let me. Which I'm not sure he would, since no one will ever be good enough for his little girl. He already told me that. Of course he was joking.

Jill smiled.

But if I did like boys, which of course I secretly admit to you because we're telling the truth, I MIGHT like Josh just a little more than anyone else. Now you have to tell me a secret. Can it be about Morgan? Write soon. Kelsey

Kelsey's entire tone was upbeat and chatty compared to the last letter. She would match that tone in her reply.

Dear Kelsey, I'm glad you had fun with Josh. He sounds very nice.

Not many boys would handle a sensitive subject like baldness so well. His sister's illness must have tempered him. That was always how it was. Experience, hardship, suffering broadened and developed people so much more than prosperity.

He might be just the kind to convince your dad to rethink his position.

As Morgan had won over her own father until they crossed the line and ruined it all. Somehow she doubted Kelsey would make those mistakes, but then, Jill sighed, she'd been awfully naïve herself.

I'm trying to think of a secret you would enjoy. Maybe I'll start at the beginning.

It would be hard not to think and write about Morgan, with his presence today still haunting the very air she breathed.

I knew Morgan through cheerleading at his football games, running track, and student council. We actually campaigned against each other for class president one year. (I won, but only because Morgan told everyone I'd do a better job.) Even before that, I had a serious, though secret, crush. All the girls in the school were crazy about him because he wasn't stuck-up or mean like many of the good-looking guys. He had a way of looking at you that made you feel beautiful.

Jill closed her eyes, remembering. She had thought other guys were cute, but Morgan was different.

I was not beautiful. First, I had been accelerated a year, so I was younger than anyone in my class. As a freshman I was dubbed "Sprite." I was tall and nicely streamlined for athletics, but, ahem, the other girls had figures.

A rueful reality throughout her entire adolescence. But Morgan had noticed her anyway. He did call her Sprite like everyone else, but he almost made it endearing.

For some reason, Morgan considered me a challenge. We vied for top grades, sports records, and volunteer projects. For one talent show he dared me to sing with him the duet, "Anything You Can Do, I Can Do Better." And I think he meant every word.

She smiled now to think of it.

Morgan enjoyed competition, wanted to be challenged. He would not give up. But if he did lose, he never made excuses. When I scored higher on the PSAT, he said, "Way to go, Sprite. I knew there were brains in there." He was a natural encourager.

Maybe that's what she missed most in the man he had become. Jill bit her lip. Don't get morose. Keep it light. This is Kelsey, not a diary.

> *In our senior year we were nominated king and queen for the homecoming dance. You can imagine my excitement when he asked me to be his date, but there was a glitch. I wasn't allowed to date until I was seventeen. Since I had been accelerated, I wouldn't turn seventeen until November, two months past the homecoming dance. My begging accomplished nothing until Morgan himself asked my father's permission. He did it so respectfully, impressively, my Dad agreed not only to the dance but other events as well.*

To this day Dad held up that instance of acquiescence as an example of giving the enemy a foothold.

> *"Go against what you know is right, give in just a little, and reap the consequences."*

He blamed himself for putting her at risk. That was why he'd been so ugly to Morgan and his dad. She sighed.

> *I guess the best thing about Morgan was that he cared about what you thought and believed. He liked to talk, really talk, unlike most guys his age. He wanted to know what was inside. And if something was wrong, he wanted to fix it.*

Jill pressed her fingers to her eyes. As he was doing now. As he must have wanted so badly to do from the first. She fought the tears.

> *That's why he wants so much to help you.*

Her throat tightened painfully.

> *I'm praying for sweet dreams for you tonight.*

No pain or illness. How she wanted Kelsey to be past it all.

> *Oh, here's a secret for you. When Morgan has his marrow drawn, I'll be with him. He knew how much I wanted to do it for you myself. God bless you, Kelsey. Jill*

————

By the daylight, Morgan guessed he'd woken early; then he remembered he was in the Midwest and it could be later than it seemed. He rolled to his side and read the clock. 5:41. He yawned and stretched. Not the time of morning he usually rolled out, but the sooner they had it over with, the better.

He took a quick shower and brushed his teeth, packed his overnight bag, and checked out. Then he drove back to Jill's. Not much chance she was still in bed if the running shoes he'd noticed yesterday were any indication. Six-thirty had been her running time. Well, he'd brought gear of his own and had dressed in that just in case.

Sure enough, she was on the stoop in a sport tank and shorts, ankle socks and powder blue Nikes when he pulled up. "I was just going to run."

He climbed out and set the car alarm. Though he worked with a personal trainer, he had not since high school considered punishing his body this early in the day. Yet he raised his foot in his Adidas running shoe. "I'll go with you."

She looked up from stretching her left Achilles tendon. "You will?"

"Yeah. We'll run to Starbucks." He gave a cursory stretch to his own calves.

She smiled. "Think you can handle that distance?"

"Think you can touch my speed?"

She bit her lower lip, smiling. "We'll see, won't we?" She pushed her headband slightly higher, then took off.

Morgan settled beside her at a comfortable pace. She was only warming up. But she was obviously a morning person. He remembered that.

It had been a long time since he'd jogged beside Jill Runyan, but he knew her stride. They left the complex behind and ran along the neighborhood street, block after block of quiet, well-tended homes. People were stirring, but no one else was running. A few dog walkers, one pair of cyclists. They reached the first stoplight and ran in place until it changed, then took off across the street together. The strip mall came in sight, but it was still half a mile away. Total distance couldn't be much more than two, two and a half miles.

Jill picked up her pace. Morgan matched it. Distance was not his long suit, but he'd kept in good enough shape over the years to do this, even at an ungodly hour, without throwing up. He hoped.

The air was thick, too. He'd grown used to the coastal air, not exactly the thin, arid air of the Rocky Mountains, but nowhere near the wet blanket now filling his lungs. At the next light he was tempted to bend low and suck wind, but he kept his legs moving and his chest high. They crossed, and her nose smelled the finish line. She always finished strong, but he was sure he had a sprint left in him.

They reached the block of the strip mall, and he leaned into his speed. She almost kept pace but fell back as he neared the Starbucks door. Reaching it, he did bend and grip his knees. Why had he crawled out of bed? She reached him, slowing and walking the last few paces. He pressed his back to the outside wall and waited for his chest to recover.

She smiled. "You all right?"

"No."

"Shall I call an ambulance?"

He winked. "Just perform mouth-to-mouth resuscitation." She didn't have to look that startled. "It was a joke, Jill." He pressed his hand against his side.

She pulled open the door. "I hope they have something cold."

"I hope they have something strong." He ordered his usual morning blend. She had a mocha Frappuccino. They sat together by the window. Her eyes were too clear to be called stormy but definitely on the gray side of blue. He was glad she didn't babble this time. He started his mornings slow. It wasn't exactly an amiable silence, more a lack of anything to say. But he did like to drink his coffee in peace.

Halfway through her Frappuccino, she pushed it away. "I forgot to mention why I don't drink coffee."

He cocked his head. "Feeling it?"

"On an empty stomach, I am definitely getting the shakes." She stood up and paced as he took his last swallow.

He was feeling it, too, but it was resurrection. "You don't intend to run back, do you?"

She glanced over her shoulder. "I planned on it."

He stood up and tossed his cup. "What if I beg?"

She dropped her chin and eyed him. "Fast walk?"

"That I can handle." He held the door for her. She was definitely caffeinated, rising to her toes and jogging in place at the corner of the parking lot while they waited for the light. She took off her headband and shook her hair, then replaced the band and struck out the moment the light went green. Maybe he ought to let her run it out. He could recover later.

He started to jog, then run, not quite the pace they'd kept before, but close. This time he was not sprinting to the finish. Jill could reach the townhouse first; he just needed to make it without a heart attack. She kept the pace even all the way to her door.

"Mind if I use your shower?" He definitely needed to wash the sweat and midwestern film from his skin again.

She hesitated, then, "Go ahead. I'll take Rascal over to Shelly's."

He took his bag from the trunk and went inside. Maybe it was presumptuous to use her shower, but his options were limited. He hadn't meant to drive her out of the house, though. He soaped off quickly with her apple-scented body wash, the only soap he could find, rinsed, and shut off the water. He toweled dry and dressed in khaki shorts and a navy Polo T-shirt, ran a comb through his hair, and stepped out of the bathroom.

He didn't have to wonder if Jill was back, for she stood in the hall, hand extended, his cell phone in her grasp. "It was ringing in your bag, so I answered."

He took it. "Yeah?"

"Morgan?"

"Hey, Todd. How's it goin'?" He mouthed, "I'll take it outside."

Todd's response was mildly encouraging as Morgan walked out to the front stoop to give Jill some privacy. He told him he was getting to watch TV and grudgingly added that he was also using the reading program.

"Glad to hear it." And he was. He needed some good news.

"And guess what?" Todd went on. "Rick's gonna show me how to train the foals."

"Yeah? That's great. Just don't let him make you break 'em. Too much pain."

Todd laughed. "I'm not getting on any horse."

Morgan said, "You might like it."

"No way."

"Aw, c'mon. If Stan can do it . . ."

Todd snorted. "I *could* do it if I wanted."

Morgan smiled. "I bet you'll be riding barrels by summer's end."

Todd laughed again. It sent a pang to Morgan's heart. "You eating well?"

"Better than before. I'm glad you got Marta."

"I thought you'd be."

"Are you with your daughter?" That question sent another pang. Obviously vulnerable this morning.

"No. She's in a treatment center in Connecticut. I'm in lovely Iowa, with the cows and the corn, but I'm heading home today."

"Through here?"

Morgan half smiled. "No, Todd. Sorry." The silence drew out. "But maybe sometime you could come see me on the coast."

"Really?"

"It's up to Stan." Morgan smiled again. Had he inadvertently given Todd a reason to toe the line with his foster dad? "It can't be for a while." Not while he was donating bone marrow and figuring out his life. "But if you and Stan get along, I'll bet we can work it out sometime."

"Excellent!"

Morgan laughed. "Who's paying your phone bill?"

"I'm working it off."

"Then I'll let you go."

"Okay. Bye, Morgan."

"Bye, kid." He turned off the phone and found Jill lingering in her doorway, toweling her hair.

"Who's Todd?"

"A foster kid who's staying at Rick's ranch this summer. Having a hard time."

Her eyes searched his face, then, "I'll just get some things packed up."

He followed her in, zipped closed his caramel-colored leather bag, and carried it to his trunk. While he rearranged things to make room for Jill's luggage, a police cruiser pulled into the lot and parked. Jill's bodyguard, Dan, climbed out, muscles flexing inside the stiff uniform. He took the few steps between them. "Leaving?"

Morgan pressed the trunk closed. "In a little while."

Dan inspected the car with a mixture of appreciation and irritation. Love the machine; hate its driver.

Morgan understood.

Dan rested his substantial palm on the Thunderbird's windshield. "Is Jill inside?"

"She's packing."

Dan's hand on the windshield clenched, but he showed no surprise. "Haven't you messed her up enough?"

Morgan's throat tightened. Yeah, he probably had. But things weren't finished between them.

Dan pushed off from the windshield and went to Jill's door. He opened it with familiarity and confidence and went inside. Morgan got into his car and drove up to the strip mall for gas.

———————

Jill flattened one last shirt into her bag, wondering again if she was doing the right thing. Was it truly her chance to be part of Kelsey's cure? Or was it just that Morgan had asked? She couldn't be with Kelsey, but she could be with him. She had told him she would go, and now she heard him behind her. "I'm almost done."

"Have you completely lost your mind?"

She spun to find Dan, not Morgan, behind her.

"You're throwing all your principles to the wind to run off and give comfort to this guy. . . ."

He must have talked to Shelly. "I want to be part of Kelsey's healing. It's not about Morgan."

"Does he know that?"

She nodded. "He just offered me the chance to be involved. With Kelsey's cure."

He shook his head. "You are the real thing."

"What thing?" She reached down and tugged the luggage zipper.

"The ultimate innocent. This man got you pregnant, Jill. He probably didn't bother to protect, then left you to deal with the consequences."

"It wasn't like that."

"Then I don't know you at all, 'cause I sure don't think you seduced him against his will."

She jerked the zipper hard and shot her gaze to him. "You know what I did, Dan? I went to my senior counselor. I told her I was in love with Morgan and didn't know where to draw the line. She told me if I loved him, I needed birth control pills. Only I knew that my parents would die if they found me with birth control." She didn't expect Dan to understand.

"So I didn't get the pill. But when things got too serious with Morgan, I lied. I told him I was on it." She swallowed the humiliation of saying that out loud again. "Because the adult I trusted told me if I loved him—and I did—I would have done that."

"What else was she supposed to do?" He spread his hands.

"How about reinforce chastity? What I'd been taught at home and at church."

"Oh, come on, Jill. Do you think that would have stopped you?"

She glared. "Yes, Dan. I do. She could have told me true love waits, and it was all right to respect myself and Morgan enough to say no."

Dan looked away. "So what now? You have this respect?"

Jill's heart stabbed. "Trust me, Dan. There's too much pain between us for anything to happen."

"I trust you. Not Morgan Spencer."

"Well, it isn't your problem." She hauled the bag off the bed and set it on its wheels.

"Jill, I meant it when I asked you to marry me."

"I know, Dan. But we have no philosophical basis for that kind of covenant." She walked past him. "I hope we can be friends when I come back."

"*If* you come back."

She closed her eyes and dropped her chin. "I'll be back, Dan. And I'll probably need a friend."

She pulled the suitcase down the hall, saw Morgan through the window leaning against his car, waiting. "I need to lock up."

Dan passed her with a final exhaled breath that said he'd done his best. He went out, glared at Morgan, then got into his cruiser and drove around to pick up Brett for their shift.

Morgan took her bag. "Everything okay?"

She sighed. "He's afraid I'll seduce you."

Morgan slanted her a glance. "I can take care of myself."

"Whew." She passed the back of her hand across her forehead and gave him a wan smile. "Then I guess it's fine."

He closed her luggage into the trunk and walked her around to the door. "Everything's covered at work?"

"Oh, definitely. It was even done for me." Where was that cynically flippant tone coming from?

"Jill?" Morgan must have caught the edge.

She shook her head. "I'm ready. I won't be gone that long, and my life"—she looked up at the townhouse before settling into the seat—"will be here waiting."

Morgan joined her in the Thunderbird. "Let's go."

19

J ill's stomach knotted as Morgan turned the car out of her parking
lot and started down the street. The sky was a muted blue, but the
forecast had said rain, and already the milky moisture was thickening.
They might not have the top down long. Her stomach knotted again.
Stormy days were hard on her kids.

Today her students would get the news that she was gone for more
than just yesterday. Rascal would try to adapt to Shelly's place, and
Dan would grumble all day to Brett. She'd become the storm cloud in
all of their lives, but she pushed the thought away and focused on her
purpose. She was going for Kelsey, to be part of the cure for her daughter. She had dragged Morgan back into it, and the least she could do
was walk through it with him.

The smell of cut grass wafted as they passed the droning mower
and approached the corner where a bony-kneed scamp waved a lemonade sign their way. "It's cold! Only ten cents!"

Jill smiled at the girls behind him, sitting at the plastic table,
primly holding the pitcher and the stack of flowered Dixie cups as their
front man jumped out at the car.

Morgan swung to the side and stopped. Before Jill could react, he
climbed out of the car and squatted in front of the sign waver. "So
you're in business for yourself now."

"Ten cents." He couldn't be more than six or seven.

"Well, let me tell you something. Ten cents doesn't cover your costs." He tipped the sign to see the back side. "You make a new sign and ask a quarter for that size cup." He reached into his pocket for his wallet. "We'll take two." He took out a dollar and glanced at the girls. "If any of you can tell me at twenty-five cents a glass how much my change would be, I'll let you keep it."

The girl in braids who was already pouring their cups full said, "Fifty cents."

Morgan clicked his fingers. "You got it." He took the lemonades, gave the kids a wink, and got back into the car. Jill took the cup he handed her.

"Do not spill a drop." He gave her a sidelong glance with the admonition and drank his glass in one long draught.

Cold, sweet, tangy. Jill closed her eyes and drank. It was just what her stomach needed after the Frappuccino and no breakfast. The knots eased. Five hundred percent profit on their first sale. Morgan had just made their day. Three little kids he'd never seen before, yet he'd be the topic of discussion over their peanut butter sandwiches.

Morgan always left an impression. She remembered the day after their first dance, sitting on the porch with Mom while Dad was still at the church for a deacons' meeting. She had hardly kept her eyes open through the service, and every time they closed she saw Morgan. She was dreaming of him the moment Mom's soft voice said, "Morgan Spencer certainly thinks a lot of himself."

Jill had startled. "What do you mean?"

Mom shrugged her eyebrows. "Just the way he carries himself as though he's got the world all figured out already." She couldn't believe how much it hurt that Mom would say something critical of Morgan after only meeting him once. But that had been her impression, and she never wavered from it. Looking at Morgan now, it seemed she'd been right. He did have the whole world figured out, while she was still floundering.

He nested her cup in his and headed for the nearest trash can, the gas station at the strip mall. When he reached I-80 west, he set the cruise control. Jill glanced over as Morgan slid in the CD that was resting in the player, and the strains filled the car even with the roof off. What had he paid for such a stereo? And the music . . .

She turned. "What is this?"

"Beethoven's Last Night."

She raised her brows. "Not exactly the Beethoven I know."

"Trans-Siberian Orchestra. The story's in the case there. It's a modern rock opera."

She picked up the case and pulled out the pamphlet paged like a book. As the music surrounded and filled her, she read the story of Beethoven's last night, how in the last hours of life he was given the chance to change anything he wanted. But with each change, he would lose the music composed out of the pain of that situation.

She read, entranced, as Beethoven chose again and again to retain the wounded reality of his life rather than lose the music it had drawn from him. And the voice of the woman he had deserted, believing she couldn't love him deaf, sang out her longing and confusion. Tears stung, and Jill blinked them away, reading how Beethoven realized in his last moments on earth that she would have loved him, had indeed continued to love him always, and he glimpsed what might have been.

She closed her eyes and dropped her head back as the music continued, strains of Beethoven and Mozart woven together and played as neither of them could have imagined. It was hauntingly beautiful and drew from her soul a response too full for words. When it ended, she sat in the silence, the world speeding past. But for his pride and misunderstanding, Beethoven could have had that joy he'd glimpsed.

Morgan said nothing, but she sensed his soul beside hers. Tears filled her eyes and she turned away, staring at the fields filled with corn as they passed. Why was she doing this? What pain would she awaken?

The music had laid him open unexpectedly. He'd heard it enough to resist, but he hadn't resisted. Hearing it with Jill had shaken him—not that he let it show. His hand on the wheel was relaxed and easy, the wind of their motion catching his hair back from his face.

She seemed devastated, though, and he recalled the impact his first hearing had on him. He left her to her silence. She'd be all right once she finished contending with all the might-have-beens. If she didn't want their baby, she could have given her to him, to his family even. But that would have kept them connected. That was what she hadn't wanted.

After a while he reached for the radio, but she said, "Don't."

He left it off. "Powerful, isn't it?"

"Haunting."

He glanced over. "Are you okay?"

She nodded.

"Hungry?"

"No."

It was nearer lunch than breakfast, and the lemonade had tweaked his hunger. "I am." He'd seen a sign for the upcoming exit and its fast-food offerings. Normally he eschewed those places, but on the road they sufficed. He took the drive-thru of the Hardee's and ordered a burger. "Get something, Jill."

She ordered a chicken sandwich and iced tea and managed to eat most of it as he drove on. She collected their trash and folded it all into the bag, having obviously caught his concern for the interior of his car. They drove in silence for a while; then she said, "Tell me about Noelle."

"Where did that come from?"

She shrugged. "You two are close."

He stared straight ahead. "I was in love with her."

She caught the hair back from her eyes cased in sunglasses. "But she married Rick?"

"That's the short of it."

"Tell me the long."

He rested his wrist on the wheel and described Noelle's arriving at Rick's ranch. He pictured her standing in the breeze like a Dresden figurine, more statuesque, more classically beautiful than Jill. "I was seriously smitten. Rick, of course, was not. He doesn't date his guests."

"Then how . . ."

"Don't rush me." He told her about the summer he'd spent wooing Noelle, the hikes, the dinners, the dancing. "She was really something."

"Then why—"

"What I didn't know was why she'd come. There was some reason she resisted my charm." He threw her a careless glance. "But I couldn't break through and learn what. I got a contract and left, never dreaming that while I was gone Rick would make his move."

"Did he? I thought you said . . ."

"He didn't date her, didn't actively pursue her. But he did what I couldn't. He learned she'd been molested as a child and run away from the other jerk who beat her up." Morgan's throat tightened. "When I joined them at my folks' place for Christmas, the damage was done. She loved Rick." He laughed low. "I knew it, but I made it as hard on her as I could."

He let that sink in. Jill should know how he really was.

"She seemed anything but resentful."

"Well, the story doesn't end there." He explained how the ex-fiancé had found Noelle before the wedding, traumatized her so badly she'd run back to New York and left Rick devastated. "I'd never seen him like that. He just stopped living. He made the motions, but even his faith was shot."

"I can understand that," she murmured.

Morgan switched wrists on the wheel. "So I found her in New York and reminded her how much she loved him."

"Him? You convinced her she loved Rick when . . ."

"When I loved her, too?"

Jill nodded.

"Well, I've done smarter things."

Jill sat silently, then said, "So Rick married her."

Morgan nodded. "Yep."

"Would you have?"

He rubbed his temple. "Probably."

"She loves you."

"I know. Just not the way I wanted."

Jill watched Morgan drive, letting his words sink in. She'd seen the story in their interaction, known there was more between them than the friendship of in-laws. But to hear Morgan say he'd loved her, probably loved her still . . . It should not hurt.

After this week when the transplant was over, they'd go their separate ways. She had to be careful, so careful. But she couldn't stop herself. "Have there been others?"

He glanced sideways. "Others?"

The point was to get the pain up front, to know what she faced. "Just wondering."

"If I need a date, I get one."

No doubt. But that wasn't what she'd asked. She studied his profile, then looked away. So he had his walls, too.

He asked, "What's it like, teaching special ed?"

A safer subject under normal circumstances. But with her status up in the air . . . She sighed. "Mostly heartbreaking. This past year I was responsible for twenty-one students. They vary in type and degree of disability. The hardest is a boy named Joey. He presents with autistic behaviors, and we went with that label because it's the closest we could come in order to get him into the program. But unlike a true autistic diagnosis, his condition is more likely due to the fact that he was kept practically caged inside the house until he entered kindergarten. He came to us more like a jungle boy than anything we could categorize."

"Aren't there laws against that?"

"He wasn't abused or neglected as far as physical needs. His parents didn't know what to do with a child who didn't respond. Or ignoring him and allowing him to run wild taught him not to respond. Neglect and autism present the same ways, so my first inclination is to assume a medical condition. In Joey's case I'm just not sure." Her heart squeezed to think how he might be reacting to her absence.

"So what do you do for him?" Morgan sounded sincerely interested.

"Well, there are several schools of thought and new research all the time. We try one thing and if it brings improvement we build on that. When we started working with him, he had almost no language, though he could fixate on a computer for hours on end. Since then he's learned two- or three-word phrases to express most of his needs."

Morgan shook his head, no doubt thinking that didn't represent much progress.

"Those phrases are hard won for a child who's overwhelmed all the time by auditory and sensory stimuli. I've used applied behavioral analysis to give him structured ways to interact, so that if someone says, 'Hi, Joey, how are you?'—he can do more than holler, 'No, no, no.'"

"Wow." Morgan breathed. "And I thought Todd was challenged."

"Next year I want to try auditory discrimination therapy. I've been reading about results through that program. It uses music to teach autistic and ADD kids to differentiate phrases and notes and ascribe levels of importance to the sounds in order to filter out some of the overload."

This was probably way more than Morgan needed to hear, but he'd opened the box. "There are also dietary connections between wheat gluten and dairy protein. I recommended Joey's mother learn what she could about that, but it was too much trouble for them to change their eating habits. I still think it could help. Joey is nine and only conditionally potty trained."

"Conditionally?"

"Under conditions he approves, he has marginal success. But if a broken routine or something else upsets him . . . well, we're not sure yet if it's actually a way to strike back or just stress. But I think there's also a digestive strain that could be lessened with a change in diet."

Talking about Joey churned emotions she hadn't faced yet. How could she not go back and work with him? He'd been part of her life the last four years. *Lord, can that truly be your will?* Nothing was settled. She'd been elbowed out for the summer, but that didn't affect next school year. "He's made so much progress. I pray for him every day."

Morgan made no response to that.

"Then there's Angelica." She told him about the child's determination to learn and willingness to try, even in areas she would never succeed in, short of miraculous intervention. "I'll have to call them when I get back. I should have done it before we left."

Morgan nodded toward his cell phone. "Use mine."

"It would be long distance from here. I'd need to talk to all the families."

He reached down and handed her the phone.

She held it a moment, unsure she could make those calls now, on the road, next to Morgan, even if he could afford it.

"Or you could e-mail them tonight from my laptop."

Jill smiled. "That would be great." She would let them know she was out on a family medical emergency, but they could still reach her by e-mail. She had always given her kids that access as well as her phone number. She could also pick up her mail, Kelsey's letters especially.

Morgan replaced the cell phone. "Sounds like more than a professional concern."

She nodded. "I don't separate professional and personal very well. With me these kids are very personal."

He didn't answer right away but finally said, "You must be good at what you do."

Jill sighed. "My principal would never concede that point. He's trying to make me quit."

Morgan turned. "Why?"

She explained their various altercations, religious and otherwise. "He's already hired my replacement, though he can't actually fire me. Not even he can fabricate cause for that."

Morgan took that in silently.

"I'm just not sure where to go with it. Does God want me out of there? Is it His hand behind it? Those kids are my life." Her voice broke as the emotion sneaked up and caught her. She hadn't meant to say so much, and probably shouldn't have, judging by the clench of Morgan's jaw. She turned away and battled down the loss. Could the Lord really take her work and her kids away? What did that leave?

They stopped for gas and used the rest rooms, which were surprisingly clean for a roadside gas station. They bought a small bag of apples, and Morgan got coffee.

The thought of so much caffeine made her head swim. But maybe he hadn't slept well. She said, "Do you want me to drive?"

He cocked his head. "Well . . . no."

"No one touches your mean machine?"

"Nothing personal." He opened her door.

"Suit yourself. I have charge of the apples."

His eyes dropped to the bag in her lap. "I have ways of getting what I want."

Her breath caught sharply, and she pulled one from the bag and handed it over. He tossed it lightly, then took a bite and started around to his side.

Jill chose an apple of her own, a little mushy inside, but sweet and juicy. "Do you have any music that isn't heart-wrenching?"

He opened his CD case. "Take your pick." Then he swung the car out and around, and they resumed their journey.

They checked in to a Marriott in Denver, which was not as far as she had thought they would get. But it was eight o'clock at night and it felt good to stop. She waited beside Morgan, credit card ready, but he told the clerk to put both rooms on his.

"Morgan, I'm—"

He slid her card back at her and winked for the desk clerk to do as he said. When he turned from the counter and handed over her key, she said, "I don't expect you to pay my way."

"Mm-hmm." He stooped to lift both of their bags, no bellhop required.

"I mean it, Morgan."

"Consider it wages, then."

"Wages?" She stalked behind him to the elevator.

"Know any nurses who work for free?" He pushed the button.

Jill expelled her breath and followed him into the elevator as soon as the doors opened. "I'm not your nurse. I'm doing this to . . ." She caught the rail as the elevator started up.

"To?" He fixed her in his indigo gaze.

"It's for myself as much as anything. To be part of it. You shouldn't pay for that."

He just pulled a slow smile. "Well, regarding finances, I have you beat."

She raised her chin. "I didn't pursue teaching to get rich."

"And aren't you smugly self-satisfied? Shallow Morgan Spencer flashing his money."

She flushed. "I didn't mean that. I knew you'd be successful. I think it's great. I just—"

"You're above all that, I know." The doors opened and he stooped again for their bags, checking the room numbers as he stepped out.

"I'm not above it, Morgan. It's just not what defines me."

The corners of his mouth deepened.

She stammered, "I don't mean it defines you. I don't know what defines you. I . . ." She swallowed the irritation driving her mouth down the rabbit trail. If she could think straight, she'd say what she meant.

He stopped outside her door and reached for her key. She mutely produced it.

"We'll just tuck the bags inside and catch the restaurant before they close."

"Dinner's on me."

"Wanna bet?" His smile was as smugly self-satisfied as any attitude he'd accused her of. What was he trying to prove? Better yet—she applied her assessment skills—what was his motivation for this particular behavior?

In the restaurant, he seated her with the brush of his hand across her shoulder. Torture, perhaps? She had broiled salmon with glazed carrots and garlic mashed potatoes. That should ensure nothing untoward happened between them, although Morgan's words were a better indication. *I'm long past need, Jill.* Was he trying to show her what she'd missed?

But when they had finished and were taking the elevator up, he asked, "Want to catch a movie?" He held up his card key, and she realized he meant to watch it in the room. The elevator stopped, and he took her elbow and walked her out.

She shook her head. "I guess not, Morgan."

A shadow of some emotion she couldn't place passed through his eyes. "Just a movie, Jill, to unwind. You can have one bed, I'll have the other."

She could not even imagine putting herself in that position. She sighed. "No thanks." Did he honestly think she would? No doubt his intentions were innocent, but he would have no idea how critically she avoided any semblance of impropriety, how conscious she was of what people might have guessed or suspected of her past. Feeling like a fool, she started for her own door as Morgan let himself into his room.

She opened her door, stalked to the bed, and unzipped her bag, pulled out the pajama shorts and spaghetti-strap top she slept in, her toothbrush, and facial cleanser. Once ready for bed, there would be no second thoughts. And she would sleep just fine without unwinding, thank you.

Arms full, she headed for the bathroom when the knock came on her door. Which part of no did he not understand? She jockeyed her load and pulled the door open.

Morgan held out the laptop. "You wanted to do your mail."

She looked from his face to the computer he offered. She would have remembered that the minute she sat down to pray, would have kicked herself for not asking to use it while she had the hotel phone lines for the modem. "Thank you." She had no hand free to take it.

Morgan stepped in and set it on the luggage holder under the wooden hangers. "You're welcome." He let himself out while she still stood, arms full, looking after him.

They definitely needed to find some middle ground where they could operate without triggering old thoughts and feelings. And his polite veneer only went so deep. She washed and changed, then went online and accessed her account.

Kelsey wondered a moment if it was disloyal to write to Jill without Mom's knowing. On the one hand, she shouldn't do anything that she knew would hurt someone, especially the person she loved so much. But Mom had introduced them and allowed her to guess the truth and address it. If she asked, Mom would say she could write, but just now she didn't want to add any more grief or concern. The strain already showed in Mom's face, though she tried to seem so positive.

Hi, Jill, Kelsey's fingers flew on the keyboard. *I've been so sick today I thought I would sleep like a rock, but I'm wide awake. If I close my eyes it feels like I'm in a rowboat in a storm. Everything I eat tastes like dirt. I know I shouldn't complain because the treatment is helping my army, but the angels don't have to eat. I can't even blame the hospital food. Dad brings me whatever sounds good, but when I put it in my mouth it doesn't taste anything like it's supposed to. Gripe, gripe, gripe.*

A wave of nausea brought a hand hard to her mouth. Kelsey grabbed for the plastic kidney-shaped dish and knocked it off the tray. *Hold it down. Fight. Don't lose the little food you actually got into your stomach.* Her instructions battled down the wave and she returned to her keyboard.

I'm giving my angels serious orders to mount an attack in my stomach. But could you pray, too? I'm sooo tired of feeling like throwing up, almost as much as actually throwing up. I know that's gross to talk about, but I try really hard not to complain to anyone else. Lucky you, huh?

Do you know what I find really comforting right now? That banquet waiting in heaven. Please don't think that's depressing, Jill. I think about heaven a lot. More than most kids, I guess. I imagine what it'll be like and sometimes I look forward to it.

She paused, almost deleted that whole last part, then refused. She'd promised herself to be honest here, to say whatever she wanted. She might never see Jill again. She wasn't stupid. Rachel was dying, and she might, too.

Rachel's brother Josh came to see me today even though she is still in the ICU. The doctors aren't hopeful for her. I'm praying for a miracle, and so is Josh. We didn't do much laughing. In fact, we cried. Do you think it's okay that I hugged him? And now came the really risky part. *I guess what I really want to ask is, was it wrong to want to kiss him? Please answer. Kelsey*

In the middle of writing the letter to Joey's mom, the message came up saying she had mail. She clicked it immediately, trying not to hope too much. She'd already been disappointed not to find anything from Kelsey when she opened her account. But this was Kelsey, and she must have just sent it. Jill's heart fluttered. Three days in a row now. *Thank you, Lord.*

Then she started to read, feeling Kelsey's nausea in her own stomach. Why did it have to be so hard? Couldn't the Lord take the sickness away? *Please, Jesus.* And then she read Kelsey's thoughts about heaven. She closed her eyes against the sting of tears and pressed her fingers to the keys of Morgan's laptop.

Dearest Kelsey, You can look forward to heaven, but not anytime soon! This is going to work! I know you're miserable and ill, but in a few days, less than a week, they will give you Morgan's bone marrow. You wanted fresh angels. Well, that will be a whole army, and they will not be coming to carry you to heaven.

Maybe it was a risk to speak that way to her daughter. But she would not consider the alternative. She read the next part of Kelsey's note and stopped cold on the last line. Then she reread the paragraph and pictured Kelsey typing it. She wanted to kiss him? And she was fourteen?

Jill bit her lip, admitting she'd thought about it herself at that age, though never once been in a situation to actually consider it. Did Roger and Cinda know? By Kelsey's tone, she doubted it. For some reason, her daughter had chosen her as the one to whom she could ask or say anything. And hadn't she given her that permission herself?

She considered carefully, then wrote,

Kelsey, I'm glad you were there for Josh. It must be devastating to face losing his sister. I'm sure your hug was a great comfort. To answer your question, I have to say I'm not a very good one to ask. My heart led me into kisses that were not in the Lord's plan, and I made poor choices because of it. Your faith is very strong. Trust what you know, not what you feel.

Her fingers poised above the keyboard, then she signed it, *Love, Jill.*

She sent the mail and returned to the letter she was composing, but her mind would not switch subjects. A moment later the mail message flashed again. She clicked.

Dear Jill, I do know what you mean. But are you sure those kisses weren't God's will? Except for that, I wouldn't be here.

Jill jolted. She hadn't meant to give Kelsey that message. Well, since her daughter was obviously online . . .

Kelsey, you were the great good that came from my wrong choices. God takes even our mistakes and turns them to good. I would never wish one single kiss away, now, if it meant you would not be alive.

She sent it and this time waited for the reply.

I know you mean that, because I saw how much you wanted to help me. But if I hadn't come out of it, would you still wish you hadn't kissed Morgan?

Jill's heart lurched again. The child was certainly direct. She did not want to give her daughter the wrong message, and she did not want to think about kissing Morgan. She pressed her fingertips between her eyebrows. *Lord, what do I say?* The truth. She had promised Kelsey the truth.

Kelsey, I loved Morgan very much, too much. I thought about kissing him long before we ever did. The trouble was, I didn't know where to stop. No, the truth is I didn't want to. Honey, some doors are not meant to be opened too early. Be patient.

Again she sent it and waited.
The answer that came broke her heart.

What if I don't have time?

20

J ill woke, got dressed, went down, and found what passed for the exercise room. She ran on the treadmill for an hour, then hung the towel over her neck and went back up to her room. When she had showered, she applied enough makeup to hide her lack of sleep and the tears Kelsey's question had brought. She dressed in white capris and a slate blue shirt, slipped on her sandals and finger combed her hair.

She wasn't hungry, but she needed some juice to boost her blood sugar after the workout, so she went down to the restaurant. The waiter brought her a menu, but she said, "Just some orange juice, please. Do you have fresh squeezed?"

"No, ma'am. Just regular."

She drank it gratefully anyway, then sat alone with her thoughts. Her reply to Kelsey had been nowhere near adequate. A blind assurance that the Lord's plan for her life was perfect. What messed things up was turning away from His love, His directions. *Jesus knows the desires of your heart,* she'd said. *Trust Him to fulfill them.*

Jill went back up to her room. She hadn't remembered to bring her Bible, so she checked the drawer and took out the one placed by the Gideons. She sought the gospel account of the Lord's own words. She read the parable of the sower and pictured a tall, lanky figure in rough, gauzy robes walking his land, one hand reaching to the bag, then tossing seed.

Maybe she was shallow ground, allowing fear for Kelsey to gain a stronghold. The Lord couldn't take root because her stones and poor soil wouldn't hold the surety that Kelsey would live to kiss a young man, to harbor the dreams that were only now beginning to take form.

Then again, maybe the fear and doubt were weeds and thorns choking out the confidence she had in Christ's love. *I want to believe, Lord.* But Shelly's words came back to haunt her. *"Well, from my point of view, those of you who believe are not in any better position than those of us who don't."*

That couldn't be true. Faith was deeper than outward appearances. It was what went on inside the heart in spite of sickness . . . and death? She trembled as the birds came and plucked away her assurance yet again. *Jesus, make my heart fertile.* Then she turned her prayers to Kelsey's needs and the roommate who might already be with Jesus and the brother, Josh, who had come to mean something to Kelsey. So fragile, all of them.

She clasped her hands and rested her lips on the knuckles. "And bless Morgan for disrupting his life to save the child he's never seen." The magnitude of his gift was immeasurable. She replaced the Bible in the drawer beside the bed and looked at the clock. 8:10. How long would Morgan sleep?

She packed her things and set the bag beside the door, then turned on a morning TV show and waited for him. An hour passed. Shouldn't they be on the road? It was another eleven hundred miles to the coast. She clicked the button on the remote and turned off the TV. Then she went to Morgan's room and knocked. She was turning away when he opened.

"Mmm." He rubbed his face.

She'd woken him. "I'm sorry, but I thought we should get going."

He stood in athletic shorts and nothing else. His torso was tanned and lean.

She averted her eyes. "It's nine-thirty and we have so far to go still. I've already exercised and—"

He winced. "I get the picture." His breath had an acrid tang, and he did not appear to have slept well.

"If you need some time, I'll be in my room."

He nodded and closed the door. Not exactly Mr. Cheerful in the morning. Maybe he hadn't slept at all. Maybe he was sick. She shouldn't have knocked, should have simply waited. She went back to her room and noticed his laptop still on the desk. She booted up and went into her e-mail account. May as well finish the letters she'd been too upset to complete last night.

Nearly an hour later, Morgan knocked. This time he smelled of coffee, but his eyes were still hollow and hooded. "Let's go." His bag was on his shoulder.

"Give me just a second to shut down the computer." She did so as she spoke, then packed it up and carried it, since he had shouldered her bag with his. Morgan leaned on the wall of the elevator, eyes closed. He must have had a miserable night.

"Do you want breakfast?"

"No." He left the elevator and started for the desk.

"Are you all right?" She rested her hand on his arm.

"Mostly."

"Morgan, are you sick?"

He slid his key onto the counter and reached for hers. "I'm fine, Jill."

When they went outside she was sure something was wrong. "What's the matter? Does your head hurt?"

"You could say that." He squinted in the brightness. "Here." He handed her the car keys.

"You're letting me drive?" Now she was really concerned.

"Just the first leg. 70 west." He stuffed the bags into the trunk, then settled into the passenger seat and covered his eyes with his hand.

"Did you take some aspirin?"

"I don't need nursing yet, Florence. Just drive."

She turned the key in the engine. She had never driven a car like this, but something in her reveled. "Music?"

"No."

"Would you like the top down?"

"No."

She took I-25 a short distance to I-70 through the western side of the city, toward the mountains that had been visible from their hotel. It was the road she had taken to Rick's ranch, cutting directly up into the mountains. Morgan's car handled the grade and curves with ease, far better than the rental she'd driven the last time. She could get used to this.

After a little more than an hour, he stirred, took his hand from his eyes, and watched her. "How do you like it?"

"It's great. Like driving a cloud. Very posh."

"Mm-hmm." Now that his eyes were mostly open, he kept them that way, mainly trained on her.

She sent her glance up the canyon walls as often as she could look up from the road. "This is so beautiful."

"Mm-hmm." But he didn't look out. "Not many women can wear a short haircut like that."

She shot him a glance. "I meant the—"

"Did you cut it for the reunion?"

"No."

"Just before, though."

How could he know that? "I wanted a change. And how did you know that anyway?"

"Your pictures."

She screwed up her brow.

He shifted higher in his seat, seemingly waking up. "You had a package of photos on your counter. And they were dated."

He was right. She had picked them up the day before he came. The police department picnic. "You looked at my pictures?"

"Some great shots of Dan."

She cast him a glance. "They were good, weren't they?"

"And your pool pose. Nice swimsuit."

"Thank you." She refused to blush.

"Could have seen it better without Dan hanging all over."

"Does this have a point?" She couldn't help frowning.

He laughed softly, then rubbed his temple.

"Is it a migraine?"

"No, Jill. Just the usual Crown Royal variety."

Crown Royal. He had a hangover? Morgan? "Oh. I'm . . . so you . . ."

"Did it to myself?" He snapped his fingers. "There go all the sympathy points."

She had no idea where to go from there, so she said nothing.

After a while he said, "Pull over at the next turnout. I'll take over."

"I'm fine."

His eyes trailed her slowly. "Yes, you are. But I'd like to drive."

This time there was no stopping the flush up her neck. What had gotten into him anyway? "Morgan, I think it would be better . . . it makes me uncomfortable . . ." *When my mouth and my brain disconnect?*

She could give a flawless PowerPoint presentation for the entire school and never miss a word.

"Here's one on the right." He pointed.

She slowed into the turnout and brought the car to a stop. They both got out and Morgan waited at her door until she slid in. Then he closed the door and walked around.

"I'll be glad to drive again."

He slid into his seat. "That's already more than anyone else has done."

"Don't I feel special." Then when he didn't answer, she stammered, "For getting to drive the car, for being the only one who . . ." She clamped her lips shut.

Wrist draped over the wheel, he turned to her, indigo eyes like the night sky over Antarctica. "It didn't mean anything."

Of course it didn't. If there were a hole handy she'd climb right in. Maybe the drop-off would do. But she nodded mutely, her throat squeezing, then focused on the scenery as he pulled out much faster than she would have dared.

He knew exactly what she had intended to say. Don't do or say anything that might suggest there was something between them. "*It makes me uncomfortable . . .*" The throbbing in his head had dulled to a nagging burn—nothing he couldn't deal with. What he couldn't deal with were her flippant remarks. "*Don't I feel special?*"

He shoved his breath out through his teeth, then wove out and around a slower car plugging along the divided mountain grade, letting the silence of the road take the edge from his mood. How much time would he give Ascon, Inc. to respond? Another month, possibly. After that Marlina Aster could find another turnaround specialist. He had more pressing concerns at the moment anyway.

Last night's call to Bern Gershwin had set things in motion financially. "*Are you crazy? You're liquidating that kind of money to gift a foundation without—*"

"*I want it ready, Bern. The procedure is on Thursday. Two hundred and fifty thousand dollars to start with. The funds have to be there.*"

"*Paternity is not legally established. You're throwing in the only card you might hold in order to force an interview.*"

Those words had sunk in. "*I can't worry about that now.*" He could sue later if it came to it, show that they had accepted his gift.

"*Well, here's what you can worry about. If you sell those tech stocks*" *now when they're in the basement, that's a hit you will not recover from. Your portfolio is less than half its worth already."*

"Thanks for the reminder."

"You're not thinking this through, Morgan. Get with me at the first chance. I'll make room. Someone needs to be objective."

"That's a luxury I don't have." But he promised to play racquetball when he got back in town.

No, he was not objective at the moment. His daughter needed more than his marrow, and the funds had to be transferred for Kelsey's care to go forward. Try to handle that objectively. Jill had placed her in a family that scratched by, had mortgaged everything already for her care, and couldn't even find decent insurance. *Drywall.*

He darted out around a van huffing along in the left lane and noticed Jill's knuckles pale on the edge of her seat. There *was* quite a drop-off to the right. He slid back over smoothly. He had no intention of putting them over the edge. Not before his marrow was safely inside his daughter.

Of course, there was still the agreement to be available for several more years if further draws were necessary, and more immediately for plasma and the like. The fewer different blood factors she had to deal with the better. And all of that took money, and most of his money was accounted for in nonliquid assets, such as his mortgaged four-million-dollar home, and growth stocks that had flattened for the moment. He had seen the tech-market crash coming and held only the ones he thought would rebound. They hadn't yet, and this was not a good time to liquidate.

But no one had consulted him. He eased up on the gas and sensed Jill's relief. He hadn't been that far over the top, but then she probably had little experience with the Rocky Mountain curves and plunges.

He put in an Eagles CD and cranked up "Hotel California." He was almost ready to eat, and Jill had to be, too. He glanced at her again. That fierce control was worse than her insouciant remarks. He reached over and touched her hand. "Are you hungry?"

"I guess."

"Fast food, or do you want to go in somewhere?"

She swallowed. "It doesn't matter."

Something besides hunger twisted his stomach, something like guilt. Oh, there was always guilt connected with Jill. But he had been harsher than he intended. She was only trying to get along. As the needle of his speedometer reached ninety, he eased off the gas again and put the Thunderbird on cruise. He settled back in his seat and realized there would not be many food opportunities for a while. Well, she hadn't sounded famished, only hurt.

He sighed. This madcap idea was proving harder than he'd thought. At least she stayed focused on the scenery, which gradually changed from forested mountain slopes to stark red mesa canyons through Glenwood Springs and beyond. In Grand Junction, he exited and found a Taco Bell drive-up.

Jill said, "I need to use their rest room."

"Okay." He pulled through and parked instead. They could stretch and take care of all their needs with one stop. She was out before he had the engine turned off. He watched her cross the parking lot on her long, fluid legs in those halfway-down-the-calf pants. If anything, her legs were more defined and shapely than before. Not that it helped to notice.

He climbed out and took in the towering stone walls that surrounded the area like a bowl, desolate eroded cliffs with flat mesa tops surrounding the green land of the irrigated valley. The edge of civilization was stark; one side of the highway lush with grass, trees, and orchards, the other rutted peaks of dirt, stone, and heat. Amazing.

He went inside, visited the men's room, and met Jill at the counter. She'd already purchased a couple tacos, accomplishing her intention of going dutch. He ordered three tacos and a Pepsi, and by the time he joined her at the table, she was halfway into her first taco.

As she reached for her water cup, he caught her hand. "I'm sorry for being irascible."

"It's all right. Morgan . . ." She tugged her fingers in his hold. Touchy, wasn't she?

He caught it between both of his. "You said friends. Dan was way friendlier than this."

Her eyes flattened. "It's hard to eat tacos one-handed."

He smiled. She did have a point. He let go and bit into the crunchy taco, warm spicy meat and cold lettuce with a touch of cheese. He chewed it slowly, studying her face. He still had two left when she finished, but she got up and cleared her trash, then seemed lost whether to sit down again. He stood and motioned her to the chair. "Don't worry, I only bite in the morning."

She sat down, probably wishing she had not rushed through her meal and left her hands with nothing to do.

"Would you like something more?"

She shook her head. "No thanks."

"Did you get your letters done?"

Her gaze finally lighted. "Some of them. I had some mail to deal with, as well." A flush crept over her features.

Must have been personal. "Dan?"

Her brow puckered. "What? No, it wasn't Dan. Morgan . . ."

"I know. Off limits."

"It's just not what you think."

He cocked his head. "Those photos were strongly incriminating."

Another flush. "Well, Dan is . . . physical. But we're not . . . we weren't . . ." She huffed her frustration.

"Intimate?"

She snatched his taco wrappers and wadded them, shoved them into the bag, and wadded it so tightly it popped.

He caught her wrist. "Do you think I care whether you and Dan got it on?"

She jerked her hand away with a look somewhere between kicked puppy and attack dog. Obviously not a wise choice of words.

"Jill, your love life is your business. I was just making conversation."

She got to her feet, stalked to the trash bin and deposited the bag, then walked out. Morgan took a last drag on his soda, then tossed it in the trash and followed her. She stood at the car, way more shaken than circumstances warranted.

He had the keyless remote in hand, but he didn't unlock the door. "Jill." He fingered the buttons on the remote. "I don't know what has you so frosted."

She turned her face away.

"Why don't you tell me so I can avoid it next time." He hadn't meant to be cruel. If he had a clue, he'd undo it. "Did you want me to care? Is that it?"

She pressed her hands to her eyes. "It was your automatic assumption."

He backpedaled and met her thoughts. That she and Dan had something going? So what?

She sucked a jagged breath and faced him. "I've spent fifteen years avoiding indiscretion. Rebuilding trust and respect."

He searched her face, catching her thrust.

"Dan hugged and kissed me. Nothing more—with him or anyone else."

232 || KRISTEN HEITZMANN

It shouldn't hurt, but it did. Jill was too warm, too loving to have closed herself off in some attempt to recapture her virtue. Fifteen years avoiding indiscretion? No wonder she was so uptight. "Why didn't you marry someone?"

Her breaths came sharp and quick. "I just . . . there wasn't . . ."

He pulled her softly to his chest and closed her into his arms. "All right, don't try to talk. Just breathe."

"With you holding me?"

Smiling, he cradled her head. "Aw, c'mon, Jill. What are friends for?"

"We don't do friends well, Morgan."

True. He wanted nothing more than to turn her face up and kiss her. That would probably merit CPR. He pressed his cheek to the crown of her head, trying to understand what she'd told him, and understanding too well. The trauma of their relationship had rendered her unable to accept another.

He closed his eyes, knowing that trauma too well.

"Please, Morgan."

He let her go and touched the button to disarm the alarm and unlock her door. She slid in with obvious relief. There ought to be something more he could say, but silence stretched between them. After twenty minutes of driving, she was asleep.

21

Jill woke with a jolt, and Morgan soothed her with a hand to her arm. She cleared her throat. "Where are we?"

"South of Richfield, Utah. I-15. We'll take it down through Nevada and stay the night in Las Vegas."

"Can't we make it all the way in?"

He glanced at her. "It would be really late."

"I can drive some of it." She rubbed her face, coming awake. Another night in a hotel was not a good idea, especially in a place like Sin City. She wanted this trip over.

"We'll stop in Vegas."

Maybe when they got there, she could convince him to go on. She looked around her. "You said Utah?"

"Mm-hmm."

"How far are we from Salt Lake?"

"Way south. There's a map in the glove box."

She opened it and pulled out the map. A small square fluttered to the floor. She picked it up and stared at her own senior picture, the one she'd given him in exchange for his.

Morgan frowned. "That was for the reunion. So I'd recognize you."

She looked from the picture to his face. Had he really doubted he would? His features were so impressed on her, she could never have forgotten. She would never need a photo to know him.

"If you open up the map, you'll see we're down near the bottom of the state and heading southwest. We'll clip the tip of Arizona, then enter Nevada."

But she slid the map back into the glove box, along with her picture, and snapped it shut. Her sleep had almost driven away the tension between them, but even now she felt his arms around her, his chest hard and strong against her face. Why had he bridged that gap? Because she admitted hugging Dan?

He turned up the music.

She didn't recognize the CD he had playing. "What group is this?"

"Scorpions. This song's 'Rock You Like a Hurricane.'" He showed her the case.

"I haven't heard of them." She listened mostly to Christian groups. Morgan, it seemed, had more varied and harder tastes.

But that song ended and another began, a slow, melodic electric guitar intro, then a male voice softly sang about time, needing time to win back the love he'd lost. Jill leaned her head to the side as the melancholy strains whispered to her ears that he would be there, he would be there. She did not want to hear another love song with Morgan, but its beauty was hard to resist. And with it came thoughts of all they'd done wrong. "I'm still loving you. . . ."

Jill ached. Much more of this, and she'd wish she had stayed home. She couldn't even suspect Morgan had chosen that song intentionally because he looked as melancholy as she. Yet he played it to the end, saying only, "They're a German group, although they record in English. You can hear it in some of the words."

The scenery they drove through at the tip of Arizona was stunning, the road weaving through the massive stone formations in sweeping curves. Morgan had put the top down once she woke up, and the sun blazed in a cloudless sky, dropping slowly as they entered the Nevada desert region.

"Are you hot?"

She nodded, and he closed up the car and turned on the air. But it had been wonderful going through that awesome landscape with nothing overhead to limit the view.

"We should be into Vegas by dinnertime."

"I really think we could go all the way. Why start again in the morning?" Especially with the slow, painful starts he made.

Morgan draped his wrist over the wheel. "I booked two rooms at the Bellagio for tonight."

"The Bellagio?"

"A little place on the strip. It's got some paintings you'll enjoy." He sent her a glance. "Oh, and I got tickets to a show."

"What show?"

"O."

She gathered her brow. "What?"

"Cirque du Soleil aquatic theater. Tenth row."

"Oh my gosh. I can't believe it."

"Still want to drive through?"

She gripped her hands together. "Well . . . no." She laughed. "Cirque du Soleil. Oh, Morgan." She should not encourage his extravagance.

"Just don't tell Tara."

The sister she'd met when she went to see Celia. "Would she like it?"

"She's crazy about acrobatics."

Jill pictured her vibrant face. "I can imagine." At his puzzled glance she said, "I met her when I went over to get your address."

He frowned but didn't fume. "She's an imp. Way too much like me."

Jill smiled. "How?"

"Well, for one thing she's a ham. Give her an audience and she *will* perform. She's got an opinion on everything, and her mouth's hinged in the middle."

"I'm sure you've spoiled her rotten."

"I've given it my very best shot."

Jill loved the tone in his voice when he talked about his family. "How's your dad?"

"He never changes. I think he's Moses or something. Just keeps tapping his staff and all manner of things go right."

Jill pictured Hank Spencer. Morgan had gotten his deep blue eyes from him. So had Kelsey, then. "Have you spoken with them since . . ."

"You dropped your little bombshell? No."

Her spirit sank. "I didn't know what else to do. You only list a post-office box, and I didn't want to tell you everything in a letter. Why don't you have a street address?"

"I do. I just don't let it out."

"Your mother was very kind, once she got over the shock."

He switched hands on the wheel. "Nowhere near the shock I'd

give your mother showing up at her door."

Jill blanched. "Morgan . . ."

"What's the matter?" He threw the mock question with a wicked grin.

"Swear to me you will not do that."

He eyed her a long moment. "So they're not apprised of this situation."

She swallowed hard. "They don't know anything about Kelsey. They don't even know I made sure my aunt would give them my number if she ever wanted to find me."

"They think you're off with me on a pleasure trip?"

She rubbed her face. "They don't know I'm out of town. I forgot to call."

"Forgot?"

"All right, avoided. Morgan . . ." Again her mind would not send the words to her mouth.

"That's okay, Jill. You can perform your act of mercy in secret and return with no one the wiser."

"It's not that. They just wouldn't understand." She loosened the seat belt across her chest. "They would take it personally."

"That you've consorted yet again with the devil?"

Pain broke over her at his words. She wanted to deny it, but it was far too close to their perception. "They blame both of us."

"Really."

"It's true. It has taken everything in me to win back the modicum of respect I have."

He frowned. "Maybe I should have that talk with them after all."

"No." She gripped his forearm without thinking.

He looked down at her hand. "You're shaking."

She drew her hand away. "It's just . . . difficult."

"It's been fifteen years, Jill. They're still punishing you?"

She drew a jagged breath. "I think it's me. I can't get past how I hurt them."

"*You* hurt *them?*" He almost spit the words.

This was not good. She had touched a nerve. "Can we talk about something else?"

"Oh, sure. Let's move on to something cheerful like our daughter's leukemia."

Jill jolted, dropped her face to her hands.

He expelled his breath. "I'm sorry. That was way out of line."

She was shaking, with no indication of stopping anytime soon.

"I'm really sorry. I can't believe I said that. This is hard for both of us, but it's nothing compared to what Kelsey's up against. I just can't get a handle on that part."

She raised her face from her hands. "It's okay, Morgan." She had Kelsey's e-mails, the visits, the sound of her voice, and the touch of her hand to make it real for her. He had none of that. She bit the side of her lip and watched him for a moment, then said, "I'm thinking of a word that rhymes with hat."

He gave her a full turn of his head on that one. The lines eased between his brows and alongside his mouth as he returned his focus to the road. "Is it a pitiable state of corpulence?"

She smiled. "No, it's not fat." One thing she had mastered were the escape routes from thoughts and emotions that were too volatile to linger upon.

Morgan followed her lead, but after several rounds of guessing the rhyme he said, "Feel better?"

She sighed. "Not really."

"Tell me your darkest sin."

"What?"

"Come on." He twisted the lid from a water bottle, steering with his knee. "The thing you're most ashamed of." He drank, then held it out to her..

She shook her head, then answered, "Doubt."

Capping the bottle, he raised his brows. "What do you doubt?"

She moistened her lips. "God."

"That He exists, or His goodness?"

It surprised her he would take it seriously. "I doubt His love."

He mulled that a moment. "Why?"

"I don't feel it. And I don't see it in my life." She looked down at her joined hands. "I don't seem to pass it on very well. I've been a believer since I was nine, but I still don't get it."

Morgan nodded. "The puzzle of God."

"What do you believe?" She would not have been so bold if he hadn't brought it up.

"I believe God exists, and He is good, and He is love."

She had not expected that.

But he added, "That's why I'm certain I'm damned."

His words shot through her. "Why?"

"Dichotomy. Goodness cannot abide its evil twin."

She searched his face to find the joke. Why would he say that? To shock her? To make her value her own salvation? In fact it did. Without that assurance, how could she face life? She shook her head. "I don't know what to say."

"Normally it triggers a desire to resurrect the dead. I'll save you the trouble."

She shifted to face him. "I can't believe you're that terrible."

"Nature requires balance. For every action, reaction."

"But God is above nature—both justice and mercy. Jesus accomplished justice so we could experience mercy."

"*Qué será, será.*"

"But, Morgan, have you asked forgiveness, sought salvation?"

He smiled. "There you go." He touched the turn signal and moved out around a loaded RV. "The point is, you must actually believe God's love, or you wouldn't want it for me."

He was right. It hit her with amazing power. If she didn't know inside that there was something better, why would she feel such despair for him? That despair opened like a chasm when she recalled it hadn't always been that way. He hadn't used the same Christian lingo, but his reverence had run deep as a well. How had it evaporated?

They drove in silence through miles and miles of dirt and lumps of scrubby growth, with Joshua trees, like crippled prophets, shouting to the wind. As the sun sent its last lingering rays across the desert, empty and flat, Jill's soul spread out, exhausted. Then the lights of Las Vegas beckoned like a carnival of attractions. They were almost to the end of the strip when they reached the Bellagio. She had no energy to argue.

The bellman took their bags, the valet their car. The "little place on the strip" was immense and extraordinary, a casino as large as a city block, glamorous and elegant and so far removed from Jill's experience it might have been another world. The entry ceiling alone, covered with giant multicolored glass flowers, cost five million dollars, according to the desk clerk. The floor was all mosaic tiles, and flowering trees and draping planters produced a powerful perfume wherever they walked. They took the elevator to their rooms on the twelfth floor. Morgan's was across the hall and he tipped the bellman for both rooms.

Jill stood in the room, more tastefully elegant than any she'd set foot in to date, including places she'd lived. The king-size bed took only a small amount of the space appointed in tones of gray and rose with sitting chairs, lamps, and decorative tables. The bathroom alone was worth spending time in, with its soaking tub separate from the shower and a telephone handy. A courtesy robe hung in the closet.

This was not real. It was some wonderful dream, only her mind would never have imagined it. She had barely unpacked when Morgan tapped her door. His hair was damp, and he'd changed to an impeccably tailored suit. She stared. "Morgan, you look—I don't . . ."

He stroked his chin. "A speech pattern you've picked up from your students?"

"Very funny." She pushed his arm. "I'm trying to say I didn't bring anything fancy enough to accompany you looking so . . ."

"Ye-s?"

She frowned. "You know exactly how you look."

"Stroke my vanity." The amusement was deep in his eyes.

She studied him boldly. "Sophisticated, debonair . . ." She faltered and looked at the wall. "Way too handsome."

"What was that last part?"

She jutted her chin back at him. "Egotistical."

He straightened his silk tie and shrugged. "Humility is overrated."

"Well, my choice of outfits is humble at best. You didn't say I needed anything like this."

"There are shops downstairs. We can get you something appropriate."

Without her summer income and the extra pay for the coordinator position given to Pam, she'd be hard pressed to pay her mortgage. "It'd be cheaper to order room service."

"And miss Cirque du Soleil?"

She should have brought the black sheath, but she'd had no idea she'd need it. She had packed practically for a few days of assisting Morgan in his home. Disappointment tugged.

"Dress size six?" He looked down at her feet. "Shoe size seven?"

"And a half. But, Morgan . . ." This was insane. She hadn't even considered shoes. She sighed. "There's cash in my wallet." From what she knew of hotel gift shops, it would probably wipe that out.

"Just give me your key."

She handed it over. "You'll charge it to my room?"

He smiled. "Freshen up. I'll be back."

She should just say no. As much as she'd love to have dinner and see the show—but he was already out the door. She pressed her fingertips to her forehead after he'd gone. So she was buying a new dress and shoes. Hardly something to lose sleep over. If Morgan's own attire was any indication, his taste was exquisite. He would choose something nice. So why did it seem so imprudent?

Because she was completely out of her element. Midwest Cinderella at the ball. If she and Dan were from different planets, at least theirs were near and terrestrial compared with Morgan's gas giant. But it was done now. She went into the bathroom and filled the tub for a quick soak. Lowering herself in, she wet a washcloth and held it over her face, breathing slowly and letting out the stress of the day.

And there had been plenty of it. But there had been good moments, too. Morgan was wonderful company. He always had been, and even now with their circumstances between them . . . but she couldn't linger too long. She didn't know how quickly Morgan would accomplish his mission, but she did not want to be still soaking when he returned. She toweled dry with the thick plush towel, then slipped into the terry courtesy robe.

At the lighted makeup mirror, she applied the sort of look she imagined this level of sophistication called for. While keeping it subtle for her natural coloring, she darkened her eyelids and lips more than usual, blush a little bolder along the cheekbone.

She applied perfume and tossed her hair with hairspray, curling a few tendrils into place, a far more glamorous look than she'd ever attempted. When the knock came at the door, she called from the bathroom, "Just leave it on the bed."

When she heard the outer door close again, she went out. A tissue-wrapped parcel, shoe box, nylons, and even a silver clutch purse. She grimaced. The man had no concept of budget. Shaking her head, she unfolded the tissue from the hanger and stared at the dress.

Beautiful did not describe it. It was understated elegance. Steel gray with a slight shimmer, sleeveless with a gathered scoop front and a similar, though lower, scoop in the back. It was fully lined, requiring no slip and the cut allowing no bra. But it was modest in spite of that, thanks in part to her scanty endowment. *Thank you, Lord.*

Then she saw the label. Giorgio Armani. Though she'd never seen an Armani label, she knew the Italian designer was expensive, the kind of expensive famous people could afford, not Iowa schoolteachers. What was Morgan thinking? She searched for a tag but found no price anywhere. Maybe it was better not to know until after the show.

She slipped on the dress, nylons, and silver heels she would never have dared wear before tonight. She closed her eyes. "I'm Jill Runyan. I teach special ed, drive a secondhand Honda, and live in a townhouse with my cat." Then she looked into the mirror and swallowed hard.

She didn't expect to find Morgan in the hall, but there he was, leaning back against the wall, hands lightly in his pockets. His eyes testified.

She swallowed. "I lost Jill Runyan, and there's only this woman in an Armani dress."

He smiled. How come he was still Morgan, no matter what he wore? He removed a small box from his pocket, opened it, and took out a pair of coiled silver earrings. She had brought no jewelry at all, seldom even wearing it to work, given the nature of her kids. Morgan must have noticed.

"Allow me."

Jill stood without moving as he slipped them through the unadorned pierce in her earlobes, his touch whipping her heart to a frenzy.

"Ready?"

"I'm an imposter."

He smiled. "No one would ever know."

They went downstairs and Morgan tucked her hand into his arm. "French or Thai?"

"You decide, Morgan." She was too overwhelmed to choose.

"What do you think of Picasso?"

"The artist?"

"Come on." He took her to the Picasso restaurant within the Bellagio. The walls were actually adorned with original works by the artist.

"He's not a personal favorite of mine, but they do have great food here."

Jill looked at the menu featuring items she'd read about but had never actually encountered and wasn't sure how to pronounce. Foods such as poached oysters garnished with osetra caviar in vermouth sauce. In fact, that was the first thing Morgan ordered, though she chose the warm quail salad with sautéed artichokes and pine nuts, and at Morgan's urging, she followed it with roasted pigeon crusted with honey and nuts. It was incredible food, as exotic to her palate as to her mind.

Morgan cut her a bite of his medallion of fallow deer in Zinfandel sauce. It was almost too much to absorb, food so fabulous it was an art form. And she'd given him tossed greens and artificial crab.

Morgan watched her with amusement. "Do you like it?"

"I don't think a prosaic word such as *like* can be applied here."

They had to pick up the tickets for O an hour prior to their ten-thirty show time, but Morgan took her through the conservatory containing a sweeping staircase, trees, and a reflecting pool with fountains surrounded by botanical gardens and little statues clothed in flowers. They toured the fine art gallery, then made their way to the theater. The show spoke to everything creative and artistic in her, not to mention an athletic appreciation for the difficulty of such perfect synchronization of choreography and the stunning effects of costume, color, and flame all performed in or over the massive pool.

After the show they walked outside in the desert night. Jill closed her eyes as they stood at the railing around the Bellagio fountain under the stars. The water danced to the strains of whimsical music, forming patterns and motion to complement the sounds. First the meal, then the show, now this. Every part of her was exhilarated and enraptured. She would never forget it.

Morgan rested his hand on her lower back. "Glad we stayed?"

She leaned her head against his arm. "I've never done anything like this."

His hand curled around her side. "You look good in Armani."

"Who cares if I'll be paying it off for the next three years?"

The corners of his mouth deepened. "It's all paid."

"No it's not." There was no way she'd allow that. "I want the receipt."

"I'm terrible with receipts."

She turned to face him. "Then I can't keep it."

"You can't return it."

"Morgan."

His eyes went to her lips. "Indulge me."

She hoped the darkness hid the flush that burned up from her toes.

He smiled. "I don't often get to buy for someone else."

"How much was it?"

He laughed low. "If you have to ask, you can't afford it."

"I hate that cliché."

He turned back to the fountain, but his palm on her lower back was warm and gentle. "Just let it go, Jill. You worry too much."

"Oh, after all, it's just an Armani gown, shoes, purse, nylons, earrings."

"Things. They don't matter."

Looking up, she saw the poverty in his face.

His night eyes reflected the fountains. "We're just playing anyway."

Was that all it was? One incredible night of make-believe? How could it be anything more? Her throat tightened.

He brought his hand up to her shoulder and stroked her upper arm. "The next fountain show is in fifteen minutes. I think it's the classical one. Do you want to wait?"

"Why not?" Let it last as long as it could. Make a memory that wouldn't fade.

"Let's walk around the pool." He let go and gave her his arm again.

It was so natural to slip her hand along the soft fabric of his sleeve. *We're only playing.* In less than a week, she would be back in Iowa fighting for her job, her kids, and her sanity. He covered her fingers with his as they walked. It conjured memories too painful to probe, and worse, engendered dreams too impossible to entertain. They both knew it.

When they'd viewed each of the fountain shows and her eyelids were starting to droop, Morgan brought her back inside and somehow navigated the immense and circuitous gaming floor to the correct elevator to reach their rooms. Funny, she had thought Las Vegas was all about gambling, but they hadn't gambled at all. Or had they?

Morgan stopped outside her door. "Here's where I say, 'Let's have a drink in my room.' And you politely decline."

"I had a wonderful time, Morgan."

His eyes dropped to her lips. "You know I want to kiss you."

She trembled. "Please don't."

His throat worked and his good-night rasped.

"Sleep well, Morgan."

He stepped back, crossed the hall, and went into his own room.

Jill closed the door behind her, achingly aware of what she'd lost. Not the glamor of Armani or the wonder of the place, but the warmth of Morgan's fingers over hers and his pleasure in giving.

She dropped her face to her hands. No tears came, just the drought of soul she knew too well. She took off the dress and hung it carefully inside the tissue. She took off the earrings, feeling Morgan's fingers there again. What sort of man put a woman's earrings on for her? She laid them on the dresser and went to bed, completely cognizant that sleep no longer knew her name.

The wine at dinner had not begun to touch it. But the bourbon he took from the minibar was real medicine. He poured it over the ice scooped into his glass, closed his eyes, and drank.

His bone marrow harvest was in two days, but the doctors had not forbidden alcohol. He'd have to fast before the procedure so tomorrow night he'd be stone sober. But tonight cut too close. After the first drink, he changed out of his suit. After the second, he brushed his teeth and lay down. After a third he would stop counting, so he left the ice melting in the glass and slipped into sleep.

He woke up at eight o'clock without Jill's assistance. No doubt she'd already run laps around the Bellagio, but he only gargled to clear out the lingering taste in his mouth and showered. Then he brushed his teeth and brewed a cup of French roast just to make him human.

He booted his laptop, remembering he had meant to offer it to Jill last night. She could use it when he was done. They'd have five or six hours on the road, but it didn't matter when they got in. He brought up his mail. There was a reply from Ascon wanting to go forward and several from Denise making certain he'd gotten that word and reminding him of other pending contracts. *What will your schedule allow?* Ordinarily, *she* told *him* his schedule. But he had thrown her off with Kelsey. Well, Ascon would have to wait now until he recuperated.

He scrolled past several dozen hits from previous clients that he would address when he returned, then stopped at a message from Todd. *Stan said its free to talk to you this way but then I have to type it. the good thing is the spell checker fixes my spelling. are you still driving? We rented the Fellowship of the ring. I watched it with Stan. i thought he might faint when the orc came out of the mud. I laughed. Are you going surfing? I told him you said I could come. when can I come? Todd.*

Morgan jotted a reply. *Not yet. Morgan.* Then he retrieved it and added, *Soon, but I have a client breathing down my neck*—now that Marlina Aster had finally made up her mind—*and I have the medical procedure for my daughter. Not sure how soon I'll be surfing. Glad you were there for Stan.*

He powered down the computer and closed it. Dressed in beige slacks and a raw silk woven shirt, California style, he took the laptop to Jill's door.

She answered his knock immediately, wearing the blue shorts that made her legs a mile long, sandals, and a white knit top. Not the sophisticated look of last night, but in a way even more appealing. Dangerously so.

He leaned on the jamb. "Want to do your mail before we check out?"

She reached for the laptop. "That'd be great. Do you think we could have breakfast? I've been up awhile. . . ."

"Hitting the slots?"

"Just the treadmill." But she smelled fresh and looked fresher.

"You run every day?"

"Mostly."

He leaned on the doorjamb. "Which first? Food or e-mail?"

She glanced at the computer. "Let me check one thing. Then I've got to eat."

"You could have already." He followed her into the room, though he hadn't been invited. Her drapes were open wide and the room awash with sunlight. He settled into one of the gray pin-dot chairs and waited while she plugged in the phone cord and booted up. What mail was more important than eating when she was hungry?

Her hair seemed lighter and a little flyaway this morning as she leaned over the laptop and brought up her account.

"Anyone I know?"

She startled. "Um . . . no, not really."

Not really? Now that was interesting. A wash of pleasure touched her features. If he didn't know better, he'd guess it was a love letter. Then again, he didn't know better. She'd sworn Dan was only a friend, but her pictures had been full of him, and he'd been full of her. She moistened her lips and read, then typed a steady reply and sent it.

"Made his day?"

"It's not a man." She exited her account, shut down and closed the computer, looking . . . uncomfortable?

He pulled and released his lower lip, certain now of her discomfort.

She glanced up and away, then met his gaze. "Ready?"

He stood, stretched. "For coffee at least."

He managed half a blueberry muffin, while Jill ate from the buffet and still looked uneasy.

He sipped his coffee. "You may as well just tell me."

"What?"

"It's going to bother you until you do."

She dropped her chin. "It'll bother you."

"I have a heart of steel."

Her eyes were the soft gray of a pigeon's breast with hues of lavender and blue. "It's Kelsey. She's started writing me—I guess to have a sounding board for things she can't say anywhere else."

He swallowed that. Not at all what he'd expected. Kelsey and Jill in direct communication, but he couldn't have one look. The woman who'd pawned off their daughter got daily missives, when he would have—

"I warned you."

He stared at the coffee in his cup.

She expelled her breath. "I'm sorry. I shouldn't have taken it in front of you. It's just that I felt bad for not checking last night, and . . ."

"What does she say?"

He'd put her on the spot, and she looked worse still. But she answered, "Mostly she tells me when she's feeling bad—sick or frightened. Sometimes she asks questions."

Something in Jill's tone . . . he looked up and studied her face.

"She's asked about you."

A hollow opened in his chest. So much for steel.

"What did you tell her?"

Jill forked her fingers into her hair. "How we were before. Student council and sports . . . homecoming."

He nodded silently. Good. Then he wouldn't have to start from scratch when he saw her himself. He finished his coffee. "Ready?"

She nodded. He caught the server's eye and she brought him the check to sign. Then he took Jill's elbow lightly and walked her to the elevator.

"I'm not sure how to pack my dress."

"I have a garment bag." It held his own Armani power suits. When he had gathered all his things, he brought his bags to her room, added her dress, and called for the bellman.

Driving through the remainder of the desert, Morgan kept the top up and the air-conditioner on, but as they neared the coast, he opened it up and breathed in his California air. This was just right. Jill looked around her eagerly as he drove them up the coastal highway. Her eyes reflected ocean and sky as she took in the gulls, boats, and breakers.

"Like it?"

She sighed. "It's beautiful. I haven't seen this coast since I was eleven. And then it was mostly sand castles and Sea World."

They tooled down along the coast on smaller roads to better enjoy the landscape, at last entering Santa Barbara. Unlike the big cities, L.A. and San Diego, the central coast had maintained a sense of normalcy, which the residue of his midwestern upbringing appreciated. But it had a culture and climate unequaled. He turned onto his semi-private road half hidden by trees and shrubs, drove down a short distance, and stopped at the gate.

Jill's eyes widened as he entered the code and the gate swung open. Now she'd understand why he didn't give out his street address. He drove around the dozen shoreline homes atop the cliff overlooking the ocean, then pulled into his driveway and activated his garage door. Jill looked mildly shell-shocked as he parked between his Corvette and SUV.

He turned off the engine and stretched. "Home sweet home."

CHAPTER

22

I t was not the Bellagio. In a way it was more incredible because it was real. This was Morgan's home—this gracious Mediterranean with manicured lawn, pool, garden, and what looked like a guesthouse. They had walked out of the garage into the back, where his yard overlooked the ocean. A pure white gull rode a breeze and dipped toward the water below. The air was scented with jasmine and lilies and other flowering trees and bushes she didn't know. She didn't smell the sea, but she could hear it.

Morgan, too, breathed the air like a hound scenting home, then said, "Want to go in?"

She turned and faced the house. The back side was mostly windows, gracefully arched and many with flower boxes tumbling color down the off-white walls. "I think so."

He opened the French door and let her inside a game room, which held a pool table, home theater, bar, and a plethora of comfortable-looking furniture, much of which faced southwest toward the view she had just left.

A woman in a crisp designer suit of lightweight lavender fabric and stiletto heels came through the arched doorway of the adjoining room and stopped. She had been primed for something, by her expression, but had probably not anticipated a stranger.

Morgan motioned toward the woman. "This is my professional

assistant, Denise Fisher. Denise, Jill Runyan."

"How do you do," Denise responded. Then, "Morgan, I've a dozen things for you to look at." Her finely chiseled face looked stark with the blond hair pulled back into a twist and neatly barretted. Morgan had mentioned his assistant, but Jill had not formed a mental picture.

He sent Denise an easy smile. "Where's Consuela?"

"Upstairs, I believe."

"Have Juan unload the bags." His touch on her elbow was light, but Jill moved with him to the stairs.

"I haven't seen Juan. And, Morgan, there are several items—"

"I'll be with you shortly."

Jill said, "It was nice meeting you, Denise."

Denise gave her a curt smile. "And you."

Morgan's fingers just touched the small of her back as they mounted the stairs. "Hungry?"

"Yes."

"If I can find Consuela, we'll have an early dinner. I'm starved."

They reached the kitchen, and he plucked a bunch of grapes from the bowl on the long white marble counter. He handed them to her and turned at the sound of singing from the long hall at the end of the open area. "Aha. This way."

Jill stopped outside the door where a black-haired, full-bodied woman shook out a sheet and tucked it neatly in at the foot of a white-washed four-poster bed while she filled the room with song. Morgan went in and reached toward her shoulder, but at that moment she straightened into him, screamed and spun, spitting Spanish at a furious rate.

Morgan stepped back, arms spread in innocence. "*¿Qué tal, Consuela?*"

"*¡Diablo!*" She pressed her chest. "You stop my heart."

"You didn't hear me come in. And what was that lovely tune?"

She waved her hands at him. "Don't you see I'm busy?" Then she saw Jill. "This is your guest?"

"Consuela, meet Jill Runyan."

Consuela reached both hands to her, which was awkward, since Jill still held the grapes. "I will have your room finished in a moment."

Jill glanced around at last, noticing the room. It was nicely appointed in muted reds, moss green, and gold, a Thomasville ensemble she'd envied from afar.

Morgan said, "Finish this later. We're starved."

"I make the tamales you like."

"Marvelous. Where's Juan?"

"Juan is not here. He is working."

Morgan raised his brows. "Then his leg is better."

"Sí. It is better."

"Then fetch those tamales."

Jill had to smile. He must be very hungry after only part of a muffin and coffee. They had driven five and a half hours without a stop. But he seemed energized, playful. Probably glad to be home. Who wouldn't be?

"*Uno minuto.*" Consuela waved him from the room.

Jill tore one sprig from the bunch of grapes and handed him the rest as they went back down the hall. He ate the grapes and tossed the stem into the sink, then took her hand. "Come here." He led her out onto the wide balcony from his great room over the walkout lower level. "This is my personal haven. If I'm alone out here, my help leave me that way." He gave a short laugh. "You may have noticed I don't get much respect otherwise."

Jill stepped up to the wrought-iron rail and looked out past his well-ordered yard, to the Pacific Ocean glittering in the sun. A warm breeze caught her hair and spread the scent of citrus from the orange tree just below the balcony. She breathed in softly. "It's so beautiful."

The sun's reflections danced from the water like golden sprites. She didn't know what she had expected. Of course Morgan had done well; she'd already guessed that. This wasn't movie star opulence, but it numbed her nonetheless. A home like this on the shore? Domestic help who obviously adored him, no matter what he said. It might not be deference, but Morgan inspired devotion.

"I'm glad you like it."

"Did you think I wouldn't?"

"It's not for everyone. Dad feels like he's falling off the country. He'd rather be comfortably centered."

Jill smiled, then sobered. "I wish you'd call and tell them what you're doing."

"If I die, you can fill them in."

She jerked her head up. "Morgan!"

"It's not a big deal on my part, Jill. Not like Kelsey's end of it."

"It's a big deal to her that you're doing it."

He narrowed his gaze over the water. "She can thank me when we meet."

Jill ducked her chin. "I know you want that, Morgan. But—"

"It *is* going to happen."

Jill struggled for words. "She has a long fight ahead."

"I've read all about it, been briefed by the shrinks, the MDs, and my lawyer."

Jill startled. "Your lawyer?"

"Bern plays a part in all my major decisions."

She wasn't sure where he was going with that. Why would he need a lawyer in order to help Kelsey?

"I always enter negotiations with a full deck."

Jill shook her head. "Morgan, what are you talking about?"

"The Bensons' refusal to let me see Kelsey."

Her heart sank. "It's their decision. My agreement with them was noninterference until Kelsey was legal age."

"Your agreement was made without my consent." His voice was cold steel.

Dismay coursed through her. "What do you mean?"

"I never terminated my parental rights."

Her heart went into a slow, lumbering beat. "Morgan . . ." She had no idea what his rights were, but if he wanted to make things difficult, she had no doubt he could.

He turned to face her. "My bone marrow could give her a second chance at life. My money is paying for that chance."

A clumsy leap of her heart. "You're paying—"

"That's right. I've transferred enough funds to the foundation to cover the transplant and more."

"How? When?" They'd been on the road since he heard about Kelsey's foundation.

He only smiled. She should be thrilled. Hadn't she seen that as God's plan, the perfect details falling into place? But what if Morgan meant to use it as a weapon? She couldn't believe he would, but what did she know? From what she'd seen already, he moved in circles the Bensons had never imagined.

"Then you know what's involved for Kelsey. You know her battle. Please don't do anything to make it harder."

"Do you think I would?" His eyes chilled. "But up to now every decision's been made without me. I want you to know that's over."

Her hand shook on the rail. What would he do? What could he do? Jill's voice shook. "This isn't a merger or, or whatever you do. It's a little girl—"

"My little girl."

"No, Morgan. She's not yours. Or mine."

He turned his back to the rail and stared into the house.

"Roger and Cinda are her parents." She had to make it real for him. "They've raised her from the day she was born."

"I only want to see her."

"I wouldn't have seen her either if—"

"But you did."

Jill swallowed the tightening in her throat. He was right. Roger and Cinda had given her more than they were willing to offer Morgan. In their minds she had carried the child, given them their daughter, and Morgan had not been part of the decision. She hadn't given him the chance.

Jill dropped her forehead to her fingertips. "Please leave it alone. At least until she's recovered."

He didn't answer.

"Morgan?"

"I'll be a little busy the next few days anyway."

She sighed. "We all appreciate what you're doing."

"It's not about gratitude." His voice was rough.

She knew that. She reached a hand to his forearm. "Be patient and let God work."

He slid her a sideways glance. "You have to subscribe to receive benefits."

"So subscribe."

He stretched a half smile. "My membership ran out."

"There's no expiration date. It just rolls over into eternity."

He stroked her fingers on his forearm. "I believed that once about other things."

Her throat tightened. "I know. God's the only sure thing."

He cupped his palm over her hand. "Ah. Here's Consuela with heaven."

She came out with a large platter of tamales wrapped in cornhusks, what looked like charbroiled chicken fajita strips with wedges of avocado in soft homemade tortillas, chips and hand-chopped salsa. She set it on the galvanized circular table on the left side of the balcony. Morgan held Jill's chair, then took his own.

Jill closed her eyes and whispered her thanks, then dug in with gusto. It was authentic Mexican food that made Taco Bell a thin pretender. Especially the tamales. "These are wonderful."

Consuela smiled as she filled Jill's glass with water and a wedge of lemon. "It is my grandmother's recipe." She moved to Morgan's glass. "And Señor Morgan's favorite."

"I have lots of favorites, Consuela. You spoil me." He filled his mouth with tamale and dabbed a drip of the rich red sauce from his lips.

"Sí, it is true."

Jill turned to him after Consuela left. "How long has she worked for you?"

"Four years. Juan only came a few months ago. I haven't arranged his green card yet. Wish I knew where he was working."

"Are they legal?"

"I made sure Consuela was. Her husband and two sons died five years ago from some wicked intestinal disease. Probably cholera or dysentery. He lost his job and they were living off the dumps south of the border."

"How did you find her?"

He leaned back in his chair. "One of the neighbors asked if I needed domestic help. They knew her situation."

"And Juan?"

"He was hit by a car trying to cross the border illegally by way of the interstate. He got word to Consuela, and she asked to bring him here." Morgan shrugged. "Unlike Consuela, he doesn't speak English and isn't awfully motivated to earn his way." His eyes narrowed. "That's what puzzles me about his being at work now."

"Can't you ask Consuela?"

He finished his bite. "I let them be as autonomous as they choose. With Consuela, it's not an issue. She's family. With Juan . . ." He wiped a dab of avocado from his finger and raised his eyebrows. "We'll see."

Jill savored a bite of the chicken fajita. "This is so good. It's amazing you're not immense with this kind of food every day."

"I skip more meals than I eat. And I'm away a lot. My job is mostly travel."

"It must be hard to leave all this."

"It's just a place." Again the tone that expressed so much emptiness.

He straightened. "And speaking of work, if I don't catch Denise now, it will get ugly." He stood up. "Take your time. Make yourself at home."

"May I use your phone? I'll reimburse the—"

"Jill. Just use the phone." He walked away, obviously annoyed by any reference to her paying her part. Maybe that was his soft underbelly, or maybe just his generosity. He could afford her phone calls. Voted most likely to succeed, he'd done just that. So why did she sense a silent desperation underneath it all?

She stood to clear her plate.

Consuela was upon her instantly. "No, no. I will do it."

Jill didn't argue, just thanked her for the wonderful meal. In another situation she would insist on helping. But this was so foreign, she didn't know what was polite or appropriate. She wandered into the large room off the kitchen. Most of this level was open, one room flowing into the next. She picked up a fine German woodcarving, a Greek vase.

Two paintings were French, or at least the artist was French and the scenes. No surprise that Morgan was widely traveled. He'd just said his work kept him moving. And his tastes had always been eclectic. It did surprise her that he worked out of his home. She had imagined a large office in a posh high-rise, not a downstairs room with a single assistant.

She ran her hand over a marble statuette on a side table. Roman or Greek, no doubt. She looked over her shoulder at the vast tasteful room. Morgan's home. A less aesthetic man wouldn't bother to create such a complex environment in a home he scarcely lived in. But Morgan had always been attuned to that sort of thing.

She wandered down the hall to the guest room Consuela had prepared for her. The walls were a muted mustard that she would never in a million years have chosen from a paint chip, but were surprisingly pleasant and perfectly complemented the Thomasville bedding and window treatment. Beside the bed a profuse bouquet of fresh-cut red lilies and yellow freesia scented the room. She lowered her face and breathed the sweetness.

The bathroom was papered in dulled green with a floral border that matched the bedroom tones. It had been stocked with everything she might receive in a fancy hotel: a basket of shampoo, lotions, and mouthwash, a coarse-textured handmade soap, a beautiful glycerin shell. In a wire basket were a selection of Bath and Body Works products, body gel, bubble bath, and vanilla lotion. Had Consuela purchased all of that for her? At Morgan's request?

Jill washed her face and hands, flipped her damp fingers through her hair, and went back into the bedroom. She made a space in the collection of decorative throw pillows on the bed and took up the phone. She had promised Shelly a call.

"This has to be you, Jill, calling from Santa Barbara, California."

"How's Rascal?"

"He and Dan are pining."

Jill pouted. "Are you cuddling him?"

"Rascal, yes. Brett draws the line at Dan."

She didn't want to talk about Dan. "Am I getting you from dinner?"

"Nope. You forgot the time zones."

Jill glanced at the clock. It would be 8:50 in Iowa. "I am a little off-kilter."

"I bet." A tone rife with meaning.

"Well, we got in just after four and had an early dinner and—"

"Is he wonderful?"

She stared around the room, everything prepared for her comfort, no expense spared on any leg of the journey, no request denied. And Morgan himself . . .

"I know that sigh. Start from the beginning. I want it all."

"Shelly . . ."

In Shelly's best mad-hypnotist voice, "You will tell me everything, e-v'ry-thing."

"He let me drive his car."

Shelly laughed. "Go on."

Jill described their night at the Bellagio, perfectly aware that Shelly would read more into it than there could be. "It was incredible—dinner, the show, even the fountains. I always thought Vegas was just trashy. But then you have to be in a different echelon to experience it as we did."

"No quarter slots?"

Jill smiled. "I don't really know. We walked through the gaming floor but didn't play anything."

"Did he kiss you?"

Something large and winged fluttered inside. "No."

"No?" Shelly was clearly shocked.

Confession time. "I asked him not to."

Shelly's moan could be heard over the ocean.

"That's not why I'm here. Morgan is helping Kelsey. He's allowed me to be part of that."

"I'm calling the tribal headshrinker. Your brain has departed your skull."

Maybe so. How else could she explain this total escape from reality? "Shelly, I'm a midwestern schoolteacher. That's what I do. My kids need me, and I need them."

"They give you meaning and purpose?"

She didn't like Shelly's tone.

"Because you have none outside of that? Hello? It's a job."

Defensive anger rose up. "It's more than a job. They matter to me."

"News flash. They're not yours."

Jill's chest constricted. "I know." And if things continued the way Ed Fogarty planned, they'd be less and less so.

"Let me propose an outrageous thought. What if Morgan wanted you there for more than Kelsey's transplant?"

"Morgan wants to see Kelsey." Enough to take drastic action. "He knows I have contact with her and the family. I'm another card in his hand."

"Oh, how foolish of me. I hadn't realized he, too, was devoid of human emotion."

There it was again. Ice queen in another form. Fine. Let Shelly believe that. "Anyway, I wanted to let you know where to reach me if—"

"Rascal needs you?"

"Yes. Anything. You made me promise to call."

"That was when I considered you sane."

"Even crazy people need friends."

Shelly laughed. "You're right. But I'll be tossing pillows tonight."

"Don't hit Brett."

Again Shelly's laugh. It was definitely her finest feature.

"Bye, Shell." Jill hung up and dialed Cinda's cell phone. She got the voice mail option and left Morgan's phone number as her contact point with a brief explanation that she was assisting him during the bone marrow harvest. They would know where to reach her for any reason. As she hung up, it settled even deeper inside, the difference between her connection and Morgan's. She didn't deserve it. He was the one whose marrow worked. She was superfluous.

She got up and looked out the window. Her bedroom faced the front with a view of the other homes in the small gated cluster, cloaked now in long shadows. Who were Morgan's neighbors? Other rich professionals? People accustomed to this graciousness, the creature comforts that required a post-office box address. This was not her world.

She sighed and went outside. The breeze was surprisingly cool. Wasn't California supposed to be beach-combing paradise? Surfing babes with Coppertone tans? Morgan didn't even do California the normal way. She wandered his yard, beyond the pool to the winding path through locust, Chinese elm, palm, and mimosa trees, tasteful patterns of color from blooming things throughout.

She reached the guesthouse and peeked into the front window. It was decorated in seascape tones of blue, beige, and aqua, the furniture contemporary, the pictures stylized seascapes, and a white painted staircase to the loft. Why hadn't Morgan housed her there?

She turned at steps behind her and saw Morgan's assistant, Denise. "Hi."

Denise smiled crisply. "Hi." She stepped past and inserted her key in the door.

"I'm sorry. I didn't realize you lived here."

"Yes. I do." She went inside, brittle and cold.

Now that she thought of it, Morgan could have meant Denise lived there, as well, though she'd only assumed the woman worked there. Jill followed the path away from Denise's space and found Morgan just past the pool.

"Your yard is beautiful."

"Thank you."

"I didn't know the guesthouse was Denise's."

He glanced that way. "She's been there awhile." At her curious look, he said, "It's a long story. Hold on a minute." He strode into the house and came back with a soft fleecy sweatshirt and handed it to her. "Let's walk down."

She pulled the sweatshirt over her head and rolled the sleeves. In his Birkenstocks, loose cotton pants, and lightweight gray sweatshirt, Morgan looked very California. She followed him onto a steep path, cutting down a crevice in the cliffs thick with a low ground cover with brilliant multicolored blooms. She caught the scent of the sea as they descended single file to the shore. There was only a narrow strip of sand beyond reach of the waves, and even it looked like it was submerged at times.

"High tide." He took off his sandals and walked in the damp sand, giving her the dry.

They walked a short way and the beach broadened out somewhat, but Morgan stayed just beyond the creep of the thin foam that rushed in, then sighed back out, chased by sandpipers on skinny legs.

"You were going to tell me about Denise."

He nodded. "She moved in eight months ago. I guess you can say it's sort of a safe house."

Jill looked up, surprised.

"We did have office space in town, and she lived ten minutes inland with her boyfriend. I honestly do not get what it is with women and jerks." The depth of his frustration brought her eyes to his face. "I told her two years ago the guy was trouble. Not that it should have been a great mystery—he was already beating her. Just not so that it showed."

No wonder she'd seemed so brittle. "I'm surprised he let her work for you."

Morgan's brow drew tight. "Well, that was a rub for sure. The problem was I paid her well, and he liked to snort." He reached down for a small stone and tossed it into the waves.

"Cocaine?"

"I didn't know that until the night I found her bloody with a cracked skull."

Jill stopped and stared. "You found her?"

"She called me. Lying on the floor, barely able to lift her finger, she speed dialed my number and I went over."

"Was he gone?"

"Luckily for him. By the time she came out of the hospital, I'd moved the office to my house and her things to the guesthouse. To keep her job, she signed the complaint against him and received a restraining order."

"To keep her job?"

"I told you I don't get it. That threat was my only means of making her see reason."

Jill shook the sand from her sandal. "You can't think she'd go back to him."

"I'd be surprised if she ever wants a relationship again. But he could guilt her into it."

"Why?"

"Because she has other issues. She's always been extremely tight-lipped, but when I saw her in the hospital, she opened the dike, talking, talking, talking. I'm not kidding. She went on for hours about stuff as far back as she could remember. It would make you sick."

"She looks so . . . . professional."

"She is. She personally manages the work of a small staff, keeps the teams on track, and me, too. She's beyond competent, and I now understand her obsessive need for control. She keeps her thumb on every detail. I drive her crazy sometimes when I go incommunicado. But believe me, I need it." He stopped and turned her with a hand to her elbow. "Look."

Jill had been so caught up in his story she'd lost sight of their surroundings. Now she realized the ocean was afire with golden light. Strips of cloud caught the color, tossing it across the sky, and at the horizon a scarlet flame kindled. Amidst the gilded water black dolphins leaped, then vanished, and only the sky remained. The sun would not go peacefully; its dying strength seared a memory in her mind.

Morgan took her hand and stood in silence. He'd been so good to Denise, rearranging his life for her protection. For Consuela as well, and Juan. It didn't seem strange at all now that he would do everything for Kelsey. His profession might be to turn around flailing corporations, but his purpose was saving lives. No wonder God had chosen him.

The last of the fiery orb sank into the sea, splashing out across its surface in molten glory. It was gone, but the water would remember, and the sky, now rose and peach, then yellow fading to gray. Sandpipers still scurried, pecked at the sand, then rushed back as the new froth chased.

Morgan turned her to him, slid his fingers along the side of her neck, and caught them in the strands of her hair. "Don't say no."

"Morgan . . ."

He lowered his face and kissed her.

Her heart hammered. Why was he doing this? Both his hands cradled her jaw as his kiss deepened. She remembered too well. *Lord!* She broke away. "I cannot do this again. I can't."

"It's just a kiss." His voice was raw.

"Not with you."

His face tightened painfully. "Jill."

She pulled away. "This is about Kelsey. I want to help but . . ."

"It's not about Kelsey."

She stepped back. "It is for me." She hated the pain she saw in his face. Didn't he see? Couldn't he realize it was futile? The thread between them had snapped. It had been too fragile and had tangled irreparably. He had rejected God; she craved the Lord's presence. He lived in a dream world; her world was all too real, and the thought of reintroducing Morgan too terrible to consider.

He let her go when she turned and headed back the way they'd come. Why did he churn up emotions better left dead? And then it hit her. She was the ice queen.

23

Need crawled inside him, morphing from the passion of their kiss to a different mind-consuming desire. One night. He had to get through one night. A twelve-hour fast in case they needed to use full anesthesia. But the sweet slide to oblivion called to him with a siren song. He should have stayed inside and drunk to Jill's health and prosperity instead of standing together with her, the sunset hues igniting her hair and tingeing her skin with gold, her lips like melted roses tempting his.

Ache and longing. How could he want her so much? Dusk stole over him. One drink. What difference did a few hours make? But in this mood one drink would lead to two and blur the line at three, and he had responsibilities. He jerked the sweatshirt over his head and tossed it to the ground. Next, the pants. In his boxers, in the dusk, he left the sand, fought through the first cold waves and dived low beneath them, then pulled hard until he passed the place where they broke.

The water was rough with seaweed until the floor fell away. He broke the surface and shook his hair back. Treading, he scanned the deepening darkness. How long could he tread? One hour? Two? He put his face down and stroked parallel to the beach. He knew this shore well, though he'd swum at night only a handful of times.

Always alone. He would not risk anyone else in dark water

haunted by sea creatures who wondered at his audacity. If a shark took him tonight, it better leave enough for them to still draw marrow from his bones. Almost subconsciously, he worked in closer to shore.

The cold Pacific had taken the sting from his mood, and as his feet touched bottom, he hurled himself forward past the breakers to the shore. He walked out drenched and chilled, scooped up his clothes, and climbed toward the house. Something skittered in front of him and took refuge in the rhododendrons.

He went into the bathroom in his lower level, took a towel from the cupboard, and wrapped himself in it. Then he went upstairs. The house was quiet, and he could almost pretend it was a night like any other. But it wasn't.

He approached Jill's room, considered knocking, then passed by. She'd made it clear why she was there. He went into his bedroom and refused to think of the decanter table in the corner. Not tonight. If he couldn't get through one night without a drink, he had a problem.

He went into the bathroom and realized his toiletries were not there. Still in the car? He stripped off his wet boxers and put on a spare robe from the hook on the door, then went down and took the keys from his desk in the office. Either Juan had not come home from his job, or he'd not been instructed to unload the car.

Morgan went out and took the bags from the trunk, including Jill's. What had she planned to sleep in? He hauled them upstairs, left Jill's outside her door, and gave it one quick rap. Then he took his own things to his room, unpacked, and showered. He pulled on a pair of shorts and wrapped again in the navy velour robe.

The night stretched before him. He should ask Jill to join him for a drink—no, a chat, to clear the air. But then he didn't want to discuss what had happened earlier. He'd lost his head to the magic of the sunset, crossed a line neither one of them could face.

He turned on his stereo and tuned it to the classical station. No lyrics to taunt or tempt. He paced his room as a lion its den. He should ask Consuela about Juan. He glanced at the clock. Nine-forty. Early. But she always retired early. He clicked the TV remote, flipped through several channels, and turned it off again. Then he walked down the hall and tapped Jill's door, noticing the bag was no longer outside it. Maybe she wouldn't answer. Maybe she was asleep. But it opened a crack and she peeked through.

"Will you sit with me? I promise to behave."

Surprise and concern filled her eyes. "I'm dressed for bed."

"There's a robe in your closet."

She stood so long without answering, he was sure she'd refuse. But she agreed and appeared a minute later, wrapped and tied tightly, the sleeves bunched up. He led her out to the balcony. The night was chilly, even though he was mostly dry except for his head, which was still a little damp. The sound of the breakers formed an immutable rhythm as he lit the candle in the glass globe on the table.

He seated her and pulled a chair from the other side of the table for himself, drawing the peace of the night inside him. A snifter of brandy would be the perfect complement, but he fought the urge.

Jill looked out over the water. "What are those lights?"

"Oil rig. *Swift of Ipswich.*"

"It's actually pretty."

"They call them crystal ships." But that wasn't what he wanted to discuss. "Tell me about Kelsey."

Jill crossed her arms over her chest. "She's beautiful, Morgan. You saw that much in her pictures." Her voice tightened. "Even though her hair is gone. She has such sweet expressions and a smile you can't resist."

He leaned back in his chair and let the breakers center his mind. "You said she was smart."

"She came from us."

He nodded. Intelligence did seem to have some genetic connection.

"She's very spiritual." Jill smiled. "She loves the Lord. Such a pure faith."

Morgan studied the stars over the water. His daughter loved the God he actively eluded. A smile brushed his lips. Touché.

"She designed her own Web page, calls it Kelsey's Hope Page. She answers questions from other kids with cancer and shares her faith, the love of Jesus. It's a wonderful page."

Kelsey's Hope Page. Maybe that was the place to start knowing his daughter. A cold, impersonal knowing, yet he could contact her, ask her if—no, that would put her in a hard position. Still, the site would give him something of her. "Has she written you tonight?"

"I don't know. Your laptop . . ."

"It's in the office. I'll get it." She looked as though she might stop him but didn't. He paused at the door. "Do you want something to drink? Are you hungry?"

"A little."

"Help yourself in the kitchen." He had meant to offer it earlier, but the sunset beach had distracted him. Just because he had to fast didn't mean she did. He went down and brought the laptop up, using his wireless LAN to open the Internet.

Jill returned with an apple and a handful of whole-grain crackers. She went to the railing and looked out over the moonlit sea, obviously in no rush to check her mail, even though he'd booted up the computer. She couldn't be that fascinated with the lighted ships, but he gave her space.

Gazing on the water, she said, "It looks cold."

"It is. I just got out."

She half turned. "You went swimming?"

"Needed something to cool me down."

She turned away.

"So tell me more."

She sighed. "I don't know, Morgan. It's not as though I've known her all these years. They never sent pictures or letters or anything like that. It was pretty much a closed adoption, except we knew each other's names. The first contact I had was the letter telling me she had leukemia."

"That wasn't the first contact."

She glanced over her shoulder.

"You carried her to term. You birthed her."

Jill dropped her chin with a wounded look. Was she surprised he would resent her having had that much? "I held her for half an hour when she was born, memorized each finger, each wisp of hair. Her eyes were your color even then. She was so tiny, so incredible. But that was all I had."

Morgan sensed her loss. "Why didn't you keep her?"

"I could never have brought her home."

He pictured her father, firm, upright, narrow. An illegitimate grandchild would not go over well. "I'm sorry." And he was. She'd lived all those years knowing her child was out there, wondering, imagining . . .

He stood up and joined her. She didn't pull away from his hand on her back. Maybe she sensed it was no more than comfort, what little he had to give.

The door opened behind them. "*Perdóneme.* Señorita Jill, you have a phone call." Dressed in a floor-length house gown and robe, Consuela handed her the cordless phone.

"Thank you." Jill took the phone. "Hello? Hi . . . Kelsey." Her eyes darted to him.

Morgan tensed. His daughter was on the phone.

Jill shifted away from his hand. "How are you?"

He checked his watch. Almost one in the morning on the East Coast. Why was she calling? Had they changed protocol? Kelsey wouldn't be the one to tell them. Certainly not in the middle of the night. And how did she have his number? Jill must have given it.

Jill's voice continued. "No, I haven't. Actually I was just going to check my mail now. The computer's booted up, but I hadn't gotten in. I didn't think about the time change or I would have done it sooner. I should have."

She sounded nervous. Did she want him to leave?

"Yes. How did you know?" She listened for a moment, then, "Oh."

It was frustrating hearing only her awkward answers. He wanted to grab the phone and say, *Talk to me, Kelsey. Let me hear your voice.*

"Yes. At least I'll be at the hospital and drive him home." She moistened her lips.

Him? They were discussing him.

Jill met his eyes. "Honey, I don't know. You need to decide that."

His breath paused. What was Kelsey deciding? Something to do with him?

"Okay." She held the phone out.

His heart made a slow flip.

"She only has permission to call me, but she wants to talk to you, and—" Jill smiled—"she's adolescent enough to stretch it."

Morgan took the phone, brought it to his ear. "Hello?"

"Hi." The voice on the other end was impossibly sweet. "I know this is weird." She paused just long enough for him to grasp that it was his daughter's voice. "But I wanted to thank you beforehand. You won't be feeling good tomorrow, so I thought it might help to know I appreciate it."

She was worried how he'd feel? "I'm glad to help, Kelsey." His throat was raw.

"You'll be less glad tomorrow."

He swallowed. "You're wrong. Even more so tomorrow, and the next day, and especially when it starts to work."

She drew a slow, labored breath. "Can I ask you another favor?"

"Of course."

"Will you send me a picture for my room?"

He nodded, though she couldn't see him. "A picture of what?"

"Of you."

His throat closed painfully. "Sure. If you want it."

"Thanks. Mom thought it would be hard for me to talk to you. But I'm glad I did."

"Me too."

"And I'm glad Jill's there, that you're together."

Morgan glanced at Jill, who was watching him pensively. "Me too."

"Bye."

"Good-bye, Kelsey." He closed his eyes and turned off the phone.

Jill's arms came around his waist, and he slowly wrapped her shoulders, laid his jaw against her head, playing back Kelsey's voice, her words. *"I thought it might help to know I appreciate it."* Jill must feel the crazy beat of his heart with her head resting against his chest. He had no idea it would affect him like this to connect with Kelsey. There was so much he'd wanted to say, but none of it had come to his mind while he had her on the phone.

I wouldn't have abandoned you, Kelsey. I wanted you and Jill and me to be a family. I just wasn't mature enough to do things right.

Jill took the phone from his hand, stepped back from his embrace, and looked up into his face. "Are you all right?"

Not by a long shot. He sucked in a breath. "How did she know you were here? With me?"

"I left this number with Cinda, who told her she could call me. She'd actually asked about talking to you in her e-mail, only I didn't get it."

"Get it now." He took her hand and brought her to the table. He wanted more.

Jill brought up her account and clicked through the messages until she came to Kelsey's. And though it might be presumptuous, he read over her shoulder.

Hi Jill, I know you're right about Josh. I don't think I would actually kiss him, even if he does come back. But I'm glad I admitted I wanted to. I have all these feelings going around inside me. It's not as easy anymore to know how to be, what to do, what to want. I know what people want for me, to be well and grow up and stay alive. But I will never have a normal life. I don't talk like this to Mom. It would break her heart. But it is the truth. I can't marry or have children. I feel so weak already, and I'm afraid of what will happen with the transplant.

Sensing Jill's distress, Morgan rested his hands on her shoulders, stroking softly with his thumbs as his own heart wrenched.

Jesus is so real right now. I sense Him every day. His love is all that keeps me going when I get so sick I can't take it. Dad said it's okay to cry. He cries with me.

Morgan's throat filled with ache. The man she called Dad, crying with his daughter. Jill reached up and touched his fingers.

I cry because I'm too sick to stop it, not because it helps. Only prayer helps. I know you're praying, too. Is Morgan?

His fingers stiffened on Jill's shoulders. He hadn't prayed for Kelsey since he thought she'd been destroyed as a fetus. He hadn't prayed at all since then.

Do you think I could talk to him? I understand Mom and Dad's point. They don't want me hurt or my energy drained. But I'd like to thank him. Before, I mean. In case I can't after the transplant. They didn't actually say no, just that they didn't think it would be good for me. So do you think I should? Hurry and tell me since it's tomorrow, you know. Love, Kelsey.

Jill drew a shaky breath. "She made up her own mind."

Morgan didn't answer. She'd sounded so cheerful. He was glad he hadn't seen this before he heard his daughter's voice. He would have known she was forcing it. He squeezed his eyes shut.

Jill pressed his hand to her shoulder, stroking with her fingers. Now it was she comforting him. "She's so strong. These letters don't show it. They're her chance to let down, but inside she's . . ." Her words trailed away.

"She thought I wouldn't be glad I helped."

"Only that it'll be painful for you."

He shook his head. "She has no idea."

Jill stood up and faced him. "She will, Morgan. As soon as she's strong, she'll see you. She'll make it happen, just as she did with me. You don't have to force it."

He cupped her shoulders. "I won't."

She rested a hand on his heart. "I would never have done this to you, if there was any other way."

He covered her hand with his. "It's out of our control."

She nodded. "Morgan?"

He did not like what he saw in her eyes.

"Will you pray for her?"

"I can't."

Her brows drew up painfully. "Why not?"

"It wouldn't mean anything."

Her palm on his chest was warm. "It would mean everything."

He cupped the back of her head, the soft short hair like kitten fur on his fingertips. "It's been too long, too hard."

"She needs you."

"I'm doing all I can."

Her eyelids drooped, then rose again. "I guess that's my part, then."

He smiled, drinking in her face in the moonlight. "Maybe between us, we'll get it right this time."

She reached her fingers up and touched his lips, and it was more intimate and visceral than any touch he'd experienced. No wonder he'd never gotten over her.

———

Jill waited in the UCLA Medical Center after Morgan had left her with a cavalier smile. She didn't know how long it would take before she saw him again, or what condition he'd be in when she did. She only knew she was glad now that she hadn't matched and Morgan had. That he had the chance to do what she had wanted to. *Lord, your ways are above mine, flawless and right. Bless this process now.*

"Praying for someone?"

Jill opened her eyes to the woman on the chair across from her to the right.

"Yes."

The woman had to be eighty at least. She waved a small reptilian hand. "When you pray, all heaven prays with you. That's a mighty army."

The imagery was suddenly strong in her mind, matching Kelsey's so well. "Yes."

"I'll pray for you, too." The woman sat back in her chair.

"It's not me, it's—"

"You will be sifted, but hell will not prevail."

Jill stared at her. How did one answer that? When the woman closed her eyes, Jill reached for a magazine and opened it. The article was on gardening with color themes and made her think of Morgan's yard. When she finished it, the woman was gone. But what had she meant, sifted?

24

Morgan seriously needed coffee. He'd been up since six to make the drive into L.A. and get registered for the harvest scheduled for nine o'clock, to ensure plenty of time to transport the marrow to his daughter.

While he waited he considered all that had gone into the process so far. The blood tests, then the counseling and physical exam, including an EKG and chest X-ray. Not sure what that was for. Probably anesthesia, which posed the only possible danger to him. And they'd taken a unit of blood at that time to be given back during today's harvest.

He looked around at the other people awaiting their procedures in the outpatient unit. Were any of them using their own bodies to save someone else? The thought was immense. He'd accomplished a lot, turned entire corporations around, saved jobs for hundreds of workers. But nothing meant more than what he was doing now, giving Kelsey another chance to live. They'd been forthright with the statistics. It wasn't a sure thing by any gambler's odds. But without it, she had no chance at all.

A nurse came, directed him to a cubicle, and instructed him to change into the hospital gown she provided. It was designed to ensure the patient felt utterly vulnerable. He was then instructed to empty his bladder and remove all jewelry and dentures or partial plates.

The nurse glanced up. "Do you wear contact lenses?"

"No." No dentures or partial plates, either.

"Have a seat on the cart, please." She wheeled him into another room. "This is the pre-op holding area." She took his arm. "I'm inserting an introducer needle for an IV to administer fluids during and after the surgery."

He did not watch as she tied a piece of rubber tubing around his arm and felt for his vein, then inserted the needle. At least she knew what she was doing. They hadn't given him some nurse intern who needed practice, as was probably the norm in a teaching hospital. "The anesthesiologist will be in shortly." She untied the tourniquet.

The anesthesiologist was a bullet-shaped man with hair on the underside of his arms. "How are you?" He pumped Morgan's hand. "Had a spinal block before? Probably not unless you've birthed a baby." When he'd finished laughing, he went on to describe the procedure. "Ready to go forward?"

Morgan smiled dryly.

"Now hunch over and roll your back for me. Don't move at all if you can help it. This is the worst part, after which you'll feel nothing but pressure during the harvest."

The needle went in. Morgan held his breath, hoping the comedian knew his way around a spinal cord.

"Might notice an electrical sort of shock in your leg."

He'd already noticed it, and it was not pleasant.

"That's it." The doctor drew the sides of the gown back together. "Now lie down on your stomach." He eased Morgan's legs up and back while the nurse connected the IV tubes to his arm.

In a short while he was wheeled into the operating room where he lay for nearly two hours while they punctured the upper ridge of his hip bone several times on both sides. Though there was no pain, he felt the pressure of multiple bone punctures for each position of the needle. They'd explained to him that only a couple teaspoons of marrow could be taken from each bone puncture, and they'd draw between one and two liters of fluid to obtain enough healthy stem cells for Kelsey.

Kelsey. Her voice had stayed with him all night, and somewhere around three he had gone to her Web page and absorbed every word of it. Her newsletter was chatty and droll, a sense of humor mirroring his own. He had to wade through her faith-in-the-spiritual-promises section, though he was glad she had faith. That joy for her was obvious, and he wanted her to have anything that helped the pain of what he saw in the pictures that followed.

Elfin features and a quirky smile didn't change the bald head, the fragile limbs, or the machines in each photo performing the various procedures that the text beside the pictures explained. She'd used her own treatments as a text for other kids to see what it was like, and her tone was frank and encouraging. *Can't say I prefer catching rays in the radiation lab to lying on the beach, but it wasn't as bad as I'd imagined it.*

It was the same voice she had used with him on the phone, but not the way she had written to Jill. Jill got the truth, the real child, the one who let down and cried. His throat tightened. Her page was intended to relieve fear, but Kelsey was afraid of what might happen. He was, too. They'd been way too forthcoming with possible complications of the transplant process that could not only cause the harvest to fail, but in itself, threaten Kelsey's life.

He did not want to go there, even in his thoughts. Maybe he couldn't pray, but he'd control his doubts and fears the best he could. He tried to picture Kelsey now and imagine her thriving because of this. It was so little compared to all he would have done for her. Then he remembered himself at eighteen and wondered. Maybe Jill had done the loving thing. Two mature parents, desperate for a child . . .

Could he have gone to Wharton? He could have brought Jill and Kelsey and lived in some sort of married housing. His scholarship would have covered something, though he would have had to work and might not have done as well. Or Jill could have stayed with her parents—no, his. Mom would have welcomed them once she was over the initial shock. She would have loved his daughter, her grandchild.

He closed his eyes. Fifteen years. Not that he couldn't have married since then and provided other grandchildren for his mother to love. Well, Rick was filling the bill. Good, do-it-the-right-way Rick. And beautiful Noelle.

He was getting drowsy when they at last removed the needle without reinserting it. The doctor said, "We'll dress the surgical site now, Mr. Spencer, and take you into the recovery room. It looks like a very good harvest, and the marrow will be sent to your daughter. You've done a wonderful thing."

Morgan lay still as they wheeled him into another room. He was tired, but then he'd hardly slept the night before and still had no coffee, only sugar water, in his veins. He closed his eyes and dozed until the pain in his lower back notified him that the spinal block had worn off. He tried to roll over and moaned.

A hefty brunette nurse, not the blonde who'd helped him before, laid a hand on his shoulder. "Let me help you sit. The doctor's ordered an oral pain medication if you think you can keep it down."

He didn't feel nauseated and nodded. She dropped the pills into his palm, and he swallowed them with the small cupful of water.

"You can take extra-strength Tylenol or ibuprofen over the next few days. Call for a prescription if that doesn't cover it." She then questioned him on his overall condition—dizzy, stomach upset, headache, fogginess?

"I'd just like to go." Jill had been waiting, and he'd as soon be in her care as Nurse Bertha's, though she was kind and less severe than the blonde.

"You'll need to change the dressing on your hips tomorrow, clean the area with Betadine. You need to keep it dry and covered three days to a week, depending on how quickly you heal." As she spoke, she removed the IV from his arm.

He rubbed the Band-Aid on his inner elbow. "Thanks." He changed back into his clothes, feeling better just for that.

The doctor ordered his discharge, and an orderly arrived with a wheelchair. Though he'd rather not be wheeled out like an old man, Morgan settled into it and let the man take him to the waiting area. Jill stood up immediately. Morgan's heart did a slow thump. Dangerous ground having her watching like that, especially after last night's tenderness.

She joined them. "Are you finished? How do you feel?"

"Like clearing out of here." He tried to stand, but the orderly pressed him down by the shoulder.

"I'll wheel you down. Hospital rules."

Morgan settled back. Even that much strain had sent knives to his lower back. The painkiller had not taken effect. Soon, he hoped, wishing they'd driven the Thunderbird instead of his Corvette. He'd been showing off, taking the Vette, but its ride would not be kind.

Jill drove, unsure of herself and concerned over every bump of his high-performance shocks and chassis. He smiled. He could get used to that sort of concern. But he said, "It's not that bad."

"Do you think they're flying it now? Your marrow?"

He looked up at the pale coastal sky. "They'll filter it first to clean out bone fragments and stuff. Then someone will deliver it by hand to Kelsey's doctors."

"Then what?"

"Since the match is only a single haplotype, they'll remove most of the T-cells. Then they'll begin the rescue, infusing my marrow into Kelsey's chest catheter."

"And then it migrates to her marrow and engrafts," Jill finished.

"That's the idea." Hopefully. "It'll be weeks before we know for sure."

"I spent all night in prayer. I know the Lord's working."

He gave her a faint smile. "Good."

"And I prayed for your recovery."

His smile stretched again. "I feel better already."

"Don't mock me." She pushed his knee, then sucked a breath when she realized it hurt. "I'm sorry."

He rubbed his forehead. "I need some coffee."

"Do you want me to pull off?" Jill searched the heavily trafficked highway.

Morgan checked his watch, then closed his eyes. "No. Just get us home."

———

When they reached the house, a stocky Mexican met them in the garage and opened Morgan's door. Juan, Jill guessed, and it was confirmed by a brief introduction. Morgan spoke to him in Spanish. Juan nodded, then went inside. Morgan climbed slowly out of the car and leaned on the door. "My legs don't want to work."

"Let me help you." She hurried around the side and curled his arm over her shoulders. Holding his waist and careful not to bump the bandaged area just beneath, she helped him inside and eased him into a chair in his game room, facing the ocean. "Is that okay?"

Morgan nodded.

Juan stumped back in with a cup of coffee and a glass of juice on a tray. His hair hung into his eyes in the front, though the back was cut fairly short. His features were chunky, without Consuela's charm, but she could see a resemblance. He set the tray on the table between Morgan's chair and the next. "¿Está bien?"

"Sí." Morgan nodded.

Juan eyed her briefly, then headed up the stairs.

Jill glanced toward the open office door. "Is Denise . . ."

"I told her I wouldn't be worth much today."

Jill knelt beside him, resting her hands on his knee, facing him at eye level. "Not worth much? You just gave our daughter a new chance at life, gave her hope, something to fight back with."

"I wasn't speaking figuratively."

"Well, Morgan, I don't know your net worth, but from what I've seen, I'd say it's substantial."

He chuckled. "Or financially."

"And you may not be listening these days, but the Lord chose *you*, not me or anyone else."

He glanced away. "Or spiritually." He shifted position and winced. "Only physically."

She sat back on her heels. "Well, that's why I'm here."

He smiled and covered her hands with his palm. "So it's not a hundred percent Kelsey?"

"Not completely one hundred percent."

"But my stock's trading at a loss."

She smiled. "Drink your coffee, Morgan. You look peaked."

He reached for his cup. "How come you look so fresh?"

"I had juice and a muffin from the vending machine. Are you up to eating?"

"I have something coming." Morgan motioned to the chair beside his. "Stop kneeling at my feet."

"Oh, come now. You tried for years to bring me to my knees."

His low laugh caressed her. It was her chance now to bless him as he had blessed so many, though he wouldn't see it that way or choose that word to describe it. She took the seat he offered. It was a soft, suedelike leather, wonderful to sink into, to stroke with her fingers. The sort that would not handle spills or wear but was certainly a sensuous sitting experience. Morgan liked comfort. He could afford it, and now she thoroughly believed he deserved it.

He softly slurped his coffee. "I will soon be human."

Jill drank her cranberry juice. "I see you've remembered my preference."

"And the adverse effects of caffeine on your system. Didn't want you bouncing off the walls."

She drained her glass. "You didn't want me running circles around you in your depleted physical state."

"Jill, you run circles around me at the best of times."

"Not true." She laughed. "Though I did notice you've lost your edge. You ought to keep me on as your personal trainer."

He fixed her with his Spencer blues. "Name your salary."

Her heart stilled. She'd been speaking lightly, joking. But there was nothing light in his expression. Of course, he brought people into his circle all the time and kept them there. And here was Consuela to prove it, with Juan behind her.

Consuela held two filled plates while Juan set up a pair of teak-wood TV trays. The aroma of thin sizzling flank steak and roasted scallions filled the room and triggered instant starvation, the vending-machine muffin notwithstanding. The accompanying ripe red strawberries looked and smelled as though they were fresh from the ground. Jill's mouth watered. She could get used to this. Her heart made a slow thump.

As Juan and Consuela went back up the stairs, Jill folded her hands. "This feast deserves a prayer."

Morgan waved a hand graciously. "Pray away."

"Father, thank you for your goodness. And for Morgan's. Bless this food for our use, and speed his recovery. And especially bless and heal Kelsey. In Jesus' name. Amen."

Morgan sliced a bite from the thin panfried flank steak. "You could also fill the position of spiritual director. Whip my soul into shape between workouts." He savored the bite a moment before chewing.

Jill's own soul stirred. She had no stellar track record with her witness, but she'd been bolder with Morgan than anyone else, and far more constant in prayer since he arrived at her door. But even if he was serious, there were too many obstacles. "The problem is I have a life."

"You'd have one here."

She would not even allow that picture to form. "My kids need me."

"I need you." He said it with perfect candor, but not the poverty she'd witnessed in his unguarded moments.

"Oh, I don't know. It seems your needs are pretty well met with the staff you have already. Denise and Consuela and Juan."

"You don't see Consuela urging that last mile from me, do you?"

Jill laughed, then tasted her meat and seriously reconsidered her argument.

"Another of Consuela's specialties." Morgan was playing all his cards.

"No fair hitting me at the point of hunger."

"All's fair in love and war."

And which one was this? "You said yourself you're hardly home."

"You'd travel with me."

Her heart tumbled over a major hurdle. "In case you had spiritual questions in the still of night?" No, that didn't sound right.

His gaze intensified. "Isn't that mainly when they strike? The dark night of the soul and all that?"

Her throat tightened. "I guess yes. It seems that way. The mind is too busy otherwise."

"Then you ought to be at hand if you expect to make any headway at all."

"Morgan."

"I'm serious. We can fly Rascal out. You already said your job was all but shot."

"That doesn't mean I won't fight for it." She should not have started this.

"You want something to fight for?"

She laid down her fork before he could see her hand start to shake. "Please don't."

He dropped his chin for a long silent moment, then went back to his meal. She was supposed to be cheering him up, giving comfort, not distress. If only reality didn't keep getting in the way.

She ate the steak with the lightly scorched scallions and the strawberries that were as juicy and sweet as she'd expected. Morgan ate his with a refinement that surprised her. But, then, she was used to sitting across from Dan. She pushed her plate aside and said, "I think I'll take a run on the beach later."

"You won't get far on our strip. The cliffs take over. But you can drive south to the real beach and marina. About four miles."

"I'll just use the street then. How do I get through the gate?"

He pulled a sideways smile. "Now there's an interesting thought."

She raised her chin. "I will not be held against my will. Rascal cannot ransom me."

"Then I'll have to keep you."

How had he brought it right back around again? "Do you want to get some air? I can help you outside." She indicated the bench outside his French doors. It would not be comfortable, but a change would do them both good.

She moved the TV trays out of the way and helped him up. He was so stiff it took him a few moments to get going, but he bore his weight better this time. Probably nourishment and maybe the pain meds. He stood awhile without settling onto the bench, just looking out across the narrow portion of his yard between the French doors and the cliff overlooking the sea.

He said, "Smells good out here. There's nothing like the sea air."

"I like the smell of the earth and trees and rain in the fields."

Morgan glanced down at her. "The sound of the surf, the cry of the gulls."

"Cricket song, crows in the morning."

"Fresh exotic flowers every day."

"Corn snapped from the stalk, boiled and buttered."

He rested his arm across her shoulders. "You ought to see what Consuela does with corn."

"No fair."

He laughed. "Help me sit."

She eased him onto the bench, and he tugged her down beside him, then curled his arm once again over her shoulders. She refused to give in to the embrace. Comfort and assistance. That was her job, her reason for coming, her part in Kelsey's rescue. That and prayer. She prayed now.

Lord, guide and sustain me. This is treacherous water. I don't want to drown.

"You're as stiff as this bench."

"I'm sorry." She softened her position.

"It feels so good to hold you."

Way too good being held. "It'll only make it worse."

The Adam's apple moved in his throat. "So you're convinced there's no chance." His voice was once again impoverished.

She dropped her gaze to her hands as her heart lumbered. "We blew that long ago, Morgan."

"And there's no redemption."

How did he mean that? "There's forgiveness."

He formed a wry smile. "What good is it?"

"It puts you right with God."

He stared across the yard, lips pursed. "Would you get Juan for me?"

She glanced up startled, then stood. "Sure."

She found Juan sitting on the front step, a weeding claw beside him but not much evidence it had been used. "Excuse me."

Juan slowly raised his head. "¿Sí?"

Oh, great. She knew no Spanish. "Morgan wants you." She

indicated with her head. He should at least recognize the name of his employer.

He rubbed his palms on his pants, then pushed up by his knees to stand. She would not depend on him in a fire. She started walking, hoping he would follow, and he did. They went around the house to Morgan on the bench. Morgan spoke in Spanish, and Juan went inside.

"I didn't realize you were fluent."

"Far from it. Just enough to communicate the important things."

Juan reappeared with a squat glass of ice and some strong liquor by the smell of it. Morgan took the glass and sipped, said something else to Juan, and he returned with the bottle. When Juan left, Morgan raised his glass. "This puts me right with God."

She frowned. "How?"

"Removes all pretense." He drank.

She had no idea what to do with that. "You shouldn't have that so soon."

He held the glass up and studied the liquid. "Trust me, it's never too soon."

Frustrated, she pressed her hands to her hips. "I guess I'll run now."

"There's a panel on the inside right post of the gate. Press the button; it'll let you out."

He was obviously no longer interested in keeping her in. Well, she'd made that happen. "Do you need anything before I go?"

"I have everything I need."

A chasm opened between them, a chasm she'd dug and he widened. She went inside and changed into her shorts and sport tank. She tied on her Nikes and stretched her muscles, then went out through the front door, past Juan still enjoying the view, and jogged to the gate. The button opened it just as Morgan said, and she took off running up the small private drive to the coastal road.

Milk had spilled across the sky and muted the earlier sunshine, but the air was warm and bees hummed in the verdant growth beside the road. Sweet calla lilies bowed and nodded. Palm tree shadows were stubby one-legged men with bushy beards standing among the sprays of leaf shadows across the road. A gull winged toward the water that was no longer in view from the road.

Somewhere Morgan's bone marrow was being flown to Kelsey, treated and prepared to work its miracle. And behind her, God's instrument was removing all pretense.

This was it. Kelsey watched the marrow flowing through the tube into her catheter. There was no pain, not even the nausea they had said she might experience. The marrow was a brilliant, beautiful red, and for some reason that encouraged her. Not that she was discouraged, she wouldn't say that. Only . . . resigned? No, that seemed like quitting. It wasn't a quitting feeling.

She hadn't figured out the new emotion yet, but it had started when Rachel died. She hadn't come out of ICU, only shut down one part at a time until there weren't enough parts working to keep going. The nurse had told her Rachel died. She hadn't seen Josh since. But it seemed now like death wasn't the giant abyss she had pictured. It was just a thin crack that took very little effort to cross.

The marrow bag was emptying, and she wondered if Morgan was in pain. The bone puncture was always painful, and he'd have had lots of them to get out so much marrow. She was glad she'd called. His voice was nice, and she could tell he did want to help.

Of course, there was the other miracle. He'd paid for it all. Mom had told her this morning. She wished she had known last night. She would have thanked him for that, as well. All the prayers people had prayed for financial help, and then Morgan just did it. Kelsey smiled. He must know Jesus.

She closed her eyes and pictured the face that was always there now behind her eyelids. Long hair, bearded but smiling. Brown eyes, warmer even than Dad's, with no vacant, superspiritual look. Just an intense love. *Hi, Jesus. I'm glad you're here.*

His smile deepened. *Always. To the end of time.*

Morgan's chin was on his chest, his mouth slightly ajar, and one side of his lower lip shiny with saliva. He looked achingly vulnerable as Jill approached, fresh from her shower after the run. He still held the glass on his thigh, but the ice had melted, and the liquid in the bottle was not that much lower than it had been.

She guessed his sleep was brought on as much from the procedure and loss of bone marrow as from alcohol in his bloodstream. Maybe even the combination of that and the pain meds. As she removed the glass, he opened his eyes. He looked blank for a moment, then reached up and wiped his lip with the top of his hand.

She smiled. "That position can't be comfortable."

He cleared his throat and shifted. "I didn't notice." He nodded at the glass. "Would you get me fresh ice?"

"Morgan . . ."

"Save me finding Juan."

She stooped down beside him. "I don't think you should have more with the medicine you've taken."

He drew a breath in through his nose, caught it at the top, and expelled it with a slight moan. "I'll be the judge of that."

"How about some cold water or juice?"

His eyelids drooped and rose. "Either get me the ice or find Juan."

She dumped the water from the glass. "You wanted a nurse. Now my orders are—"

He caught her wrist. "Stop playing games."

"I'm—"

"We both know it's irrelevant. I did what I needed to for Kelsey. Now let me live my life." He released her.

She picked up the bottle. "This is your life?"

He swallowed, then glared. "Who do you think you are?"

"Someone who cares."

He snorted. "Man, you make me want to drink."

"Well, I'm sorry to hear that. But you're in no condition for more." She took the bourbon into the house and set it on the bar, then opened the refrigerator and took out a can of pineapple juice. She shook it, filled a tall skinny glass, and brought it out to him. "Here."

He eyed the juice like poison. "Listen, woman—"

"No, you listen. You asked me here, and I intend to do my job."

"I never said nursemaid."

She raised her eyebrows. "If the situation warrants it . . ."

"What are you going to do, slap my hand next?"

"I am trained in disciplinary measures."

He leaned his head back and studied her.

"Ready for your juice?"

He took the glass and drank it all, then handed it back. "Satisfied?"

"A little less lip next time."

He stared at her, then his yard, then back. "All right, Nurse Ratched. All these healthful fluids have created a rather pressing need. Suppose you help me up." He walked fairly well to the bathroom, though she stayed beside him just in case. He paused in the doorway. "I might faint."

"I'll call Juan if you do." She closed the door.

———

Leaning at the sink, Morgan washed his hands. There probably was some chemical interaction happening in his blood. He hadn't drunk enough to make him drool. Oh well. He rubbed his wet hands over his face, then dried it all. Hanging the towel, he leaned another moment on the wall. It seemed he'd enlisted a nag—and one with no vested interest. Smart, Morgan. He sighed and left the bathroom.

Jill waited by the French doors, turned when he came out. "Need a hand?"

"No."

She approached. "Want one?"

"You already turned me down."

She caught his elbow and helped support him. "I'm here for a few days at least."

Definitely a two-edged sword. He settled into the soft leather chair.

She folded her hands and hung them at her waist. "Would you like to watch a movie or something?"

"Or something."

"What would you like?" Her forced cheerfulness was like ants under his skin.

He cracked a wry smile. "Why don't you kneel at my feet again."

She frowned. "I reserve that for moments of heroism."

He shook his head. "Nothing heroic in surrendering my posterior to an elephant-sized needle."

"Does it hurt?"

"Not at the moment." He patted the arm of the chair next to his. "Sit down."

She did.

"Have a nice run?"

"Yes. I got in sight of the marina." She flipped her bangs back with her fingers.

"Want to take my boat out?"

"One of those is yours?" Before he could answer she threw up her hands. "What am I saying? Of course, one of those is yours. Probably the biggest one."

"The biggest ones belong to companies. Mine is nice, though. Do you mind?"

She stood up and paced the room. "Why should I mind? It's just not . . ."

He carefully stretched out his legs. "Not what?"

"Real."

"Well, I do pay a docking fee, maintenance, fuel . . ."

"Do you even notice?" She spun on him.

"What?"

"The expenses."

Interesting question, especially on the heels of his detrimental financial decision on Kelsey's behalf. Oh yes, he would notice every expense for some time to come. He might in fact be selling that boat. "You want me to apologize?"

She pressed her index and middle finger between her eyebrows. "Can I ask you something?"

He spread his hands in permission.

"Is there anything you want? No, think a minute. Do you ever just want?"

Way too loaded a question.

"Look at this place." She waved her arm. "Is there one thing missing?"

"They're just things."

"Then why do you have them?"

"Why not?"

She flounced back down in the chair, clearly frustrated. "And your cars? One man needs three cars?"

What on earth got her on this tangent? "The SUV is for camping and to pull the boat when I take it to Tahoe. The Corvette is my status car. I admit the Thunderbird was redundant, but fun." He captured her gaze and held it. "What's the matter, Jill?"

She actually blinked back tears. "It's no wonder you don't need the Lord. You don't need anything."

He swallowed the automatic rejoinder. He had bared himself enough. "Is need some sort of aphrodisiac? You can only get it on with someone in debt?"

Her eyes flashed as she jolted up from the chair. "I don't 'get it on' with anyone, in debt or not."

"I am a hard act to follow."

Her face went like stone. He'd gone too far, revealed his mean side. Her spine was steel as she climbed the stairs and left him sitting alone. Well, that was what he'd wanted, wasn't it? To drink in peace?

———

It was the alcohol speaking; she knew that. This was the third time he'd shown his fangs, either under the influence or after the fact, and she did not have to stand there and take it. He wasn't loud or abusive, just melancholy and mean. But when had he turned to booze? And why? Then she realized with a sinking thud that she did not want to know, nor even guess.

Jill paced the room, its elegant muted reds and greens and mustard walls closing in as the thought persisted. No, she would not take that on. She had not driven him to drink. When she knew him he didn't drink, had never taken a drink. Why should she think she had in any way contributed to his choice? *Don't I have enough guilt, Lord?*

She stopped at the window and stared out. Morgan made his own choices, always had. If he cared to spend an afternoon in his own home anesthetized by his beverage of choice, what was it to her? Yet . . . *What is it you want, Lord? I've done what I came for. I held them up in prayer, and heaven prayed with me, as the old woman said.* The morning had been powerful. She'd felt close to God, grateful to serve in the way He allowed. Not what she had wanted, but what He had allotted for her. She had prayed for Kelsey, prayed for Morgan . . .

A jolt. She paced again. *What is it Lord; what am I missing?* She had prayed for the process, for Kelsey's healing, for Morgan's quick recovery. What else? She circled the room slowly. Something had agitated her spirit while she ran; aggravation with Morgan certainly, but something else, as well. Something that made her look at his environment, see it differently, critically. A hollow opened up inside. He was empty, so empty.

Jill pressed a hand to her chest. She had criticized the symptom but ignored the disease. She closed her eyes and his wound opened before her. He had lived with her lie, with the belief she had destroyed the fruit of their love, rejecting him as she rejected the infant from her womb. She had stricken a mortal blow, and he had not healed after fifteen years. Even now with the truth of Kelsey's existence revealed, the wound festered.

My God. She clutched her hands at her throat, where sobs built and shuddered, and tears burned behind her eyelids. *What can I do? I've spoken more boldly than ever before. I've shown him his need.* She wished she had brought her Bible. She went out to the library off the great room. Many of the shelves were decorated with items to match the room décor, but the others held books. She scanned them, mildly hopeful but without expectation of finding anything religious. On the lowest shelf, she noticed a photo album and pulled it out. There were very few photographs anywhere in Morgan's house. Art on the walls that reflected his personality, but nothing personal.

She sank cross-legged to the floor with the album. Okay, so it was snooping. Then again, it was in a public area, not like going through his dresser drawers or something. Albums were meant to be perused. And she needed something to go on. She opened the cover. Morgan's family smiled out at her: the little girls and Rick, Morgan in his letter jacket perched on the white rail fence, his arm hooked over the top in the nonchalant posture she remembered so well.

He couldn't be much older than eighteen in that shot. And when she turned the page, she saw herself. Morgan in his tux, his hand on her waist. She looked like a baby, wide-eyed and dazzled. Her heart thumped in her breast at the sight of a dried white rose, pressed flat, lying in the crease. She picked it up and brought it to her lips, remembering her fingers pinning it to his lapel. Men kept such things? Men like Morgan. She looked again at the picture.

Her pictures of him had been lost. Burned most likely or torn to a million pieces when she was gone. No doubt for her own good. She had none but the yearbook snapshot, and in the same book the photo of them together on the football field, all pompons and shoulder pads.

This picture had been taken at the dance when they were crowned, all the envious and adoring peers looking on. She had thought that night was the beginning of her life. Had Morgan felt the same? They'd been bantering three years, competing and challenging each other, laughing and crying over every event in the hypersensitive way of teens. She had dreamed of more, but that night opened his eyes and something changed between them, subtle yet intoxicating. That night he kissed her. She touched his face in the photo.

How do I help him, Lord?

The memories were painful. Why keep them fresh? Especially now that it was obvious they could not reconstruct what had been damaged beyond repair. The thought hurt, but she forced herself to face it. This interlude would last only until Kelsey recovered. Then she and Morgan would return to their lives and stagger forward. An aching loss gripped her.

Why? If she was fulfilling God's purpose for her life, why was there so little joy? Wasn't joy a fruit of the Holy Spirit? The Lord never promised constant happiness. But He did say He came to give life abundantly. Was her life abundant?

If she still had a job to go back to, she would throw her energy into it, though in fact all of that had scarcely entered her mind these last days—amazing, given her previous obsession. That was peace, wasn't it? Trust, that the Lord would look out for her, safeguard her job, her livelihood, the kids who mattered so much when her mind wasn't too full of personal crisis.

She had good friends—Shelly and Brett, and, she hoped, even Dan. Maybe Cinda would allow her to keep some contact with Kelsey. She could get more involved at her church, volunteer somewhere, and somehow, find the joy she had lost along the way. Daddy's little sunshine had hidden behind the clouds long enough.

Hadn't the apostle Paul been content in all circumstances? Okay, so he hadn't given his only child away and lost the love of his life—if he even had one, which she doubted, since he wasn't too keen on women by the sound of some of his writings. Still, he'd had troubles of his own and learned to be content in the midst of them. That was the element her faith was missing. That was her challenge.

Morgan had his own. Why did she even think she could help him? She turned the page of the album. Morgan's achievement awards, graduation photos. She was there as well, in her cap and gown, his arm around her. That was before she told them. One week before they all knew. *Oh, Lord, if I could turn back time and change it all . . . but you know I can't.*

She turned page after page, looking at the moments Morgan had frozen and mounted, the people who mattered most. Not another picture of her. She was gone, and the smiles in the photos looked fragile, except for Morgan. His grew larger and more confident, his prosperity evident in the champagne christening of his boat amid an entourage of beautiful people. Morgan had done what she couldn't—found contentment.

But that didn't make sense. The pictures lied. He had turned his back on God, lost faith in his Savior. And turned to drink. That was not the abundant life Christ brought to the world. It was not the joy Kelsey found in Jesus. It was . . . desperation. Again the conviction of her complicity stung.

Lord? She fought the sting of tears. *Have I done this to him?*

He had borne the blame, the vitriolic rancor from her parents. But it was her lie that had toppled all of them into the abyss. *"It's okay, Morgan. I'm on the pill."* She had not simply allowed his advance, she'd encouraged, urged. She had wanted so badly to prove her love.

Jill closed the album and slid it back into the shelf. She could not undo any of it. Only God could. But that would be her prayer, that the Lord would repair what she had destroyed. Wasn't there something in the Bible about the year of locusts? Restoring what the locusts had destroyed? She wished now she had her concordance, as well. But she was getting the picture. She had to pray for Morgan's restoration. The conviction grew. Not prayer alone. She had to act, to repair the harm she had done him—whatever it took.

———

Morgan drained the glass and set it aside. Strange how different the result could be. No euphoria, no energizing party mania. The same liquor, drunk alone, slid him down the path of no return. He tipped his head back and closed his eyes, but there was no sleep behind his lids. It was the middle of the afternoon, on the day he rescued his daughter, and he was wiping his mind clear of sentient thought.

He should have kept Denise on the clock and sloughed off Jill. But then he *had* sloughed her off, with all the finesse of a dragon torching his damsel. He drew a slow breath and released it. Why couldn't he remain cordial with her? He faked it all the time, with people he disliked. Why fail with the person he loved?

Now, there was a root thought. But why not? He was to the point of honesty in this downward slope. *I love Jill Runyan. I've always loved Jill Runyan. I will always love Jill Runyan. So what do you think of that, Lord?*

It must be bad if he was praying. *That was not a prayer.* What was it, then? His own thoughts were betraying him, turning toward God as though He might answer, might care. This would not do. He should have planned a party, a night on the town.

The only thing getting in his way was Jill. "This is not about you, Jill. It's all about Kelsey, remember?" At the sound of his own voice, he opened his eyes, raised an unsteady hand and pointed across the room. "It's not about you."

"I know that." She spoke and it startled him.

He squinted at the chair across from him, realized she actually did sit there. Wonderful. At least he could pretend he had meant to talk to her.

She crossed and squatted down at his knee, her hand warm on his flesh. "You're going to be ill, Morgan."

"I am ill."

She took his hand. "What can I do?"

Laughing, he raised a knowing finger. "You don't do that, remember?"

"I doubt you could now, either."

Her response caught him short. No blushing, no rushing from the room. Actual repartee. What was with that? "I want to."

"Do you?"

He swallowed. Of course he did. Then he let his hand drop.

She gathered it with his other. "Do you want to lie down?"

"I will not . . . walk . . . very well."

She lowered herself to her knees. "How can I help you?"

Oh, this was rich—on her knees begging to help. Pain rose up and gripped the back of his throat. "Go . . . away."

Lifting his hand to her cheek, she shook her head. "I did that once. I won't leave you again."

Shards in the fibers of his heart. She wouldn't accept his sober invitation, but she'd stay out of pity? No, thanks. He slid his hand free. "I told you I have everything I need." He reached for the glass, dumped it onto the carpet, swung for it and missed, then left it lying.

She sat back on her heels. "I don't know if you can understand me right now, or if you'll remember anything I say."

"Probably not."

"I want to ask your forgiveness, Morgan. I lied and forced the issue between us. I was responsible for what happened, but I let you take the blame. I wanted to prove how much I loved you, but when it came to it, I loved myself more. I'm so sorry."

His throat worked over words that would not come. He couldn't understand. "What are you talking about?"

"I told you I was on the pill so you would make love to me. I didn't plan it exactly, but I knew very well what I was doing."

He hung his arm over the side, searching her face and wishing now his vision was clear. "So?"

She moistened her lips. "I let everyone, even you, believe I was led astray, a naïve child misguided. But I wasn't."

Did she think she was saying something he didn't know?

She expelled her breath, her voice rising a notch. "I knew without birth control what could happen. Maybe I even wanted it."

Now he was catching the thrust, straight in the abdomen.

"But when everything got so crazy, I couldn't admit it. I let Dad think you'd practically forced yourself on me, that I hadn't known what was happening."

Memories rushed. Words, names, his own dad weeping outside. He gripped her arm. "Do you think I care?"

She covered his grip with her palm. "I care, Morgan."

He dropped his chin and closed his eyes, his hand slipping from her arm. "I am way too drunk to deal with this."

She sniffed back tears. "Do you want me to tell you again later?"

He expelled a silent laugh. "Spare us both."

"I can't. We've lived with my lies too long."

Those lies hadn't hurt just him. He pushed her away. "My dad wept."

Her eyes flew to his, ripe with anguish. Did she really think this little episode would undo the hurt? Anger surged. "Oh, he'd teared up before. Actually he's a softhearted man, you might recall." Morgan fought a fresh rush of fury. "But I'd never seen him weep. When he got off the phone with your father, he walked out into the yard, held his face, and cried."

"I know Dad said cruel things. . . ."

"That wasn't it. He thought he'd failed, and that failure caused the death of his grandchild."

Jill clutched her hands at her knees on the floor. "I'm sorry, Morgan. Dad was wrong to lie. He's not perfect, but—"

"He's *saved*." Morgan tasted the word like something pungent.

She searched his face. "Is that why you turned from God?"

His throat worked painfully. "Do you really think, after that, I could pretend to be anything but what I was?"

She sagged.

"Now if you're through, I think I might sleep." He closed his eyes, wiping the sight of her from view, but hardly from recall. That would be merciful.

From her crouch on the floor, Jill stared at Morgan. What had she hoped to accomplish? Had she thought her confession would somehow wipe the slate clean? She pressed a hand to her face. And what had induced her to admit she'd all but planned her pregnancy? She had hardly admitted it to herself.

All she had known was that Morgan would not run out on her if it happened. They were both facing college, four years spent apart. She loved him so fiercely. What if he forgot her? Found someone else? She rested her face in her hands. Why hadn't she trusted God then?

Could He have given her such a love if it wasn't His will? Other girls were in and out of relationships all the time. No one had ever meant to her what Morgan did. Once her heart was set, it never wavered. Why hadn't she seen it as the Lord's blessing? For Morgan Spencer to date no one else his entire senior year—wasn't that proof enough that they had something special, something that would stand the test of time?

And, God help her, it had, and would continue to. Tears came and soaked into the cracks between her fingers. Morgan was too gone to notice, too jaded to care. But she cried for all they'd lost. If only there were a way to fix it now. She would give up everything for one more chance. And when he sobered, she would tell him that.

Sniffing, she climbed up from her knees. He was out cold. Alcohol, anesthesia, physical and emotional trauma; he might sleep for hours. She stood and looked around the room. A dozen choices for entertainment, to enjoy alone? No wonder Morgan said they were only things. She looked down at him, heart breaking. *I'm sorry, Morgan.*

His office was quiet. Where was Denise? In her little cottage, or had she gone into town? She found Morgan's laptop and opened it on his desk. Even if Kelsey hadn't written, she could leave her a note, telling her . . . Morgan was fine? That he'd come through the procedure with flying colors? Was overjoyed with all of it?

Jill brought up her mail. She could ask Kelsey to pray for him. The purity of their daughter's prayers would surely soften God's heart and avail much. Over the next few days with Morgan, she would do the same. Though her prayers were not Kelsey's, they were the best she could offer.

> *Dear Kelsey,*
> *I suppose by now you've received Morgan's bone marrow. I cannot tell you how hard I'm praying for this to work. Since you were concerned for him, I thought I'd let you know he came through fine. Sore, of course. But I wondered if you could pray for him. . . .*

How could she expect a fourteen-year-old to understand? But then, Kelsey was no ordinary fourteen-year-old. *Could you pray for his faith and for . . .* Jill searched for the right word. Healing, forgiveness, restoration. She settled on *peace.* Yes. If Morgan could be at peace with God, with himself, that would be enough. She didn't want to reveal too much or impugn Morgan in any way. So she left it at that and asked Kelsey how she was feeling, what the next steps were, and assured her of her constant prayers.

Resting her fingers on the keyboard, she had a sudden sensation of purpose. God's will was at work. Now if she could just keep out of His way. She raised her finger to exit the program, but the mail message came up. Biting her lip, she clicked on the message.

> *Hi, Jill. I actually feel better today than I have for a long time. The doctor said it had nothing to do with the marrow yet. They're always careful I don't get the wrong ideas. But do you know what I think? I*

think Morgan sent some of himself with it. Like good wishes or hope or love? I don't mean like he really loves me, but as I sat there with Jesus during the rescue, I was so covered in love. The Lord's, of course, and Mom and Dad. But I also sensed you and Morgan. Is that crazy?

No, it wasn't crazy. Not when she loved Kelsey so much, and after Morgan's response to the phone call . . . his tenderness had been tangible.

But I just got your note and I'm curious. You said pray for Morgan's faith? I will, of course, but I'm not sure why. Jesus loves him so much. That's another thing I sensed today. As I dozed, I had one of my visions. Okay, maybe it was a dream, but where I get this stuff if it isn't from God, I don't know. And Morgan was on his knees before Jesus, and Jesus lifted him up and hugged him really tight.

Jill's breath stilled. Her eyes closed. *Oh, Lord, thank you.* If only Morgan knew it.

So, yes, I'll pray for faith and peace. But I have a secret thing I'm praying also. It makes me very happy to think about it. Oh, guess what? Josh came to the hospital. I could only see him through the window, but he threw me a kiss. Now that kind of kiss is O-KAY. Kelsey

Jill smiled and typed her reply. *More than okay. How kind of him to come. Did he know this was your big day?*

After a moment, *Yes, he knew. My smile is hurting my face.*

Jill laughed softly, typed, *I love you, Kelsey.* And sent it before she could think too hard. She waited, breath held, praying she hadn't overstepped.

I love you, too. Don't let Morgan forget my picture. I want to compare it to my dream vision.

Jill had to smile again. At close to Kelsey's age she'd had dream visions of Morgan, too. She didn't share that with her daughter, only focused on the beauty of what Kelsey shared with her. *She's the best of both of us, Lord. Please make this work.*

She wandered out to the yard, stood at the edge, and looked out at the ocean. Something dark leaped from the water, and she guessed it was a dolphin. She searched the waves for another sight of it or perhaps more of them. A large bird, skinny legs trailing, dipped down and mounted up with a silver fish flipping about in its beak. The lowering sun opalized the clouds where they thinned, but the sea had a grayer cast than the day before.

She could understand how people listened hour after hour to the ebb and flow of the waves. Even on a tape, that sound brought peace. And there was the fin again, only it wasn't a dolphin. The creature rose up and spouted. Jill sucked in her breath. She'd never seen a whale, not free out in the ocean. What a sight, though it had been so brief.

Near where it disappeared, a flock of white birds glowed over the water in a ray of sun that shot through the clouds. The trees beside her waved in a breeze, then grew still. *Oh, Lord, so much beauty. So much life.* She wanted Morgan to see it. To know in his soul what Kelsey knew without ever meeting him. *Open his eyes, Lord. Let him know your love.*

CHAPTER

26

Morgan dragged himself from what was nearer coma than sleep at the incessant shaking of his shoulder. The room was shrouded in night, too dark to make out the hand that assailed him. He vaguely remembered Juan walking him up the stairs at Jill's direction. So why was he being rousted now?

"Wake up. Señor Morgan, wake up."

He peeled his lids open, blinking against the gritty surface of his eyeballs. Consuela in his bedroom?

"It's Juan. He's been arrested. They say he broke into a car."

Morgan lifted her hand from his shoulder. "Stop shaking me. I'm awake." Her words penetrated his fog. Juan. He'd known something was up. Suspected, at least. He eased slowly up on one elbow. His back and hips ached. But it could be worse, like his head.

He slid his legs out from the sheets. Consuela was too worked up to notice his boxers or care. He sat up and buried his face in his hands. "What time is it?"

"Two o'clock. I'll make you coffee." She hurried from the room.

He hunched on the edge of the bed, feeling every poke from yesterday's needle. His head pulsated pain, and his tongue cleaved to the roof of his mouth. Juan arrested. What was he supposed to do about that? He couldn't think.

Broke into a car. There were signs in cities like Tijuana where Juan

had come from. Do not park here. Car thieves. It was something of a
sport down there. Morgan let the weight of his head rest in his palms.

Consuela was back, restoring his soul with the steam of French
roast. He gripped the mug and drank. She'd spiked it with bourbon.
He raised his brows, surprised.

"Juan called from the police station. He asked for you to come."

"I don't know what I can do, Consuela."

She pressed her hands to her face and started to cry. "If anyone can
help him, you—"

"Stealing from cars is not considered honest work up here."

"Sí. Sí." She wrung her hands like rags. "He is lazy, I know. But
he's my brother. *Mi hermano pequeño.*"

Morgan took another gulp of coffee. What was she thinking, spiking it like that? "Let me get dressed."

She went to his closet and pulled out slacks and a long-sleeved
cotton-knit shirt. She laid them on the bed beside him then went to
his dresser.

"Consuela."

She turned, one hand on his underwear drawer.

"Wait for me in the hall."

She gripped her hands against her mouth. "Gracias, Señor."

"Don't thank me yet. There may be nothing I can do."

Nodding and wringing her hands, she went out and closed the
door. His first order of business was the bathroom. Then he washed his
face and head at the sink and brushed his teeth. He poured the rest of
the coffee down the drain.

Dressing was interesting. He had old-man legs. But he managed.
Now if he could get his head cleared. He'd need all his wits to get Juan
out of this mess. He carried the empty mug to the door and handed it
to Consuela. "Straight, this time. No hair of the dog."

She nodded. "Sí, of course." She hurried down the stairs.

He made his slow way down the hall, one hand to his pounding
head.

Jill's door opened. "What is it, Morgan? What's wrong?"

"Juan's in trouble."

She stepped out wearing the robe from her closet. "I heard the
phone. I thought Kelsey . . ."

He rested a hand on her shoulder. "Just a matter of car theft."

Her eyes widened. "Oh no."

"Consuela thinks I work miracles."

Jill pressed his hand. He ought to apologize for his ugliness earlier.

But Consuela hurried up the stairs with a fresh mug of coffee, handed it over, then turned to Jill. "I'm sorry to wake you."

"That's all right."

"You will pray for Juan?"

Jill nodded. "Yes, I will."

Morgan sipped the coffee. At least Consuela wasn't pinning all her hopes on him. He released Jill's shoulder. "You may as well go back to bed. This could take a while."

She stretched. "I'm awake now. Do you want me to drive you?"

"Consuela's driving." She had pulled on a jacket. There would be no convincing her to stay behind, though a police precinct at two in the morning would not be pretty. Morgan motioned Consuela down before him, then followed stiffly.

Jill's heart steadied as she watched them leave. The two-o'clock phone call had brought waves of fear that something had happened to Kelsey, though if there were an emergency, she and Morgan would hardly be the first called. Rational thought had come with waking, then concern and curiosity.

Juan. Consuela was brave to wake Morgan—or desperate—after how stubborn and morose he'd been when she insisted Juan get him up to his bed. Yet he seemed calm now and willing to do his best. Of course. He'd made an art of rising to the occasion. The least she could do was pray. Or maybe the most. But how could she pray for a car thief? Surely not that he'd be let off, though Consuela's tearful face was convincing. The Lord's will be done, then, whatever was best. Leave the knowledge of that to the Lord.

And maybe that Morgan would see God's hand working and his heart would be opened. He must be exhausted, maybe in pain, certainly hung over, yet he went out in the night, not even waiting until morning to help Consuela's brother. Jill's impressions of Juan had not been positive. He seemed sullen, resentful even. Morgan had taken him in and was trying to obtain a green card for him. Yet she noticed none of Consuela's gratitude. No wonder Morgan had been troubled at the thought of Juan's work. He knew he couldn't work legally without a green card. Even then, he gave him the benefit of the doubt.

And here were his fears materialized. Poor Consuela. It was obvious she cared deeply what happened to her brother. But what would happen? Theft was no small matter. Jill went into her room and settled cross-legged on the bed. *Lord, comfort Consuela. Give her peace. Give Morgan wisdom. Uphold our system of justice, but be merciful.* She sank into prayer, noticing how much easier it had become once need prompted practice.

The sun was rising when they returned. Jill had dozed, jolting awake now and then at some sound or thought that penetrated. When she heard the door open and their voices, she hurried down the hall, dressed in the capris and a blue-and-white-striped top that she had put on as soon as they left. Their voices came from the kitchen, Morgan speaking low over Consuela's tears. "It's best all around. He didn't want honest work. You know that."

"Sí." She sniffed. "But . . ."

"You can't change how he is. We gave him the chance."

That didn't sound good. As Jill stepped into the room, Consuela looked up with tearful eyes.

Morgan turned Consuela toward the doorway. "Go get some rest. We'll manage in here."

Consuela smeared the tears from her eyes and nodded. She stopped at the edge of the kitchen. "Gracias, Morgan."

"*De nada.*"

Jill wanted to ask what happened, but maybe it wasn't her business. Morgan headed for the coffeepot and poured a mug. "Want some?"

"Just some juice if there is any."

He walked out to the balcony, pulled oranges from the upper branches of the tree, then came back in and worked silently, cutting them in half and pressing the halves on the juicer. She'd had fresh squeezed but never right off the tree.

When Morgan handed her the glass, she felt as though it were filled with gold. "Thank you."

He took her hand and led her out to the balcony. The sunrise was off to their left, but the water reflected its glory. The birds were already busy, flocks of tiny, pure white gulls and variegated pigeons, swallows that circled and swooped, singing their hearts out, and sea gulls with their singular cry. Jill breathed the balmy air. "What happened to Juan?"

"Juan goes back to Mexico, which is better than jail."

Jill sipped the orange juice, a sweet burst of flavor. "How did you manage that?"

He leaned his elbows on the stucco block of the banister, cupping his mug between his hands. "There've been seven cars broken into in the last two days. With Consuela translating, Juan confessed that he broke in, took cameras, CD players, and the like."

"But how can they let him go when people have lost their things?"

Morgan glanced over. "I agreed to pay for whatever couldn't be reclaimed. Most of it he already pawned off on the beach."

Jill watched him with the morning shadows playing on his face. "So you're paying for his dishonesty."

"I agreed to let him come."

"That doesn't make him your responsibility."

He ducked his chin. "I owe it to Consuela."

"You pay Consuela."

He turned, let his eyes travel her. "I find solutions. That's why I'm successful. That's how my brain works." He looked back at the sea, sipping his coffee. "It's beautiful, isn't it? I don't often see it this early."

"You must be exhausted."

He nodded.

"You should go back to sleep."

"I need to get you to the airport. Nine-fifteen flight."

It sunk like an arrow between the ribs. She hadn't seen it coming. A flight home in just hours. "Oh."

He reached over and took her hand. "I'm sorry for yesterday."

Tears stung her eyes. "I wanted to—"

"Jill." He brought her fingers to his lips and kissed them. "I know what you said. Let's not rehash it."

There was so much more she had wanted to tell him, but he had made plans for her strategic and immediate removal. He drained his cup and said, "I need a shower."

Nodding, she watched him leave, the thread unraveling yet again, maybe for the last time. What reason would they have to reconnect? She stayed on the balcony another moment, soaking in the everlasting rhythm of the ocean, the cries of the gulls, even a school of dolphins. But she needed to pack.

She went to her room and folded her things into the bag, then zipped it shut and set it by the door. She stood a moment before the Armani gown, shoes, and clutch, then left them in the closet. That was another life. Morgan met her in the hall and reached for the suitcase.

She kept hold. "I can take it. You're still sore."

"You have everything?"

She nodded. Everything that was hers.

He let her into the Thunderbird and loaded her bag into the trunk. Then he drove her to the Orange County airport, where they picked up her ticket from the counter.

She refused to cry. "Thank you for letting me be here with you. If I hear anything from Kelsey, I'll let you know."

He took a small box from his pocket and held it out.

Her brow drew together, puzzled.

"Birthday present."

More puzzled still. "Morgan, it's not my birthday."

"Belated."

Her birthday was in four months.

"A few years late."

Her throat tightened. "I don't . . . ."

"Just open it. I saved you all the tape and paper part."

She lifted the lid of the box and took out a bracelet she had admired from the shop window on one of their Beauview walks over fifteen years ago. She remembered it by the delicate silver swans connected with wave-shaped links. She'd been in her swan phase and the bracelet was the most delicately beautiful thing she'd seen.

"Morgan . . ."

"I'd already gotten it." Before she left him to go stay with her aunt. "I'm terrible with receipts."

She looked into his face. He'd kept it all these years?

He smiled. "You'd better get into the security line. It's filling up fast."

She swallowed the tightness in her throat. "I don't know what to say."

He brushed her cheek with a kiss. "Good-bye."

Tears washed in, in spite of her efforts. "Good-bye, Morgan."

He turned and walked out, with hardly any limp at all. He might not be running the next few days, but he'd be fine.

She stood in the line, waited for her bag to be scanned and her body checked for bombs and weapons, then went to the gate. It was there she realized she held a first-class ticket and was boarded ahead of the coach passengers. Taking her seat in the relative luxury of the first-class section, she slipped the bracelet onto her wrist, then fought tears the rest of the flight. By the time she landed, she was drained.

She had supposed she would have to take a taxi from Des Moines, but Shelly was waiting at the exit. "Shelly, how. . . ?"

Shelly grabbed her into a hug. "Morgan called this morning. Dan wanted to come, but he was on shift."

Thank God. She was not ready for an hour alone with him, not when the tears insisted on rising to the surface with each thought. Now, for instance, at the realization Morgan had covered even this detail.

"I would have fought him to come anyway. I know I won't get the bald truth once you have time to think. So no matter how tired you are, you have to tell me everything."

Jill settled into the seat of Shelly's Miata. After Morgan's cars, it didn't seem so special.

Shelly tapped her hand on the steering wheel. "So what happened?"

Jill looked out at the highway flanked by cornfields, and all she could think of were glittering waves and soaring gulls. "The transplant went fine. Morgan is healing well, and Kelsey will, too."

"I did not drive an hour and a half up here to settle for that. Details, sweetie."

"I don't know what to say." But she described Morgan's house and told about Denise and Consuela and Juan, recounting each one's story as she knew it.

"He's a nice guy."

Jill nodded, fingering her bracelet. "Too nice. People take advantage of him."

Shelly glanced over. "I like the swans. A little something to go with the Armani dress?"

Jill didn't answer for a moment. "I didn't keep the dress."

Shelly waved a hand. "Yeah, who wants Armani?"

Jill dropped her chin, smiling.

"When are you going to see him again?"

Jill fought back the insistent tears. "I don't think I will."

"I'm making Hungarian goulash for dinner. You can have Rascal back after that."

Jill leaned her head back, smiling again. Hungarian goulash was Shelly's comfort food for every woe. "Sounds great."

Goulash and, of course, corn on the cob boiling in the pot, the midwestern side dish for anything. But there was nothing so good as farm-fresh corn. Unless it was California strawberries and avocados and orange juice squeezed from the tree. She forced the thought away as she snuggled Rascal under her chin and let his purr rumble in her own throat, then looked up as Dan came through the front door with a bottle of wine.

"Welcome back." His T-shirt was taut over his shoulders and chest, a slight dampness around the collar. His bike shorts were snug on his narrow hips and muscled thighs. He must have ridden over.

"Hey, hey." Brett waved his tongs and continued pulling corn from the pot.

Shelly hadn't mentioned that Dan was coming, an innocent oversight, of course. He placed the wine on the counter and turned. "No suntan? I thought you'd come back bronzed like a California girl."

No, she was, after all, an Iowa farm girl. "I hardly had time for that."

"But you're back." He smiled again as though he had no control over it. "That's a good thing."

With time she might see it that way. She let Rascal down, and he scooted under the table.

Dan uncorked the wine and set it to breathe. "How was your trip?"

Mr. Talkative, wasn't he? "It was fine. The marrow harvest went without a hitch." She glanced at Shelly. "Kelsey called Morgan the night before to thank him." She tried not to visualize Morgan overwhelmed by his daughter's voice and the comfort she'd offered. That had been such a tender and hopeful night. She trapped a sigh and said, "Now we can only pray."

Dan actually nodded.

Brett carried the bowl of goulash to the table. "Pull up a chair and prepare to gustate."

"I don't think that's a verb." Shelly set the bowl of corn beside the goulash.

"Gustation, the act of tasting. If you can taste, you can gustate." Brett untied his apron and tossed it over the counter. "Don't argue with the man, wench."

"I'll wench you." Shelly bumped him with a hip.

"Where are my handcuffs when I need them? Got yours, Dan?"

Dan clicked his fingers.

Shelly glared. "You wouldn't dare. Sit down, Jill, before my he-man beats his chest."

Jill laughed. Brett was a man's man but certainly never beat his chest. Since Dan didn't think of it, she pulled out her own chair and sat down, trying not to miss the feel of Morgan's hand across her shoulders. So many things to miss. But she would not think of that now. These were her friends, welcoming her home. She had kept it light on the drive with Shelly, in spite of her friend's contention that exhaustion would gain her the bald truth. She could do the same now.

Shelly took her place beside Brett and looked across at Jill. "Dig in."

Silently Jill offered her thanks as Dan and Brett filled their plates. She took her own servings of comfort food and swallowed her first bite. "Shelly, as always, it's great."

Dan said, "I forgot the caviar. You'll have to wean yourself off it."

"Caviar?"

He shrugged. "Now that you're back with the peons."

So it was a stab at Morgan. "No caviar, I'm afraid. But Morgan's housekeeper is a wonderful Mexican cook. Tamales no American could make."

"Nothing like foreign servants. Where does the guy live?"

"Santa Barbara."

"No hovel, I guess, if he needs servants." Dan made it sound like a weakness in Morgan rather than the blessing it was to Consuela.

"No hovel." Jill described the lovely gated property overlooking the Pacific. "I saw dolphins and a whale. So many birds, and the sound of the waves was so peaceful. Oranges right off the tree to squeeze for juice. Very exotic." Dan deserved that for his caviar comment. "And they have a private beach at the base of the cliffs."

"Very posh." Dan sipped his wine.

Jill tried not to picture Morgan with his tumbler of bourbon, drowning the hurt she had caused. "I drove both his retro Thunderbird and his Corvette. Now that's posh."

Dan set the wine down. "A Vette, huh? Don't suppose he has a bike."

"I didn't see one." She met his eyes. How far would he push it?

"No one to pedal it for him?"

Jill iced him with her gaze. "He had difficulty even walking after multiple bone punctures."

Dan's face reddened. "Sorry."

She held his eyes without answering. She might have questioned Morgan's need for all his things, but Dan had no right to disparage him personally. He had no concept of Morgan's sacrifice, his hopes for their daughter, his pain, his emptiness in spite of all the things Dan envied.

"So . . . any movement in the Marvin case?" Brett tossed his balled napkin at Dan's head.

Dan turned. "Actually, yes. I'd be surprised if we don't get a confession tomorrow."

Jill took a bite of goulash. Brett might break up the fight, but their police chatter did nothing to still the defensive anger Dan had churned. At the earliest chance, she stood and loaded her plate into the dishwasher. "Thank you so much for dinner, Shell. I better get Rascal home."

"I'll walk you over." Dan stood up.

Inevitable. She nodded with a forced smile and scooped Rascal into her arms.

Outside, he said, "I was a jerk."

Jill didn't argue, just started across the lawn between the patios.

He shook his head. "The green monster's eaten me the whole time you were gone."

"I'm sorry." Rascal trembled in her arms, fearful once again of the great outdoors.

"Don't apologize. That makes it worse."

She looked into his face. "I shouldn't have rubbed it in."

"Are you in love with him?" His face was firm, yet vulnerable.

She owed him the truth. "I always have been."

He nodded. "But you didn't stay." He was fishing.

"I would have."

Dan stood a long minute, his brows pressed together. "I could learn to be second best."

"Please don't do that, Dan. You deserve to be best."

He brought his chin up and nodded, hands clutching his hips. "Good night, Jill." He crossed back to Shelly and Brett's, where she knew he would receive consolation and understanding.

She went inside with Rascal, set him on the floor and watched him run to a place where he could regain his dignity. Then her icy façade melted. She pressed her hands to her face as all the memories and emotions rushed in.

27

Bern Gershwin looked as though he'd put on a pound or two since the last time they'd played. He sweated and huffed but took full advantage of Morgan's relative immobility, smacking the ball hard and low in the echo chamber court. Morgan just managed the return and Bern put it away with a shot low and wide, then pulled off his goggles and toweled his face. Morgan set his racquet down and removed his goggles.

With only a slight gloat, Bern said, "Not too slow on your feet, considering."

"Slow enough to give you advantage."

Bern laughed. "Like I need it."

Morgan wiped the sweat from his head and neck. "I talked to my daughter."

"You did?" Bern hung the towel across his neck and checked the clock. Reflex.

"She initiated it, called me the night before the harvest."

Bern pulled the two edges of his towel taut across his neck. "Then you don't need what I got for you."

Morgan shrugged. "The thing is, I could make contact. E-mail. Phone calls. She has that much with Jill by permission, though for some reason the Bensons won't extend the same to me."

"But the girl called you."

"She called Jill and used the opportunity to thank me."

Bern rubbed his face. "But she didn't have permission."

Morgan shook his head. "And if I pursue it that way, it pits her against her parents' wishes." He'd learned that much from Todd and Stan. He ducked through the half door of the court.

Bern followed him out. "And you've spoken with the parents."

"Not directly. They communicated right at the start through the doctors that it would be handled according to donation protocol. It's part of the agreement in the donor program not to make contact within a year's time." Morgan started down the hall toward the locker room. "But that doesn't apply to relatives." He paused in the doorway. "So am I?"

Bern frowned. "Legally?"

"I know reality. Now walk me through your world."

Bern passed by into the locker room. "First off, you don't have much to go on. Since you weren't married, Jill had sole custody of the child at birth."

No surprise there, though it rankled. "Shouldn't I at least have known?"

Bern tossed his towel on the bench. "Prior to petition for termination of the parent-child relationship, all putative fathers must be notified by publication in a newspaper."

"Wait a minute. What do you mean, all putative fathers?" Morgan spun the combination lock.

"She listed you as unknown."

He digested that. As though there'd been any confusion.

"If the father is unknown or his whereabouts unknown, due process requires notification in a publication most likely to inform all potential fathers."

"I never saw anything." Morgan scowled as he tugged the locker door open.

"Did she know where you were?"

"She knew my plans. Full scholarship to Wharton in Pennsylvania."

"She posted in Des Moines, Kelsey's birthplace."

"Why would I see it there?"

Bern shook his head. "You wouldn't. That's the one scrap from the table. Due process requires her to post notice in the county most likely to reach you. Because the termination order was entered without full due process, you *could* request a court order for revocation of release of custody."

"What does that mean?" Morgan shoved his racquet into the long narrow space.

"It attacks Jill's custodial release. However, before your eyes start gleaming, let me say you must show good cause to vacate the termination order."

Morgan hung the goggles with the racquet. "What constitutes good cause?"

"Fraud, coercion, misrepresentation . . ."

"Coercion? As in her parents forcing her?"

"In the case of a minor they probably had responsibility in her decision. At least both parties could argue that."

Morgan pressed a hand to the fresh ache in his traumatized hips. "Was it fraudulent to claim she didn't know who the father was?"

"Fraud would be claiming rape, statutory in your case. You're lucky it didn't go that way."

Morgan jerked his head to stare at Bern. "Rape?"

"You could possibly make a case for misrepresentation if you could prove she did know it was you and there were no other possibilities." Bern stripped his T-shirt off over his head. Definite extra poundage, but that hadn't immobilized him anywhere near the pain Morgan was feeling just now.

He focused on the point of this exercise. "So if there's misrepresentation, then what?"

"You could request the vacation of the termination order."

"That means I'd have a right to see her?" Morgan stripped off his own sweaty shirt.

Bern pursed his lips. "You want reality?"

That didn't sound good. Morgan gripped the edge of the locker door and slacked a hip. "Go ahead."

Bern raised his index finger. "First, you can't prove you were the only possible father, even if the DNA shows you actually are. If Jill claims there was another putative in Des Moines, then she followed due process."

A putative father in Des Moines? Hardly. It must have humiliated Jill to claim "father unknown." It was bad enough to be in that position with the only person she'd slept with, but to make it seem as though she'd slept around and couldn't name the possibilities . . . Yet at the moment he didn't feel too sorry for her.

Bern raised his next finger. "Second, in the state of Iowa, age fourteen is when the child is consulted in the matter of custody. You'd be asking Kelsey to give up all she's known, and especially to deny Roger Benson as her father."

"Wait a minute. I'm not talking about changing custody."

Bern's thumb stuck out. "Third, the judge will consider the best interest of the child, including avoidance of disruption in relationships. So basically, you don't have a chance."

Morgan dropped his chin. "So I have absolutely no right to see my daughter."

"Under the law she isn't your daughter. She can only have one legal father at a time."

He swallowed. "Can't we do anything?"

Bern drew his brows together. "I could draw up a letter to the effect that you intend to challenge the termination. We both know you haven't a chance, but it might give you room to talk about settling the matter directly with the Bensons."

"It could give me some leverage?"

Bern shrugged. "It might get you in the door."

He'd just donated marrow to their daughter, covered their medical bills. But he'd have to threaten legal action to get through the door. What was wrong with that picture? He jammed his fingers through his hair. "Write the letter, but don't send it. I'll hold on to it just in case."

With the hot water dribbling down his chest, Morgan scrubbed his skin. Why couldn't the club get any decent water pressure through the showerhead? And would it have been so much to give a guy elbowroom in the stall? He shut the water off and stepped out, grabbed his towel, and scrubbed himself again. Bern had gone to steam himself in the sauna. Morgan just wanted to get home.

Pain stabbed Kelsey, totally unrelated to any physical cause as she read the question from her Hope Page. *How can you claim Jesus loves me when He let this happen to me? I'm a freak and everyone hates me and stares at me and says there goes that kid with cancer. It's a stinking lie that Jesus loves me and you are the big liar. Darren*

Kelsey closed her eyes. Yes, kids were cruel. They couldn't help it. They didn't know how to be around someone who was dying, whose hair had fallen out, who tired easily, bled easily, cried easily.

Sometimes she wished she could hold an assembly and say, "Look, here's how it is. Say this, and don't say that, and don't stare, but please, please don't look away as though we don't exist."

Tears filled her eyes for Darren. *Please let me know what to say, Jesus.* She started to type. *Hey, Darren. Yes, you're a freak in some people's eyes. So am I. We all are. Do I understand why we were chosen for the no-hair club? No. But it's a very exclusive group. No one can just apply. You have to be chosen. That makes you mad, I know. You didn't WANT to be chosen; you didn't ASK to be chosen; you'd give anything NOT to be chosen. But reality is, you were.*

The question is what do we do now? Can you make it go away? No. Can you spend the time you have hating everybody and being miserable? Yes. But why would you want to? Personally, I think we're on a mission. It's so important that we may not make it back. But what we accomplish will be worth it. So here's your mission, should you choose to accept it.

Find Jesus. Pour out your heart, all your hurt and anger and fear and wishes and dreams. Learn who He is. You can read about it in the Bible. I like the gospel of Luke because Luke was a doctor. And when you know Jesus, if you can still say He doesn't love you, then you can call me the biggest liar who ever lived, because . . .

Jesus loves you and so do I. Kelsey

www.kelseys_hope_page.com

With renewed spirit, she went to the next question.

Dear Kelsey,

Why do I have to be alone? No one can touch me. I want my mommy.

P.S. Mary is five years old. She asked me to write that message when I told her about your page and how she could ask anything she wanted to know. Please answer soon, and bless you for the hope you give. Nurse Becky

Again the tears came. This was going to be one of those days.

Dear Mary,

I know how hard it is to be alone. The doctors have good reasons for keeping people away so germs can't make you sicker. I'm alone right now, too, for the same reason. But when you feel very lonely, close your eyes and picture Jesus. He said, "Let the little children come to me." He will hold you on His lap and cuddle you. Your mommy and daddy want to be with you, but when they can't, Jesus always is.

Jesus loves you and so do I. Kelsey

www.kelseys_hope_page.com

Kelsey dabbed her nose with a tissue as she read the next message and wrote:

Dear Joanie,

Don't be afraid of the doctor. Jesus chose her for you and will help her know what to do. Jesus never wants you to be afraid. He said perfect love makes fear go away. And His love is perfect. I know some of the things the doctors and nurses have to do hurt a lot, but let Jesus love you even then because He hurt a WHOLE lot for us when He died on the cross. He knows how hard it is to be brave, but He forgave everyone who hurt him, and they didn't even have a good reason. They were not trying to help, heal, or save His life. Your doctor and nurses are.

Jesus loves you and so do I. Kelsey
www.kelseys_hope_page.com

And another one on pain.

Dear Jeremy,

The bone tap hurts, but if you know the people are trying to help you, the pain is not so bad. Each procedure is a battle that requires courage. You are only a little soldier, but I know you can be brave. Trust in Jesus.

Jesus loves you and so do I. Kelsey
www.kelseys_hope_page.com

She was so tired. She had not managed any food or drink by mouth, only the ever-present IV fluids. Her progress would be measured in part by her ability to take nourishment, but nothing would stay down, and if it did, it only caused more trouble in her intestines. Nor had she been out of bed yet. Tomorrow she would try to walk, but now she was just too tired. The stationary bike across the room was a joke, she was sure.

She drew a slow breath. She would just rest a little, then answer the others. Tomorrow she would have more energy. She wanted to write to Jill, though, since she hadn't for a while. Maybe that much she could manage.

———

For the third night since returning home, Jill checked her e-mail for a message from Kelsey. She didn't expect the child to write every night, but she didn't want to miss one if she did. And all the other messages became insignificant the moment she noticed Kelsey's. Plus there was the added excitement of sometimes finding Kelsey online.

Most of the time, as soon as she sent a reply, Kelsey came back with an instant response. The child must use her computer a lot, or maybe she kept it online to answer whenever something came in. Jill wrapped her arms around herself and tried not to hope too much. But the truth was she could not get enough of this remarkable girl she and Morgan had created, and Cinda and Roger had raised.

It was all she went on these days, as the ache for Morgan howled at her mind, demanding entrance when she knew she could not stand it again. If she had known how hard it would be to leave him, she would never have gone out there. Not even to be part of Kelsey's rescue. She had this relationship with Kelsey already. Yet she had allowed the wolf that devoured her joy back in.

Wasn't it her mission to find joy, to demonstrate it, to live in victory so others could see the benefit of Christ? She had accepted that challenge, taking Shelly's words to heart—and proceeded to lose everything she found purpose in. She missed her kids. She had gone by the school briefly, but the moment the kids saw her they began acting out, destroying order for the new teacher, Don Daley, who, according to Ed Fogarty, had done marvelously so far. She couldn't help that they didn't understand why she had abandoned them, or that they wanted the connection back. Don might be the nicest man alive, but she and her kids had history.

Soon she would be back, planning for next year under Pam's direction, and fighting for her job when every wrong turn would be celebrated by Ed Fogarty and gleefully added to her employment folder. It would probably be easier to give up the job and look elsewhere. But there were Angelica and Joey and Sammi . . . the others who needed the silent prayers and many hugs she offered.

She sighed. She could let it go for at least a few moments if there was a note from Kelsey. Just thoughts of Kelsey were balm, filled with so much hope. Her daughter deserved a miracle. And Jesus loved her so much. It came through everything Kelsey said. Jill had never known anyone so intimate with her Savior. She had a quick breath of anticipation as Kelsey's e-mail came up. Jill bit her lip on a smile, wondering if Kelsey knew how these letters sustained her.

Hi, Jill. I now know what a stock animal feels like sitting in a stall all day. But isolation is not too bad when you can barely lift your fingers. I guess I spoke too soon. The doctors said I'm crashing, but not to be alarmed because it's expected. I guess words like crash are no longer alarming, not compared to fail or die. They also said I exhibited signs of veno-occlusive disease, VOD, during treatment before transplant. It's about the blood vessels to my liver. So they're watching very closely for lovely yellow eyes and skin. If I swell up like a balloon, they know I have it.

Jill tried not to picture Kelsey with either symptom. But her daughter's tone was definitely less upbeat.

I'm trying not to be discouraged. I have so much to be thankful for. I've been answering the letters on my Web page. I get so many now, and some of the kids have become good friends even though we've never met. But lots of them are frightened and angry, and I want so much for them to know about Jesus, and how His love casts out fear. His love is like breath to me.

Jill's own breath caught. To have such a love, such a deep sense of her Lord.

And that brings up why I really wanted to write. Please don't think I'm weird like a prophet or anything, but I was praying for Morgan the way you asked me to, and I realized that even though Jesus loves him so much, Morgan doesn't know it. Or believe it or something. And then I got this idea like there was something in his life that kept him from knowing that love. So I was praying against it, and I just knew God wanted me to pray for him to get sick.

Jill reread the sentence, but Kelsey had actually said what she thought.

I told Jesus I could not do that. Not after Morgan did so much to help me get well. That would not be fair or nice. But He said, "Do you trust me?" And I said yes. Then He said, "Do my will." I know this sounds really crazy, but I have to obey. Jesus really wants me to pray that prayer even though I don't know why. Could you please tell me if you understand? Kelsey

Jill stared at the screen, making certain she understood what Kelsey had said, but there didn't seem to be any doubt. Kelsey was praying for Morgan to get sick. Jill pictured him sick all too easily, after seeing him hobbling in pain, then drunk and hung over. Why would Jesus want him worse off than he already was? *Lord?*

She typed, *Kelsey, I'm sorry I don't have a better answer. I don't know why Jesus would want that prayer when we've been praying for healing. It doesn't make sense. But I do know that God's ways are above ours, and there have been so many things I didn't think were right, and then they turned out to be perfect. If you know that's what the Lord wants of you, then I agree you have to do it.*

A pang of remorse and serious betrayal stung her. She did not want Morgan to suffer more than he had. How could she condone her agreement? She should tell Kelsey no, she must have heard wrong. Pray for healing. And if Kelsey prayed for him to be sick, and she prayed for him to be healed, weren't they at cross-purposes? Would God contradict himself?

Just be certain you heard right. And I don't think you're weird at all; I think you're wonderful. And so does Morgan.

But would he if he'd read this e-mail over her shoulder? Jill closed her eyes, remembering his hands on her shoulders, the ache in his eyes as he spoke with Kelsey and heard her voice. What if she'd said, "God wants me to pray for you to get sick." How on earth could he answer that?

Jill sent her answer and prayed she had not just made another mistake. When no answer came back, she squelched the flicker of disappointment. With Kelsey so weary, Jill was thankful she'd taken the time to write at all. She would trust the response, though she questioned everything these days. Prayer was coming easily, but understanding was slow. She'd had more misfortune this past month than since the last time her life fell apart. If this meant another fifteen years of misery, she was not sure she would handle that gracefully. She could take lessons from her daughter. But, then, who couldn't?

28

Two weeks of preliminary action with Ascon had actually proved both productive and enjoyable. Marlina Aster was not the snob she'd at first appeared. In fact, she'd been quite cordial, and at the end, provocative. Morgan's mouth quirked. Marlina was not used to having her invitations refused. But a scrupulous professionalism seemed to be his current mode.

He turned the Corvette into the garage and parked. No Juan to carry his bags, so he unloaded his own power suits, shirts, and ties. Even Consuela had conceded it was better that way, though she did send a portion of her income to Juan in Tijuana to try to keep him from provoking the *federales*. Morgan shook his head. He was willing to give anyone a chance, but some people wanted more than a chance. Juan wanted a free ride.

He hung his suits in the walk-in closet and turned at Consuela's knock on the open bedroom door. "Hello, Consuela. How's the world?"

"Eh?" She shook her head. "Your world or the rest of it?"

"Let's start with mine."

"Are you staying home tonight?" She put both hands to her hips.

"I am."

"Then I'll start your supper."

Morgan nodded. "You do that."

"You want something special?"

"Anything you make is special." He was easy tonight. Working hard and applying himself, not to mention attacking a problem and projecting viable solutions, had unshackled his tension like nothing else. He had two weeks free while Ascon made adjustments, then he'd assemble a team and go back in.

"Señorita Fisher is waiting."

"I'll see Denise in a moment."

"She wanted me to tell you."

He had sneaked inside to unpack before Denise laid the new load on him, one of the drawbacks of a home office and an overzealous personal manager. "Yes, Consuela. I'm on my way."

"I will unpack your things."

"Thank you." With a sigh, Morgan left her and went down to Denise.

She stood up from her desk as he entered the office, always preferring to address him eye to eye. "Welcome back. Ascon went well?"

"Very well."

With hardly a breath between, she outlined her past two weeks, and all the things he had not addressed via e-mail, and the things requiring his personal attention. As usual he had driven her crazy.

"Thank you, Denise. Efficient as always."

"Explain again why it's impossible to answer your e-mail while on assignment."

That dance again. "You know the answer, Denise. On the initial consult I don't want to be distracted, nothing cluttering my focus. Other concerns take my mind from the issues at hand. I put one hundred percent into that first thrust."

She slid her gaze to the side, unimpressed. "It would help to know when you're returning."

He had left it open ended as he always did when he hit the road, a habit that irked Denise to no end. Morgan picked up the sundry envelopes from his desk. "Then I'd be held to a timetable. Allow me my nonconformity. It's why I work for myself." And not for her, though she tended to forget that.

She amped down a notch. "Will you at least reply to Malta Systems? That's a very good opportunity, and one which—"

"I'll do that first thing tomorrow. You've had a long day. Why don't you call it quits?" He booted the computer to show his good faith and went into his mail, quick-scanning for anything Denise might consider life or death. Jill's name flashed. His heart skipped, then ached. Why would she write?

He glanced up as Denise slipped her purse over her shoulder and stopped at the door. "And the—"

"I'll do it tomorrow."

She pursed her lips. "Morgan, sometimes I wonder if it's healthy working for you."

"I pay well for your aggravation." Not to mention a roof over her head and relative safety from far less healthy situations.

"That's exactly why I'm still here. That, and how much you truly need me." It might have been a joke from anyone else. But believing that was essential for Denise.

"No argument." He smiled. "I'll see you in the morning." He was already opening Jill's message.

> Dear Morgan,
>
> I heard from Cinda this morning and thought you might appreciate an update now and then. She said the doctors are concerned over several aspects, but generally optimistic, whatever that means. The danger of infection is the main concern, so Kelsey is isolated. She did develop an initial fever, which they anticipated, but they were able to control it with antibiotics. It's too early to know how well the marrow is engrafting, but the immunosuppressive drugs are causing some side effects. Cinda didn't go into detail.
>
> I just read what I've written and it sounds so clinical. But, Morgan, I spoke with Kelsey for a few moments, and she's so brave, though mouth sores made it painful for her to speak. She tried to be cheerful and even made jokes. What a spirit she has.
>
> Are you well? I'll write with anything new,
> Jill
> P.S. You promised her a picture. If you send it to me, I'll see she gets it.

Morgan jolted. How could he have forgotten? The one thing his daughter asked! He wasn't used to it. After the frustration of meeting with Bern, he'd plunged into Ascon in his normal unidirectional mode, forcing everything else out.

He left all the other messages unread and headed upstairs. Where were his photos? "Consuela." He stopped in the kitchen. "Where do I keep photos?"

"The library."

He turned back to the room he had just left, then entered the library. Jill's message was more than a week old. Maybe Denise had a point. But then so did he. He would have thought of nothing else. Just over two weeks since she'd left. He wished he didn't recall so clearly the look on her face when he announced her morning flight. It had been abrupt and unkind, the arrangements made the day before in anger. And he'd regretted it as soon as he left the airport. What would a few more days have hurt?

He pulled open the lower doors of the whitewashed maple cabinet and found a box with loose photos. Most were places around the world. Some included him, but not many were close up, and quite a few had one woman or another included. Just people he'd met along the way. He wasn't even sure he could name them.

He pushed the box back into the shelf and reached for an album from the lowest shelf. He opened it. The photos were too old to send Kelsey, but he remembered what was on the second page and turned it. His throat tightened when Jill smiled out at him, crowned and jubilant.

That night had started it. He'd dated Jill exclusively their entire senior year, and, yes, they'd gotten in trouble. Would he want that for Kelsey? If she were a normal teen, would he want some handsome devil to claim her heart so completely she couldn't say no? He swallowed. No wonder Jill's dad wanted blood. Regardless of her claims of guilt, he hadn't been innocent himself.

He closed the album. At this rate he'd have to find one of those quick picture booths and send Kelsey a mug shot. He stood up and slid the album back into place, then noticed the stiff paper standing along the side of the shelf. He pulled out the watercolor Noelle had painted of him. It had a roguish quality to the expression but was a remarkable likeness. Especially considering she'd painted from memory and some few sketches she'd made.

He held it a long moment, recalling Noelle's face when she'd presented it at Christmas with his family. He had brought her perfume from Paris. Extravagant. Yet this picture had gone straight to his heart. If he gave it to Kelsey . . .

He sighed. Noelle was Rick's wife. It was time to let go. He carried the painting to his office, found a padded envelope large enough, and slipped it inside. Then he took a sheet of letterhead and wrote:

Dear Kelsey,
   This painting was done by my sister-in-law. It's a close likeness,

but if you prefer a photo, just ask. I hope you're doing well.

He held his pen poised, then added *Love, Morgan.*

He slipped the note into the envelope and sealed it, put that inside a FedEx same-day mailer with an extra prepaid mailer for Jill to send it on to Kelsey, then took out his wallet and the card that held Jill's phone number and address. He could probably send it directly to the cancer treatment center, but that might get tricky with the Bensons. He addressed the envelope to Jill and put it in the tray for outgoing mail. Then he picked up the phone.

Jill ran breathlessly inside from the tag football game with her neighbors. "Hello?"

"Hi."

His voice stroked her heart, and it lay still a moment too long. "Morgan."

"I just got your message."

She'd sent it almost two weeks ago and been disappointed when no reply came. "Were you gone?"

"Consulting in New York."

"Oh." So he hadn't been offended or simply blown her off. She wiped her forehead with the back of her arm and leaned against the kitchen counter.

"Were you running?"

"Football with the neighbors. You started it."

"I recall a sound trouncing." She heard his smile.

"One touchdown difference is not a trouncing."

"All it takes is one."

"To win. A trounce requires at least three." She pulled out the stool and sat, hoping he'd stay on long enough to warrant it. "I hope you don't mind that I wrote. I just thought since you were so instrumental . . ."

"I don't mind. But next time why don't you call? I'm easier to reach that way."

And far more devastating.

"You have my cell?"

"No, I don't think so." She reached for her phone pad, and he gave her the number. "Morgan, did you send Kelsey a picture? She hadn't gotten one when—"

"I have it on my desk to send. It's a painting Noelle did a year ago last Christmas. Do you think she'll mind?"

"I think she'll love it. From what I saw of Noelle's work, I'm sure it's wonderful." And if Morgan was the subject, she could envy Kelsey.

"There's a rakish cast to the expression, but she might miss it."

Jill laughed. "I doubt it. Your daughter is very astute, especially about human nature." *Your daughter.* It had come so naturally, as though they were a happy couple teasing and preening over their off-spring. Yet they were anything but.

"I miss you."

Her heart staggered, and she could not go there. "Have you talked to your parents? Do they know?"

"That I miss you?"

"That you helped Kelsey." Her fingers shook as she forked them through her hair.

"What is it with you and that question?"

She filled and cleared her lungs. "They ought to know."

"Do yours?"

"That's different." She stood and walked the length of the kitchen.

"Why?"

"Because I wasn't the one who matched."

"So you're telling me if you had done the harvest, they'd have the play by play?"

She could not begin to imagine it. She had come home to a concerned message from her mother and blithely explained that she'd taken a brief sojourn to California, but she was sorry she'd forgotten to tell them she'd be gone. A play by play on Kelsey and Morgan was not reality. "I guess not."

"Then let it go."

"Okay." But it wasn't the same for his family. They knew part of it already, certainly wanted to know more.

Morgan said, "There are three dolphins leaping just past the breaking surf. And the sun on the water is dazzling."

The image leaped to her mind. "Are you on your balcony?"

"No. Under it by the orange tree. A gull is pecking the life out of some poor sand crab it carried to my yard."

She could almost smell the salt air, hear the rhythm of the waves. Tears stung her eyes. "What color is the sky?"

"Pale blue with a smattering of thin, wispy clouds."

She had touted Beauview the last time they compared

environments, but now that she was back, she found little to commend. "I'm sure it's beautiful."

"It's nicer with someone to share it."

"Morgan . . ."

"I should have stuck to the original gate idea." Why was he doing this, when he'd all but shoved her out the door?

"I should go."

"All right."

"Bye." She hung up the phone and caught the sobs before they took hold. Tenaciously she fended off the emotion and grabbed the phone again while she flipped open the directory and found the number she needed.

"Hello, Celia? This is Jill Runyan."

When she hung up that time, she felt as though a weight was lifted from her heart. Morgan's family knew now what he'd done for Kelsey, and she'd been invited for supper tomorrow night. Longing and trepidation warred inside her, but she had accepted.

———

Morgan stood alone in the warm air and watched the gull demolish the tiny white crab. The scent of lilies lent peace to the brutal scene. The songbirds in the orange tree ignored the death below, one crab among millions. The waves washed them up, the birds carried them away, cracked their shells, devoured their meat. The cycle of life.

He slipped his cell phone into his pocket, crossed the yard, and descended to the beach. His two weeks in New York City had been invigorating. In addition to the whirlwind hours of his initial attack on the project, he'd taken in a show with Marlina. He had even spent a few moments with Noelle's father, William St. Claire, just to connect.

But even though he'd told Jill it was just a place, this was home. He had adopted it completely. There was energy here, the sound of the waves, the grit of the sand, the heat of the sun. No smothering humidity, just balmy, living air. The palette of the sky above him grew interesting. *What color is the sky?* Why wasn't Jill there to see it herself? He imagined her on the beach with him, hand in hand.

"Hello, Morgan. Home again?"

He turned at the greeting to meet the wide, sophisticated smile of his neighbor. "For a while."

"You work too hard." She brushed the long red hair from her

shoulder with melon-colored fingernails cut square and sporting white palm trees and a jeweled sun on each. "Just like Eric."

"Where is he this time?"

"Japan." She shrugged. "Home of the geisha." Her gaze intensified. From conversations with Eric, he knew her suspicions were well-founded. And from conversations with her, she didn't waste time suffering.

"Want to come over for a drink?"

He tucked his hands into the pockets of his slacks. "No, thanks, Suzanne."

She raised her brows. "He'll be gone all week." She stepped close and touched his arm. "I see you out here all the time. Why do you want to be lonely?"

"What makes you think I'm lonely?" He stepped back half a pace.

"You have the look." She studied his face. "No one as attractive as you should ever be alone."

He crooked a smile. "Thank you. But in fact, I'm not lonely, just pensive. My mind's been on overdrive and it's gearing down."

"Forget your mind." Her eyes traveled him brazenly, and he realized how a woman must feel under his own scrutiny. Another incriminating thought about actions he'd scarcely considered suddenly spotlighted.

Discomfort seeped in. Women came on to him all the time. It had never bothered him before. What was this attack of conscience? But he wanted out of there, away from her, from everyone. He raised a hand. "I'll see you."

"You know where to find me. I'm the girl next door."

The *wife* next door. He took the path up to his house and got a bottle of gin from the bar. He poured it into a martini glass with a splash of Rose's lime. All of his neighbors were married, except for one. Alex was living with the fifth long-legged blonde he'd brought there since Morgan moved in. Several of the other marriages were second or third efforts. It was natural that he, the lone bachelor, would be Suzanne's mark, though truth be told, marriage hadn't stopped some of the others.

He drank the gin and lime and circled his game room restlessly. He was just so tired of it all, and talking to Jill had awakened the pain. Why not join Suzanne, wrangle all night, and have no remorse in the morning? He drained the glass and refilled it. Because he would have remorse and it changed nothing. He'd hardly slept or eaten for two weeks, thoughts of all his bad choices troubling him every moment he let down. It was an assault, his soul in rebellion.

He gripped his head with splayed fingers. His stomach churned. He went to the bathroom and emptied the booze from his belly. Another symptom of late. He'd switched from bourbon, thinking the last over-dose when Jill was there had caused some kind of allergic reaction. Now it seemed the gin was doing the same. If he didn't know better, he'd think something conspired against him, something large and ruth-less like the gull with the crab. He washed his mouth and face at the sink, staggered to the wall. This was not good.

It had to be a bug, some virus. He'd tell Consuela to forget supper.

Her expression clouded the moment she saw him. "Señor Morgan . . ."

"I've got a virus or something. Don't make me food." He waved her off and went to his room, collapsed on his bed, and stayed there. Sweat leaked from his pores. A very good thing he had not accepted Suzanne's offer. His stomach turned at the thought.

"God . . ." The word was out like a prayer. Did he mean it that way? Morgan swallowed, his chest heaving painfully. He jerked back the coverlet. Hot. At the tap on his door, he said, "I don't want any-thing."

He closed his eyes. Maybe his immunity had been compromised from the loss of bone marrow. Fine. He'd caught something. It would pass. He pressed his face to the pillow. In the meantime he was mis-erable. "God . . ."

29

A stockier, grayer Hank was in the yard when Jill drove up the next night. He set down the trimmer he was using on the front bushes and pulled off his work gloves to greet her. Drawing a deep breath, Jill climbed out of the car and met him halfway across the walk. How warm his smile, deep in the eyes so blue like Morgan's.

He held out his hand, and she took it faintly, then found herself curled into his arm. "How are you, Jill?"

She expelled her breath. "A little nervous."

He squeezed her hand and let her go. "I'm glad you accepted Celia's offer."

"I was too surprised to refuse."

He laughed. "Good." Then he stood a moment looking at her. "We appreciate your call. Of course, we assumed Morgan would do what he could, but when we never heard . . ." He spread his hands. "We wondered if there'd been anything he could do."

"It's too early to tell for sure. Engraftment can take weeks, but—"

"Save that, if you don't mind. Celia will want to hear it, too."

Jill looked at the door, bracing herself to go inside and face Celia again.

The girl she'd seen before opened the door. "Hi. I'm Tara, if you don't remember."

Jill smiled, recalling Morgan's assessment of his youngest sister. "I remember."

"And you're Jill. Unless you want me to call you Ms. Runyan. Mom said I had to ask, but it makes me feel like a little kid to say it."

"Just call me Jill." She laughed softly. No wallflower this one.

They ushered her inside and Celia met her at the entrance to the living room. Her smile did not embrace her as Hank's had, but it was there. "Hi, Jill. I'm glad you could come. We're waiting for Therese, but you remember Stephanie and Tiffany." She motioned to the girls coming in behind her.

Yes, she remembered them but as little girls. They would have been four or five? She couldn't remember, and she must have looked confused, because the nearest one said, "I'm Tiffany. That's Steph." Sthphanie had Hank's firm jaw. Tiffany's hair was as dark as Morgan's. Both were lovely young women.

Jill smiled. "You were pretty little when I knew you before."

"I remember you," Stephanie said. "But you had long hair and wore it in a ponytail."

Jill raised her eyebrows, surprised. "You're right. I just cut it this summer."

Steph flipped her thick braid over her shoulder. "I'd seriously like to cut this, but I'd look dreadful with it short."

"My hairdresser has a gift for finding the right cut for the face. I'll give you her name if you want."

"Great."

Celia said, "Why don't you sit down? Would you like some tea or lemonade?"

Jill smiled. "Lemonade sounds great."

Tara plunked down beside her on the couch. "Well, I think it's really cool I'm an aunt."

The thought startled her. Of course, each of Morgan's sisters would be Kelsey's aunts. Oh, how the ripples spread. "I'm not sure how that works with adoption, Tara."

"I know."

"And Kelsey's almost your age. Are you sixteen?"

"Yep."

Jill reached for the lemonade Celia handed her. "Thank you."

The front door opened and a tall, slender brunette came in. Therese. Jill recognized her, but then she'd been six at least. A young man followed, about the same height with a triangular face and arched brows over gray eyes.

Hank stood up. "Jill, this is Therese and her fiancé, Steve."

"Don't get up," Therese said, coming in. "We're just family."

Hank gave Steve a side hug and patted his back. "Long classes?"

"My mind is mush."

Therese sat down on Jill's other side. "It's been a long time."

Jill nodded. A lifetime.

"Mom filled us all in, so we know about Kelsey. I'm glad you had the baby."

And here she'd worried about being careful what she said. "I couldn't do anything else."

"How's Morgan?" Again right to the point.

"Do you mean from the bone marrow harvest?"

Therese shrugged. "Everything."

Jill settled back in the couch, gripping the glass between her palms. "Well, he handled the harvest well. It's not an easy procedure. But I spoke with him last night and he sounded good." *I miss you.* Why had he said that? His actions had spoken quite the opposite.

"Tell us how all this works," Hank said.

"I'm no expert, but I think I've read every Web site and quite a few books since I learned Kelsey had leukemia." She started by explaining the sort of disease that threatened Kelsey's life, then the treatments they'd already tried. Last she described the marrow harvest and rescue.

Tara hunched forward. "Is it for sure? The transplant will cure it?"

Heart sinking, Jill shook her head. "Because Kelsey got leukemia at an older age, the prognosis is not as good. Also, the disease is tenacious. They had hoped to do a minitransplant. That means they administer lower doses of chemotherapy and sometimes avoid total body irradiation to destroy most but not all of Kelsey's own marrow. Her cells and Morgan's would coexist, and his cells should combat the cancer in a graft-versus-tumor effect. But the cancer was too resistant and she needed standard myeloablative therapy, which wipes out her immune system completely."

"So could Morgan just give more bone marrow if she needs it?"

"It's part of the protocol for the donor to agree to successive transplants if necessary. I know he'll do whatever it takes." Jill pressed her hands together. "But it's a difficult and involved process. So many things can go wrong."

"I think we should pray." Celia's voice was calm but warm. She reached a hand to Hank, who joined with Steve, and as one, they formed a circle with their hands. Jill's were clasped in Tara's and Therese's as they bowed their heads and prayed for Kelsey's healing, for her adoptive parents, and for Jill and Morgan, as well.

Warmth and hope seized her as she joined them in prayer. Maybe this evening would not be so difficult after all. In fact, it was boisterously pleasant. Jill talked about her work—though not the current situation, which she had yet to confront—the others about their plans and activities. There were no lulls in the conversation, and by the time she left she felt thoroughly filled up.

She got home and found a FedEx same-day envelope on her door. The return address was Morgan's and she scooped it up eagerly. Letting herself in, she set her purse on the couch and studied the envelope. She probably could readdress it and send it on, the way it was packaged.

Jill pressed it to her breast. Was it wrong to just take a look? She turned on the lamp and gripped the tab of the envelope. The phone rang. She went to the kitchen and answered, "Hi, Shelly."

"No, Jill, it's Mom."

Jill's heart made a guilty thump, having just left the Spencers. "How are you? Is everything okay?" Her breath came too quickly, but that was ridiculous! She was thirty-one years old. She could visit anyone she wanted.

"Oh, we're fine. I just keep missing you every time I call. Are you working the summer again? You need time to relax, keep your perspective. They ask too much of you."

"I actually have it off." Through no choice of her own. *Thump, thump, thump.* She pressed her hand to her heart. What was happening, a panic attack? She'd never had one, but it felt like she'd run too hard and long.

"I'm glad to hear that. It's such draining work. I don't know how you do it."

"I love working with the kids. But it is hard." Not as hard as praying and fighting for Kelsey, or explaining that to her mother.

"Jewels in your crown, Jill."

Kelsey was her jewel. "Mom . . ."

"What is it, dear? You sound different. Is it stress?"

She had to be honest. Who was she to lecture Morgan when she couldn't be frank with her own mother? "I've had some stress lately."

"Nothing dangerous, I hope. I hate you living alone."

Jill straightened. "Mom, I live across from a police officer, for heaven's sake."

"Speaking of which, are you still dating Dan?"

And what a wonderful segue into the meaty part of her confession. "Not really." *Coward.*

"Well, your father and I met a young man at church whose wife died of cancer. Two years ago, I think he said. A little older, he's forty-three. But such a nice man."

"I'm sure he is."

"We told him about you."

Sure you did. All except the dark parts.

"You're thirty-one, Jill. Work can't be everything forever."

At least her heart had stopped thumping through her chest. Because she wasn't going to mention Morgan's name? "I'm not really interested right now."

"We could have the two of you over for dinner."

"How subtle."

"You don't have to be sharp."

Jill sighed. "I'm sorry. I know you mean well."

"You're my daughter and I want . . . what's best for you."

For a moment Jill thought she would say for her to be happy. "I know, Mom."

"Think about it, will you?"

She didn't want to lie. "I'm not in a very good place for that now."

"Because of Dan?"

Say Morgan. Just say it. "It's not a good time, that's all."

The sigh. "Your father sends his love."

"Mine to Dad, too. Good night, Mom."

Jill hung up and went back to the chair, calling herself every kind of coward. She picked up the envelope and tore it open, taking out the inner padded envelope. She wasn't cheating Kelsey; she would get it to her at the earliest opportunity. She peeled it open and pulled out the stiff watercolor. Morgan's face—rakish, yes, but irresistible.

Breath leaked from her lungs and left an ache. Noelle was talented. She had captured not only the form but the substance. Jill closed her eyes and saw it still. And now the price of her nosiness; she didn't want to let it go. She had so little of him.

She opened her eyes again, crossed to the couch, and slid her purse onto her shoulder, then drove to the twenty-four-hour copy shop. The sorts of machines they had now should suffice. "I'd like the best possible copy of this," she told the clerk, laying the painting on the counter. It took less than five minutes.

Then with the copy and original, she drove back home. She had felt so close to Morgan at his family's house. Eating around their table had almost brought tears to her eyes, listening to the chatter that had matured but not diminished. She had told them more about her visit with Morgan, about the incident with Juan. They seemed to hang on every word. Why wouldn't he talk to them? They were so receptive and desirous.

She took out the copy of his portrait, studied his broad but roguish smile. His family did not hide the past or cover his flaws. They didn't pretend he was some perfect offering for a widow at church.

Dinner with the Spencers had not been peaceful, but it had given her hope, and she'd enjoyed getting to know the girls again. She had sensed a true affection from Hank and a softening on Celia's part. Most of all, their prayer together had filled a dry well inside her, wakened again that sense of purpose. God was moving.

She refused to let her mother's phone call get in the way. *Lord, I don't know your purpose.* Her heart leaped to prayer in its new manner. *Whatever way you can use me, I'm here.*

Morgan shivered. If he could just get warm. The only good thing was this hadn't happened when he was on the job. But then his focus had been too complete. Coming home was dangerous. He was not a brooder by nature, but he'd done enough of it these last weeks to brew up a major illness. He clutched the sheet and cover around him, aching up his spine into his head, his arms, his legs. He should never have let down.

He'd spent last night with dry heaves. Consuela had tried to help several times throughout the day. He hadn't let her through the door. He couldn't focus his thoughts; nothing held his attention. Malta Systems. His meeting with Bern, and what to do about Kelsey. His favorite night spots, his upcoming prospects.

His stomach seized. He hadn't eaten since the airplane from New York. Maybe he'd been poisoned. He kicked off the covers as heat radiated from his skin, tried to lift his head, then let it fall. It was night again. The moon's silver glow shone through his skylight. A knock on the door.

"Señor Morgan."

"Let me die in peace."

She opened the door.

He whisked the sheet over himself. "Do you mind?"

"I had a husband and two sons. What haven't I seen?"

She hadn't seen him. But she came right in and pressed her palm to his forehead.

He clutched the sheet. "It's running its course. Let me be."

She set a glass beside the bed, its fizzing crackling in his ears and a slight scent of lemon-lime. "You need the liquid." She was probably right.

"Tomorrow, I call the doctor." She pressed a holy card into his hand. "Tonight, I pray."

"Whatever you say." *Just go away and leave me alone.*

"It's an attack of the evil one. You helped too many and drew his eye."

He rolled to his side, dragging the sheet with him.

"I will light the candles."

"Mm-hmm."

"You are a good man. It attracts the notice."

"Consuela . . ."

She patted his shoulder. "I go now."

He nodded. *Good.*

"You drink."

If only he could. He nodded again. She left, and he reached for the glass, brought it to his lips, achingly thirsty. The soda was crisp and sweet. He took one gulp and let it settle. His elbow slid on the laminated visage of the holy card, rays of light shining from the heart of Jesus.

Closing his eyes, he sank into the pillows. Sweat beaded his forehead. If he was poisoned, it would soon be purged from his pores. His stomach tolerated the soda, so he took another gulp. He must be dehydrated. But the third gulp sent warning signals.

He set the glass down and clutched his stomach, curling up like a worm. He thought of the crab pecked at mercilessly, dashed against the walk, and ripped apart. Had God removed the kid gloves and decided to go at him in earnest? A hard ache balled his stomach.

What do you want? He writhed, rolled to his feet, and staggered to the bathroom to lose the soda. One hand pressed to his face, he shuffled back and dropped to the bed. He set the Sacred Heart next to the soda, then buried his face in the pillow. If he could just sleep.

"*You are a good man. It draws the notice.*" His sweat soaked the pillow. Thank God he hadn't gotten this before the bone marrow harvest. *Thank God?* Why not? At least his daughter would heal. Had his marrow engrafted? Was it making new cells, teaching her body to live? There was a thought he could cling to. *Don't waste Consuela's prayers on me, Lord. Use them for Kelsey.* He sprawled to his stomach, kicked off the sheet, and tried to sleep.

Kelsey stood up, determined to accomplish the "hall walk." Since she had not yet managed food, she slid her IV pole alongside and made it to the doorway. The mask over her mouth crinkled when she smiled at the nurse watching her progress. It was Jackie who usually did her daily measurements of waist girth and weight, drew the blood for the bilirubin and blood-sugar checks, and monitored her blood pressure, like any of that told them something they didn't know.

Her face was shaped like the moon, her waist like the lollipop girls. For someone who couldn't eat she was certainly putting on weight, and by the looks on everyone's faces it wasn't a healthy glow her skin had developed. It burned like a sunburn and itched.

"How did the ultrasound go?" Jackie pushed the door wide to fit the IV pole through.

Kelsey shrugged. "Haven't seen the pictures, but I'm hoping for a bouncing baby liver."

Jackie smiled. "You know this is all in the expected range."

"Oh, I know. Wouldn't want to disappoint the experts." She took a step down the hall, then realized how sharp that had sounded. That was another thing; her moods were all over the place and it was really hard not to give in to them. "Sorry, Jackie."

"That's okay. How far are you going to go?"

Kelsey looked down the hall. "To the bulletin board and back."

"Good goal. But this is your first time. Be gentle with yourself."

Meaning Jackie didn't think she could do it. *All right, army, fight off those lying spirits. I am making it to the bulletin board and back.* Her mouth was on fire, a side effect of the methotrexate, and even though she sponged her teeth and gums to avoid splits that might get infected, she had developed painful sores. She fought tears, but they came anyway. *Why are you doing this, Jesus? I don't understand.*

She swiped the tears so she could see where she was going and kept plodding. *Guess I misunderstood. I thought we were praying for me to get well and Morgan to get sick.* And that was such a snippy thought, she immediately repented. *Actually, could we both just be well now?* She felt too terrible to wish illness on anyone.

She sniffed. "I'm sorry, Jesus," she whispered. But for once there was no answer. Maybe the medications had blocked her ability to communicate spiritually. They had adjusted the drugs, but nothing was the same. "I know what you asked. But I'm sick enough for both of us."

She caught her foot on the roller and gripped the pole to steady herself. *It doesn't make sense anyway. Nothing makes sense.* But the message had been so clear: pray for him to get sick. That much she could remember even with her mind foggy. She looked down the hall. The bulletin board was too far. She might get there, but she'd never get back.

I don't want to make him sick. It wasn't as easy as it had seemed when she told Jill. Jesus had been so clear, and she had trusted Him so completely. Now ... She frowned at the stupid bulletin board. She couldn't make it. She turned around and there was Josh in gown and mask and gloves.

"Need a hand?"

She looked into his freckled face and started to cry. Of all the stupid things to do in front of him. But the tears would not stop. "It's the Prednisone."

His eyes smiled. "Your mask is soggy."

"It's the new style."

He laughed.

She dabbed her nose with her finger. "How'd you get through security?"

He took her elbow. "Bribed the nurses."

"With what?"

"Fudge."

"Don't offer me any."

He nodded. "Still not eating?"

"You'd never know it, I'm such a blimp." They were almost back to her door, and her legs were in revolt—just like her stomach and kidneys and liver.

"It'll go away."

"Will it?" She lowered herself to her bed. "Because I don't know that. Every day they come in with something else that's going wrong and right now—" She stopped at his pained expression and pressed her hands to her face. "I'm so sorry." She peered between her fingers. "I didn't think. I'm so sorry about Rachel. I didn't get to tell you." She dropped her hands to her lap.

His eyes had teared up. "I'm really sorry, too. I miss her. I miss teasing her." He tried to smile.

"I guess she knows that. I bet Jesus lets her watch and listen. If she wants to, I mean."

His sigh billowed the paper mask. "Maybe. That's why you have to get well for both of you. So she can see it and be glad." He looked around her room. "I was going to bring you flowers, but they said you couldn't have any."

Kelsey raised a pair of monster hands. "Fungus amungus. No fruit or veggies, either. At least not fresh. Of course, what goes down must come up, so I'm just as glad I can't have them." She could not believe she'd actually said that, but Josh laughed again.

"I really like that about you."

"What?"

"You're funny."

It surprised her to realize her own mood had lifted. "I'm glad you came." And the burn that rushed to her face had nothing to do with leukemia. "How'd you get here?"

"Guess."

"I don't know." She leaned back into her pillows.

"I drove."

"By yourself?"

He nodded. "Got my license."

"You mean you're sixteen now?" It suddenly seemed impossibly old.

"Yesterday. And I got my license so I could come see you."

She was not thinking clearly. "Did you know cyclosporine causes female facial hair?"

He cocked his head. "No, but I like bald, bearded girls."

Kelsey sputtered a laugh through her mask. "You do not mean that."

Jackie tapped the door. "Sorry, Josh, but it's time."

Kelsey drew her brows together, but she knew they'd already bent the rules. Probably because of Rachel. He didn't live far, right in New Haven. Maybe he would come again. "I'll see you, Josh." She tried to sound casual.

"I'll try to get through again. The others aren't as easy as Jackie."

"I heard that." Jackie put a hand to her hip.

Josh stood another moment, then gave a little wave and walked out. Jackie tossed her a smile. "Good job on your first hall walk."

Kelsey nodded. If Josh came back, she wouldn't even use her feet next time.

30

Morgan sat on the side of the bed, a limp slug, but at least the cramping had left his stomach and his head no longer throbbed. It did, however, rest on his palms, braced by the elbows on his knees. He moaned at the knock. "I'm alive, Consuela."

"It's Denise, Morgan. I have a wave of e-mail messages from a Todd Marlin? He insists you promised to meet with him. Are you in any condition to deal with it?"

Morgan grinned at her tone. He'd enjoy her expression more if she knew it was a thirteen-year-old kid making the demands that had her in a lather.

"Morgan?"

"You're right, Denise. This one's important. I'll be down shortly." Since when did his secretary roust him out of bed? Something was wrong with that picture. Of course, he'd been out of commission two days after promising to catch up.

He pushed himself up and stood still, checking his equilibrium. Not bad. The top stayed up, the middle didn't waver, and the legs held firm. Good. He went to the bathroom and took a shower, cleaned his mouth thoroughly, and even shaved. He dressed in a crisp shirt and slacks, though no tie, and went downstairs.

He waved Consuela off in the kitchen. "Just coffee, strong." Then he went downstairs to the office. He passed Denise without comment, booted up the computer, and got into his mail. He almost felt human. When Consuela arrived with the coffee and he took the first swig, he knew he'd live.

He pulled up the seventeen messages Todd had sent, surprised the language hadn't clued Denise. But then, many players in the high-tech field were equally illiterate with anything beyond acronyms.

He typed, *Hey, Todd. Cool your jets. I've been flat on my back dog-sick. Wouldn't want to pass you those germs. How about this weekend? Think you can make it? Ask Stan. Ask nicely. Morgan.*

He sat back from his desk and looked at Denise. "I'll meet with him this weekend if he works it out. Can you arrange a flight for one, first-class from DIA?"

"Transportation from the airport?"

"No, I'll pick him up."

"Morgan . . ." He knew her objection. She hated the image of him meeting a prospective client at the airport himself.

"Trust me on this, Denise."

She turned back to her desk. "There's Malta Systems."

"I'm on it."

"I've printed the ten top prospecti for—"

Morgan quirked an eyebrow. "Did you say prospecti?"

She sent him the stare. "The prospects you tagged before leaving. They're on your desk to the left. On your right, you'll find several follow-up issues, one from Techstar that requires prompt attention."

"Thank you, Denise."

"Are you over your . . . flu?" Something hard in how she said it. Did she think he'd faked it? Played hooky?

"I seem to be. No more fever, chills, or bellyache."

She snorted softly.

He stood and walked to her desk. "Am I missing something here?"

"You could at least do your drinking after hours."

He frowned. "What are you talking about?" Did she think he'd been on some two-day bender?

She rotated her chair. "You remind me of my father."

By some of what she had told him the night in the hospital, that was not a compliment.

Her face hardened. "I admired him more than anyone I knew. Admired and despised him. He had so much promise, genius even." She waved her hand. "Except, of course, when booze made him an idiot."

"Which part are you reminded of?"

Her gaze chilled. "Both."

"Well, now that we've cleared the air . . ."

"I watched him destroy himself."

"I get the point, Denise." And she was crossing the line.

"That's one reason I thought it would be safe to work here alone with you."

"Because I drink?"

"Because I'd never get involved with an alcoholic." No parley, just stab.

Morgan clenched his fist. "Only a crackhead."

Her eyes blazed. "I did not know."

"You stayed with him after you did know. Even when he beat you."

"Well, I had plenty of practice with Dad."

Morgan rubbed his face. "Why are we doing this? I had the flu."

"Dad puked his guts out and swore it was the flu more times than I can count. That man had every flu ever invented. And in between he was brilliant."

Morgan fought the urge to holler. Children of alcoholics tended to see anyone who drank as problematic. It was natural. "How many times have you seen me sick?"

She turned away. Her hair seemed more severe than ever today, pulling the skin at her temples. "I haven't seen you sick. But how about all the times I can't reach you? All the hiatuses, your 'nonconformities'?"

"It's how I operate, Denise. If you can't take it, I understand. I'll give you a great reference."

She sighed. "I'm talking myself out of a job, I know."

"Only if that's how you want it."

Her face tightened. "I don't want to watch you . . ."

He spread his hands. "I had the flu." What more could he say? She thought him a drunk. Suzanne probably thought him impotent. Consuela had already sainted him. They were all wrong.

He returned to his desk, lifted the follow-up stack and perused the sheets Denise had printed. Part of his fee included six months' availability for questions, concerns that arose subsequent to his involvement. That was a good place to focus.

"Malta Systems first."

He looked up at Denise and set down the sheets. He'd line that up to satisfy her, then work on the other. Now he understood her frustration better. He could be more reachable if it made her life easier. At the very least he could answer her daily correspondence when he was away. It was his style to focus unidirectionally. But he could adapt. And if he accepted Malta Systems, he'd be gone soon enough anyway.

They worked in silence until Consuela brought him the phone. It must be a personal call or it would have rung to the office. He put the receiver to his ear. "Morgan Spencer."

"I can come!"

He smiled. "That's great, Todd. I'll e-mail your flight info. Can Stan get you to the airport? Or Rick might."

"Stan'll do it."

Morgan glanced up. "My assistant's working on your flight right now. I'll let you know the details when she's got it. Is Stan there?"

"Yeah."

"Put him on." Morgan waited.

"Hi, Morgan. I've got one excited kid."

"How long can I have him?"

"How long do you want?"

Morgan studied the calendar he'd brought up with a click. He could plug Malta in the last week of September. He would have things rolling with Ascon and begin the initial phase with Malta. But before diving into either, some time with Todd sounded good. "How about a week starting Saturday?"

"Sure?"

"Sure. I'll teach him to surf."

By now Denise had given up all pretense of not listening and turned her chair toward him. "We'll send the info by e-mail. Bye, Stan." He beeped the phone off and set it down. "Make sure the airline provides an attendant for Todd Marlin."

"He's a kid?"

Morgan let the smile only into the corners of his mouth. "He feels pretty mature for thirteen."

Her lips set tightly. "Another one you didn't know about?"

Anger surged. She must be hormonal or she wouldn't dare. "He's not mine."

She seemed to realize the line she'd crossed, and all her body language retreated. "You said Saturday?"

"That's right." He crossed to the doorway, paused, then went out. It was different having employees in his home. He allowed for that. But this . . . He forced the anger back. He had set her up to some degree, not explaining about Todd. But her jump to that conclusion, and the audacity to say it . . . She must be ready to quit.

He was weak still. He felt it in his spine. And the first pangs of hunger gnawed his belly. He crossed the game room and stepped outside to the patio. A short walk in the open air might ease the fury. So far she'd called him a drunk, a liar, and a father to the illegitimate.

He swallowed the sudden shrinking in his throat. How far off the mark was it? He rubbed a hand over his face, then followed the path to the beach, wishing Jill were under his arm. She had scolded his drinking, too, but it wasn't the same. Her censure showed she cared. He wanted her to care. Wanted it so badly it hurt. He could fly her out to meet Todd. No, that wouldn't be fair, not to any of them.

He took off his loafers and walked barefoot in the sand, thankful the strip was deserted. But as he rounded the bend he found Scott Menard, a bronzed and oiled demigod, and one of Morgan's staunchly single friends.

Morgan paused. "Day off?"

"Finished our project. Little bonus time." Scott winked at the twig in a bikini beside him on the sand. He'd said living on the beach married was like eating before a banquet. He wanted to savor the feast, not wish he were hungry.

Morgan passed by, the heat of the sun beating off the sand. He opened and rolled his cuffs and one more collar button. His shirt fell open and sweat dampened the hair on his chest, evidence he wasn't one hundred percent yet. He turned and headed back. As he crossed his yard, he noticed Suzanne next door sunbathing nude on her deck. Was this all there was? Emptiness overwhelmed him. His head started to ache. The game room felt overly chilled as he paused at the entrance, then closed the door behind him with a shiver.

Denise came out of the office, took him in with a penetrating glance. "Are you all right?"

Body temperature neutralizing, he nodded.

"Maybe you should see a doctor." She'd become a believer?

He crossed to the bar and poured a glass of pineapple juice—Jill's cure. He drank it down. The coffee had stayed put. The juice refreshed. He rinsed the glass and passed Denise on his way into the office. He could work now. He needed to.

"Morgan?" She caught her index nail between her teeth.

"You'll ruin your manicure."

She jerked the nail free, then didn't seem to know what to do with the hand. "I made the reservation. The ticket's at the Delta counter, DIA. They'll have an attendant ready."

"Good." He sat down and took up the right-hand stack once again. "Contact Malta Systems and get them on the calendar. Last week of September would be good."

She went to her desk and clicked the keys with her undamaged nails, long ovals in frosted plum that matched her tailored suit and heels. She'd never get involved with an alcoholic? It had never entered his mind to get involved with her.

It was crazy to feel guilty for doing the right thing. The Spencers had wanted to know, had soaked up her information like dry sponges. Maybe it should have come from Morgan, but it wouldn't have. Jill pressed a hand to her face. But she had to tell him. He would not appreciate being blindsided by a careless comment or even a direct communication from his family. She punched in the number he had given for his cell, then paced the front room, waiting through two rings.

"Hi." Not the abrupt "Morgan Spencer" greeting she had heard him use before. His voice had a warm syrup effect.

"Morgan, it's Jill."

"I know."

She pressed a hand to her stomach, which was taking the brunt of the ache and joy of hearing him. "How are you?"

"On the tail end of something nasty, but recovering, thank you. I walked the beach just now and thought of you."

She did not want the images that filled her mind of the narrow beach where he'd kissed her. Better to brave the dragon at once. "Morgan, I have to tell you something."

"You're not calling just to hear my voice?"

She expelled her breath. "No, I . . . I mean it's nice to hear—would you please stop causing the disconnect to my brain?"

He laughed. "It's cute to hear you flustered. Jill Runyan, star debater, lost for words."

"I am not lost for words. You distracted me."

"I like hearing yours. Just thought it might work both ways."

She sighed. "Well, it does. But that's not why I called."

"Hold on." She waited through a soft shuffling, then he was back.

"I wouldn't want Denise to get the wrong idea. She's mad enough at me already."

Jill didn't want to know. "Are you sitting?"

"If this is another of your bombshells, I'd better be."

She pressed her fingers to her forehead. "No, it's just that . . . I wanted you to know that . . ."

"Deep breaths, darling."

When his *"darling"* had just knocked the breath from her? "I saw your family, Morgan. They had me over for supper."

He didn't answer.

"They needed to know, so I called them after we spoke, and they asked me to come for supper, and it was really nice. They're so glad you helped Kelsey, and they wanted all the medical details. I told them what I could." She bit her lip as the silence lengthened. "Are you angry?"

"No." But he sounded hurt.

"Morgan, they wondered. They wanted to know. They'd like to hear from you."

"They hear from me."

She rubbed a circle on her forehead as she paced into the kitchen. The levity had certainly fled. She was a lightning bolt hanging over him. "I'm sorry if—"

"And your folks? How did they take it?"

Her throat constricted. "They don't know. They don't want to."

"How do you know that?"

She sighed. "It's been a code of silence for fifteen years. Don't mention Jill's shame. Don't think about it, and maybe it never happened."

"It happened."

She pushed off from the counter. "I know it. I tried to tell my mother I'd seen you, but . . . I just couldn't."

He laughed low. "Don't worry, I can keep a secret. Better than you, it seems."

"I don't want it to be that way."

His expelled breath rasped in her ear. "Only you can change it."

"How?"

"Tell them we're getting married."

Her heart somersaulted.

"When they learn that's not true, they'll be relieved it was only a visit on behalf of your sick daughter."

Jill sank onto the couch. He hadn't meant to be cruel, she was sure.

And in theory his point was sound. Tell them something utterly impossible and the small infraction of seeing him would be forgiven. She pressed a hand to her eyes. After a while she said, "I just wanted you to know."

"Any other sabotage in the works?"

She leaned her elbow on the arm of the couch. "No."

"How's Kelsey?"

"Everything's fine so far."

"Great." He yawned. "Guess I'm not to full throttle yet."

"What was wrong?"

"Some flu from hell."

Jill jolted. Or heaven? "How long were you sick?"

"On my back two days. But I've had some sporadic attacks. Not sure what's going on."

Prayer was going on. Jill bit her lip. "Well, you're in God's hands." More so than he knew.

"Huh. Take care."

"You too." She hung up and pressed the phone to her chest. Why would the Lord want Morgan sick? Kelsey had been more assured than ever that it was exactly what Jesus wanted. She was steadfast in her conviction and faithfully praying for it, and it seemed to be working. Jill realized once again how very little she understood the mind of God.

Kelsey opened the package from Jill that Mom had brought her. It was flat and stiff and she guessed what it held, though it was much bigger than she had expected. Instead of a photo, she pulled out a watercolor and stared at the face smiling back at her. Jill was right. Morgan was handsome. It wasn't the same, seeing him in a painting, but it was cool. She held it out to Mom, who took a long look of her own.

"I wonder why he didn't send a photograph."

"Maybe he didn't have any." Kelsey thumbed her father. "How many pictures would we have of Dad if you didn't drag him to the studio?"

"I'd take lots of pictures if it weren't for this big nose."

She loved his big nose, and the ears that stood out just a little too much, his broad shoulders he used to carry her on, and his big rough hands that were so gentle when he stroked her head. Masked now and gloved, wearing scrubs and slippers, he looked like a big blue bear.

Mom handed him the picture, and he held it back a little to take a look. "I know this guy. He's the one all the women faint over."

"Daddy." Kelsey giggled, though Morgan did have that sort of movie star appearance. Pierce Brosnan and Tom Cruise together.

"You want me to hang it, honey?" He looked over her walls covered with pictures of her friends and the people praying for her.

Kelsey considered it. Morgan looked near enough the person she'd seen in the Lord's hug to know she was on track with that part of her mission and also the secret part. She wasn't exactly sure the Lord had directed the other part, but she was praying for it anyway. And since she was feeling a little better, she had renewed her efforts on both accounts. She smiled at Dad. "Okay." Morgan might not be praying for her, but she was sure praying for him.

Mom nudged him. "It's a shame to put tape on that art. Why don't we set it on the table for now, and I'll pick up a frame later."

Kelsey leaned back in her pillows. "Thanks, Mom." It hadn't gone over too well when she told them she had not only called him but asked for a picture.

"Kelsey, that's very presumptuous when we've made it clear there won't be any contact." She had apologized, and she did feel bad that they were not happy, but she didn't really regret talking to him. And she was glad she had the picture. Its being a painting actually made it stand out, though she wasn't sure yet whether that was a good thing.

She didn't want Dad or Mom to obsess on it, though they were trying not to show their discomfort. She wanted to tell them she was just curious. But maybe it was more. Everything got more important when she thought there might not be much time left.

They had determined her problems were not merely side effects of the immunotherapy drugs but acute GVHD, graft-versus-host disease, striking in spite of the drugs. Basically it meant Morgan's bone marrow had realized her body wasn't his and had decided to attack it. The "sunburn" now covered three quarters of her body, and though she was eating a little, the stomach and intestinal problems had worsened.

Dr. McGraine said there was also a graft-versus-tumor benefit to GVHD, and kids who got it had less chance of relapse. So they were all waiting for it to burn out with as little damage as possible to her important organs. Today had been a little better, and she dared to hope it was turning around.

"Guess who came to see me."

"You had a visitor?" Mom sent her a surprised and curious look. They knew no one in New Haven except the hospital workers, who were now becoming like family.

"Josh. Remember Rachel's brother?"

Mom smiled. "Of course, I remember. He came on the day of your transplant."

"He came again, but he could only stay a few minutes."

Dad seemed puzzled. "Who's Josh?"

"My friend." Kelsey pictured Josh's eyes filling with tears, then laughing at her silly jokes. "He likes bald, bearded girls."

Dad draped his hands between his knees. "He knows my little girl's the best thing going."

"Sure, Dad. I'm shaped like a pickle." The fluid leaking from her liver into her body cavity not only made her uglier than before, it was putting pressure on her lungs and making it hard to breathe.

"That's the VOD," Mom said. "Now that they're restricting salt and fluids, it'll get better."

"It has to." Dad waved at her walls. "Just look at all the people praying for you, Kelsey."

She'd felt the prayers today. She'd been much more hopeful and less tearful. Getting Morgan's picture was a bonus. Now she needed one from Jill. The two of them had given her life. That had new meaning now—even with Morgan's bone marrow making trouble inside her. The fluid buildup from the veno-occlusive liver disease, caused by the high conditioning levels of radiation and chemotherapy, the symptoms of the GVHD, her burning, peeling skin, blurred vision, and stomach and intestinal distress—it all amounted to an assault on her body that frankly made the leukemia seem tame. The enemy inside her had recruited fresh bullies, and her angels needed all the prayers people sent.

And now it was time for a fresh platelet infusion. Mom and Dad went back to the hotel apartment, and Kelsey lifted her laptop to her lap. A lot of leukemia kids had Web pages that told their story, but hers was the only interactive page for questions and answers that she knew of. It was her ministry, her way to use this nightmare for God's glory.

Not that she was any holier than the next kid. It was just that she had no chance at a normal life. It was easier to be close to Jesus when you had nothing else. The kids with everything would not understand. But the ones she wrote to needed hope and someone who would not laugh or turn away embarrassed or avoid them. Jesus came for the sick.

31

Jill sat with Brett, Shelly, Dan, and his date in the high school bleachers. A definite fifth wheel. Yet she was ready for some all-American small-town fun to take her mind off everything else. The afternoon rain had been enough to clean and cool the air without ruining the field for tonight's game. The diamond was combed and chalked, and Beauview's varsity team stood ready in the dugout for this exhibition.

Dan's date was a petite redhead named Melissa. Her freckles were actually cute, as were her toenails painted hot pink, the hand wrapped around Dan's substantial bicep, and her little kitten teeth. She was the new EMT, and they'd met at a car wreck.

But Jill did not let any of that distract her as they stood and faced the flag while the band played the national anthem. The crowd hollered when the local boys were called out one by one to wave their hats and grin at the fans. Dan settled back and watched the first visiting batter take the plate. He crushed peanut shells, dropped the nuts into his palm, and tossed them into his mouth. Melissa carefully pulled apart the shells, rubbed the skin from each nut, then tucked them into her kitten mouth.

This was ridiculous. She was glad Dan had an interest in someone else. It not only took the pressure off but also dispelled the guilt. It was just that she felt long and gangly and her nails were their natural selves and—

She jumped up and cheered when the first batter was thrown out at second.

"Does that mean he's out when the man jerks his thumb like that?"

In her peripheral vision, Jill caught Dan's surprise and silently clicked her tongue. His favorite sport, and Kitten knew nothing about it.

"Excuse me. I'm going to the bathroom." Jill stepped past Dan and Melissa to the aluminum stairs between the sections and rattled the bleacher with her steps. At the bottom, she circled the low wire fence surrounding the outfield, passed the third-base dugout, and reached the gate area near the bathrooms and concession stand.

Inside the damp concrete stall, she closed her eyes and begged forgiveness for her critical spirit. She washed at the sink, noticed the towel holders were empty, and shook her hands as she exited. *Lord, don't let me become one of those bitter people who can't stand for anyone else to be happy.*

She waved at several people from church, a couple fellow teachers, and some parents, then fixed her eyes on her group of friends and climbed to them. Dan took her hand to help her past and looked surprised to find it wet.

"No paper towels."

He smiled. "Oh."

She settled back in between Dan and Shelly. "Melissa, has Dan taken you out to Finnegan's Pond? It's a nice bike ride."

Melissa glanced from Dan to her. "No, but I don't have a bike."

"You'd be welcome to use mine. We can lower the seat." Jill took a peanut from Dan's bag, cracked the shell and tipped the nuts into her mouth, then returned her attention to the game, hoping there was something the two of them could enjoy together.

They all jumped to their feet for the foul ball arcing right to them, but the heavy man three rows down came up with it.

Dan sat back grumbling. "I'm going to watch what he drives."

Jill laughed. "Poor sport." She really did enjoy Dan, and maybe now they could be friends. She turned to Shelly, who'd been remarkably quiet, and tucked her head to catch her friend's gaze. "Are you okay?"

Shelly raised her chin, the setting sun turning her face pink. "I'm pregnant."

Jill caught her hand, staring. "When? How?"

"Don't ask me. They said it wouldn't happen, that the endometriosis was too advanced."

Jill knew all about the pain, the surgeries, the poor prognosis. "Shelly, that's . . . it is wonderful, isn't it?"

Shelly glanced at Brett munching a handful of popcorn. "If it works."

Jill squeezed her arm. "I'm so happy."

Shelly leaned against her. "Good. I'm too shocked to be."

Jill knew that feeling, shock and terror that what was inside her would change her life forever. And it did. "I will pray for your baby every day."

Now Shelly smiled. "Throw in a few for me. My stomach is no longer my friend."

Shelly had asked her to pray! "I will. I remember how that is."

"I'm not encouraged to think the memory's fresh after fifteen years."

Jill held her own waist. "Some things you never forget." She chewed her lower lip and tried to figure out what on earth was happening in the game. A baby. Shelly was having a baby. Tears stung her eyes, and she prayed no baseball flew her way until they cleared. But then, Dan would snag anything that came within a hundred feet.

———

Morgan raised a hand to Todd as the kid cleared the secure area of the John Wayne Orange County Airport, a flight attendant at his side. Todd grinned but kept his slouch until Morgan thanked the woman and took Todd's shoulder in his hand. "Hey, kid."

"What's with the baby-sitter?"

The lack of an adjective proved Todd wasn't really mad.

"Thought you might need a shield in case of terrorists."

Todd looked to see if he was serious. "I'd take them out with my bare hands."

Morgan squeezed his shoulder and let him go. "Did you bring swim trunks?"

Todd shook his head. "Don't got any."

"Then that's the first order of business." They reached the luggage claim and caught Todd's bag from the carousel. "This it?" Morgan shouldered the bag.

Todd nodded. "You look different."

"How?"

"Tanner. Skinnier."

"I told you I was sick. And I went sailing with some friends yesterday." His athletic trainer, Mick, and two friends from the club. Choppy water and a cooler of beer had proved his stomach was still not up to par. "And I'm not skinny, I'm lean."

"Stan's skinny."

"Well, he's tall." They headed toward the exit for short-term parking.

"My dad had a gut."

"Heard anything from him?"

Todd didn't answer as they passed through the doors from the air-conditioning to the California sun. Then he said, "He sent me a letter."

"Did you answer?"

"No."

They rode the shuttle to the parking lot and disembarked. Todd froze in place when Morgan led him to the Vette, disarmed the alarm, and said, "Get in."

"Sweet!" Definite improvement in vocabulary. "Is it yours?"

"Yep."

Morgan tossed his bag into the trunk and got behind the wheel.

"You sold your other one?" Todd felt the gear shift like a puppy's head.

"No, I have them both."

"I like the Vette better." Todd grinned. "Make it squeal."

Morgan laughed. "Maybe later." He meandered out of the parking area, paid his fee, and took the highway toward home, surprised how good it felt to have Todd along. "You like tacos?"

Todd nodded. "Yeah."

He had told Consuela to think along thirteen-year-old-boy lines for this week's meals. With the traffic congested, they'd be good and hungry when they got there. Todd seemed content to stare at everything with the wind in his face and, if he only knew, a little-boy grin plastered on his mouth. Morgan zoomed the last stretch of road and squealed the turn to his private drive, then coded the gate to open.

Todd shook his head with another grin. "I thought you were lying."

"About what?" Morgan cruised past his neighbors' homes.

"How rich you are."

He pulled into the garage. "I don't lie to you, Todd. But every-thing's relative."

"What's that mean?" Todd closed his door and immediately scoped out the backyard through the garage window.

"Means there are guys with more, bigger, and better." He nudged Todd toward the back door and they stepped out into the yard.

"A pool?"

"Yeah."

"I could stay here."

Morgan let him into the game room. "I'm not home much. And you have something with Stan you wouldn't get with me."

"What?" His tone was purely skeptical.

"A family."

"You could marry someone."

He'd hit the family nail on the head. "Well, I haven't. Let's make a deal."

"What deal?" Todd headed straight to the pool table and rolled the cue ball at the form holding the rest of the balls.

"You don't bug me to stay past the week, and I'll see if I can get you back out here soon. Maybe all four of you."

He looked less than enthused about that.

"And I've got an all-day pass to Disneyland."

Todd glared.

"Ever been there?"

He shook his head.

Morgan smiled. "Good. Hungry?"

Todd shrugged.

Morgan sighed. "Listen, Todd. I'm not taking Stan's place. You've got a family that cares for you. Think of me as your godfather. You come here once or twice a year to get spoiled, then toe the line for Stan the rest of the time."

Todd kicked the toe of his tennis shoe on the carved mahogany leg of the pool table.

"You can spend this week sulking, or we can have some fun. It's up to you."

Todd looked sidelong. "Okay."

Morgan gripped his shoulder. "Let's see what Consuela's done for us."

She had done tacos, corn, gazpacho—which Todd wouldn't touch, but Morgan thoroughly enjoyed—and chocolate sheet cake with chocolate-chip ice cream for dessert. Todd was coming into some growth, Morgan noted, and ate accordingly. Good. Maybe before the school year started he'd have a little size on him.

While the evening was fresh, they went to town and rented movies and bought Todd swim trunks. "Tomorrow you can check out the waves. Ever bodysurfed?"

"I never saw an ocean before." Todd stared at it in the distance from where they stood on the sidewalk in town.

"Well, come on." Morgan drove them home, then walked Todd down to the beach. It wasn't the same as sharing the sunset with Jill, but it swelled his heart to see Todd dash around barefoot when the purling waves chased in on him, then stoop to pick up every broken shell along the way. The week's end might be just as hard on him as on the kid.

———

Jill jolted up and stared at her alarm clock. 1:30 A.M.—11:30 P.M. on the West Coast. Dream images raced through her head, keeping time with her heart. She glanced at the phone. It was crazy to call. What was she going to say? Morgan, I had a bad dream? But what if it was more than a dream? It was potent enough to be a premonition, though she'd never had anything like that. She pressed a hand to her eyes and prayed for the fear to leave her. The images were too real. She had to know he was all right.

She slid over and picked up the phone. He was a night owl; their time together had shown her that. But his cell phone kept ringing and each ring increased the dread. She gripped the front of her nightshirt. Six rings and his voice mail answered. "Morgan, it's Jill. Please call." She hung up. *Lord God, please.* It was Saturday night. He could be out, probably had a date.

Her phone rang and she snatched it up. "Morgan?"

"Is it Kelsey?"

It took her a moment to still her breath, and then she said, "No, no, it's . . . you're all right?"

"Last time I looked."

"You didn't answer your phone." She released the wadded ball of nightshirt.

"I was on the balcony, barely heard the cell from the office."

She swallowed. "I'm sorry."

"What's wrong?"

She released a long breath, chagrined that he sounded so calm, so safe and fine. "You'll think I'm silly."

"Just tell me."

She stuffed a second pillow under her head. "I had an awful dream."

He made a small shuffling noise as he settled in somewhere. "Want to share it?"

Could she say it out loud? "It was so real. I've never dreamed anything so kinesthetically."

"Translate."

"I felt it, the impact."

"You were falling?"

"Not me. It was you, Morgan, in your Corvette. You crashed through the guardrail and onto the rocks below."

"Oh, not my Vette." The sound of sipping came over the line.

He was making a joke of it. He couldn't realize the shock she'd experienced. "It was a horrible sound and it hit so hard. I couldn't breathe."

"It's only a dream."

Like no other dream before. "You couldn't survive. How could you survive?"

"It's not real, Jill. But it's nice to know you care."

She closed her eyes. "I told you I did."

"We just can't let it out."

"Morgan . . ."

"Don't worry. I rather like this clandestine phone affair. Like a fiber-optic Romeo and Juliet. We're safe as long as no one checks my phone records."

"Please don't."

"It's actually a nice change from women who want the world to know I'm theirs."

She cradled her face in her hand. "Did I take you from one?" She could too easily picture him sharing the moonlit view from his balcony.

"No. I was out there alone, attempting a glass of Cognac."

"Attempting?" That was an odd word choice.

"This bug seems to have an aversion to alcohol in my system."

Jill sat up. "Really?"

"I hear your disappointment. But be assured I'm trying everything I can to overcome it." Another long sip.

"Is it only alcohol?"

"At this point food is no longer a problem."

Kelsey's words came clear. *"I got this idea like there was something in his life that kept him from knowing that love. So I was praying against it, and I just knew God wanted me to pray for him to get sick."*

Jill covered her mouth to hide the sudden exultation. Was such a thing even possible? His daughter's prayers could have such an effect? If it was directly ordered by God! *"Jesus really wants me to pray that prayer."*

"I don't think you should fight it, Morgan. There could be a reason."

"Some purpose in the stars?" A clearly cynical tone.

"Some purpose, yes."

He sighed. "I have news for you, Jill. There is no purpose."

"You're wrong, Morgan." And she suddenly knew it in every part of her.

A long pause, then, "There. Cognac successfully imbibed. I think I'll toast my next one to purpose, in your honor."

She regretted what he had in store, especially if she added her prayers to Kelsey's. "Don't drive."

"No fear. I'm rather attached to that Corvette."

Morgan refilled the cordial glass. Finally a liquor his body didn't resist. And just in time with Jill's sweet concern still warm in his ears. So she was dreaming of him—dead. An interesting twist of the subconscious. He drew the Cognac into his mouth and savored it. It probably would be easier for her that way.

No, he was not wallowing, merely pensive. Would she get on with her life if he were permanently removed from the picture? And when had his focus shifted? His intention had been to see his daughter. Jill had been his means. He wanted that still, though his legal possibilities were flimsy at best. And somehow it had gotten complicated. Talking to Kelsey, being with Jill. It was no longer cut-and-dried. His daughter had reached out, and he was still not recovered from her sweet voice, her thoughtfulness.

"I wanted to thank you in advance." Would she thank him for making trouble? For throwing his weight around and using his resources when he knew better than anyone the Bensons could ill afford to compete financially. He could force a meeting with Kelsey, but at what

cost? Maybe he should contact her through the Web site, let it be her choice. But he knew inside that wasn't right.

And now the past had seeped in and made it murkier still. He had put Jill on a plane to stop the freefall of his heart. He had not expected letters and calls, not the sound of her voice in the night, fearful and concerned for him. As long as no one else would know. Fiber-optic Romeo and Juliet was right on the mark. A passion to die for. But all in the dark. He drained the cordial glass like a shot. Only in the secrecy of her balcony.

He poured another slender crystal glassful. The Cognac was hitting a mostly empty stomach. Todd had talked him into delivered pizza for dinner, and one slice of that had sufficed. He welcomed the buzz that blurred his Juliet's sweet visage. Raising the delicate glass, he anticipated the burn, then took the Cognac once again in a single draught.

Careful now. Don't overdo the first precious succor allowed him by his traitorous flesh. Time for bed. He got up and steadied himself with a hand to the chair. In the dark, he groped past the pool table and knocked his shin on the curve of its leg. "Aah." He held the shin until the pain subsided, then gripped the banister, looked up the stairs and called, "But soft, what light through yonder window breaks? It is the east, and Jill is the sun."

He climbed two stairs and wavered. "The brightness of her eyes would shame the stars as daylight doth a lamp." He steadied himself at the top, crossed the shadowed great room, and started down the hall. "Oh, that I were a glove upon that hand that I might touch that cheek." But one touch leads to another. Better to keep his hands to himself.

He passed the room where Jill had slept, then paused at the next one on the other side of the bathroom. There was movement inside; maybe Todd couldn't sleep. Morgan tapped a knuckle, then opened the door to check.

A missile slammed the wall beside his face. He flung the door wide and threw up a hand.

"Get out! I hate you!"

Something else smashed against the wall, and Morgan staggered back.

Todd charged to the center of the room, wielding a wooden hanger. "If you hit me, I'll bash your head in."

Morgan gripped the doorframe. "I'm not going to hit you. Why on earth would I hit you?"

Todd's face screwed up. "You stink. Get out!"

"I just wanted . . . I was checking to see if you were okay."

Todd threw the hanger and Morgan ducked. "You're drunk!" He ran full force and slammed the door shut.

Morgan stood in the hall, vaguely aware that Consuela had appeared and was flapping him toward his own room like a hen on a chick. He dropped to his bedside while she tugged off his shoes. "You are drunk, señor. You scared the boy."

He'd scared Todd? All he did was check to make sure the kid was all right in a strange room. *"If you hit me . . ."* Hit him? Consuela reached for the buttons of his shirt and he caught her wrist. "Go away."

She stepped back. "You go to bed now. No more poison."

Morgan looked at her blurred brown face. "Make sure Todd's all right."

"Sí. I will check on him."

"Tell him . . ." Morgan pressed a hand to his gut.

"Go to sleep." She went out, and Morgan fumbled with the buttons of his shirt, pulled it off, and dropped it to the floor. He did the same with his pants, but sleep was out of the question. His stomach twisted, knotted, and balled itself into a fist. He staggered to the bathroom and retched. This was ridiculous! He hadn't had enough to be sick on.

He splashed cold water in his face and washed out his mouth even as fresh waves struck his belly. He gripped his torso with his arms. Tomorrow he was seeing a doctor. There had to be an explanation. He staggered to the bed and collapsed.

"If you hit me . . ." Lying sprawled, he tongued the corner of his mouth. All he knew about Todd's dad was he'd killed a man in a bar fight and Todd wanted nothing to do with him. Had he beaten the kid when he got drunk? Sure sounded that way.

Morgan pressed a hand to his face, starting to sweat. He gripped the sheets with white knuckles. The bed felt like yesterday's sailboat. Gripping his head, he curled off the bed and went like a penitent to once again pay homage to the porcelain gods.

Afterward, he stuck his head under the shower and braced himself against the stall walls. He'd frightened Todd just opening the door. Todd knew before it opened what condition he was in, or he would not have had his missile ready. He shut off the shower and hung his head, watching streams, then drops hit the shower floor. He straightened slowly, then dried his head and hung the towel over his neck. He should talk to Todd. But not now. In the morning. They'd talk in the morning.

CHAPTER

32

J ill woke to the drum and flow of rain on her roof and drains. Normally she loved the sound, the smell, the presence of rain—washing, nourishing, rejuvenating rain. This morning she lay still, wishing it could wash her clean of cowardice and deceit. Clandestine phone affair. How wrong was that, to call Morgan with her fear, her concern for him when all the while he knew she would not acknowledge what was in her heart?

But what was in her heart? The residue of a tragic union aborted without closure? Or an abiding love for Morgan in spite of his self-destructive flaws. She had maintained a distance from Dan since he did not profess her faith, share her world view, understand her limits. No unequal yoke for her. But wasn't that something like her cheerleading clique all over again? Only perfect people need apply?

Didn't that rule her out? How precious it would be to have kept herself pure, to have married Morgan or even someone else and never fallen from the grace assured her by acceptance of her Savior. Salvation did not guarantee she would not fall to temptation. She was forgiven, but that did not stop all the ripples that spread even now from her rock in the lake.

She thought of the widower at Mom's church. She could almost hear her mother's whisper. "Now, Jill, he doesn't need to know about that other business. That's over and done." Jill pressed her fingertips to one eye. It was not over. But was she willing to make that known? Secrecy had become a second skin to her.

It was Sunday morning. She was expected to teach her class, then sit among the faithful and worship. She had the right. They were all sinners sanctified by the blood of Jesus. But this morning the act just seemed too hard to perform. She groped for the phone and notified the coordinator she couldn't make it, then rolled over and pulled another pillow onto her head as the rain played its rhythm on her roof.

Morgan raised himself slowly. His head would hurt more if he hadn't purged the night before—some small consolation. The smell of chorizo sausage permeated the room, probably the entire house, but his stomach did not revolt. Oh no, it had the audacity to send a hunger pang to his brain.

He rose and washed himself thoroughly, brushed and gargled twice, then spritzed cologne. He dressed in shorts and T-shirt, slid on his Birkenstocks, then stood at the door of his room and prepared to face the dragon.

The dragon was thin and weary-eyed and hunched over a plate of scrambled eggs and sausage buried in shredded cheese. He looked up darkly when Morgan crossed the kitchen and poured a cup of coffee. Morgan rested his hips in the corner of the counter and eyed the boy back.

Consuela sliced a melon and laid a chilled green crescent on Todd's plate. He bit it in the middle, leaving a wet smile on each cheek that did not reach his eyes. "Guess you're not eating."

"I'll eat." Though he was not generally a breakfast person, he would do it today.

Todd scooped a forkful of eggs into his mouth, pinching off the cheese connecting it to his plate. Morgan took his cup and sat down with a glance at Consuela. He sipped the coffee. She did make a perfect cup of coffee. Consuela set a plate before him with only a sprinkling of cheese but additional green onions Todd must have opted against. She set the bowl of homemade hot sauce beside the plate. He was actually tempted to use it.

He took a forkful, aware of Todd's surreptitious attention, and stuffed it into his mouth. Flavor, texture, heat, he processed instantly. No rolling of the stomach, no warning signs. Of course, he had sweat and purged even the fumes of Cognac from his system last night, so there was no reason for his stomach to complain.

Todd took another bite of melon, working from the center toward one point. "We surfing today?" For a kid who thought his life was over last night, he seemed flatly unconcerned this morning.

"I thought we might." He took another bite, all the while trying to get a bead on Todd. Had last night been a trick, some bid for attention? No, there'd been terror and rage in his eyes. Morgan washed his bite down with coffee and methodically finished his plate. Todd left a portion of his but had made a decent job of it. Consuela cleared the dishes and refilled his cup.

Morgan breathed the steam and sipped. "I guess we need to clear the air."

Todd sniffed. "You cut one?"

Morgan fought a smile. "Metaphorically speaking."

"Meta-what?"

"Talk about last night." He met Todd's eyes.

"What about it?"

"Why you thought I wanted to hit you."

Todd pushed his milk glass away and scraped his chair back, getting up so quickly he banged his thigh. "I just did, that's all." He rubbed his thigh. "I'll get my trunks on now."

"What's your hurry? We've got all day. Got all week. I cleared my schedule for you."

"Consuela said the best time to find shells is early morning."

Morgan glanced up at her. "She's right. Especially after a storm. Get a rough sea overnight, you'll find all kinds of things washed up."

"Then let's go." Todd had mastered avoidance. Also confrontation, and you never knew which one to expect. Maybe he was embarrassed he'd overreacted.

Morgan took one last swig and stood. "Okay."

Todd scurried to his room and Morgan changed into his own trunks, rummaged two beach towels from the closet, and met him in the hall. They walked down and stepped out into the balmy air.

"It smells different here."

"You have an acute sense of smell." Morgan led the way down the path.

"What's acute?"

Didn't they teach vocabulary anymore? "Sharp, strong, finely tuned." At least he hadn't told him he stunk this morning.

"Well, there's no horse manure, for one thing."

Morgan smiled. "True."

"And all these flowers and orange trees and something else."

"The sea. You smell the ocean."

Todd passed him at the bottom of the path and ran onto the sand, then turned. "The beach is bigger today."

"Low tide."

"Hey, where's the surfboards?"

"We're not using boards today."

"Then how're we gonna surf?" He planted his hands on his hips, jutting out his pointy elbows.

"Bodysurf. Helps you learn the feel of the waves. If you haven't swum in an ocean, you need to learn its rhythm."

Todd slacked a hip. "I can swim. What's the big deal?"

Morgan spread the towels side by side on the sand. "Walk out there twenty feet or so, where the waves are breaking thigh high."

Todd walked to the water's edge and splashed up to his ankles, then stopped. "What's with the quicksand?"

"Keep going."

He moved in up to his calves and the next wave splashed over his knees.

Morgan watched his surprise as the water pulled against him even while the new one rolled in. "That's the undertow."

Todd raised one foot, lost his equilibrium, and splashed it down.

Morgan had forgotten how disorienting it could be the first time, how the water rushing back out while you stood still fooled the brain and made you dizzy. He stepped into the cold water and plugged through to Todd's side. "Feels strange, eh?"

"It's sucking the sand out under my feet."

"Come on." Morgan battled the breakers. Normally he ran and dove low, but Todd wasn't there yet. He was still turning his back to every wave that came. Morgan grabbed his arm when one breaker almost toppled him. He righted him in the lull. "Hurry now and we'll get past the break point to the swells."

Todd tried but couldn't pull hard enough against the water to get far. Morgan saw the next wave cresting and grabbed hold of the boy. The force of the breaker tumbled Todd, but Morgan kept hold of his arm and dragged him up from the foam, laughing at the outrage on the kid's face. The language was predictable.

"Better move. The next one's coming."

Todd twisted. "I'm getting out."

"Just hold on." Morgan tugged him. "Grab my arm."

Todd put a death grip on his forearm, and Morgan clutched him when the next wave crashed. It splashed over Todd's face but didn't tear him loose.

"Now. Dive down and swim."

"I can't."

"What do you mean?"

"I can't swim when the water's pulling and smashing me into the ground."

The peak was over them already, sharpening into its curl. "Turn forward. Put your head down." Todd's arms circled him like a boa constrictor.

Morgan pulled them under before it broke. Todd's feet left the ground with the swell and Morgan dove, pulling them both into deeper water. They surfaced a moment later in the relative calm where the water peaked and rolled. Todd still gripped him.

"Can you stand?"

"No." Even as he answered a wave lifted him like flotsam and passed them by.

"Let go and tread."

"I can't."

"I thought you said you could swim." He was losing circulation in his arm.

"I can. If the water holds still."

Morgan pried Todd's hands loose and caught him around the chest. "Don't fight it. Feel how it rises and drops?"

"But it's pulling me, too."

"You'll be fine." Morgan's feet left the ground with the large swell that rolled by. He kicked them out a little farther and let Todd go. Immediately the hands clawed on to his arm. Morgan took hold of Todd's wrists. "Let me see you tread."

"I can't. I only swim where I can stand."

Morgan turned Todd to face him. "If you can stand, it isn't swimming."

Todd glared. "So sue me."

Morgan caught him around the chest. "Make like you're sitting and kick out slowly with your legs. Relax. The stiffer you are, the quicker you'll sink." They rose and dropped again. "Now use your arms in a breast stroke out and together."

"What's a breast stroke?"

Morgan showed him with one arm. "Cup your hand, you'll push more water."

Todd moved his arms.

"Now the legs. Bend up your knees like I told you. Pretend you're sitting. Now you can either do a slow bicycle or just kick. Gently." He caught a heel in the thigh. "That's right." He let go and Todd kept moving, riding forward a little with the wave.

"I'm gonna die."

Morgan laughed. "You're not gonna die."

"I'm ready to go back now." Todd's arms jerked.

"You'll have to get through the breakers."

Todd spun his head to face him. "You mean get smashed again?"

"Unless you can ride a wave in."

"I'm dead."

Morgan splashed him. "What's that talk? I thought you were here to surf."

"I thought we'd paddle around on surfboards."

Morgan stretched onto his back. "Who needs a board?" Water sealed his ears with a dull *woam, woam,* as the waves rocked him. He only rested a moment before squinting over to make sure Todd was still treading.

"My legs are getting stiff."

Morgan righted himself and took Todd's arm. "So get on your back and rest."

Todd lay back with surprising ease. Someone had taught him that much at least. Morgan looked toward the shore. He was a little concerned about getting Todd back on solid ground. The kid was not physically strong and was a very weak swimmer. Not that they were in danger of a riptide or anything, but you could get beaten up by a good wave.

Todd's float only lasted a moment, then he bent and jerked up, shivering. Morgan caught him, treading for them both. "Now, listen. You can let the wave work for you, push you all the way in. But you have to swim strongly enough at the start or it leaves you behind. Do you know the front stroke?"

"Which one is that?"

"Front crawl." Morgan demonstrated with his free arm.

"Kinda." Todd looked away.

"We'll work our way toward the beach, then when we're in a good place, we'll catch a wave and swim hard. It'll carry you. Just stay on your belly until you hit bottom or start getting sucked back. Then get up and pull through to the shore."

"I'm dead." Todd nodded.

"I'll be right by you. Ready?"

Todd rolled his eyes. Morgan held his elbow as they moved, then kept him steady when they'd reached a good spot. "Wait till I say." He watched a good-sized wave rise, but it peaked right where they were. "A little closer." They moved with the flow, and the next rose even higher. "Now!" Morgan thrust Todd forward and dove himself, feeling the rush, then at last the grate of sand against his knee.

He stood up against the tug and saw Todd halfway back battling the water and losing. Morgan splashed back and pulled him out. Sand coated his feet and ankles as they reached the towels. Morgan lifted and shook one as Todd did the same. Rubbing the sun-warmed towel over his face, he realized his headache was gone. He'd been too focused on keeping Todd alive to worry how he felt. Todd had wrapped the towel around himself and stood shivering, probably as much from fear as cold.

"I think we're experiencing a lack of communication." Morgan wiped the towel briskly over his own chest and arms and back.

"You said surf. You never said swim." Todd swiped a drip from his face with an edge of the towel still wrapped about him.

"What did you think you were going to do if you got knocked off a board?" He used his towel on Todd's head, causing a surprised look.

Todd didn't answer but reluctantly rubbed himself dry.

"You did fine out there once you let loose and gave it a try. But I think we should do some stroke training in the pool before we tackle the waves again."

Todd wrapped the towel back around his shoulders with his typical slump. "Yeah. I might drown or something."

"That wouldn't go over well with Stan." Morgan elbowed him.

"You wouldn't care."

"Oh, really."

"You'd just get drunk and forget all about me."

Morgan folded his towel. "This must be roast Morgan morning. I hadn't realized." He studied the kid. "Last night you thought I was the ax murderer."

"No I didn't."

"What, then?"

Todd picked up a rock and threw it at a gull, which fluttered up, then settled back down.

"Your dad?"

"You smelled like him. Sounded like him, too, falling up the stairs talking stupid."

Morgan formed a keen memory of his Shakespearean eloquence. "Well, I had too much. That doesn't mean—"

"Just shut up."

Morgan closed his mouth and studied the boy. Every angle was sharp, shoulder hunched between them, no eye contact. "So when he got drunk, he hit you?"

"I said, shut up."

"Well, in case you haven't noticed, I'm the adult."

Todd yanked the towel off and threw it down. "In case you haven't noticed, you're a jerk and a drunk and I hate you." He kicked the sand.

Morgan sputtered as the sand struck his face, and Todd ran toward the path up to the house. Morgan rubbed the sand from his eyes and grabbed their towels. And he'd asked for this?

He plodded up the path, recalling the previous night. Falling up the stairs and talking stupid. Not a bad description. But no way had he intended any harm to Todd. The kid was projecting. He reached the house, addressed the concerns Denise caught him with inside the door, then headed up.

Maybe bringing Todd was a mistake. He'd thought it would be fun for both of them. So far he felt like scum and Todd was not happy. He found the kid pulling the leaves off the potted fig beside his bedroom window. He stopped just inside the door in a nonthreatening posture. "You want to leave?"

"You want me to." Todd kept staring out the window.

"If you have concerns, you ought to address them directly."

Todd jerked a whole branch of leaves. "I'm just a kid."

"Well, you are a kid. That doesn't mean what you have to say isn't valid."

"Why can't you . . ." He crushed the bunch of leaves in his fist.

"Why can't I what?"

Todd spun. "Be like you are all the time."

Morgan tried to decipher what he meant. "You mean, be like this?"

The kid was shaking, his breaths making shallow jerks in his bare chest. The wet trunks clung to one leg.

"Do you really think I'm going to hurt you, Todd?"

"Not now."

Not sober. Morgan sat down in the chair beside the door. "There's a guest robe in your closet."

Todd walked over and pulled on the blue-and-white-striped terry robe. Its midcalf length reached the floor on Todd and he swam in the sleeves, but at least his teeth would stop chattering. What did he know about troubled kids? Only that Todd wanted something from him, and he'd started it in the first place. He'd never had to approach Todd on that porch, not been forced to take him hiking or to the movies or exploring. He had wanted to do it, seen the need and responded.

Todd slid down the wall and sat beside the window. His face was wary.

"You don't want me to drink, is that it?"

"Like that would happen."

Morgan drew and released a slow breath. It was like reasoning with a recalcitrant pup. "Not everyone who drinks gets mean."

Todd rolled his eyes to the side and found a leaf on the floor. He tore the tip off, then piece after tiny piece.

"Is that why you won't talk to your dad?"

Todd swore.

This was going nowhere. Morgan rubbed his face. "You seem to think I'm like him."

"You are. You're a stinkin' drunk."

Anger flared. Morgan gripped the arms of his chair. "And you're a foulmouthed, self-centered kid." He stood up. "Why am I wasting my time with you?" He went to his room, showered the ocean salt from his skin and hair, dressed, and went down to the office to work. Todd could take a hike for all he cared. He skipped lunch and methodically addressed all the professional issues he'd intended to put off until the next week. Denise was as perplexed as she was pleased.

Consuela demonstrated neither pleasure nor acceptance and made regular trips to the office that she usually avoided. "Your guest is watching the movies." "The boy is sitting in your car." "Todd is throwing oranges at the house." "He's going to the beach."

Morgan looked up at that one. "Alone?"

Consuela spread her hands. "Who would be going with him?"

Sighing, Morgan left his desk and went out the lower door. He didn't see Todd in the yard and stalked toward the path. From the top he saw him walking along the shore with a stick. He hurried down, then sauntered after Todd until his longer stride caught up. Todd stopped and poked the translucent remains of a sand crab.

Morgan said, "I'm sorry."

Todd flicked the crab into the speckled foam and watched it wash away, then lodge again in the sand.

"Come on. You gotta give me somethin', Todd."

Todd threw the stick into the shallow breakers. "Why don't you send me back?"

"I will if that's what you want."

"It's what you want."

Morgan fought his frustration. Was this what he'd missed all these years? No-win conversations with someone who thought him alternately God and the devil? Some roller coaster of emotions too illogical to define? "Could we get on the same page?" He stepped around to Todd's front. "You're putting stuff on me that doesn't belong. I drink alcohol because I like it. I'm not answerable to you for that choice. I already agreed I had too much last—"

"Every night."

"How would you know?"

Todd looked at him then. "Because I do. I know what it looks like. I know what it sounds like."

Another person putting their experience on him. Twice now he'd admitted to Todd that he'd overindulged. Two times, the kid knew of. With that he'd labeled him a stinkin' drunk? And he hadn't even been drunk when Denise did her suspecting. He'd been sick, plain and simple. He rubbed a hand through his hair.

"You don't see it." Todd bit his lip, such a vulnerable, little-boy thing it hurt Morgan's heart.

"What don't I see?"

"How it changes you."

Why did that hurt? Morgan swallowed, spread his hands. "So I won't drink while you're here." It wasn't agreeing with him anyway. A week off might be just the ticket to get his system back on track.

Todd shook his head and started walking. Morgan clenched his teeth, fighting the irritation. Why was he trying to please some punk who wouldn't meet him halfway? It wasn't even his own kid. He'd never seen his own, never been allowed to. Todd sure couldn't fill that slot. "Maybe I should send you back," he called after him.

"You'd rather drink anyway."

"You know something? You're right." Morgan turned his back and stalked up to the house. He'd call Stan and tell him it wasn't working.

Good luck and good riddance. Since he couldn't leave Todd at the shore by himself, he sent Consuela down to keep watch. He might just go to town, but when he went around the front of the house, his neighbor Dana raised a hand in greeting and crossed the street with her young teenage son.

Morgan returned her greeting and added, "Hey, Matt." Her son was the likeable sort. But then, his life was pretty good. "What's up?"

"Go ahead, Matt." Dana nudged him.

The boy raised his blond, freckled head. "I have to interview someone for a youth group assignment."

"Someone he finds interesting and knows personally," Dana added.

Morgan kept eye contact with Matt. "What's the slant of the interview?"

Matt frowned. "I don't know. Just stuff about you, what you do, that sort of thing."

He wanted to interview a stinkin' drunk? "Okay."

"Go get your notebook, Matt." Dana turned after he hustled back across the street. "Thanks, Morgan. He was nervous about asking."

"No big deal. I'm glad to help." That's all he'd wanted to do with Todd.

They sat down on the front porch furniture amid the crimson geraniums emitting their not-so-fragrant perfume. Morgan answered the basic questions, then elaborated, even leading Matt to questions he hadn't prepared. He might not understand slant, but he'd get a more interesting biography with some direction, some angle, not just rote facts.

At last Matt smiled and said thanks. Morgan got an idea. "Hey, Matt. I've got a kid here about your age. Would you like to watch a movie tonight, keep him company?"

"On your big screen?"

"Yeah."

"Cool." Matt turned to his mother. "Can I?"

"If you have your biography written." She turned to Morgan. "A relative?"

How much should he tell? "No, he's a friend. Met him at my brother's ranch. Actually . . ." The truth seemed right. "He's a foster kid. We hit it off a month ago, and I invited him out here." Morgan watched Dana's face for the protective-mother look he expected to precede the backtracking.

But her smile was gentle. "That's nice, Morgan. Boys need men to stand for them."

"Well." He ran his hand through his hair, knowing what Todd would say to that. "He's not keen on me just now."

Dimples appeared in her cheeks. "How would it be for Luke to come, too?"

Morgan pictured the next son up, maybe fifteen? "Sure, if he wants to. We'll fix up a mess of munchies . . ."

"The movie needs to be PG or better."

He hadn't considered that. Todd's own language could violate that rule.

"Why don't I have Luke ride down to the video store and choose something?" Dana suggested.

For a sweet-faced petite woman she certainly took control of a situation. Maybe he should send Todd to her. "Sure." He smiled.

She turned to Matt. "You'd better get writing."

He got up. "Thanks again," he called as he headed across the street.

Dana stood also. "That might not be what you had in mind."

Morgan shrugged. "I hadn't planned anything."

"We don't budge on that rule."

"It's fine. But . . . Todd's not too predictable. And his mouth . . ."

She nodded. "I'll talk to the boys."

For the first time that day, he felt peaceful.

33

J ill opened the door, surprised to see three friends from church. She had spent the morning and part of the afternoon cleaning her place and preparing plans for the upcoming school year, assuming she had a job and would be allowed the autonomy she needed to do the best she could for her kids. It had depressed her to think they might not even give her the same caseload. If Mr. Daley's expertise was severe and profound, she could see him skimming the kids like Joey from her schedule.

The rain had lessened, but the large green umbrella Pat held over all three friends ran streamlets onto the threshold. "Surprise," Pat said with her trademark smile.

"Hi. Come in." She hadn't planned for company, but the house was clean and fresh. Now if her mood only matched.

After the others stepped in, Pat closed the umbrella and left it standing on the porch just outside the door. "How're you doing?" Her deep brown eyes were surrounded in lashes that curled almost back on themselves over caramel-colored lids that hung at half mast, giving a sultry expression she never intended.

"You never miss your class." Deborah glanced quickly around the room. "We thought you might be really sick."

Gina held up a can of Campbell's. "We brought the chicken soup."

Jill sighed. "I'm not sick. I just . . . wasn't up to it today."

Pat nodded. "I hear you. Some days are like that."

Were they? Did these women curl up like worms awaiting the next deadly peck?

Pat said, "I just added your flock to mine. But they were all askin', where's Miss Runyan?"

"Do you want something to drink? I can make some iced tea."

"Sure, honey. That sounds nice."

Gina carried the soup jar to the counter. "Hope you don't mind us barging in. With some people we wouldn't think twice if they missed their class. But you're like clockwork."

As a teacher, Jill knew firsthand the hardship of an irresponsible absence. But it had seemed more phony and irresponsible to pretend to be something she wasn't.

Deborah touched her arm. "Hey, this is a cheer-up party."

Jill tried a smile, then set the kettle to boil. Pat glided in, taking the pitcher from the counter. "Want me to fill this with ice?"

Jill nodded. "Sure."

Gina said, "The truth is, we've been worried about you for a while."

Jill turned from the stove. Had she been so transparent? Was the whole church talking about her?

Pat slid an arm around her shoulders. "If you're bearing a burden, that's what friends are for."

Jill stood silent. She couldn't begin to tell these women the burden she was bearing. They knew the Jill Runyan she pretended to be, the soft-spoken Sunday school super teacher. She was such a hypocrite, but that didn't mean she could step up and confess to the world. She'd almost worked up the courage to tell her parents. But these women . . . she had to work with them, see them every week, impress them.

"You don't have to tell us." Deborah touched her hand.

Gina said, "We just want to cheer you up. And if you'd like to share what's got you down, we're here."

It was there before her, the chance to let go of the secrecy. She heard Morgan's mocking tone. *"We're safe as long as no one checks my phone records."* Had she actually called him, shown her concern, prolonged the impossible?

Pat squeezed her shoulders. "You think you're the only one with stuff? Think again, girl."

Jill sighed. "My stuff beats your stuff any day."

"Maybe." Pat's smile warmed the kitchen. "But God doesn't see it that way."

Jill turned and took down the box of decaffeinated green tea. How would it feel to just tell it all? Stop pretending? She lifted the lid of the steaming kettle and dropped four bags in. The relief would be immediate, but it wouldn't last. Shelly knew, and Dan and Brett, but they didn't hold her to the same standards as these women. And there were other people to consider. Her parents most of all. She could not risk word getting back to them, even if these friends did understand.

Jill opened the cabinet and took down glasses. "I would just appreciate your prayers, for me and two others."

"That works," Pat said.

Jill smiled for real, thankful they didn't push. She hadn't considered these women friends, not the hang-out-together sort, though she knew they were close to each other. To her they were church friends, Sunday friends. Well, it was, after all, Sunday. She poured the steeped tea over the ice. "Do you like it sweet?"

The answers were mixed, so she got the sugar canister and let them doctor their own glasses.

"Why don't we all sit down." Pat stretched one dark elegant arm toward the living room.

They settled in with the rain casting the room in grays. Jill turned on the lamp next to her giraffe chair. Sweetly and without pretense, the women prayed for her unspoken concern. Their willingness to support her even without knowing the situation was a balm to her spirit.

Pat crossed the room and knelt before her. "You need to remember what you are."

Jill looked into her eyes. "What am I?"

"A daughter of the King. A bride of the Bridegroom. Beloved."

Tears welled up. The words held so much love.

Deborah came to stand behind Pat. "And know that all things are possible with God."

Jill shook her head. "I just wish I knew what was supposed to happen."

Pat smiled. "Then fall on your knees and ask, and when the answer comes, listen. Then do."

Jill swallowed. "That's the hard part."

"I know it." Pat squeezed her hand. "But you gotta let people uphold you. Who you got praying? You standing alone?"

"I guess so. Mom might be praying for me, but not about any of the rest. She doesn't know either." Not the new aspects that would dredge up the old.

Gina rested her hands on her hips. "You need to tell her. Not because she needs to know, but because it's hurting you to keep it in."

Jill winced. Altogether too perceptive. If it was time to bring things to light, that was the place to start. But sometimes it seemed it would be easier to shout it from City Hall than voice it to her mother. And Dad? No way.

"Don't let the enemy steal your courage." Pat covered her hand with the other. How could she know what had just gone through her mind? "Let's just take authority over that right now." And she prayed.

Jill closed her eyes as something eased inside her. Maybe she would call her mother, see if there was a time they could talk. She was not fully confident but encouraged enough by the time they left to do her daily devotional, then get on her computer and journal, then check for mail from Kelsey. The letter was brief. *Jill, could you please send me a picture of you? I want it next to Morgan's. Love, Kelsey.*

Halfway through the movie, Stan called. Morgan left the boys tossing popcorn and peanuts and went into the office to talk freely.

Stan's voice sounded as if he was using a cordless phone in a tunnel. "Just calling to see how Todd's doing."

If he'd called a few hours earlier, Morgan would have said he was catching a morning flight home. But Todd had actually warmed to Dana's sons and not shocked them so far. It was a good move on Dana's part to send her older boy, Luke. Not only was he gregarious, but Todd related at a different level than with shy, innocent Matt. They'd played a game of pool in which Todd waxed them, and Morgan wondered how many pool halls he'd frequented.

"He's doing all right. We've had some ups and downs." The downs being like a bungee jump from the Golden Gate Bridge.

"Well, that's Todd. I have to say, I miss him. I've been home with Melanie and Sarah for the week, but I think Todd and I were making some headway." Stan sounded eager for affirmation.

"I guessed as much. He's talked about you in positive terms, and when we're not knocking heads, he's eager and amiable. Whatever you're doing, it's making a difference."

"Lots of prayer."

That would be Stan's modus operandi. "He's got his sore spots."

"Which ones have you poked?"

"His dad."

Stan was quiet a moment. "Well, he beat him up pretty bad. Once the mother left, he just went off the deep end, bender after bender, and Todd took the knocks. It's all in his case history, but I don't usually tell it."

It didn't take a genius to figure it out, the way Todd had reacted. But it was all the more frustrating that the kid made the parallel between that kind of man and him.

Stan cleared his throat. "I wasn't easy about sending him out there. But he just came alive talking about it, and when I prayed it seemed the right thing to do."

"I understand your hesitation. You have a heavy responsibility." He'd been surprised himself.

"One of the checks is, I need to talk to him every night."

Morgan glanced through the crack in the door. "He's watching a movie with some neighbor kids, but hold on, I'll get him." Morgan brought the phone to Todd. "It's Stan."

Todd sagged into the couch in his typical attitude and took the phone. "Yeah? Yeah. Yeah." He rolled his eyes. "Okay. Bye."

Morgan would have offered the office, but the conversation was over. He checked, and Stan had hung up. Morgan leaned on the arm of a chair and watched a few minutes of the movie, then went to return the handset. He noticed Todd's gaze follow him to the base at the bar.

He had told him he wouldn't drink, but Todd obviously didn't believe him. Well, Todd had grounds for his distrust. He hung up the phone and rejoined them. Seeing Todd relax sent a pang. The kid didn't need any more stress in his life, certainly no more fear of being hurt. And he suspected the emotional hurt and betrayal was as bad as any beating.

The movie Luke had brought was an older sports story called *Rudy*. Todd seemed to relate to the main character's struggle, maybe being undersized himself. Morgan thought the end a little farfetched, where the dogged bench warmer scores the winning touchdown in the last play of the season, but it was supposedly true—at least based on a true story—and the message was one Todd could use. Don't give up.

After the neighbors went home, Morgan sent Todd to bed and made a point of going up himself. He sat down on the bed and rested his hands on his thighs. It felt like ages since he'd woken with a headache and faced one insult after another. But it had been good to help Todd in the water and see him enjoy the evening. What a precarious age thirteen was. Or fourteen.

How was Kelsey doing? How long would it be until he heard? Had the marrow engrafted? How was he supposed to go about his days as if nothing were different? He'd thought having Todd would take his mind off it. In a way it had, but in a thousand other ways it triggered thoughts and questions.

Seeing Todd's thin, bony legs made him try to picture hers. Had Kelsey ever swum in the ocean? Searched for shells in the sand? What if she were down the hall? They'd say more than four words to each other. There was so much he wanted to know.

Did she wonder about him? Or was the dad who raised her the only man she cared about? One phone call. He'd heard her voice. Why didn't he ask her for a picture?

He sighed heavily. Sleep would be good. He'd need his energy for tomorrow. Maybe at Disneyland, Todd would lighten up and stay off his case.

Jill snuggled Rascal under her chin the next day as she lay on the couch for another gray morning. Setting aside the educational journal, she buried her fingers in Rascal's fur and stroked him with her nails. His purr was surprisingly smooth, which meant he was not only content, he was peaceful. The rain had softened overnight but not stopped, and it still fell steadily, making the water run off the gutters in streams. She'd spent a few hours reading, escaping, occupying her mind and wondering if she should have bared her soul to Gina, Deborah, and Pat the day before.

Sitting up, she settled Rascal onto the couch where he arched up in a luxurious stretch and fluffed his tail, tempting her to settle back down with him and doze. But now that she was up, she had to do something. She'd missed her run again because of the rain. It was not worth the mud. But she wanted to do something.

The phone rang and she snatched it up. "Hello?"

"I have to talk to you." Shelly sounded breathless.

"Are you all right?"

"Yep. Can you come over?"

Jill looked outside. "Sure. Be right there." She unfurled her umbrella at the patio door and ran across the yard.

Shelly closed the door behind her, then pulled up her shirt, baring her belly. She pointed with her finger. "They got a heartbeat."

The smile broke into Jill's face. "That's great. I didn't know you were that far along."

"Look." Shelly kept her finger in place. "Don't tell me you thought that was all me."

Jill laughed. "You're doing it the healthy way. I weighed less at five months than when I started."

"Figures." Shelly poured them each a glass of milk and set out a plate of cookies with thick chunks of chocolate and walnuts. "This baby demands chocolate."

Jill raised skeptical brows. "Really?"

"I read an article that said you need to anticipate and respond to your baby's needs. I'm only complying." She bit a chunk from the edge of a cookie.

Jill took one from the plate. "What's my excuse?"

"You don't need one." Shelly drank her milk. "So do you want the nitty-gritty?"

"Every detail." Jill savored Shelly's baking. Mrs. Field's, eat your heart out.

Shelly went over her doctor's appointment in detail. "You should have heard it, this whooshy sound, then clear as a bell this little heartbeat. Of course you'd never know that's what it was until they told you." Shelly snatched up another cookie, then got up and motioned. "Come here a minute."

Shelly led her into the bedroom. "I found the best book." She lifted a coffee-table-sized book from the bed. "It's all these photographs of babies in the womb. Look at this one." She flipped through, then back, then found the page. "He's sucking his thumb."

Jill stared at the picture, one she'd seen before in documentaries and magazines. Still, to see the cartoon-shaped baby with his thumb in his mouth made her tremble. To think she might have destroyed that precious life inside her. But she hadn't. And that was the grace in all of it.

"And this one." Shelly showed her a much earlier picture. "That's about how big Brett Junior is now. It looks like a tadpole with wings."

"Brett Junior?"

Shelly bit into her cookie. "We won't actually call him that."

"Especially if it's a girl."

"If it's a girl, I'm calling her Natasha." Shelly swallowed and flipped the page.

"Boris for a boy?"

Shelly sent her a look. "Very funny. But I kind of like Rocky. And knowing Brett, his first Christmas gift will be boxing gloves." She popped the end of the cookie into her mouth. "Rocky Barlowe has a ring, don't you think?"

"What does Brett think?"

"We haven't talked about names yet. He's been working swings in addition to his shift." Shelly rubbed a crumb from the corner of her mouth. "They've had a rash of burglaries, drug related they're pretty sure. He and Dan have been working like crazy." Shelly plumped down on the bed. "Jill, are you and Dan done for good?"

"Why?" Jill settled across from her.

"He's seeing a lot of Melissa."

Jill turned the page of the book to a full-page photo, all red and amber. "I think that's good."

"At the game it seemed like he wished it was you hanging on his arm."

"We're friends." She looked up. "I'm glad we could keep that. He's not a bitter sort of guy. I wonder what went wrong for his marriage."

"Liz."

"Oh, Shelly, it's never black and white." Jill shook her head. "I've been seeing that too clearly."

"Maybe. But you didn't know Liz." Shelly dragged another immense book onto the bed. "Look at this one. I found it in the same section of the store. It's Anne Geddes." She flipped open the cover. "She has all these babies inside flowers and stuff."

They looked through the book, exclaiming over the newborns in pea pods, on rose petals, in tulips. Jill's heart swelled for Shelly, who not only seemed past her disbelief but engrossed in anything to do with babies. She grabbed her hand. "I am so excited for you. And Brett."

Shelly's entire face smiled. "I just thought it wasn't for me. But now my whole mind is changed, and I haven't even had him yet." She sobered. "Will you be there with me? Would it be too hard for you?"

Jill looked down at the baby sleeping on a leaf, stroked it with her finger. "I'd love to." She swallowed. "I only got to hold Kelsey for half an hour."

"You can hold mine anytime you want. You'll be his auntie."

Jill smiled. "I can't wait." But could her heart bear it? She slowly paged through the book again, amazed and enthralled by the beauty of the impossibly small beings, curled up or hunched like caterpillars. The flower parts were artistic, but nothing matched the miracle of those tiny, tiny babies. It rushed in on her so potently. Kelsey's fuzzy skin, her curved, wrinkled arms and little bowed legs, the heel of her foot hardly larger than a thumb.

A chasm of longing opened up for a baby inside her like Shelly's, the flutters and kicks, even the groans and strain of pushing her out, then holding her, holding and never letting go. *Oh, God.* To look into the face of another baby with Morgan's eyes.

She stood up. "I better go."

"Can't you stay and have lunch? Brett's gone and I took the whole day off."

Jill looked out at the silent rain.

Shelly caught her elbow. "You don't want to go out there. Let's put on a chick flick and eat hoagies and ice cream."

Jill laughed. "Sounds pretty good." Twice now, friends had stemmed the tide. Maybe that was God's hand, invisible yet real, loving her through Pat and Gina, Deborah and Shelly. And she needed all the love she could get, since she was having dinner tomorrow night with her parents.

Morgan laughed with Todd as their jeep careened down in front of the giant rolling stone, tipping them into its path, then diving underneath. There was enough little boy in Todd to respond to the magic of Disney in spite of himself. When they finished that ride, Morgan asked Todd and Dana's two sons if they'd had enough.

No, it was back to Splash Mountain, Morgan trailing behind. Bringing the other kids had been a good move. It avoided awkwardness and made it more fun for Todd. What adolescent wouldn't rather have friends along than a thirty-three-year-old man? There had been a few nice moments, and Morgan wondered if Todd was trying to make up for his rudeness.

Morgan boarded the Splash Mountain raft, this time riding with Luke, with Todd and Matt sitting together. He was a little surprised Todd had gravitated so easily to the neighbor boys. He'd have guessed at a prickly personality that made friendship difficult. Maybe it was a vacation syndrome, a nonthreatening, convenient friendship. Maybe it was Luke's and Matt's congenial natures.

They had eaten hours ago and the park would close soon. But the boys were wound up and going strong. It would be hard to match it tomorrow. Maybe Todd would welcome a low-key day after this one. Wishful thinking.

Not until the rides had closed did they join the streams of die-hards leaving the park. Definitely a successful day. They had taken the SUV to comfortably seat the four of them. He drove home, guarding his smiles as the boys talked about the rides and events of the day, picked at each other for being scared of silly things like the Pirates of the Caribbean or the hippos in the jungle ride. Todd seemed quieter now than the other two. Morgan pulled into the neighbors' driveway and let them out.

Their dad, Mark, opened the front door. As Matt and Luke filed inside, he called, "Thanks for taking the boys. They behave?"

"Better than I would have." Although he had been taught courtesy and generally used it, a day at Disneyland with two buddies and a nonparental sort . . .

"Good." Mark smiled, obviously expecting that answer. What if he'd said they were holy terrors?

Morgan waved a hand and pulled across the street with Todd, the quiet of the night closing around them. "Think you'll sleep tonight?"

Todd shrugged. "I see roller-coaster tracks every time I close my eyes."

Morgan caught his shoulder in a companionable grip. "Did you have a good time?"

Todd nodded, then glanced sideways. "Thanks."

Morgan fought not to show his surprise. It was the first time the kid had thanked him for anything—not the movies they'd seen, the things he'd bought, the places they'd gone. Maybe Disneyland was finally big enough. Or the other boys' manners had worn off. "You're welcome."

As he let them into the house, Consuela met them with two mes-sages, though she had normally retired by then. Both were Stan, and Morgan directed Todd to return the call, though it would be late in Colorado. He should have told him what they'd planned and maybe he would have let one night pass without the check-in.

Consuela laid a hand on his arm. "You survived it?"

He smiled at Consuela's choice of words. "I did."

She signed herself with the cross. "Better you on those rides than me."

He cocked his head. "Aw, they're harmless. It was keeping up with three teens that has me weary."

"And your stomach?"

Morgan pressed a hand to his flat torso. "Fine." It had handled lunch and dinner and all the rides without complaint. "I'm making headway."

"Good." She shuffled off to bed.

It was the perfect time for a slow-sipping whiskey on his deck. But he'd promised Todd, and as the kid came back from making his call, there was a light in his eyes Morgan wouldn't dim.

"Did you tell him about it?"

Todd shrugged. "Kinda."

It couldn't have been the long version. "Did you wake him?"

"No. He was waiting up."

Morgan jerked the side of his mouth. "We should have thought of that. It's an hour later in Colorado."

Todd shrugged again. "His choice."

Morgan ruffled Todd's hair. "Better get some sleep."

"What are we doing tomorrow?"

Recovering. "What would you like to do?"

Todd grinned. "Take your boat out."

Morgan considered that. "Sure. If you think you can handle it." He touched his fist playfully to Todd's jaw, but the kid shied and scowled. Morgan withdrew his hand, fingers splayed in surrender. "Let's get to bed."

"I'm not tired."

"Well, I am." He was tired of second-guessing every motion, every word.

"I'll watch a movie."

Morgan considered his collection. He wouldn't have thought twice before Dana's comment. Now he wondered how positive most of the choices would be for a thirteen-year-old kid. "Not tonight, Todd."

Todd's expression darkened, the brows lowering over glaring eyes. "Why do you want me in bed so bad?"

"Because it's late, and I'm tired." *Don't spoil what we've had.*

"So go to bed yourself and leave me alone."

Morgan ticked off in his mind the minutes since they'd come home. Exactly when had the amenable Todd disappeared? When he threw his play punch? How was he to know that would freak the kid out? Was this some power play now?

"If you want to take the boat out, we should get a good night's sleep."

"You won't sleep. You just want me out of the way so you can get drunk."

Fury surged. "I told you I wouldn't drink while you're here."

"Yeah? So what?"

"Are you calling me a liar?" Morgan forced an even tone.

"You'll say anything."

Morgan cocked his jaw. "Go to bed, Todd."

Todd's hands fisted as he stormed up the stairs. That kid could drive anyone to drink. Maybe there were two sides to his dad's story. Morgan ran a hand through his hair. He'd spent the whole day playing Disney tour guide, and this was what he got? It was his house, his life. He wished he hadn't told Todd he wouldn't drink.

But he had. And if he took a drink now, he would be a liar. Oh, wouldn't the kid be smug then? Well, he'd done his time. He could call tomorrow and arrange an early flight back. If Todd wasn't grateful or even appreciative, that was his problem. Morgan took the stairs equally stormily. He was tired, but after he'd stripped and groomed for bed, he paced his room, frustrated.

He had not been so personally scrutinized since leaving home. And it was wearing thin. If Todd would quit projecting . . . but maybe the kid couldn't help it. Morgan opened his door and listened. Nothing. He crossed the hall, put his ear to Todd's door. What was that? Not normal breathing. Crying? He tapped the door, opened it, and leaned in. "Don't throw anything."

Todd sniffed. "Go away." He was huddled in the corner of the room, gripped in his own arms.

Morgan walked in, halted some five feet from him. "What's up?"

Todd didn't answer.

"Is it me?"

Todd shook his head.

"Are you homesick?"

The kid swore.

"I thought we were friends."

Todd swiped his hand under his nose and gasped a jagged breath. "Leave me alone."

"I don't think you want me to."

Todd didn't answer.

"Todd, tell me what's wrong."

"Just stuff."

Morgan sat down. "Your dad?" He anticipated blows.

But Todd nodded, sniffed his running nose. "One time he took me to a carnival. I was excited, but he brought a bottle. He puked on the second ride and hit me for watching. It made my nose bleed, and I got scared and ran away through the booths. He just kept bellowing, and I knew if he found me he'd beat me up." Todd swiped his face again.

Morgan tried not to picture the scene, but it was all too vivid.

"I didn't know where to go. The carnival was closing, and all these guys that looked . . . bad teeth and stuff, were watching me. I thought I could just hide in a ride or something. But when I tried to get on the carousel, Dad caught me. He slapped me so hard I wet my pants."

Morgan's chest constricted. Was that what Todd saw in him? It chilled him down the spine. He reached out and gripped Todd's forearm. "You're out of that now. Stan won't hurt you, and neither would I."

Todd leaned into the wall. "Stan doesn't drink."

Morgan squeezed his arm and let go. "You can go back tomorrow."

"I don't want to." Todd looked up sideways.

Morgan spread his hands. "I don't know what else to tell you. You either trust me or you don't."

Todd rested his head against the wall. "The stupid thing is, I loved him."

"It wouldn't hurt if you didn't."

Todd put his elbow across his knees and buried his face. Morgan moved closer to hold his shoulder while he cried. And Todd's dad had probably loved him, until he'd messed himself up so much he couldn't. Morgan fought a wave of disgust. *You don't even see it.* How much didn't he see? At that moment, Todd was a mirror, and Morgan couldn't help but look.

CHAPTER 34

The next day was perfect to be on the water. They'd lubed on
sunscreen, filled a cooler with watermelon, chips, and turkey
sandwiches, and hit the waves. Now they floated, engine silent,
Morgan's arms tucked behind his head, ankles crossed. Looking sideways at the boy sprawled on the cushioned seat, he felt a fresh stirring
of affection.

He'd been surprised Todd wanted to go out alone without the
neighbor kids. But he was glad. Last night seemed to have opened a
door, and as the honesty poured out, he hoped it would transfer to
Stan as well.

"Do you fish?"

Morgan shook his head. "Nah. But I like seafood."

"Why don't you want to catch it?"

"Most of the fishing done around here is sport fishing. I can't see
battling some creature to the limits of both our strengths just to say I
won."

"You could stuff it and stick it on your wall." Todd picked a scratch
on his leg. "My dad had lots of stuff on his walls."

"He hunted?" Every mention of his dad was worth drawing out.

Todd nodded. "He took me once before Mom left, stuck me in a
tree. I watched him shoot a deer."

That was the first mention of his mother. "What did you think of that?"

Todd shrugged. "He was excited cuz it had four points. But it was all bloody when he cut it up."

"Did you eat it?"

"No. He just took the head and had it stuffed."

Morgan took the chance and pushed a little. "When did your mom leave?"

"Five years ago. I was eight." He pulled up his knees in what Morgan now recognized as a defensive posture.

"Why'd she go?"

He shrugged.

"Your parents had problems?"

Todd slanted him a glance. "Duh."

Morgan smiled. "Do you talk to her?"

Todd shook his head. "She never even called."

There had to be something intrinsically wrong with that picture. What mother could walk away from her own kid? Then his throat constricted. Jill had. She'd birthed their child, then handed her over to strangers. Here you go—special delivery. He stopped that train of thought and nudged Todd with his toes. "You want to drive?"

"What?"

"Take her closer in and bang some waves?"

Todd looked out at the water. "I dunno."

"You can do it." Morgan stood and led him to the helm. He started the boat and showed Todd how to bring it around the direction he wanted to go. Todd would enjoy this, even if he didn't think so at the moment. He just needed encouragement.

He had guessed right. By the time they headed home, he was a tired but happy kid. Now if they could avoid his evening transformation to Spanish Inquisitor, it would be the best day yet.

Jill buttoned the short-sleeved pink cardigan to the circular neck. With the cream-colored loose capris, it was casual but stylish in an understated way her parents would approve—in spite of the sassy haircut that they would not. She had asked to come over for a bit and chat, but Mom had suggested dinner, of course, taking any overture as a chance for overkill. Jill only hoped they wouldn't have lost their appetites by the time she was finished telling them about Kelsey—and worse, Morgan's involvement.

She drove to her parents' modest home, neatly manicured lawn, a few shrubs and flowering pots, a sprinkler in one corner sending a thin oscillating fountain that made her think of the Bellagio. Her skin warmed. How on earth would she get through this? Dad must have a new car. She passed the navy Chevrolet sedan in the driveway. He'd even changed allegiance from Dodge.

She knocked on the door and waited for admittance. Mom arrived all smiles, then eyed her hair. "Oh, Jill. You cut your hair off."

"Only some of it."

"It's so . . ."

Fashionable. Daring. Attractive. Fun.

"Short." Mom pushed the door open. "But it'll grow."

She had just had Crystal trim it up. But Mom's hair was neatly swept back into a stylish twist, as it had been from Jill's earliest memories. "So Dad finally bought a Chevy?"

Mom looked perplexed. "What, dear?"

"The new car." Jill motioned behind her toward the driveway.

"Oh. That's not ours."

Prickles crawled up her back.

"Come on through. I'll introduce you to Glen."

Jill stopped and hissed, "Mom, you didn't."

"Well, when you said you wanted to come, I thought you meant . . ."

Fury surged. "No, you didn't. I said I wanted to talk."

"You said chat. A little get-together that I thought might be just the chance to get to know Glen a little." Could Mom really believe the fantasy world she lived in, where daughters never disappointed?

Jill moistened her lips. Oh, how she wanted to tell them everything right in front of Glen. But of course she wouldn't. She followed her mother to the back patio, where Dad sat with a pleasant-faced man, a little thin and needing some time in the sun, but nice looking nonetheless.

"Glen, this is our daughter, Jill. She's just had her hair cut, so it's different from the pictures."

They'd shown him her pictures? But, then, they were sprinkled around the house. "Hi, Glen." Jill held out her hand.

He stood and took it. "It's very nice to meet you, Jill. Your parents have talked a lot about you, the times they've had me over lately."

"I'm sorry about your wife. It must be very hard to lose someone you love." As she had lost Kelsey and now feared for her life.

"Thank you. It is. But it's been two years, and time does ease the sting."

So you're ready and willing to move on.

"Have a seat, Jill. I'm just finishing in the kitchen," her mom said.

"Oh, I'll help you, then." She didn't leave time for argument but led the way back inside.

Her mother's face sharpened. "I know you didn't expect this."

"Didn't expect it? I said no." Could the fact that she'd refused even enter her mother's mind?

"Oh, Jill, just give him a chance." Her mother's face was so piteously hopeful.

"Don't worry, Mother. I can be polite."

Mom went to the oven and took out a roast. "I'll let your father carve this. The potatoes are in the warming oven. They can be put on the table."

Jill did as she was told, then spent the evening under Dad's searching gaze making small talk, mostly about her work with the kids at school, which Mom elevated to near Mother Teresa's efforts in India.

Glen smiled. "It does take a special person to work with challenged kids. I'm challenged enough with my own." Then he told a couple humorous stories about his eleven- and thirteen-year-old boys.

He did seem like a nice man and hardly looked forty-three. After dinner and a reasonable time over coffee, which Jill did not drink—she would be sleepless enough—he walked her out to her car. "I really enjoyed meeting you, Jill."

She knew what was coming.

"Would it be all right if I called you sometime?"

She took her keys from her purse. "I don't suppose Mom told you I'm not really dating right now."

"Me either. But . . ."

"And I have some things that I really need to focus on."

"Oh. Okay. Well, maybe I'll see you again sometime. Do you go to church?"

"The big one on the corner of Elm."

He nodded. "I've heard the pastor a few times."

"We have three now."

He smiled. "Guess I'm more of a small-church guy."

Where everyone knew everything. She returned his smile. "Well, it was nice meeting you, too, Glen." She pulled open her door and slid in. "Good night."

No one could say she hadn't tried. Mom had probably panicked when Jill mentioned she wanted to talk. Maybe specters of that first horrible revelation had filled her mind, and Glen was the only defense she had. Maybe it was kinder after all to keep them in the dark. The tension she'd held in check all evening washed away, leaving a sense of failure. But she could not be blamed. Pat and Deborah and Gina had meant well with their encouragement, but they did not know how it was. Nothing penetrated Mom's code of silence.

———

Kelsey lay as though run over by a tank, her skin yellow and blistering. Every breath was work, her lungs laboring under the fluid pressing her down. Dr. McGraine's face was blurred as he spoke to her and her parents. "The GVHD has escalated to severe. Her bilirubin and alkaline phosphatase indicate liver damage, possibly treatable by increased levels of Prednisone and cyclosporine, but that is in turn toxic to the kidneys, which are already failing."

He looked at Kelsey, and she wondered if she should not have insisted on receiving all the medical updates with her parents. "I wish I had better news for you, Kelsey. It's a balancing act. One thing that helps here . . ." He held up his left hand. "Hurts here." He raised his right. "We can attack, but that opens new battles."

She nodded. "So there's nothing you can do?"

He shook his head. "I'm not saying that. We will try everything available to us. I just want all of you to understand what we're up against." He turned to her parents, who were holding each other at the side of the room. "I don't recommend raising the drug levels because the pressure on her lungs and heart is already extreme and dialysis can only do so much for the kidneys. But that means in addition to the veno-occlusive disease, the GVHD will probably increase. There may be permanent damage to the liver especially, and the stomach and other soft tissues." Back to Kelsey. "It could burn out within days or continue to escalate."

"Burn out" is exactly how it felt, her skin peeling off, her mouth cracked and bleeding, her belly swollen to twice its size. She drew a slow thick breath. No one had been allowed in except the medical staff and her parents. Her energy was so low she hardly responded to them.

"The best news we have is lack of infection. You're handling that like a pro, Kelsey." He smiled.

She tried to smile back but only shut her eyes. When he left the room, arms closed around her. Not Mom's and Dad's—they knew it hurt too much. But arms so soft and strong and embracing they could only be her Lord's. *It's too much, Jesus. I can't do it anymore. I can't make it good.*

No smile on His face this time but tears in His eyes. The shortest verse in the Bible. *Jesus wept.* She didn't want Him to cry for her. *It's okay. I'll try. If you help me.*

Jill turned off the computer. No message from Kelsey. Nothing since the brief request for a photograph, which Jill had sent immediately. She tried not to read more into it than the fact Kelsey probably didn't feel well and had her Web page to keep up with and her family and friends. Maybe she no longer needed to gripe. Maybe it was all going so well she could only rejoice. And that part she did easily enough with Cinda. The thought encouraged Jill enough to face her day.

Normally the preliminary meetings for the upcoming school year had her focused and energized. This year the tension and uncertainty almost spoiled the anticipation of working once again with her kids. Or maybe her reality had expanded, her focus no longer limited to that small part of her life. Her past had converged with her present, and her future was no longer the day-to-day existence she'd managed before.

As long as she focused on Kelsey healing and Morgan recovering and her own—

The phone rang, and she crossed to answer it. "Hello?"

"Jill, this is Cinda."

Her heart accelerated. "Cinda. Are you home? How is Kelsey?"

The pause seized Jill's belly and twisted. Cinda's voice sounded flat. "No, we're not home, Jill. Kelsey's not doing well."

Jill gripped the counter for support. "Did she reject the marrow?"

"No. Her immune system can't reject anything. It's the opposite. GVHD."

GVHD. Jill had read about it, graft-versus-host disease, Morgan's marrow identifying Kelsey's body as foreign and attacking. "They expected that, didn't they? It was part of it, I thought. An anti-tumor effect and . . ."

"It's life threatening, Jill. They're not sure they can control it. And there are other complications. Liver and kidney failure. She's very weak. But she wanted me to call and ask for your prayers."

No. Jill slid down the kitchen wall. It wasn't possible. Morgan's marrow was supposed to heal her. "Can you give me details so I can address them in prayer?" How could she sound so calm?

"She has acute stomach and intestinal distress, her skin is blistered and sloughing off, extra fluid all over. Also her vision is impaired, and the drugs cause confusion. But the worst is the damage to her vital organs. Her stomach is hemorrhaging. Pray—" Cinda's voice broke. "Pray for a miracle."

Jill sat stunned, unable to fathom so many things wrong with her daughter. She'd imagined, pictured her healing, growing strong, getting well. She pressed a palm to her heart where the ache grew. "Thank you for calling, Cinda. Would it be too much trouble to continue to let me know how she's doing?"

"I'll try."

Jill hung up the phone and gave in to sobs. Everything else paled. It couldn't be happening, but Cinda's voice left no doubt. *Lord, why? She loves you so. How could you do this?* She didn't care that she was questioning God again. Where was the reason in it? If Kelsey's faith counted for nothing, then Shelly was right.

With trembling fingers, she touched the numbers on the phone, got his voice mail. "Morgan, this is Jill. Please call me."

Then she cried until her stomach hurt, her eyes ached, and her throat burned. But none of it was close to what Kelsey suffered. Kelsey wanted prayer, but how could she? Her spirit was a sieve and faith drained through it like water. *God, forgive me.* She had to pray, whether she believed or not.

"Jesus, Kelsey loves you. She trusts you. She knows you. You worked miracles before. You can do it now. Please . . . please . . ."

She didn't care that the meetings had started at school. She stayed on her knees and begged. She had given up her daughter once; she was not ready to do it again. *You can't have her yet. She has too much life to live.* "How can you want her now after what I went through to bring her into the world?" It wasn't fair. It wasn't right. But God was sovereign.

No. She shook her head. She would not accept this. She would batter His door until He heard and answered. She might be helpless, but she would not give up.

Morgan picked up the phone and dialed Jill. The sound of her voice on the message sent ice through his veins. "Jill, it's Morgan."

She said nothing, just broke down and sobbed.

Worse than he'd expected. Something horrible had happened. Kelsey?

He tried to speak, couldn't, then tried again. "Jill, what's wrong?"

"She's so sick, Morgan. So many things wrong. Acute GVHD. I've prayed and prayed but . . ."

GVHD. His marrow attacking Kelsey's system. They had counseled him extensively on not taking the blame for the all-but-inevitable occurrence. Especially with a mismatched transplant. The question was not whether it would occur but how bad it would be.

Jill sniffed. "Cinda called this morning and said liver and kidney failure, soft tissue damage, her skin is peeling off. Kelsey wants our prayers. But, Morgan, I can't believe. I'm so angry and I feel so betrayed. How could God do this?"

The cold spread to his spine. He knew only too well. It was his marrow they'd had the audacity to use. He pressed a hand to his face, thankful only that he'd seen Todd to the airport that morning, which was where he had been when Jill called. "Are you home?"

"Yes."

"Is anyone with you?"

She hesitated, then, "I can't face anyone. If I tell Shelly what I really feel, she'll know what a lie my faith has been."

Morgan swallowed. "This isn't your fault, Jill."

"I want to scream and kick and break something."

"Go ahead."

Instead she started to cry again. Did she have any idea how help-less that made him? "Hang in there." He hung up. With luck he could find a seat on something heading east. Luck and lots of money.

By the time he arrived at her door, he was not sure she was home. Maybe she had gone to Shelly after all, or to Dan. But then the door opened. Her face was dry but bore the streaks and swelling of too many tears shed during the hours since they'd talked. She stared up with a look of astonishment and dismay, then burst once again into tears.

Remembering her neighbor, he stepped inside before pulling her to his chest, then held her. At least this time there wasn't half the country between them. Jill was not a crier, but he supposed too many years of held-back tears left her raw now. He pressed his face to her head and cupped the back of her neck.

After a while she wiped her tears. "I'm sorry. I don't know what to do."

"How quickly can you pack?"

"What do you mean?" She looked up.

"We're going to Connecticut."

She searched his face, incredulous. "Morgan, we can't just show up. They won't let us in."

"Just get your things."

She shook her head. "They didn't ask us to come. Cinda and Roger have enough to deal with, without us trying to force—"

"We're not forcing anything."

She caught his forearm. "I know you, Morgan. You won't stop until you accomplish what you went for."

He gave her a careless smile. "I'm very diplomatic."

"But—"

"She's our daughter, too. If she's in a fight for her life, I want to be there." Needed to be. He cupped her face. "And I know you do, too."

She pressed her hands to his chest. "I don't know if I can." Pain passed over her features. "Maybe God was right, that I could never have handled what was ahead for Kelsey. What if He gave her to Cinda and Roger to . . ." She shook her head. "To undo it?"

Undo it? He tipped her face up and studied it. He'd never seen her so fatalistic and hopeless. That was his role, wasn't it?

She sagged under his hold. "What if we did it to her?"

He gripped her shoulders. "Did what?" His voice was raw.

"Caused her illness, made it happen."

The same thing had haunted him since Jill came to him with the news, but had he faced it, voiced it, given it substance? "Genetic predisposition?"

She looked up. "Or spiritual."

Way too close to the mark.

"What if we set it all in motion? Like David and Bathsheba. They sinned, but did God strike them?" The tendons in her neck were ropes. "Their baby died, Morgan. And Pharaoh's son, and all the firstborn." Her chest rose and fell with hard breaths. "Not by any fault of theirs but by the sins of their parents."

He shook his head, anger brewing. That was taking it too far. God could do as He liked with him, but to make Kelsey pay? "She's not going to die. I won't let that happen."

Jill expelled her breath. "Do you think you can change what God has determined? I've spent today begging for her life. You don't even talk to God."

"I intend to do more than talk."

"What, then?"

He caught her face. "Whatever it takes." Maybe he was crazy, but he was not going to sit back and do nothing. "Don't give up."

Fresh tears washed into her eyes. "It's just that . . . it's like it was before. I wanted her so much. I prayed and prayed, but I was powerless. I had to give her up." Jill started to shake. "But I didn't let them take her. I couldn't bear that. I gave her myself."

Morgan lowered his hands from her face to her shoulders. He didn't want to imagine Jill giving their child away. But for the first time he realized how terrible it must have been. That wound was paralyzing her now, trapping her into a fatalistic surrender.

But he would not go there. He had not believed Kelsey dead for fifteen years to lose her now, before he ever laid eyes on her. "Don't let go of her this time, Jill."

She swallowed but made no reply.

"Come with me."

She closed her eyes. "I don't know what to do."

Once again he drew her into his arms. It would be better by far if Jill came along. She had some relationship, at least, and direct communication with both Cinda and Kelsey. More than that, he wanted her with him. He kissed the top of her head.

She pressed into him and sniffed. "I didn't expect you to come here. I just had to tell you."

He stroked her back between the shoulder blades. "You did the right thing." What if she had called when it was too late? He threw that thought aside. There had to be something more he could do, something to make up for what his marrow was doing to Kelsey's body, some way to stem the tide, reverse the course of nature . . . resist God's will? Yes, if that was what it took.

"Pack your bag, Jill. Come with me."

She stared up into his face. "Okay. But I need Shelly to keep Rascal and . . ." She shook her head. "I can't think."

"Need to cover yourself at work?"

She half laughed. "I missed the planning meetings today. I never even called."

"Give me a number."

"Umm . . . You could talk to Ed Fogarty, the principal." She drew away, then said the number.

He took up the phone and punched it in. A school secretary answered. "Ed Fogarty please." Then, "Mr. Fogarty, this is Morgan Spencer."

"Morgan Spencer of *Fortune* magazine?" The man said it jokingly.

"Actually, yes." He gave him a moment to let that sink in. "But I'm calling on a personal matter. For Jill Runyan."

"Is this some kind of joke? Because I've had all I can take from Ji—"

"It's no joke at all, Mr. Fogarty. Jill's daughter, my daughter, has leukemia and we're flying out immediately to do whatever we can to help her stay alive."

There was silence on the other end, then, "What year did you graduate from Beauview High?"

"Class of '88. You can check the article, and you've probably already deposited my check from the fund-raiser this past June."

An even longer silence. "You said Jill Runyan's daughter? Saint Jill?"

Morgan wished for ten minutes alone with the man. "I also said my daughter. I'm requesting a leave of absence for Jill. She's been devoted to that school more years than you've been in Beauview."

"How long a leave?"

"However long it takes. I understand you're well staffed."

"The truth is, I don't really need Ms. Runyan."

Morgan steamed. This little power trip of a man was the sort he'd love to take down. "That will be Jill's decision."

"Have her see me when she's back. I'll try to work her in."

"She'll have my lawyer's number with her."

"There's no need for threats. Now if you'll excuse me, I have a school to run."

Morgan hung up and turned to Jill, who looked as though someone had sucked the breath from her.

Jill couldn't breathe. Had Morgan just told everyone she knew about Kelsey? All those years of "summer mission trip" concealment, extreme protection of reputation, personal projection of virtue . . . How long before the whole school knew? Minutes, if she knew Ed Fogarty. Then the small-town ripples. Then Mom and Dad.

A chill seized her. Morgan had also identified himself. They would know he'd been there. She should have told them. But they had made that impossible. Slowly air seeped back into her lungs. Fine, then. Let everyone know. She was not ashamed of Kelsey. She was proud of her—desperately, achingly proud. She said, "I'll go pack."

Morgan picked Rascal up from rubbing his legs. "I'll take Rascal to Shelly."

In the bedroom, Jill tossed several outfits into her bag, hardly caring what she packed. Morgan was right. They had to fight. This time she could not surrender. It didn't matter what Ed Fogarty or any of the teachers or anyone else thought. Nothing mattered but Kelsey. Maybe it was wrong, but this time she would trust Morgan.

She bit her lip on the smile that came when she recalled his tone informing Fogarty that she'd have his lawyer's business card. Once again she was thankful for his clout, not that she would sue to keep her position—it would be intolerable to work under those conditions—but that Ed Fogarty would stew over the possibility and experience a little of what she'd gone through these last weeks.

She zipped the bag shut and rolled it to the front room. Should she call her parents? There was time still before word reached them. She could soften the blow and let them know what she was doing. She dragged herself to the phone, dialed, and got the machine. No way was she leaving it all on a message. She hung up. A call from New Haven might not be too late. Or from the airport if there was time.

Shelly came in with Morgan. "You're lucky I was home."

Jill realized that was true. All sense of time and schedule was shot. "Why were you?"

"I've cut down my hours since Brett Junior has made smelling the lollies less than enjoyable." Shelly headed into the kitchen and collected Rascal's food from the cabinet and his feeding dish. "Brett will have to handle the litter box. There's some contamination that is *ix-nay* for pregnant women."

"I'll get it," Morgan said. He fetched the litter box from the bathroom in the hall, then took the rest from Shelly and went back out.

Shelly grabbed Jill into a hug. "Are you all right?"

Surprisingly all her tears must have been spent, or maybe it was just a habit not to show Shelly her pain. Jill nodded. "Did Morgan tell you?"

"Only that you were going to see Kelsey in New Haven."

"Maybe." Jill swallowed the pain. "She's very, very sick."

Shelly studied her face. "So sick she might . . ."

Jill closed her eyes. "I'm praying for a miracle."

"I will, too."

Jill opened her eyes.

"Look, if I can get pregnant when every law of nature says I can't, then maybe there's something bigger than nature."

She squeezed Shelly hard. "Thank you."

When Morgan came back they loaded her bag into the rental car and left Beauview. As they drove once again to Des Moines, Jill broke the silence briefly. "What article did you tell Fogarty to check?" The details of that conversation were still spinning in her head.

"*Fortune* magazine."

"You're in it?"

"On the cover. They called me the success guru, a nickname Noelle coined."

She smiled. "That will frost him. He's of the socialist mind-set, that no one should have more success than the next guy."

"I'd like to see him pay for his computers."

Jill sat back in her seat. *Do not gloat.* It took only a moment before any personal victory she felt was overshadowed by the horrific struggle ahead—and the reality of what they were doing. Thoughts of seeing Kelsey excited and terrified her. She knew better than to expect the imp who had guessed her identity and stretched the rules to contact Morgan. She might not be able to speak to them, if they got in to see her at all. And Jill was not sure they would, even if Morgan was the "success guru."

As it turned out, they had no time to speak of in the airport. Morgan had chartered a jet and the pilot was waiting. Jill had never flown in a private plane, much less a Learjet. Morgan seemed perfectly at ease. She settled into the seat beside him, and he took her hand as though it were the most natural thing in the world.

"You okay?"

She shook her head. "I'm terrified."

"Of the plane?"

She shook it again. She couldn't speak the fear for Kelsey that rose up and filled her. But she didn't have to.

Morgan took her hand and pressed it to his cheek. "We're doing what we can."

She realized that was the key to his success: his persona, probably his nature. Morgan did what he could. She studied him now, seeing him for the first time since his second surprise arrival at her door. "You look tired."

"I had Todd all week."

"At your place?"

He nodded.

"I bet he loved it."

Morgan slid her a glance. "It was like taming a tornado."

She smiled. "Tell me about him." She listened for the next half hour while Morgan regaled their misadventures, starting from their time at Rick's ranch. She glanced over, surprised when he described Todd's reaction to his drinking. She would have thought Morgan might keep that to himself.

"Don't look so smug. Todd dragged his life experience into our interaction. But . . ." His pause was long enough for her to anticipate anything. "It did make me step back and look. That, coupled with my stomach's rejection of anything harder than apple cider, has pretty much clinched it."

"You are thin, Morgan. Are you still sick?"

"Like I said, anything nonalcoholic, even Consuela's tear-jerking green chili, sits like milk in my tummy."

Should she tell him? No, not when he was going to see Kelsey for the first time. A fresh stab to her chest. "Morgan, do you think they'll let us in?"

His swift follow of her switch in topic showed the subject was not far from his own thoughts. He squeezed her hand. "We'll get in."

Why hadn't she let him handle things from the start? Let him take care of her as he'd promised, her and Kelsey. But that wasn't the same. What he'd become at thirty-three was colored in part by the same decisions that made her who she was now—the decision that made them outsiders to Kelsey's struggle. Morgan was determined to get in, but she had to consider Roger and Cinda and Kelsey.

They sat in silence, hands still clasped, Morgan's slow, occasional stroke of his thumb the only communication. She moistened her lips. "I guess Mom and Dad will hear."

He glanced over. "From Shelly?"

A smile touched the corners of her mouth. He really had forgotten small-town dynamics. He had no idea what he'd done to her life. "From you."

"Me." He frowned.

"You told Ed Fogarty about Kelsey and identified yourself. That was as good as saying to the whole town this is why Jill Runyan disappeared fifteen years ago."

The realization penetrated his expression. "Oh." He swallowed. "I guess I should apologize."

"Are you sorry?"

"No." Both his face and tone had an edge.

"I didn't think so."

The lines of his face sharpened and his grip tightened. "Actually I'm glad."

"You don't have to live with it."

"Wanna bet?"

She leaned her head on his shoulder. After a while he rested his cheek against it and gave a soft laugh. "How many hours do you think you have?"

Jill nestled her other hand over his bicep. "I'd guess by dinnertime it'll make juicy table talk."

"Except for your folks."

She shuddered, picturing the aching silence that would shroud their table.

He snorted. "You'd think we sold our souls."

She pressed her face against his arm. "That's pretty much how they see it." Yet hadn't he? Turning his back on God, living in rebellion . . . Was that any worse than the lie she had lived?

He stroked her head. "You don't have to go back. You can stay with me."

She didn't try to pretend that wasn't what she wanted. But it was impossible. Especially now when everything was falling apart. "That would be running away all over again." She almost felt the pain in his sigh and looked into his face. "I don't know how to make it right, Morgan."

He nodded, swallowing, then drew a slow breath. "Then right now we focus on Kelsey."

Appreciation flooded her. Morgan might see himself as wicked and doomed. But did he know how many times he gave precious solace and hope? She should let go of his arm, remove her head from his shoulder. But these moments were numbered, and she would not waste one.

Jill's hand in his was moist as they navigated through the immense hospital. He understood her anxiety. His stomach felt like a boa constrictor had taken up residence, and he was far less certain of his strategy than he let on. He had wanted to communicate directly with the Bensons as Bern suggested. But timing made that impossible. He had no intention of suing for custody or making trouble for any of them. But if he could make the hospital recognize his right to see his own daughter . . . He had finessed situations before, yet none like this. But if he imagined it as the same sort of challenge he faced in business . . . Other people's money was a far cry from his own flesh and blood, but Jill was counting on him.

They reached the oncology center and the secured section where they would have to be buzzed through by permission. He went up to the desk and said, "We're family to see Kelsey Benson."

The nurse looked at him shrewdly. "I'm sorry. Kelsey's in ICU. It's immediate family only."

"I am immediate family." He took out the letter from Bern that announced as unambiguously as Bern had been able that paternity was in question due to false termination of parental rights, failure to serve reasonable notice, and lack of due process. That could bring into question Roger Benson's right to make medical decisions on Kelsey's behalf. Morgan knew no court in the world would interfere with that relationship in this situation, and it felt wretched to even propose it. But if it was the only way they would let him be involved . . .

The nurse looked up with something like malice in her face. "I have no authority to address this. You'll have to speak to the hospital administrator." He was definitely scum in her eyes.

Morgan checked the name tag on her uniform. "Listen, Reba. I'm not here to cause trouble. I only want to see my daughter."

"Well, that may not be possible, Mr. . . . ." She glanced toward the letter to check his name.

"Spencer. Morgan Spencer. I'm the one who donated marrow for Kelsey's transplant. They recognized my relationship when they performed the harvest."

Her expression changed. "Oh."

He caught Jill's elbow. "And this is Kelsey's birth mother."

Jill gave the nurse a smile. "Cinda called me this morning with an update. That's why we're here. To help and support in any way we can." She glanced at him.

He wished now he hadn't played the heavy. Her winsome face was far more effective than his lawyer's letter.

The nurse shook her head. "I'm sure that's the case, but the doctor's orders—"

Morgan pressed his palm to the counter. "Then ask the doctor."

Jill laid a hand on his arm. "Morgan would really like to see his daughter. If you could at least let the Bensons know we're here . . ."

Morgan frowned. He had not wanted to take that tack, to put himself at the mercy of Roger Benson. But maybe Jill was right. What he really wanted was to do everything he could for Kelsey, donate platelets, new marrow, whatever. And just see her.

"You may wait, but I can't guarantee anything."

Jill nodded with such a look of hope that Morgan almost wished he hadn't dragged her into it. He kept her hand in his and led her to a chair.

"I can't sit." She turned to him. "Morgan . . ."

"I'm not forcing things."

Jill licked her lips. "In your world it might not look that way. To the rest of us, a man who walks in as though no one ever stands in his way, with letters from his lawyer and—"

"I just wanted her to know I have legal standing. I never gave it up." He said it gently without malice, understanding now what she had sacrificed. He cupped her elbows. "They need to know I will do whatever it takes to help Kelsey, but I deserve something, even if it's just the chance to know she's really there."

Jill laid her palm against his heart. "She's here." She pressed her own. "And here."

He dropped his gaze, wishing that were enough, then started when the doors opened and the nurse returned with a medically clothed man. Not Kelsey's dad then. Must be the doctor. He let go of Jill as the man approached with purpose.

"I'm Dr. McGraine, in charge of Kelsey Benson's care. Reba's explained your request and I'm afraid it's out of the question. The hospital recognizes the Bensons' parental rights and their complete authority over medical choices for their daughter."

Morgan might have argued, but the man's tone changed.

"We have a very sick little girl who cannot be exposed to anything that might stress or traumatize her situation."

Morgan softened his own stance. "We don't intend to traumatize her. We've been part of this whole process."

"I understand that. But I have a fourteen-year-old patient and two very worried parents to consider. Any decision would be completely up to them."

Morgan drew a breath, but Jill interrupted. "We understand. We only want to do what we can for Kelsey. And let Cinda and Roger know we're here if—"

"How bad is she?" Morgan tried to keep his voice steady.

"I'm sorry. That information is for the family only. If they choose to share it—"

"Jill?" They all turned to the gray-faced man in scrubs coming through the door.

"Roger." Jill's voice was scarcely more than a whisper. She must be reading the man's condition as clearly as he.

Morgan swallowed. So this was Kelsey's dad. Large, slightly hunched, gentle sounding.

Jill asked, "How is she?"

Roger couldn't answer for a long moment. Then he turned to the doctor. "Her breathing's worse. She's really fighting. Isn't there anything more we can do?"

Dr. McGraine glanced at them before answering. "This morning's tests revealed aspergillus infection, which is causing the pneumonia. We're treating with a fairly effective drug, amphotericin B." He kept his face perfectly neutral.

"Is that going to help?" Morgan couldn't stop the question, unused to the communicational nuances in doctor-patient relations. He didn't care; he wanted to know.

Roger eyed him as though he'd just realized he was there. Morgan returned the gaze. "I'm Morgan Spencer."

Roger nodded, his eyes flicking to Jill, then back to him. "I've seen your picture."

Jill stepped between them, a small motion putting only her shoulder in front of his chest but enough to get her point across. "Roger, we came when Cinda called, hoping there was something we could do. Medically or . . ."

Roger spread his hands. "We all want that. I'd give anything. . . ." He choked up and tears filled his eyes. Surprisingly, he returned his gaze to Morgan. "You want to see her."

Morgan's throat tightened painfully, and he nodded.

"She doesn't look . . ."

"I don't care how she looks."

Dr. McGraine intervened. "She's too weak to handle a shock."

Morgan kept eye contact with Roger. "I just want to look at her. I won't say a word." It would be enough for now. Later, he'd tell her all the things he wanted to say.

Roger turned to the doctor with a questioning glance.

Dr. McGraine shook his head, then released a breath. "From outside the observation window."

Morgan grasped that he was being admitted. Something inside him trembled as Jill slipped her hand into his and they were buzzed through the doors. He walked with more confidence than he felt, realized Jill was equally vulnerable and wrapped an arm around her shoulders.

They stopped outside a glass cubicle filled with equipment, tubes, and a bed. In the bed, a person partially covered by a sheet, no way to guess at sex or age, and nothing at all like the elfish pictures he'd seen on her family's walls. Pain like nothing he'd experienced seared through him. "Why is she so swollen?" The words escaped in a whisper. Was this what his marrow was doing to her?

The doctor answered. "Her kidneys are no longer processing fluids and toxins."

Kidneys. Morgan gripped the edge of the window and turned on the doctor. "If hers won't work, I have one to spare. And Jill has another."

Dr. McGraine took a moment before saying, "She can't withstand a surgery. We're pouring platelets into her body, but even so she's hemorrhaging. We can't stop it."

"Then what can you do?" Morgan hadn't meant to holler. Jill gripped his arm, and he forced himself to calm. He turned back to his daughter and noticed the woman at her bedside. That must be Cinda, the one Jill had trusted more than herself to raise their daughter.

Morgan dropped his face to his hand, resting his forehead against the glass. "Is there anything at all?"

Roger said, "Pray." Then he went into the room and spoke to his wife. She glanced up, sent Jill a weak smile, met Morgan's eyes briefly, then returned to her bedside vigil.

The doctor seemed to debate a moment, then left them. Neither one of them moved as he walked away. Implicit was that they could stay there outside the window. Jill slid an arm around his waist, shaking with her silent tears. Morgan held her shoulders, but walls were coming up inside. *You can't take responsibility for the outcome. The odds are only ten to thirty percent that she will survive.* The counselor knew nothing about how impossible that was. His body, which had wrongly created her, was now killing her. And there was absolutely nothing he could do.

Pray. What a perversion that would be.

Kelsey burned. Drawing air into her sodden lungs took more effort than she had strength for. Her mouth was filled with pain from sores that wouldn't heal. Her mind could not focus. Her kidneys did not understand she didn't want this extra fluid.

Her palm sweated in Mom's hand, comfort passed osmotically. She could only think medically, picturing the inside of her body more clearly than the oozing, hairless skin. Images of blood cells mutating, spasming, attacking their companions. Nerves screaming overload messages to her brain that already knew but had no answer. Bones devoid of marrow, hollow, brittle reeds, filling with alien cells that made war on her.

The Lord is my shepherd, I shall not want.

But she did! She wanted smooth skin and hair she could braid. To see Josh again, to laugh with him. She wanted to sing in church, play softball, and run faster than anyone on her team. To hit a home run over the fence. She wanted to sit under the big tree in her yard and crochet blankets for the babies at the crisis pregnancy center. Babies like her who happened by mistake.

He maketh me to lie down in green pastures.

How long since she'd walked between the rows of corn, felt the hot earth between her toes? How long since the rain fell on her outstretched palms? Since she'd spun herself dizzy with the wind in her hair and the song of birds all around? Walls, steel bars, beeping, buzzing, blinking machines and tubes, tubes all over her, though most had been disconnected now.

He restoreth my soul.

Her soul cried, *Jesus. My Jesus.*

Mom's hand tightened, and there was Dad's voice. "Hey, baby. You hanging in there?"

She squeezed, drawing a damp, worthless breath, but no words came.

"She hears you, Roger."

"That's my girl."

She tried to open her eyes. Sometimes she made it.

"It's all right, Kelsey." Mom's voice like chocolate pudding. "Just rest. We're here with you. We're praying."

Yea, though I walk through the valley of the shadow of death . . .

Was this the final valley? How many more breaths must she take? She fought the urge to stop, to simply stop. It wasn't time. There was something, someone . . . She gathered strength and opened her eyes. Mom's face, and Dad. Love surged. But . . . She looked past Dad's shoulder to the window.

Jill. And Morgan. It had to be. Was she dreaming? No, their pain was too real. *Lord.* Her mind could not form the thoughts. But Jesus knew her heart.

She closed her eyes. The room had faded anyway. Angels closed in around her, a brilliant guard backing toward her until the light from their wings illuminated her skin. If she could raise her hand, she would touch the vibrant feathers. *What is it? What are you doing?*

The angels pressed closer, swords raised outward, until no space remained between them and they became a circle of light. The darkness was engulfed in their shimmering brilliance, light pure and beautiful, bathing her as she stood inside their circle. She could no longer see the enemy, yet somehow she knew it was there, stronger and more malevolent than before. Why didn't they fight? Why had they drawn back, crowded into her like a bright cocoon?

We're losing the war. The thought formulated and clung.

One massive seraph turned to look over his shoulder. *We will guard you to the end.*

But what about the others? Mom and Dad, and Jill and Morgan?

Their battle has just begun.

She wanted to help, to comfort. But she couldn't penetrate the circle of light. A moment of fear.

Again the seraph addressed her over his vigilant pose. *Do not be afraid. You will not be alone.*

And she knew that without question. *I'm not alone. I'm never alone.*

And then He was there, standing above her, and the seraphim had dropped a knee and pressed their swords to their breasts.

Talitha kum. Kelsey heard the words in her heart. Its beating no longer blocked them. *Come where, Lord? Where do you want me?*

At the answer, longing became joy. Such joy.

Little girl, arise.

She lifted her hands toward him and they were light, so light.

Come.

For one moment doubt stirred. Tears? Yes, but not hers. The tears of those she left behind. *I'm sorry. I have to go. You must see. I have to. I want to.*

Then joy. Only joy.

36

Jill stood at the window when the room changed, a machine sounding, Cinda's head dropping, her shoulders shaking with tears, Roger closing in. Kelsey's glance had been so brief, but she knew it was goodbye. She should be glad the suffering was over, but a grief too wrenching for tears tore her insides.

People passed into the room and the curtains were drawn, leaving her reflection and Morgan's on the glass. She sagged against him. *Oh, God.* His head still rested against the pane, and she knew it was more bitter still, since he had nothing but one brief conversation and that single glance.

He turned to her, eyes like broken glass. "I'm sorry."

She shook her head. He could not take this on himself.

"Let's get out of here." He caught her hand and walked her out of the secured hall and through the passages of the hospital to the valet parking, where he turned over his ticket without a word. Jill might have stayed and offered a word to Cinda and Roger, but it was probably best that they simply go.

Tears streamed unbidden from her eyes as Morgan drove them back to the airport. When would she realize that it was over? Her mind knew, but the rest of her was numb. Like a soldier on the battlefield who has no idea his limb is missing, she couldn't even question why.

The sun was setting when they reached the airport, and Morgan buffaloed an employee into finding a pilot to fly them back on whatever charter plane they had. It was dark when they landed and took a taxi into Beauview. A light turned on in Mr. Deerborne's window as Morgan paid the driver and walked her inside. Jill was so far from caring what her neighbor or anyone else thought about Morgan going in with her at one-thirty in the morning.

They sat together on the couch and after a while they dozed. It seemed disrespectful to give in to sleep, yet her system was functioning on such a subnormal level it was inevitable. She woke with her head pressed into Morgan's neck, his arm heavy across her shoulders. As soon as she stirred, he opened his eyes. They pulled apart, and she looked into his face without words. He reached up and cupped her cheek, then let his hand drop.

She cleared her throat. "You need coffee."

"Don't worry about it."

"I can . . . I have . . ."

He closed her hand into his. "There you go again."

She pressed her brows together. "I want to do something."

"You can't." The poverty in his tone this time was pure desolation.

She started to cry. Kelsey couldn't be gone. All these years knowing she was out there, growing, learning, living. Jill pressed her hands to her face, sobbing. Morgan's hand warmed the back of her neck, but nothing penetrated the chill inside her. Their daughter was dead.

Morgan waited for Jill's sobs to ease. Then he let her go and went into the bathroom. He heard her crying again, mourning Kelsey with everything in her. He could not get the image of his daughter out of his mind, her bloated body, angry blistered skin, but most of all the eyes she'd opened and turned to him. His eyes.

She had known he was there, but he'd been utterly helpless to stop her dying. He scrubbed his face and wiped it dry, then went back out and stood behind the couch. Jill's sobs had become weary sighs. She needed someone who could do something, help her in a way he could not.

He had nothing to offer. Everything he'd accomplished was dust. He had no control over anything that mattered. It was all a joke. The very marrow in his bones had failed. When she took a turn in the bathroom, he went to the kitchen and picked up the phone, flipped Jill's book open to Shelly's entry and punched in the number. To the man who answered, he said, "Yeah, is Shelly there?"

The guy hollered to someone in the room. "Brett, where's Shelly?" Then he came back on. "She's asleep. Who's calling?"

"Is this Dan?"

"Yeah, who's—"

"Jill needs someone with her." He glanced behind him to make sure she was still in the bathroom.

"What's the matter? Is she okay?"

"Please send Shelly over." His throat closed on the next words, but he forced them out. "Kelsey's dead."

The silence on the other side of the line told him Dan understood. Morgan hung up, picked up his bag beside the door, and went out. He walked along the sidewalk to the street, then took the route he and Jill had run. At the Starbucks he could call a cab in from Des Moines.

———

Jill came out of the bathroom, more composed if not peaceful. Morgan didn't need her falling apart. His grief matched hers. She stepped into the hall, pushing the hair back from her face. Dan stood in the main room and turned when she entered. She searched the living space with her glance. "Morgan?"

Dan said, "He called for someone to be with you."

Fresh pain. How could there be more? She caught the back of the couch. Dan hurried around and clasped her elbow. Where had Morgan gone? And why?

"Come and sit."

Would he leave without saying good-bye? Now that Kelsey was gone, he had no use for her? Maybe he went for coffee. But her eyes fell to the place he'd left his bag. She sank to the couch with Dan's help.

"Jill, I'm so sorry."

She nodded silently, fresh waves of pain too deep for tears. Shelly took over for Dan when he left with Brett for work, keeping her company and for once not forcing conversation. She handled phone calls until Jill asked her to unplug it altogether. She could not make herself function, and the phone was a constant reminder that all around her, life was happening. But it shouldn't be. Why had Morgan gone? And why, why had Kelsey died? It was all so useless.

Shelly brought her a cup of broth and Jill did manage to swallow it. She turned to her friend. "You were right. Faith changes nothing."

Shelly caught her hands and held them. "It helps you bear it."

Jill nodded. Maybe. But right now she didn't believe she could. Especially when Shelly opened the door to her parents. *Lord God, I can't pretend anymore. I can't.*

"Jill, I've tried to call you for two days." Mom stepped inside and took one look at her face. "So I heard right."

What had they heard, that the word was out? That people knew she'd had an illegitimate child, that she'd seen Morgan? Surely not that her daughter had died, that Morgan had done everything possible to save their child, then stood like an outcast for one brief glimpse before she died.

Jill had not risen from the couch. She hardly had the strength to hold back her tears. Her parents' indignation was a drop in the well of her grief.

Shelly gave her a quick hug and whispered, "Sorry."

Jill formed a thin smile. "Come back later."

Dad took the giraffe chair while Mom joined her on the couch. Dad cleared his throat. "I guess you know in a town this size secrets are hard to keep."

Did he have any idea how hard? What it cost her to pretend, to hold her shame and sorrow inside so tightly she could not experience joy and relationship? Mom searched the townhouse with her gaze. "Is he here?"

Jill slowly turned her head. "No. But if he were, I would beg him to stay."

"Oh, Jill, why?"

"Because after Kelsey, he's the best person I know."

Dad cleared his throat. "There's no question he's done well for himself. *Fortune* magazine and all that."

"No, not all that, Dad. I'm talking about what's inside him. How he helps people."

Mom huffed. "Well, he certainly didn't help you. Coming back here and destroying everything we've done to keep—"

"The truth from being known?"

"To keep you safe from the consequences of your mistake."

Jill's heart split. "The consequence of my mistake was a beautiful girl with features like mine and Morgan's deep blue eyes. She spent half her life battling a terrible disease but used her suffering to give others hope and tell them about the love of Jesus. Get on the Web; read Kelsey's Hope Page. See for yourself the consequence of my mistake."

"We're not condemning the child." Dad used his deacon's tone.

She turned to him. "And even though we lied to Morgan, let him believe I had destroyed his child, falsified information to obtain a termination of custody, and gave her away without his knowledge, he donated his bone marrow to try to save her. He paid a third of a million dollars in medical expenses—"

"He could afford it," Mom murmured.

Jill spun, staring in disbelief.

Mom dropped her gaze. "I'm not criticizing."

"You've done nothing but criticize him since the day you met him."

Mom shook her head. "Because I knew he was trouble."

"You judged him by his walk."

"He was so worldly."

Dad said, "We are to be in the world but not of it."

Jill turned to her father, enunciating each word like a knife blade. "Morgan's housekeeper lived in a city dump. Her husband and sons died from it. His personal assistant was almost killed by her boyfriend. He moved the office to his home and made a safehouse of his guest quarters for her. He befriended an angry foster kid and helped him believe in himself."

Dad spread his hands. "That's all well and good—"

"Morgan doesn't profess his faith, he lives it."

Both her parents were silent. Mom played with her fingernails, then looked up. "The question is what do we do now?"

Jill looked from one to the other. "What do you mean?"

Her mother moistened her lips. "People will want to know if it's true." Now Jill was struck dumb as Mom continued. "It was Morgan who told Ed Fogarty."

Lord God. Would they make him a liar? "He told Ed Fogarty the truth."

Dad clasped his hands piously. "Don't you care that your name is ruined? You teach Sunday school, Jill."

She sank back against the couch, thinking of her friends, how they'd reached out to her. "I'm not the only person who's made mistakes. I'm not worse than anyone else in this town, and I'm tired of believing I am."

Mom reached a hand to her arm. "We're not saying that."

"You've been saying it since the day I told you I was pregnant."

Dad drew himself up. "Well, it isn't something you should be proud of."

Jill's throat hardened. "Maybe not the way it happened. But I'll tell you what I am proud of. I'm proud of the child Morgan and I created! I'm proud of the lives she touched and her brave witness to truth and hope and love." Tears poured from Jill's eyes. "Yesterday I watched her die. Today I don't really care what people think of me." She pulled her arm out from under her mother's hand. "Would you please leave so I can mourn my child."

Mom looked as though she'd been struck, and for a moment Jill thought she would break down and beg forgiveness. There was regret in her eyes when she stood with Dad and walked to the door. He turned. "I know you think we're insensitive. You've resisted instruction and pushed the limits from the day you were born. Cheerleading. Flag football. Dances, dates, sex before marriage. That's not who we are."

Jill crumbled inside. "Then shake the dust from your shoes when you leave my home."

Mom opened her mouth to speak, but Dad caught her elbow and ushered her out. Jill pressed her hands to her face and cried.

———

When Morgan left the airport, he drove the Vette along the highway toward home but on impulse kept going through Santa Barbara, into the green hills with clumps of trees, all the way to the San Luis Obispo Mission. He paid the donation and went inside without a tour, just walking through to the chapel. Somewhere there had to be an answer. The question would burn his soul to ashes. *Why, God?*

Another tourist stood alone in the cool quiet of the place, and Morgan noticed the cross on his lapel. "Are you a Christian?"

The man turned and nodded. "Yes, I am."

"Can I ask you a question?"

The man shrugged. "Sure."

"Why does God make the innocent pay for the guilty?" He gave him Jill's biblical examples, then the agonizing one from his own life.

The man nodded slowly. "As C. S. Lewis put it, it's the 'problem of pain.' It doesn't seem right that a loving God could inflict or allow pain. Those were Old Testament examples, before the blood of Jesus covered our sins. Now suffering is the purest prayer there is, a perfectly good God allowing us to share in His redemptive work."

Morgan took in the words. The image of Kelsey dying filled his mind. Pure? Perfect? Good? Pain like fire rushed in his veins. He turned and walked out. Heading south, he redlined the Vette down the highway, then the curving coastal road. His marrow had burned the life out of Kelsey, and God called it good and redemptive? He swung around a produce truck, saw the VW bug in the opposite lane and veered back, but his speed was too high. The Vette left the road and plunged over the side.

Rick took the phone from Noelle. "Hello?" His stomach plunged like lead inside him as he listened, strangely unprepared for what he heard. He'd had no sense, no urge to pray, no burden weighing on his spirit. "How bad is it?"

"He's still in surgery, but his condition is critical, his injuries extensive."

How long had he anticipated this call, though he'd always expected it in the middle of the night. "Have you contacted any other family members?"

"Yours was the first number we located in his wallet."

Rick rubbed his face. "I'll call the others." He hung up and took Noelle's hand. "It's Morgan. He's crashed the Vette."

She searched his face. "It's bad, isn't it?"

He nodded. "Let's pray." They took the time to bring Morgan before God, pleading for healing, protection, and skill for the doctors. Then Rick called home.

Five hours later they gathered in the hospital. Morgan was out of surgery but had not been upgraded. The doctor came out to talk with them. She gave them a frank smile. "First let me say, by rights he should not be alive. If the car had come down on the rocks in any other position, he would have been killed instantly."

Rick held Noelle to his side, hoping the anxiety and dread obvious in her face and posture would not affect the baby inside her. It was bad enough they had flown with her due date so near. The stress and fear could not be good.

"As it is, he's sustained massive trauma to the chest and abdomen, major organ damage, fractures, and some lacerations. I can't tell you yet which way this will go."

"No head injuries?" Dad's voice quavered.

"Nothing major. Bruising from the air bag, minor lacerations. Brain function is normal, but we've induced a coma to promote stabilization."

Rick glanced at his mom and read in her face the worst of her fears playing out before her. *Lord, this is up to you. All things according to your perfect purpose and power. Don't take Morgan, yet, with his heart unturned. Give us time to reach him.*

When Morgan was brought out of recovery into ICU, they took turns at his bedside, since there were so many of them. Rick worried now for Tara, who'd always been the closest to her big brother and was clearly distraught. Her first sight of Morgan had brought a wail to her lips, and he wondered if they should have left her with friends. But she would not have stood for that. Not when it was Morgan in that bed.

Rick bent and kissed her head, and she looked up with a desperate smile. "He's going to be okay, Rick."

He smiled back. "We're storming the gates, aren't we?" When the nurse came in to get his vitals and check the monitors, Rick asked, "How high was the blood alcohol?"

She checked Morgan's chart. "No alcohol, no drugs."

Rick stared at her a moment. "None at all?"

She let the clipboard drop back against the bed. "A trace of caffeine."

Then why? The policeman who'd met with them had described a probable speed of over a hundred miles per hour before the car left the coastal road. Why would Morgan drive like that unimpaired?

Therese and Tara sat with him while the rest of them went to the cafeteria for dinner. Rick posed the question, and they batted around a few thoughts. Then Mom said, "Has anyone heard anything about Kelsey?"

Something stirred inside Rick at her words. "Would you like me to find out?"

She nodded. "This has been a critical time for Morgan with the transplant and everything. Maybe . . ." Her words faded away.

Rick searched Morgan's wallet for the card Jill had given him. It was there, next to a small copy of her senior picture. He found a phone and dialed the number. It rang twelve times before he hung up. No answers from there.

Overnight, they upgraded Morgan's condition to serious because the internal bleeding had subsided. The family set up a regular rotation, though the staff had informed them he would not regain consciousness for days, not until they had control of the many life-threatening injuries within him.

The bruising on his face blackened both eyes, and there were myriad superficial glass cuts. But it was his torso that had taken the brunt of the engine and steering wheel, trapping him and requiring the jaws of life to cut the car away. His collarbone was shattered and his sternum had multiple fractures, as did his left arm and leg. They had surgically repaired the punctured stomach and colon and spleen and removed part of his liver and his entire left kidney. That, and the bruised heart and lungs, warranted the induced coma.

Rick took his turn with Morgan in the middle of the night, accustomed already to spending such times in prayer when necessary. He insisted Noelle guard her strength and make use of the nearby suite they had rented to use when not on watch with Morgan. Rick looked at his older brother, ventilated and intravenously receiving both the drugs that kept him comatose and the nutrients he needed.

"What were you doing, Morgan? I thought you were coming around." He shook his head. "I should have said more, prayed more, done something." Well, he could pray now, pray hard, stand in the gap.

Morgan floated in a sea of soft gray down. The uncertainty of his position in space troubled him. He had so little sense of self. Had he left his body and floated now with no destination, no purpose? Was this what there was after death? Was Kelsey out there somewhere?

An image of Kelsey wholly different from the one haunting him in his last conscious moments appeared. She was vibrant, angelic, glowing with health and purity. She said nothing, but her smile sank in like glycerin, dissolving the memory of her tortured body. Her gaze was so sweet it stabbed.

I'm sorry, Kelsey. I never meant to hurt you.

The peace in her face stilled his mind and a single thought took shape. *Jesus loves you and so do I.*

Why? When he'd been belligerent and rebellious, going his own way and daring God to follow. Why would Jesus love him when his whole life was vanity? It was Kelsey who'd been good and precious. His marrow had destroyed her.

But her smile was radiant. *Jesus loves you.*

Then she was gone and he floated again, cool gray waves of mercy enfolding him, rocking him with a smooth, ceaseless rhythm, carrying the words back and forth, bathing him. *Jesus loves you. Jesus loves you.*

No simple comfort—instead, a sense of awe and deep unworthiness. Reverence and fear. He could not take in the sense of her words, but the years of blaming God came back in his face, his bitterness, his striking back. *Jesus loves you.* That was incomprehensible, but he suddenly wanted to love Jesus, to serve and follow again. To stop running, stop fighting. Utter surrender.

Other images came and went, Mom and Tara, Dad and each member of his family. He almost heard Rick's voice. And there was Noelle, ripe with child. She shouldn't be there, sounding so concerned. He wanted to squeeze her hand and tell her to go home.

But mostly he floated. Gray mist filled his mind and lungs and being, making breathing a struggle. Kelsey's last fight came clear, and the pain of it infused him, each heavy breath a reminder that hers had ceased. His heart ached as it labored, and there was other pain, though he barely touched it.

It was harder now to stay in the gray cocoon. It grew brittle and cracked open. Morgan blinked in the light. Dad was beside him, pressing his hand between his. The features waved, then cleared. Morgan tried to speak, but his throat felt stripped.

"Welcome back, son."

Morgan drew in the cool air fed into his nostrils. He swallowed. Why was Dad there? But before he could ask, others filled the room, working around him like a colony of ants, moving, touching, talking. Dad was on the phone, and soon Mom was there, as well. Had he dreamed the others?

No. When they moved him to a different room, his sisters came, and Rick and Noelle. It was to Noelle he finally spoke. "You should not be here."

She leaned down and kissed his forehead. "I'm fine. You're the one we're worried about."

"Heart of steel."

She smiled. "I believe it now. Your doctor's mystified."

"No mystery."

"Basically a miracle." Mom kissed his cheek from the other side.

A miracle. For him? Why? Why not for Kelsey? He closed his eyes, fresh pain leaking from his pores. *Jesus, why?*

"I want to talk to him, too."

The insistence in Tara's voice twitched the corners of his mouth. "Come here, imp."

She pressed her cheek to his. "You scared me to death."

He winced inside. She had no idea.

Rick spoke from the foot of the bed. "We're just glad you're back."

Was he? He would have traded his life for Kelsey's, no contest. Maybe he'd tried to. He had a momentary flash of Kelsey's angelic face. Certainly she participated in God's redemptive work. That much had come clear.

A woman with straight shoulder-length blond hair and pert features joined them. "Well, Mr. Spencer. How do you feel?"

He looked down at his casted and bandaged body. "A little beat up."

"A little?" She raised an eyebrow.

He tried to shrug. Big mistake. "Maybe more than a little."

She explained to him the seven-hour surgery she had performed and the condition they deemed him in currently. "You have a long recovery ahead. But you're very lucky to be with us at all."

Morgan gave her the smile she expected.

Rick said, "God's not finished with him yet."

It was not comforting. But then he realized it was. His old cynicism couldn't withstand the vision of Kelsey's sweetness. Maybe it was time to listen, to at least try to understand.

Morgan closed his eyes, weary enough to slip away again to that place of waves and gauze. *Jesus loves you.* But why? What had he done to deserve it?

Jill had tried to call Morgan's cell phone to tell him about the funeral. The message that it was not in service was all she got. When she called his house, Consuela said they hadn't heard from him since he left to see Kelsey. Jill hadn't had the energy for more. If he wanted to disappear, let him.

They had brought Kelsey's body home from New Haven and now almost a week after she'd died, they were laying her to rest. Jill stood at the graveside after an incredible service honoring a life that had touched so many others. The hall had been filled with cards and photos of cancer kids who still lived and those who had died, but all had been given hope by Kelsey's faith.

Jill still could not believe Kelsey was gone, but there was the casket, the cloth-covered grave. No more e-mails. No late-night calls. No chance to introduce her to Morgan. Not even the hope that somewhere in Des Moines her little girl thrived.

Jill's soul was barren. *I know you're with Jesus now. I'm glad your fight is over. But I miss you so much.* The brief moments Jill had experienced were precious enough to know a dreadful loss. She could not begin to fathom the pain Cinda and Roger must know, having shared every moment of Kelsey's life.

At the end of the ceremony, Cinda approached. Jill wanted to say something profoundly comforting. But all she could manage was, "How are you and Roger bearing it?"

Cinda hugged her. "The sorrow may last for the night, but His joy comes with the morning. I cling to promises like that."

Jill's heart filled with tears. "Thank you for letting me know her."

Cinda smiled. "That was mostly Kelsey's doing."

Jill nodded, the tears overflowing her eyes.

"She wanted you to have this." Cinda held out a manila envelope. "She asked me to give it to you if she couldn't."

Jill took it, breath stilling. One last message from Kelsey? "Thank you." She carried it to the car, sat a long moment in thought. She wanted to open it right then but didn't. When she was home, she would open it and treasure each word. She forced herself to drive the speed limit and pay attention to the road. Dan had offered to go with her, but she'd needed to do this alone. She made it home and went inside.

Heart trembling, she dropped to the couch and opened the envelope. There were three items inside. A sealed envelope with Morgan's name on the outside, the painting he had sent her, and a letter for her. Kelsey must have written it on her laptop and printed it out. It was so like her e-mails Jill smiled painfully.

> *Hi, Jill. This is one of those "if you're reading it I'm not around" letters. I guess it might be hard for you to read, but there are things I wanted to say, and I might not have the chance. First is, thank you so much for not aborting me. I know it wasn't easy for you to go through what you did, but you gave me life. Maybe you're thinking it would be better if you hadn't, since I didn't get to live very long. Don't think that.*

Jill sucked in a sob and pressed her hand to her mouth. Reliving Kelsey's suffering in dreams and pensive moments, she had thought it.

My life was not a waste. I know I lived for a reason. I've done what I was created to do. I served my Jesus the best I could, and I think others have hope because of me. I might have wanted a different life, a healthy one. But Jesus knew better. So don't be sad for what I've lost. Be happy for what I've found.

Thank you for letting me e-mail my gripes and complaints. It helped a lot to be honest, and I liked hearing about you and Morgan. My secret prayer is that you will be there for each other. I know you love him still, and he can't help but love you. I'm writing him a letter, too, but my sense is he'll have a harder time. Please help him to know Jesus loves him.

Jill pressed her eyes shut. Even dying, Kelsey's concern was for others.

Also, I'm giving you his picture. I don't think he'll mind. It gave me comfort to see his smile and know he wanted to help. Things don't always work out the way we want. The trick is to want the way they work out. I love you and Morgan. Thank you for all you did.

Jesus loves you and so do I!
Kelsey

Tears streamed as she sat and held the letter, reading it again and again. *The trick is to want the way they work out.* God's will. To want it. Want it. Jill swallowed. *Lord . . .* She couldn't form the words, but her intent was there. *Help me to want your will.* And then she voiced it.

She took the painting of Morgan from the envelope and stared at his face. Noelle had captured him so well. She hoped wherever he was he could find that smile again. But what should she do with his letter? She turned it over and found the sticky note. *Jill, please give this to Morgan personally.* Well, that changed things. No stamp and quick delivery to his P.O. box.

She picked up the phone and was told again his cell was out of service. Consuela answered the home phone, but the message was no help. "Señor Morgan is not home. No, I can't say where he is. I'm sorry."

Frustrated, Jill called his parents. Someone had to know where he was, and she had to find out, if she was going to fulfill her daughter's last request. Morgan might not want her to know his whereabouts, but . . . no answer, no recording. She found Rick's number through information, but there was no answer there, either. Had Morgan's whole family disappeared?

She set the letter aside, determined to try again every day if she had to. After six days, she reached Celia and was almost too flustered by an actual response to speak coherently. "I need to find Morgan. I have a letter for him from his daughter, but Kelsey wanted me to give it to him in person."

Celia was silent a long while. Then she spoke frankly. "You'll have to wait."

"I don't understand."

"Morgan is not able to see you."

Jill swallowed the swelling in her throat. "Won't he want Kelsey's letter?"

Again Celia was quiet. Then she said simply, "Not yet."

"But—"

"Morgan needs time to heal. Please give him that."

Jill hung up. They would all need time to heal. She looked at the letter she held. Maybe it wouldn't help, would only make it harder for him. She couldn't believe Kelsey's words would be anything but wonderful, and yet if he wasn't ready . . .

She pressed the envelope to her heart, willing and almost grateful to hold Kelsey's missive awhile longer. Though she didn't know the words inside, she guessed the message. When Morgan was ready . . .

CHAPTER

37

Noelle stepped out the door and into the glory of new green aspens and dark pines that climbed the crag, crisp blue sky, appreciating the scent of sage and the stable smells of horse manure, hay, and leather. She breathed it in, then turned her attention to the porch of the nearest cabin.

Morgan sat on the stoop, one hand outstretched to steady little William Henry Spencer. She had wanted to name the baby for Rick, but he honored both granddads instead. The toddler took a dive into Morgan's lap and he laughed, huddling over the gurgling boy, then lifting him to one knee.

She strolled toward them, her finger marking the page in the magazine she carried. Morgan glanced up with the distant, sifted look she was growing accustomed to. He smiled. "This boy is half wiggleworm."

William bent himself out of Morgan's lap and all but tumbled off the stoop. He pushed his bottom to the air, then rose back to his feet and hurtled toward her. She scooped him into her arms, the magazine flapping against his back. Little Will had Rick's walnut eyes and fine golden curls, a beautiful baby and precocious.

She settled onto the stoop beside Morgan, and immediately Will wiggled out of her arms and toddled off to examine something in the gravel. He had walked early as all Spencers did, she'd been informed, and was now one week shy of nine months. He toddled back and patted Morgan's knee with both palms, just to tease since he had every intention of escaping the moment Morgan caught him.

Morgan got him by the finger and Will tugged, then plopped down on his diapered-and-blue-jeaned bottom when the finger slipped free. "Let that teach you." Morgan grinned, then turned to Noelle. "Hi."

"I have something to show you." She opened the magazine across her knees and Morgan's face smiled out. It was actually the cover of his book at a slight angle across the glossy page. The caption read: *Money Magic by the Success Guru* a NY Times Bestseller, but has the turnaround magician done a vanishing act?

Morgan's mouth pulled sideways in a half smile. He glanced over the article that followed, which she had already read.

"Climbed to number two, huh? Can't seem to fail if I try."

"It's because they put your picture on the cover."

"It's because people want a magic purse that fills itself with gold."

She nudged his shoulder with hers. "Sounds like your next book. *Money Magic for Kids.*" When they had brought Morgan back to the ranch to recover, he'd surprised them all by accepting an offer from a publisher who'd been pursuing him for a year. Morgan worked maniacally, pouring out his knowledge, hypotheses, and savvy with a humorously irreverent tone, along with a few kicks at certain highbrow consultants who preferred to keep people mystified.

He told her he had written the book in his head during the weeks of convalescence in the hospital, a repository of his professional knowledge, which read, to Noelle, like a collection of anecdotes. She could see Morgan clearly through it all, and his verbiage was accessible and honest, but all the knowledge on the pages didn't account for Morgan's ability. That was something inside him that theories and experience couldn't match.

Nonetheless, he had completed the manuscript in three weeks. The publisher had pushed production through, and the book hit the stores two months ago, soaring to number four on the bestseller list, then climbing steadily. The New York house was ecstatic, but their expectation of speaking tours and book events had evaporated when Morgan refused to leave the ranch and in fact remained completely isolated from all but his close family. Now it seemed they had decided to capitalize on that with such phrases as "elusive mogul," "mysterious departure," and her favorite: "vaporous wizard."

She looked at him now, solid and real, yet the term did not seem too farfetched. It was as though he had transferred his old self to the pages of his book, then stepped away. It was almost a year since Kelsey had died and he had nearly followed her to the grave. She had not asked him if the accident was intentional, but she wondered. His injuries were healed, the scars of surgery fading, she knew, from the times he worked shirtless with Rick. Yet he was changed.

He had not taken a drink nor spent his nights at the Roaring Boar. He had no car with him at the ranch, yet he'd rarely voiced frustration or boredom. The quiet he once avoided seemed his solace now. The biggest surprise had been that he went with them to church without arguments or even his cynical amusement. From Rick's library he read C. S. Lewis's *The Problem of Pain* and Augustine's *Confessions* and the Bible Rick ordered for him. Yet for all that he seemed . . . fragile.

He handed her back the magazine and lifted Will to his chest. The baby tucked his head against Morgan's neck and stuffed his thumb into his mouth, sucking it in the pre-nap mode Noelle recognized so well. More times than not her son went to sleep against the chest of his daddy or his uncle. Morgan rocked him gently now, one hand cupped behind the baby's neck.

A pang tugged her heart, recalling the anguish he had tried to hide when she and Rick brought Will home. But instead of shrinking from it, he had spent every chance he got holding and nurturing her son. As much as she loved his connection, it was time for him to look ahead.

"What are you going to do, Morgan?"

Once he would have given her a flippant answer. Now he just stared across the yard and said, "I don't know."

"You need another project."

He smiled. "Denise has threatened to quit if I keep paying her to do nothing."

"It's hardly nothing to fend off the offers and requests of everyone who wants something from you."

He nodded, pressing his cheek to little Will's head. The baby's eyes were doing the slow blink. Morgan was such a part of Will's life, how would it be if he actually did go back to California and took up his previous whirlwind existence? He had lost a lot of money to Kelsey's expenses and more in canceled contracts afterward. He had sold assets rather than taken new contracts, though now the book had taken off.

It wasn't really work Morgan needed. It was some deep healing that had not come through the accident nor his subsequent return to faith. She didn't think it was an act. He appeared truly reverent, yet also . . .

chastened. His old fire was banked, and while he reached out and helped in more ways than she could count, financially, physically, and emotionally, his need never diminished.

"Do you think about Kelsey still?"

He swallowed. "Not as much."

"Jill?"

"No." He looked away, and Noelle's spirit stirred. Why would he lie?

With one finger, she stroked her baby's velvety cheek. "I should put him in his bed. Too many more naps on your chest and he'll never learn to sleep lying down."

Morgan eased the baby into her arms and she stood up. The magazine pages fluttered in the breeze. She went inside, up the stairs, past her studio to the golden-hued room decorated in chubby bears and pine trees and laid him in the crib Rick had designed and built.

"You're a blessed little baby, Will."

He scooched his bottom up and kept sucking. She pressed a kiss to her fingers and touched it to his cheek, then went downstairs to the kitchen. How could she find the address? Maybe Celia?

Jill stopped still at the table in the bookstore. She didn't usually peruse that section, but in passing by, she could not miss the dynamic display of books bearing Morgan's face. He'd written a book? And not only that, a bestseller? Naturally.

Her heart thumped within her chest as she picked it up, staring into the eyes that had last looked so shattered. This smile was confident and wry and a little droll. Probably his business persona. If the picture was new, the last ten months had been good to him.

A woman stopped beside her. "I'd buy that just to have him on my coffee table. Mmm-mmm."

Jill smiled, but inside the ache opened up. What had she expected? Letters, flowers, cards for her birthday? But not one word. And each time she checked, Consuela, Denise, and Celia continued to insist they were not at liberty to give his whereabouts, nor did he wish to receive messages. It couldn't be clearer.

Jill set the book down. On her table it would bring nothing but pain. She passed on in the direction she had intended and found what she needed for school. Amazing how that had worked out—Pam not only resigning the directorship but quitting altogether. Jill refused to listen to the gossip of a failed relationship between Pam and Ed Fogarty. Given that he was married, it would not be fair to make any assumptions, though others had no qualms. She knew what it was like to be castigated for poor choices and would have reached out to Pam if she'd had the chance.

As it was, her days were full again with her kids and their troubles. Don Daley was a good partner, and together with the paraprofessional aides, they had the program rolling well. If people looked at her differently now that they knew about Kelsey, she didn't care. She was just as glad it was out in the open. And her witness was not diminished, because now her faith had been refined. She'd passed through the fire.

She was sorry for Mom and Dad's humiliation. But the worst of that was for their having lied about it in the first place. Their church friends were hurt that they'd been misled and not trusted with the truth. Jill only hoped someday they'd realize what really mattered.

She paid for the books and went home, collected her mail from the mailbox, and with the book bag dangling from her wrist, perused the envelopes. The return address on one personal letter caught her short. Juniper Falls, Colorado. She hurried inside, deposited the rest on the table, and tore that letter open. Rascal came and rubbed her legs as she slipped the paper out and unfolded it.

> *Dear Jill,*
>   *I don't know if you remember, but we met briefly a year ago last June when you came to tell Morgan about Kelsey.*

Jill glanced down at the signature and confirmed her guess.

> *I'm so sorry for your loss. I know it must be terrible by what I've seen in Morgan these past months that he's been with us. He is healing from the accident, but there are wounds deeper than those which threatened his life.*

Accident? What accident had threatened his life? Jill frowned at the page.

>   *I see those scars healing, but he is changed. Some are changes for the better. He has found his faith, though it is a quiet and, I think, painful return. He no longer drinks nor spends long nights in town. Though he smiles and laughs and is wonderful with my small son, there is something raw beneath it. He is too quiet, and I'm afraid his spirit has been crushed.*

I'm not sure what I hope for by writing to you, but I believe I am led to do it. Morgan knows nothing about this letter. He has shut himself away up here as I once tried to do, but I hope to help him as he helped me. I believe he loves and misses you very much.
Sincerely,
Noelle

Jill held the letter, and everything in her stilled. First the book, then this. Both in the same day. But what on earth was she to do with it? Her eyes darted to the phone on the wall, but she had tried that avenue before. *I'm afraid his spirit has been crushed.* It never occurred to her that he had left like that because the pain was too great. Only that he didn't want to be with her, to grieve with her, to heal with her. And now he wasn't healing.

He had looked on top of the world on his book cover. But that was not what Noelle described. *He has shut himself away.* And everyone guarded him zealously as her attempts to reach him attested. *Oh, Morgan. Even when you're wrong they love you.* He was wrong to close everyone out and lock himself away. Did he think it was his fault Kelsey died? Hadn't he apologized as they stood outside her window and the curtains were drawn?

She should have seen it then. But her own grief blinded her. And she'd spent this year putting her life back together and trying not to think or wonder about him. She closed her eyes and sighed. *Lord.* But hadn't her focus been to want the Lord's will? Hadn't she prayed repeatedly for wholehearted acceptance? Jesus should have let her know if there was something more for her to do.

Or was He? Her heart skipped a beat. Kelsey had asked her to help Morgan know the Lord's love. If he knew it, his spirit could not be crushed. She pressed the letter to her heart. *Lord, show me what to do.*

———

Morgan reached down and lifted little Will out of the rut beside his cabin. "You don't want to go that way little guy." He set him back on solid ground, but the baby immediately toddled back to the rut, lost his balance and sat hard on his bottom. Will turned up a pouty face looking for sympathy, but Morgan laughed. "I warned you."

He scooped up the baby and dusted the dirt from his pants. Little Will automatically tucked his head into Morgan's neck, knowing he was due a hug. Morgan complied, glancing up at Rick. "We've created a monster."

Rick smiled and took his son. "He knows we can't resist him." He swung Will onto his shoulders, producing a gleeful baby gurgle. With Will patting his head, Rick strode off across the yard. He and Noelle had created something incredible. Morgan watched father and son and knew he had to stop waiting for doom to fall.

It had been almost a year now. Though there was a permanent pin in his collarbone, the rest of the injuries were healed, and he had no excuse to keep on at Rick's ranch. He had a house and business in Santa Barbara, people depending on him. He ought to kick himself back to work and practice the magic he'd preached. He leaned a shoulder to the porch post and considered leaving.

It was past time. The seasons had nearly run their course. Noelle was strong and happy, Rick as confident and steady as always. Marta would spend another summer with them to cook up her magic, then go back to her grandkids. Todd had come up for spring break and actually learned to ride. Morgan smiled at the memory of the kid's first time astride—not too different from his first time in the waves. But Rick had been patient and determined, and Todd had not only survived but enjoyed it, gaining a measure of proficiency by the time he went back to Stan.

Morgan breathed the mountain air and actually missed the scent of salt and seaweed, citrus and flowers—not for the first time, but this time the strongest. He wanted the sound of the waves through his window while he slept. Maybe then he'd actually sleep. He would miss little Will. No help for that. But he would come see him. No way he'd let that baby forget his Uncle Morgan.

But he had never intended this hiatus to be so prolonged. Writing the book had cleared his mind for other information, knowledge of things beyond commercial problems and solutions. Interesting how many of those concepts he had already incorporated into his life before he knew why, before he stopped resisting the purpose behind everything. With the early June sunshine bringing life to the mountain, he could no longer ignore the purpose in his own life. Yet the thought of returning to everything the way it had been before . . .

He turned at the sound of tires as a car pulled into the yard. His heart hammered when Jill stepped out, looking first at the big house, then catching sight of him. Her hair was still short, with soft flutters about her face, as she closed the door and walked toward him.

The clamor of his heart awakened the ghost of injuries he all but ignored these days. Or maybe this particular ache would never really pass. Here she was crashing in once again to his sanctuary. A lucky guess? Actually more people knew where to find him than the magazine article let on. His parents, every one of his noisy sisters, Rick and Noelle, Denise and Consuela, though he hadn't thought they would tell. It wasn't that he was hiding from Jill. He just had hoped she could put all of it behind her. A hope that at this moment seemed ludicrous and destructive.

How could he have thought it was the answer? As she came close, he breathed her fresh apple scent and noticed a bruise on her cheek. Without thinking, he raised his hand and touched it with his thumb. "What happened?"

"Restraining Joey. He got me with his head."

So she was back to school and functioning in her position. It must all have worked out. "Thought maybe someone had tackled you."

"I play tag football."

He smiled, wanting nothing more than to pull her into his arms and hold her. "What are you doing here?" Besides charging his heart and flooding his mind with thoughts and memories.

"I brought you something." She held out an envelope. "I would have gotten it to you sooner, but you made that difficult by not taking my calls or messages."

He wished now that he had. Even though it hurt like crazy to see her, he drank it in as a drowning man sucks water into his lungs. He tore his eyes from her face and took the envelope. "What is it?"

"A letter from Kelsey."

He jolted, unprepared for that reply. From Kelsey?

Jill touched his arm. "I tried to reach you with funeral information, but Consuela said she hadn't heard from you."

"She hadn't. I was in a coma and not communicating well."

"A coma?"

He looked up from the letter and met her eyes. "Remember your dream?"

"You crashed your Vette?"

He nodded. "Pretty much the way you envisioned it. Only I survived. Minus a kidney and plus a few metal parts that make airport security interesting."

She shook her head. "You were determined to give up that kidney."

He gripped the letter, remembering. "It was a useless waste of a good organ. Not what I intended."

"I know." Her hand on his arm was warm and gentle. He supposed she did know, if anyone did. He'd wanted so much and accomplished so little. But he wasn't in control. He fingered the envelope. The letter looked innocuous, but how could it be? "Do you know what's in here?"

"Can you see where I steamed it?"

He glanced up, but the minx was kidding. She tossed her hair back with one hand. "Well, I have thought of opening it every time Consuela said, 'No, Señor Morgan is not home.'"

Morgan smiled. He'd missed her humor, her voice, her eyes. His glance dropped to her lips. *Do not go there. She'll only say no.* She had come to deliver Kelsey's letter. "Will you sit with me while I read it?"

"I should. Kelsey asked me to deliver it in person."

"Must've been hard when you couldn't reach me."

Her eyes settled on him like doves. "That wasn't the only thing that was hard. I had so many questions. Where were you? Why didn't you call? Why did you leave?" She searched him with her eyes.

He hadn't meant to make it worse. He wasn't sure now what he'd meant. He'd been trying to make sense of it all, and maybe that wasn't even possible.

She said, "After a while I stopped asking. But there was Kelsey's letter. I couldn't forget that."

He wished he'd known. Or did he? He took her hand and drew her down beside him on the stoop. Then he opened the letter. His pulse raced as he unfolded the typed sheet and read:

Hi, Morgan,
    As I told Jill, you'll only be reading this if I've gone to be with Jesus.

His throat suddenly felt as though they'd just removed the ventilator.

    I would have liked to meet you. You sounded really nice on the phone and I'm glad we got to talk. And thank you for the painting. It's really cool. Dad said you're the guy all the women faint over.

He could tell when Jill got to that line, reading beside him. He nudged her ribs with an elbow.

    What I'm really thankful for is that you cared enough to help me. I know it didn't work out (if you're reading this) but that isn't your fault. It was all according to a plan more perfect than we can understand. Just like I didn't understand praying for you to get sick.

His raised his eyebrows and flicked a sidelong glance at Jill, which she avoided. Interesting. Kelsey prayed for him to get sick? He suddenly recalled the times his stomach had revolted against the booze, what he now considered an allergy or aversion. Way beyond anything to do with volume. It had seemed diabolical. Now he suspected the opposite.

I only knew that was what God wanted because something kept you from knowing His love. Sorry if you were miserable. I did feel bad for it but not if it worked. Do you know Jesus loves you?

The same words as in his vision of her after the accident. Did he believe it yet?

I hope you do. He loves you no matter what you've done or haven't done. He's always loved you. And no matter how bad things get, His love sees you through it. I know.

Better than anyone. Morgan lowered the letter, pressed his eyes closed at the thought of her suffering. He'd finally understood the tourist's words. Kelsey had been pure and good enough to cooperate in God's redemptive work when he'd been stiff-necked and rebellious. He'd spent these last months trying to be everything God had called him to be. He'd done it as much for Kelsey as for the Lord himself.

But now she reached back from the grave to assure him of Christ's love, love that had been there before he turned his life around, that had always been there. The least he could do was believe her. He raised the letter again.

Now for my last request. Will you marry Jill?

They reacted together, but Morgan didn't look at her. He couldn't. What impish trick was this? Of course, she would have no idea Jill sat beside him as he read. Then again, she had asked Jill to hand-deliver it. He could almost picture Kelsey peeking down from the clouds, laughing at his discomfort. He read on.

I hope so, and I've prayed hard that you will be together when I'm gone. You're supposed to be. Thank you for everything.
Jesus loves you and so do I!
Kelsey

Morgan stared at the letter, afraid to take his eyes from it, knowing they would go directly for Jill. He folded it slowly and slid it back into the envelope, then stared at that, dazed by the request that so crazily caught hold.

"I swear I didn't know that was in there." Jill's voice was low. "She didn't say it in my letter."

His throat closed on the tight breaths, and his heart and lungs were reminiscently bruised. "It was her last request."

Jill's face shot up toward his. "Morgan, it doesn't mean . . ."

He set the letter down and turned to her. "Are you happy, Jill? Do you have everything you want?" The same questions she had thrown at him in frustration. *Do you ever just want?*

The calm she had approached him with wavered. "I don't want you to think you have to—"

He cupped her face and kissed her soundly. The taste of her lips would never really leave him, nor the softness of her skin and the shape of her jaw. "What if I want to?" Wanted it so much he opened the chasm inside and let her see.

She pressed her palm to his cheek. "You don't have to do this. I only came because—"

He kissed her again. He would kiss her until she realized he meant it. The need and hurt still trapped inside was the longing for her love, for days of companionship and nights sanctified by covenant. Not just any companion, but this woman he knew so well, needed so deeply. His life was God's, but He was the one who said it wasn't right for man to be alone. Morgan pressed his lips to her eyelids. "If you don't want me, say so. I've been down roads you knew better than to travel."

She caught his face with her own hands. "I love you, Morgan."

Looking into her face, he drew the first unencumbered breath he'd enjoyed in a year. "Kelsey's right. If you can love me, Jesus surely must."

Jill's eyes teared. "She'd be so glad to hear that."

His own eyes stung as he held her face and the immensity of the moment sank in. Years of loss, the last one more acute than he could stand. He turned his face aside, battling the tears jerking his chest. He clenched his hand. "I did not intend to cry."

"You need to."

"Not in proposal mode." But his voice broke with every word.

She circled his neck and kissed him softly. "Yes."

"Yes?" Heart beating his ribs, he returned her kiss, fiercely gripping

THE STILL OF NIGHT ‖ 425

her arms and shoulders and waist, heart pounding and desire erupting like a volcano inside.

"Morgan," she gasped.

"I know." He pressed his forehead to hers and held her shoulders, clamping down the want inside. There was no way he'd mess it up again. But that didn't make it easy. "So . . ." He cleared his throat. "How do we do this? Do I ask your father's permission?"

She wilted and shook her head slowly. "Maybe someday they'll take the blinders off. I hope so." She sighed. "But I don't see it happening."

"This won't help. Can you live with that separation?"

"If I'm with you?" Her expression made it a no-brainer.

His hands cupped her face again. I won't allow any back-door wedding. We're going to have the best—"

She put a finger to his lips. "I already do."

He swallowed a fresh tightening in his throat and a new onslaught of desire. *Back off. Calm down. Think of something else.* "Tell me the truth. Did you know Kelsey was praying for me to chuck the liquor every time?"

Jill's cheeks dimpled, and there was a silver glimmer in her eyes.

He nodded. "Uh-huh. I'll have you know I was stone sober when I wrecked my Vette."

"Maybe something more sedate like a Buick . . ."

He caught his fingers in her hair. "You think I'm bringing you home in a Buick?"

She laughed. "Maybe not."

Epilogue

O
ne more time, Jill. You can do it." Morgan's hand gripped hers with firm intensity. "Deep breaths, darling."

Easy for him to say. It wasn't *his* stomach becoming a vise and crushing the air out of him. Or his skin pearled with sweat, mottled and red. He looked devastatingly wonderful as always—the bum.

"Get ready, now. This is it." He brushed her cheek with a kiss that projected all his hope, his strength, and his love.

The contraction started and grew. She stared into his eyes and squeezed down on the pain with everything in her. Then the pressure released.

"Hold it. Wait," the nurse cautioned with a hand on her abdomen. She puffed frantically as people moved into position.

Morgan's hand pressed between her shoulder blades, solid and reassuring. His other palm stroking her head. "You're doing great." Waves of comfort.

"Push now, slowly," the doctor directed.

Jill did. The sensation so unforgettable. Soft cheers.

The doctor said, "Congratulations. You have a daughter."

Jill stared at Morgan's face as he watched them aspirate their daughter's tiny nostrils, and then he cut the cord himself, tears washing his eyes a deeper shade of blue. He turned to her, his throat working soundlessly, then bent and kissed her softly. "A little girl, Jill."

The Hispanic nurse bundled the baby and tucked her into Jill's arms, then turned to Morgan. "We have a saying: Anyone can make a son; it takes a lover to make a daughter."

Jill's heart swelled. And a loving God to restore hope and blessing. Jill stared into her baby's face, enthralled with every feature and the fine black hair like a thin lace cap. She ran a finger over the infant's cheek and closed her eyes. *Are you watching, Kelsey? This is your sister.* Her tears were bittersweet.

Morgan pressed his lips to her forehead, his thoughts obviously matching hers when he said, "She knows."

Jill looked into his face and nodded, then found the face of her baby, and joy exploded inside.